TALENT HUNTER editions

THE TRUTH

Ana Teresa Silva

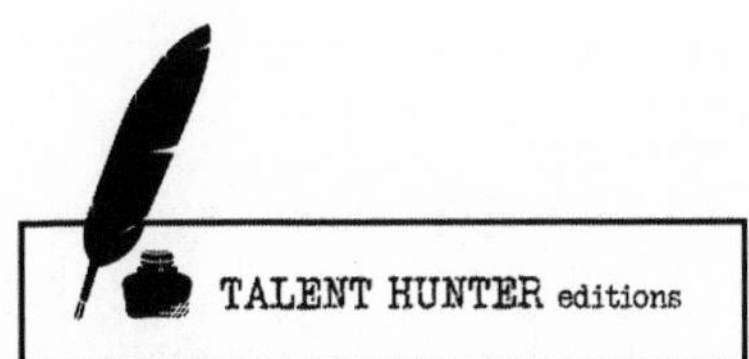

Title: The Truth
Translation: Chris Mingay
Proof reading: Fiona Philips and Derek Barretto
Cover: André Santos
Design: Silvana Vieira
Back cover photo: Telma Antunes
Photos: Paul Talbot, Tom Barrett, Zoltan Tasi, Zetong Li, Antoine Perier, Sufyan, Alonso Reyes, Gatis Marcinkevics, Rob Potter, Aarn Giri and Navi on Unsplash
Talent Hunter Editions
1ª edition: December 2023
Legal Deposit: 524 716/23
ISBN: 979-8-86-317546-1
Printed and bound: Manuel Barbosa & Filhos, Lda.

To my son, my mother, and brother; my family pillars, who are always present in my life, and to my father, the pillar of the family, even though he departed 31 years ago.

To all my 'lighthouse-friends' who keep me from losing my way in the most important things in life, and the truth of my heart.

To "my" angels and guides who make all the difference in my life.

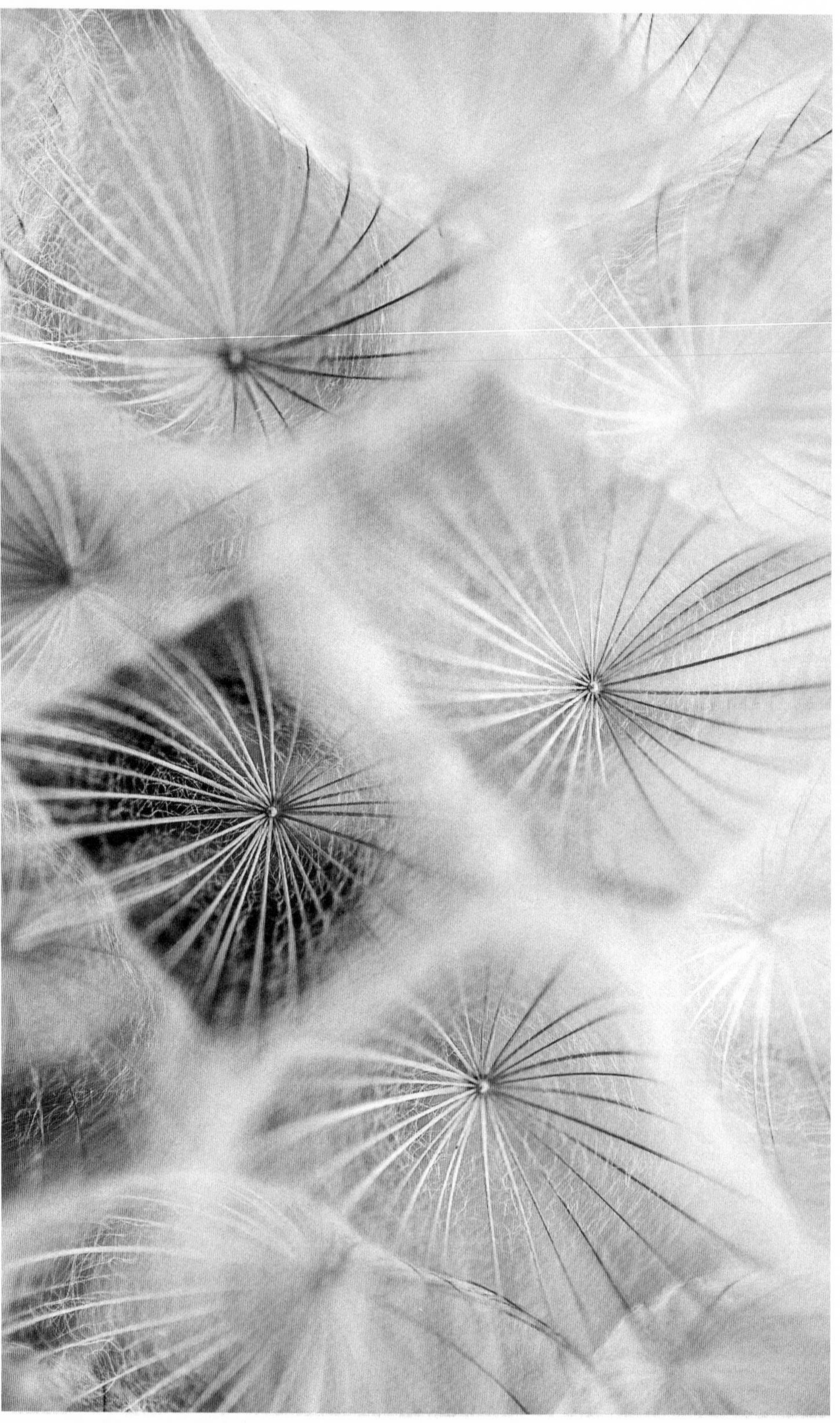

Acknowledgements

Firstly, I would like to express my deep gratitude to all the interviewees who agreed, spontaneously and generously, to share their lives, their wisdom and for discussing a topic as significant and complex as the Truth.

I know how precious time is for each of them, whose work touches so many people around the world - and, therefore, is all the more reason to sincerely thank each one for them for their dedication, their affectionate presence, their words and the trust they showed in my work.

My gratitude to (in alphabetical order):

ADAM APOLLO (Physicist, Systems Architect, Designer),

ARIEL SPILSBURY (Author of "Mayan Oracle", Founder of 13 Moon Mystery School and Sanctuary of the Open Heart),

FREDDY SILVA (Author, Documentary Filmmaker, Researcher of Ancient Civilizations),

JIM GARRISON (President of Ubiquity University),

JUDE CURRIVAN (Cosmologist, author and co-founder WholeWorld-View),

JUDITH KUSEL (Author and Soul Coach),

MARIN BACH-ANTONSON (Founder of Priestess Rising Mystery School),

MARTIN GRAY (Anthropologist, National Geographic Photographer),
PAM GREGORY (Astrologer),
PETER ENGBERG (Award-winning filmmaker),
SANDRA CISNEROS (Award winning writer)
and SARITA CAMERON (Founder of SolHenge Retreat centre).

I also want to acknowledge the inspiring wisdom of Matias de Stefano, Betty Kovacs, Anne Baring, Robert J. Gilbert, and Arkan Lushwala.

A very special thank you to the musicians and artists who, inspired by this book, created original music and songs. This union of arts reminds me of the different trees in a forest when they intertwine, across branches and roots. When scholars have asked why different species would do this, the answer came simply: together they are stronger. For me, this creative cross-fertilization brings unique landscapes to our hearts, creating new journeys, showing different expressions of the same love.

I also want to thank Ana Franco, Derek Barretto, Fiona Philips, Manuela Doutel-Haghighi, Silvana Vieira and Teresa Andrade, for all their help and friendship, my son André and my mother Laurinda for all their support, and Satya for her intuitive trust and for giving voice to this book at its launch.

We open our eyes
To see beyond what we have seen before
We open our ears
To hear what we could not hear before
Beyond limitation
Beyond the beyond
We feel a new story emerging from our cells
And rippling out into our lucid bodies
As waves of love remind us of who we really are
Dissolve us into what we have always meant to be
And the layers between us
And who we are meant to be, fade away
And suddenly we realise
We are all that we dreamed we could be
"To see without eyes, to walk without feet
and to fly without wings"
This is my prayer for you

Zola Dubnikova

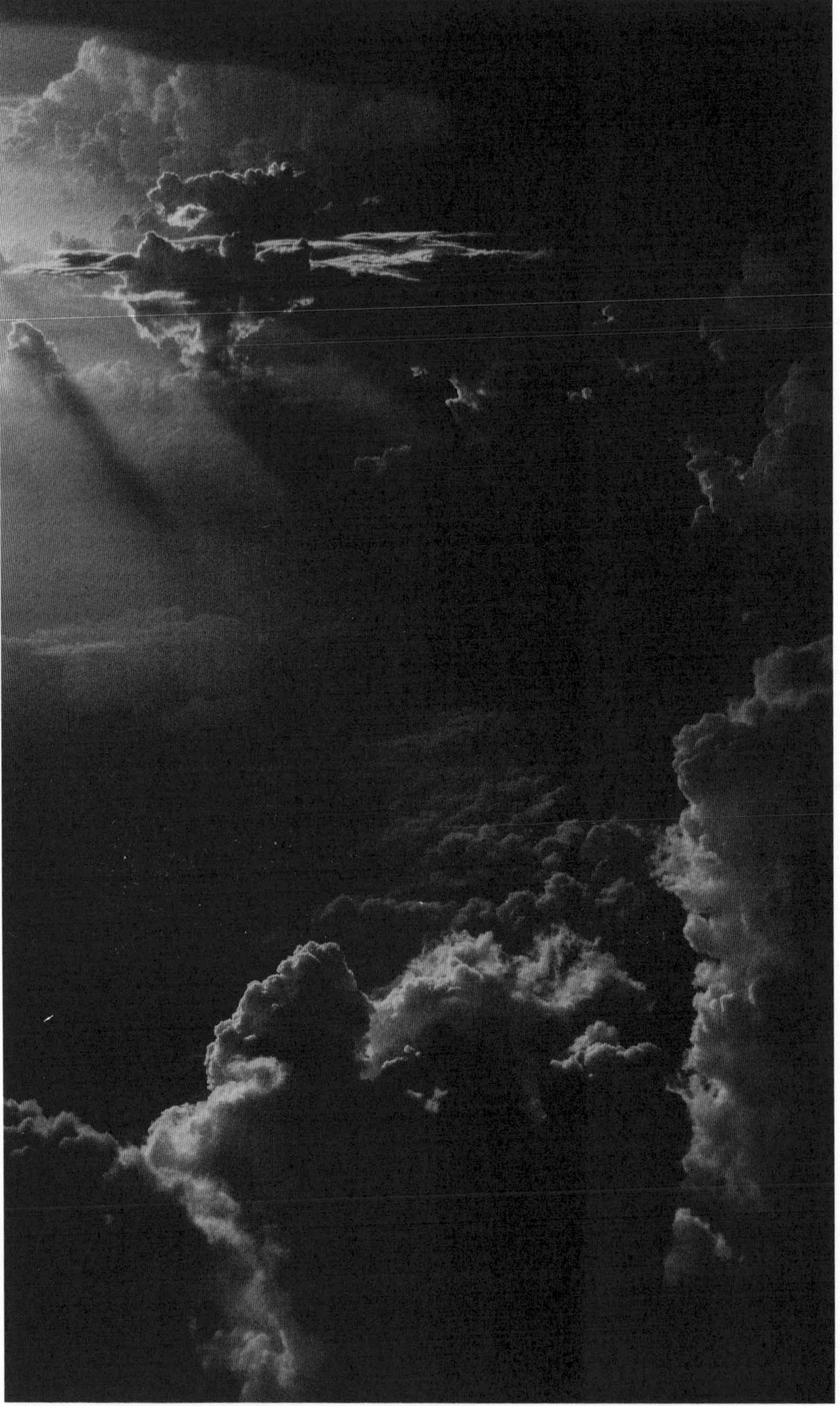

Prologue

Helena doesn't know I exist. Not consciously, that is. Our connection is a powerful one, but it transcends the visible. More questions will need answering, I know, but now is not the time. Believe me. In time, it'll all make sense. For now, though, just sink back into this story, a year in the making. To be fair, this, like any other story, began way before that, in a place bereft of time, where creation sings its song, unleashing a sequence of events that cross the generations, in a tangle of tales, seemingly spellbinding when seen from front to back.

A gentle reminder, like a murmur from my soul to yours. There are some incredible journeys awaiting us, a blur of potentials, dependent on the caprices of our choices, on the searchlight of our mindfulness, if we can illuminate, or not, certain clues, hidden in the depths of our hearts. The choice is entirely ours. Anyone who has never plumbed the fathoms of this sacred inner space might not believe that such journeys could ever exist. And, for many, this exploration is prompted solely by the punch of pain, loss, illness or darkness. With time, incalculable until it happens, it might then morph masterfully into love, light, truth, wisdom and bliss.

It's not my intention to skip the pages of time, nor to hurl you into a labyrinth, but this narrator, yours truly, does not abide by the rules of linear time. So, prepare yourself for a beginning, middle and end, but not necessarily in that order. Either you'll be in the embrace of light and love, or shoved unceremoniously off the precipice, so that, like Helena, you'll find your wings as you fall. And talking of beginning, middle and end, in this book, don't expect them to be one-offs. The way I see it, some beginnings are intertwined with middles and ends, all woven into the same fabric.

Conversely, despite this book being based on true stories, on so many real conversations, my imagination has also melded with the blend, together with the way I have been able – from where I stand – to perceive this whole journey. But such is life, is it not? How much of it is true and how much of it is the vision of someone else? And how our own vision is affected by the construct that we are?

It comes from the age-old wisdom that, with every generation, only the few are fit for the truth; only these are able to recognise it when they see it. But there are generations when the number of such people balloons to proportions never before imagined, such as now.

Life is a meld of tales, tales of many others, sourced in writing or word of mouth, books and media, family members and friends, teachers and artists, scientists and scholars. Tales of a reality oft not experienced by the storyteller, rather communicated and recommunicated ad infinitum, piecemeal, edited, improved upon, unwittingly transformed, until lost in a whirl of points, added and removed, prompting the experience of our own tale, those we experience and those we tell (to ourselves and to others) about what we live.

And not even science is spared this charade. Over the years we bear witness to discoveries, about matter, space, time, our existence, evolution, the cosmos, the mind, consciousness, the power of the heart, laying rest to the truths of old.

The experience of truth is thus bound to an ingenious labyrinth and, with the proliferation of information, the reader, and everyone currently walking the Earth, must root out their finest compass, their finest polygraph, be it of the heart or felt in the guts, to decipher tales and intentions, narratives piled high with layers and blurred with photoshop, while learning to interpret the vibration of truth, peeling back layer after layer of information inbound from afar, tossing aside old beliefs based on ideas deftly sown by men at key moments, but which are questionable; everything is questionable when the mind is curious. And when the heart is open, everything can be recognised.

Here, with each page, more than deciphering what was real, what counts is to be aware of what resonates in you as truth. As, this story, the conversations taking place throughout this entire voyage, the extraordinary intertwining events, the deep feelings weaving a singular tableau, touch your truth, your life in the present moment, your experiences, your hero's journey, with all the deconstructions and awakenings that it inevitably implies.

The Truth is like a map, and a map always depends on the person looking at it. As such, the profound journey enshrined in this story - and what you take away from it - will depend solely on you. Take notes, underline things, ask questions, let the codes inscribed in certain lines trigger reflections and feelings. There will be lighter moments, others of diving downwards, so always follow your feelings. Pause at key moments, explore and relive the words used, put on some music, dance, meditate, allowing a few phrases to echo, to (en)chant. Or read it all in one go, as only an experienced diver can do, and only then revisit the gems you've found. This is a book that is open entirely to each reader's consciousness.

It is said that the master only arrives when the disciple is ready, that we are never given greater obstacles than the strength we possess to overcome them and that, often, the truth is hidden right before our eyes, for even that cannot be hurried. "The lips of wisdom are closed except to the ears of understanding".

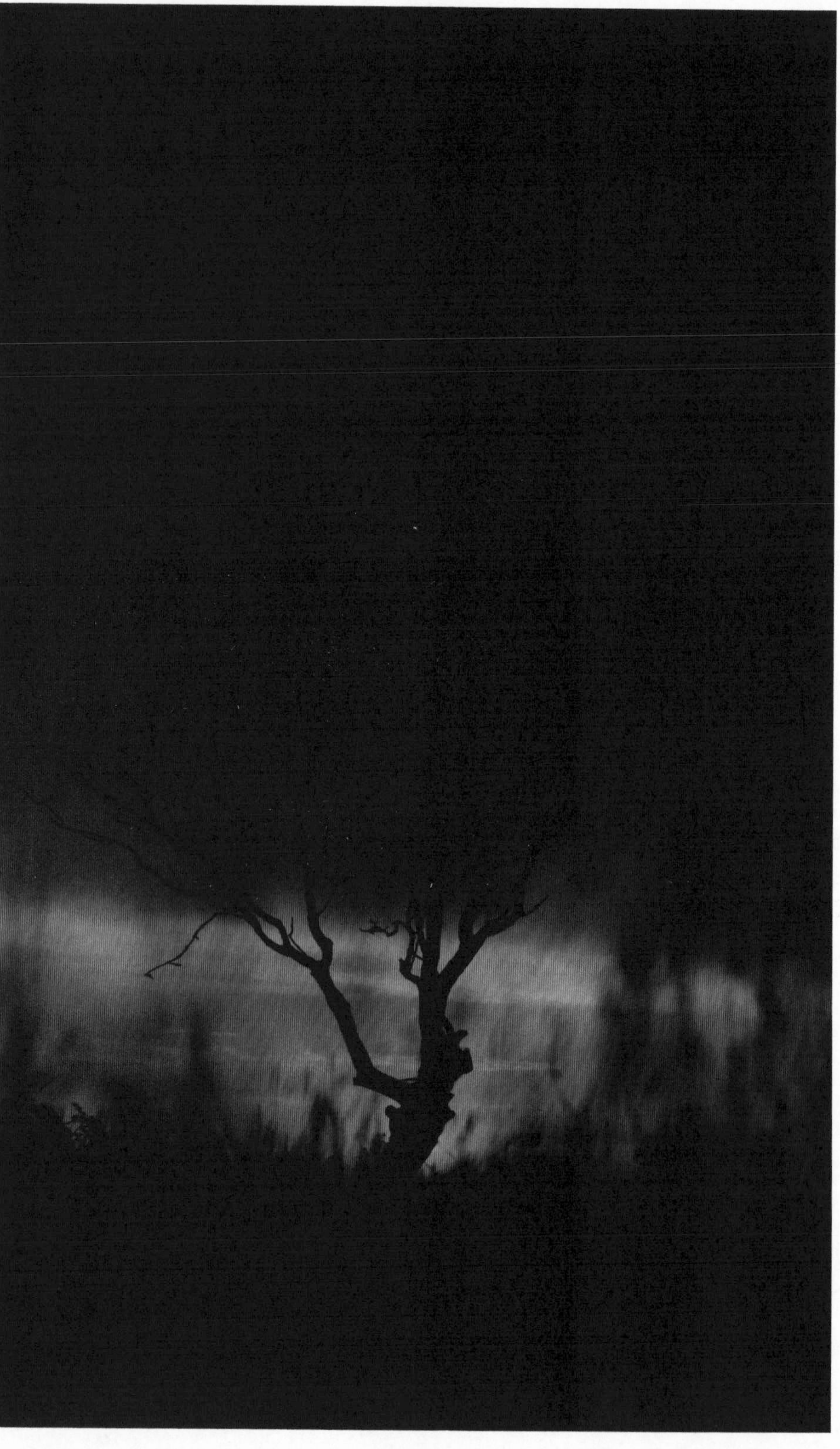

On the 3rd day of the Dark Night of the Soul

"It hurts like hell."

"I know."

"I just can't bear it."

"So it would seem."

"It's gonna kill me, like a poison," Helena said, pain in her voice.

"When you fight poison in the body, you only make it spread faster."

"I don't know what to do. I'm barely holding it together. Nothing makes sense."

"How often does it only make sense in the afterglow?" asked Adriana. "You of all people should know this. At some point in the future, you'll find the missing pieces to understand this very moment, this dark night of the soul..."

"If only I could be sure of that, right now, and not later. What guarantees are there we'll ever find them? A whole life could go by and we'd still be in the dark... And what about the pain? Where should we put that? All I want is for someone to enter my heart and pluck out this pain like a weed."

"Heart pain pluckers... What a brilliant idea. If such a person were to exist, their schedule would be packed," said Adriana, a wry smile on her lips, eyeing Helena in an attempt to charm a reciprocal smile out of her, to lighten the moment. But Helena was unfazed, wrought with personal terror, drawing Adriana back to a place of utter seriousness. "Unfortunately, only you can do that, I believe. At the right time. But, while you still need me, I'm here for you."

"Thank you so much, Adriana," she whimpered, resting her head in Adriana's lap, exhausted.

"There's no need for thanks," she softly replied, gently caressing her hair. "It does me good too, to sit here and cry with you. All this just breaks my heart. I'm not sure how, but I have this funny feeling that on your journey you'll learn how to pull out all the thorns from your heart, one by one."

"Let's hope so."

"You will, I know it."

There are times when there is no more room for words. You need to put them on mute and leave them, silenced, in the flow of sadness, with the sobs, with the bodily convulsions before the flood, together with the heavy tears of pain. And Adriana, like a flickering flame, radiating as much light as she could, braiding her hair, the best way to cure the ailments of a woman's heart, as her grandmothers would say.

In the beginning was a hollowness

As far back as she could remember, Helena could feel a hollowness in her chest, a kind of soul-ache that carried her along her journey, but she couldn't quite put her finger on it. In life, if you can't be the poet, be the poem, she would silently recall, smiling at having found that scrap of wisdom on the tiles of a public toilet. On the few occasions she had spoken about this pain with no known cause, she would relate that the minor mystery burrowed in her heart had been the driving force behind her entire life journey. Until that point. Until the moment of pain that now had a name and had shattered her heart. On the day she turned 38.

When she was younger, and whenever her father would spend some time with them, she would make the most of his being there to explore the world of secrets. Her father had one of those jobs that comes with no specific title. One, to put it as simply as possible, that involved him 'disappearing' the unwanted secrets of the rich, the famous and the powerful, in the Internet era. He challenged the expression, "once on the Internet, always on the Internet". In his circle, he was known as a 'Fixer' or 'Reputation Fixer'. But his business card simply bore the words 'Strategic Consultant'.

Helena called him the onion farmer, when she wanted to provoke him; the Daedalus of Mazes, when she wanted to praise him. When they were alone, she would lovingly call him "my mystery maker". To her, it was like her father, with his angelic blue eyes, possessed godlike powers, creating parallel realities in which to hide events and taking the common man on endless forays down countless dead ends, as if in a maze, barefoot, on layer after layer of an onion they never knew existed. And, at the same time, he had a devilish trident he could pull out, to cast away those who deserved to serve time. Helena tried to turn a blind eye to this, so as not to call her great love into doubt. Only on the fringes of some conflict, especially in her teenage years, did she use this knowledge as ammunition. But faced with the indignant accusations of his daughter in a rebellious state, Helena's father would only reply: "don't worry, this is just an illusion, because nobody can escape their Karma." To which she laconically replied: "well, you can't either."

Ever since she was little, the games she would play always had this common denominator: hide and seek. Enigmas, treasure hunts, secret codes, time travel, puzzles, spy parties, escape rooms and, later on, cracking ancient codes and ciphers, modern systems of cryptography and espionage, a world into which Helena immersed herself as if there were no tomorrow and which, somewhere in time, had led her to do a course in theoretical and applied mathematics which, after finishing, she abandoned, to do a master's degree in film studies. Not that she had lost her fascination for the magic of numbers, the attraction remained. She just wanted to travel, to lose herself in the world of research, documenting, bringing to light hidden information, not yet deciphered, new visions of the universe, new windows of thought. Basically, all she wanted was to transform her long-held interests into stories, through images and words.

A few months prior to the huge and unpredictable shattering, Helena had decided to travel to Italy. Before leaving, she went for lunch at her parents' house, one of those typical Sunday lunches. An unwavering family habit since Helena's birth. Sunday lunches and afternoons were for the extended family, not linked by blood, rather by the dreams, visions and interests of her parents, especially the arts, the 'sophies' - philosophy, theosophy and anthroposophy - and some 'logies', especially cosmology, anthropology, psychology and astrology.

Many of the guests were repeat performers, appearing sporadically throughout the Sundays of the year, as her mother had a passion and skill for fertilising friendships, seeing them grow and flourish over time. But not infrequently there were some new faces, who, in her mother's language, were new Sunday windows, opening up a new landscape to the conversation.

When she was little, Sunday was the gift-word that meant she would have tons of adults to play with, especially artists given to rolling around on the lawn, belly-laughers, but more importantly it meant that there would be other kids to embark on her adventures and exploits with her, heaven for an only child. But when she was a teenager, Sunday became a nightmare-word, which meant hiding in her room all day, with her headphones glued firmly on and her eyes fixed to the television screen, watching series after series, all to avoid the deep conversations that inevitably took place between those present, but also all the flirting, the 80s and 90s music, the dancing on the lawn at night, the drinking that led to dips in the pool: everything that she'd loved before, but which now seemed utter foolishness and not suited at all to the age of the guests. Conversations, adventures, dancing and drinking, yes, but only with her friends. The adults were all boring, square, even the ones who'd seemed cool, quirky and of great wisdom before.

As she approached her thirties, the joy of Sundays filled Helena's heart once again, and she too became a mainstay of her mother's lunches, despite living alone in a small house near Guincho. In the years spent studying and working abroad, in the USA, Cuba, Brazil, she had come to fully understand the influence and pleasure of these Sunday conversations, alongside the games with her father, and was so grateful to have grown up within such an inspiring tribe.

On that third Sunday in June, ten years since her return to Portugal, and so many stories later, Helena went to lunch at her parents' as usual. There were fewer people than normal. More down to the mini-holidays that many were enjoying than to the pandemic, which, despite the rules still in place, fears and differences of opinion, had never stopped the tribe meeting up, to embrace, to debate what was happening, argue about it even, without ever breaking the deep roots of those friendships, most of them at least, which gave her a feeling of safe haven, there, every Sunday, like a bubble of hope, helping her to stay strong and able to come to terms with the new reality.

"I'm going to Italy in a few days," she told her mother.

"Not you too! As if it wasn't enough that your father was always travelling to Italy, now you are too."

"That doesn't count. This'll be my first time there."

"I know. I'm just kidding with you."

"What are you going to do?" her father asked, entering the kitchen.

"I don't really know, yet. I've been toying with the idea of visiting the Vatican library for ages. Especially since Cardinal José Tolentino de Mendonça became archivist and librarian of the Holy Roman Church."

"Have you spoken to him?"

"I sent him an email, but he hasn't replied yet. I'm not too bothered; my ticket is open-ended. There are other people I'd like to visit in Italy. Have you visited it?"

"The library? Yes," her father said.

"And how did it make you feel?"

"It's hard to put into words the emotion you feel on entering. The silence that envelops you. The feeling of endlessness. A sea of questions soaking your pores. But I don't want to influence your experience."

"Every experience is unique, don't you worry. The Pope said that two great rivers flow through the library: the word of God and the word of men. I've always been curious about to what extent the word of men has transformed the word of God."

"That's like separating drops in an ocean," her father replied, a smile on his lips.

"Ah, I just want to dive in and feel the water... that's the plan. Then we'll see. And if, on one of these dives, I was to find a forbidden secret treasure, hidden at the back of some bookcase, then that would be the icing on the cake."

Her father laughed.

"I have my doubts. But who can know for sure what plans the universe holds for you?"

"That's exactly what I'm counting on," retorted Helena, smiling broadly.

"If you need anything, just ask," her father said, before returning to the guests with a tray of *caipirinhas*.

Helena followed her father out to the garden, where the guests were enjoying the sun.

"My daughter is going to Italy," he said to the air.

The many eyes turned towards Helena.

"What are you working on now?"

"Oh, I'm still just setting out. With an idea and no clear direction. It's like a ray of light behind a solid swathe of clouds."

"But where are you heading?"

"Oh, you'll be startled by the enormity of this word: the truth."

Helena looked around her, seeing the interest and the smiles the sound of that word had produced.

"It's a good time for that subject," said one of the guests.

"I've been going round in circles with the truth, as if in a dance. Thinking about the false premises that have defined realities for centuries... and how this affects us to this day. After all, how are we to discover the chinks through which the light can pass? How can you tell what is true and what isn't? The experience of truth in us. This thought has stuck with me: how do I experience the truth? How do we get to the very core of ourselves, how do we peel back the layers that don't belong to us? These things. I believe that the clear direction of this project will appear to me at any moment."

"Of course, it will. We've got used to your profound works, full of subtle and veiled messages, keeping us on our toes," said another of the guests with satisfaction.

"We really admire your work. And we're not the only ones, given the number of awards your documentaries have won," concluded Sofia, one of the guests who had known Helena since her birth.

"Come on, don't place the bar too high, otherwise I won't want to jump," said Helena transparently, a serene smile on her lips. "Too much expectation pumps up the pressure... and in this documentary I really want to let things flow. Especially at a time when the world seems prevented from flowing. Let the universe show me the way."

"The universe is wise. You have great guide there."

"I know. I know."

The meeting

The universe is wise, that's right. But the path isn't always revealed in the way we think it might be. Helena went to Italy. Adriana would be waiting for her at the airport, which gave her a sense of relief. Travelling during the pandemic wasn't as fun as it had been before. Although she had already become used to the paperwork, the requirements and the restrictions, after the many work trips she'd done after the first lockdown and for about a year since, she still felt an invisible burden hanging around the departure gates that constrained her. If she'd been a cartoonist, she would have drawn a grey cloud hovering above all the people hidden behind their masks.

That experience of surrendering to the unknown and the unfamiliar, with a smile on her lips, that was part of every flight she'd ever taken, now seemed impossible. Helena would never say 'impossible', but 'difficult', requiring an effort and energy she didn't feel like expending. There were invisible walls, holding people apart. Fabric-covered smiles, closing travellers into their own world, conditioned by fear and rules. And because Helena lacked the grace and lightness of former times, whenever possible she would book night flights. "Just close your eyes and when you open them, it'll be over," she would say to herself. But for a short-haul flight to Rome, an evening flight was as close as she could get.

Her friend Adriana was a comfort, bringing her reassurance. She was like a lighthouse on a stormy night and Rome was now her safe haven. Helena saw this as confirmation of the path she should be taking. She had met Adriana a few years earlier in a cacao ceremony, more precisely in an eye-gazing circle, and their relationship had remained strong ever since. Eye to eye, windows of the soul, opening a deep interchange between two people in a fraction of a second. The body responding to the reunion with eyes overflowing with tears. Then the dance. Only later the words.

Adriana was Chicana. Her father was German and her mother Brazilian. Both were wandering musicians who had rocked up in Mazunte, in Mexico, originally for a few days, before eventually staying for a few years. Adriana would often recall the sleepy mornings of Mazunte, her barefoot existence, the turquoise waters, the untouched beaches lined with dozing palm trees. Her parents had fallen for this timeless place, where there was nothing to do, but where life felt complete. That was where she had been conceived, in this little fishing village, which ensnared unsuspecting travellers in its magical net. And it was there that she had grown up, surrounded by beauty and simplicity, the soles of her feet hardened from never wearing shoes, her skin peeling in its defiance of the hot sun. A charmed life that had been suddenly cut short, when family problems meant her father had to take the family back to Europe. From then on, until her emancipation, life in Germany had been no more than a lump in the throat of her memory, a hole in her existence, her resolve trapped in a fading loop, a deep sense of helplessness and solitude.

For all this, and for everything that words cannot express, as soon as she had felt able, she set off, alone, to far away places. Like her parents before her, she too had a deep-seated wanderlust. She called herself the explorer of the faces of humanity and at a young age she had decided to spend a year in every country. Italy was her 22nd country. In the first eleven, she had immersed herself in healing and learning, and in the latter years she had already imparted what she had learnt through retreats she offered to men and women looking to explore the practices, teachings and insights embedded in feminine wisdom. Adriana had this rare talent of being able to take people to somewhere deep inside of themselves, through a deeper vision of the Divine Feminine that resides in us all, through non-dual thinking, the wisdom of the natural world, emotional intelligence and creativity.

In this moment of closing her eyes and opening them, on the flight from Portugal to Italy, Helena had revisited the life-changing emotions she had experienced on one of Adriana's retreats. She held those memories close to her heart, ready to share them in their embrace on arrival. But, strangely, Adriana was not there to greet her and her mobile was switched off. With her phone still to her ear, deciding what she should do, Helena saw an unfamiliar man coming towards her; his stride confident and his maskless face lit up by a huge smile.

"Helena?" he asked, while opening his arms for a warm embrace.

"Yes?" she stammered, allowing herself to be embraced.

"*Oh, scusa*" he said, taking two steps back, half ashamed. "I've heard so much about you over the last couple of days that I feel I know you. I'm Thomas. Thomas Gatti," he added in perfect English.

"Are you a friend of Adriana...? Sorry I... she didn't text me, or tell me about you."

"Ah, right. I haven't even explain myself. There was an emergency. Adriana had to rush off and won't be back for a few hours. She called me, worried, and asked if I would pick you up. This all happened when you were in the air; there was no time to warn you, and there's no reception where she is now. I asked her not to text you, I wanted to surprise you. I don't know what I was thinking..."

Helena laughed for the first time.

"It really was a surprise. It still is. Adriana has never spoken about you. Has something bad happened?"

"I'm not really sure. She didn't tell me anything. She just asked me to come and pick you up and to keep you company until she comes back."

"What time is she coming back?"

"In a few hours. That's all I know," he said, bending down to pick up her cases and heading towards the car.

Helena remained still.

"Shall we go?" added Thomas, seeing her hesitation.

Helena looked down at her phone, hoping for it to ring, but then she pulled off her mask, smiled and allowed herself to leave with this man she had only just met.

Only when they were on their way in the car, did she look at Thomas for the first time, at the beauty of his face, at his unruly black hair. She pondered that she hadn't met such a gorgeous man in a long time, the thought unleashing a smile.

"Where are we going?"

"Rome?" he replied with a cheeky smile, noticing Helena's unease. "Let's go out tonight, while we wait for Adriana. What do you say?"

"Sounds good. Have you known each other for long?"

"Ah, Rome and I go back forever," he continued, jokingly.

"Very funny!"

"I met Adriana quite recently, on one of her retreats. But we felt a very strong connection."

"I can understand that. The same thing happened to me."

"Maybe the three of us are connected..." his cheeky tone continuing.

"*Quiçá*?" she quipped, playing along.

"*Pas moi*," said Thomas, in perfect French.

"Wow, an Italian who speaks English and French perfectly. You are rare!"

"I like rarities, so thanks for the compliment."

"You're welcome."

"At last, I'm welcome! I was beginning to think I would never be," Thomas said before chuckling like a child. "It's just, that first hug was a little... cold."

Thomas carried on laughing. Helena smiled at her lap, a little embarrassed.

"I was caught entirely by surprise," said Helena.

"Don't you like surprises?"

"It depends."

"Am I not a good surprise?" asked Thomas.

"I'm not sure."

"Oh, Adriana thought I would be. I did too. I'm a bit disappointed..."

Helena looked over at Thomas again as they drove towards Rome. She loved spontaneity in people, seeing that inner child revealed in their gestures, but there she felt a little intimidated. Thomas intimidated her somehow. She couldn't even tell if it was because of his good looks, his confidence or his spontaneity. Characteristics that people often praised her for. Including the fact that they often found her intimidating. There, in her mirror, she became shy and insecure.

"Would you like to?"

"Would I like to what?" asked Helena.

"Didn't you hear what I said?" asked Thomas, surprised.

She had become so lost in her own thoughts. She noticed that they were already in Rome. Thomas had parked the car.

"Sorry," said Helena.

"I was wondering if you'd like to go to the Trevi Fountain?"

"You choose, I'm all yours..."

"You're all mine? Lucky me!" said Thomas, amused.

"It's an expression we use in Portuguese, maybe it got lost in translation," Helena stammered, a little embarrassed.

"I understood. I'm just pulling your leg."

"All you do is kid around," said Helena, still a little uncomfortable.

"Don't you like being silly?"

"It depends."

"Do you answer 'it depends' to every question?" asked Thomas.

"It depends," she replied, looking directly into his eyes for the first time. Thomas' green eyes gave off a soft, pure light. The impact of their eyes meeting was powerful, like a sucker punch to the gut. Her body was reacting strangely under his gaze. Where was Adriana? Why had she sent this man? It was Thomas who cut the moment short.

"If you're all mine, then come," he said, getting out of the car.

"Can we leave my things?"

"No problem. Come."

Helena followed him, looking around her. This was her first trip to Rome. It seemed strangely familiar to her... the streets, the city, Thomas. They started walking and, bit by bit, she let go of her expectations, her fears, the restraints of her thoughts, and she started to surrender to the experience, to the here and now. Her senses started to open up, as if hit only now by the smells, the lights in the windows, Thomas' gentle voice, a group of musicians in the Piazza della Rotonda, the painting of the Virgin on the façade of the Antica Salumeria, all those wooden shutters that whisked her off to an old film, the magnitude of the Trevi Fountain at the intersection of the three roads. By the time they had reached the Spanish Steps she had already let go of any doubts, any questions or strange feelings about her arrival. It was as if everything around her had changed, when it was only her who had changed, with different thoughts and words. They sat down on the steps.

"How wonderful to be here," said Helena, smoothing her dress between her legs. She had this girlish way of sitting down somewhere, only to remember later that she was a grown woman now and you couldn't go around flashing her knickers to everybody.

"It's good to hear you say that. There were times when I thought I would have to say to Adriana that I'd totally failed in my mission."

"Mission?"

"Yes, of properly greeting you. A proper Roman welcome. This is your first time in Italy, is it not?"

"It is. No idea why, though. My dad used to come here often. And although I travel a lot, I've never been here."

"Does your father have work here?" asked Thomas.

"Ah, he has work all over. But you could almost say that Italy is the head office."

"What does he do?"

"Hmmm, I don't really think I should go into that, sorry. It's not that easy to explain," said Helena.

"No problem."

"And you, what do you do?" asked Helena.

"I look at stars."

"Ah, that's amazing. So, we're doing your work right now," she said, looking up to the sky.

Thomas laughed, throwing his whole body backwards and lying down on the stairs, his eyes pointing skywards.

"This isn't a good spot, too much light pollution. I prefer the Atacama Desert or Tasmania," he replied naturally, before turning to Helena.

Helena looked into Thomas' eyes for the second time. Until then it had been simple, just to be carried along, lost in the stimuli of the city.

"You are serious," she said softly, without tearing her eyes from him.

"I'm always being serious, even when I'm mucking around."

"Are you an astronomer?"

"Astrophysicist."

"I'm impressed," Helena said with real admiration.

"If I'd known it would have been that easy, I would have told you in the airport: Thomas Gatti, astrophysicist," he said, extending his hand.

"Highly amusing."

"*Eu nasci assim, eu cresci assim*," he sang in Portuguese.

"Oh, my God, you speak Portuguese too?"

"A little. I have some Brazilian colleagues and friends. I'm always sharing information with people from all around the globe. We end up working together a lot. This science of searching the heavens is very complex... everything takes so long; we need many eyes trained on the sky everywhere to cross-reference information. Sometimes it take years to get definitive data."

"Have you ever made a great discovery? " Helena asked, curious.

"No. But I've contributed to some."

"How amazing! Tell me more!"

"I don't know... There are things that only we give importance to. Like with the discovery of the rings of Chariklo. They were discovered by a Brazilian colleague. Up till then, we had thought that only large planets, such as Saturn and Uranus, could have rings. For us this was an incredible discovery, to find out that tiny bodies within the immensity of outer space could also be circled by these phenomena. This could give us precious clues about the formation of the solar system. We're talking about an asteroid more than two billion kilometres from earth. Imagine seeing a coin two hundred kilometres away. It's magical. Have you ever heard of Chariklo?"

"As a matter of fact, I have, from an astrologer. I even know where it is on my birth chart," answered Helena.

"That's crazy! I wasn't expecting that! And what does Chariklo say in your chart?" asked Thomas.

"I don't know much yet. Chariklo is just making her debut in the astrological world. Partner of Chiron, both centaurs from the Kuiper Belt."

"Now it's my turn to be impressed. I never imagined you'd even have heard of it," said Thomas fascinated.

"I'm keen on astrology, and my mother always had lots of astrologist friends. Another way of looking at the stars... Actually, what I'd like to know is how these planetary bodies are given their names. Why Chariklo? It's just that it makes so much sense astrologically that it seems as if the name has been sent down from above."

"I don't know either. Chariklo was discovered by an American astronomer, James V. Scotti, from the Spacewatch programme, in 1997. But I have no idea why it was named after the nymph Chariklo. This discovery I was telling you about, was just of the rings, in 2013, in Chile. We knew that the asteroid was going to occult and that this might give us new insights into its size and shape... but the discovery of the rings was a complete surprise," he explained. "But, I can ask Felipe. Maybe he knows. *O cara que fez a descoberta*," he said in Brazilian Portuguese, smiling, "my Brazilian colleague."

"I'd love to know. The story is so beautiful and very interesting when you apply it to a birth chart. Until now, we only knew about Chiron, and for me it is very symbolic to only now find out about the importance played by his wife! This had me wanting to know more. But I found very little information on her in the standard sources of classic Greek mythology, which makes poetic sense; the little we know of her accords with the powerful invisibility of her presence. They say that originally, she was a nymph, who turned into a centaur. Could it be that she fell in love with Chiron and followed him to his kingdom? We know that she cared for him all her life, and dealt with the wound that he was unable to heal. The silent power of yin receptivity, of holding a sacred space. As such, she is associated with compassion, tolerance... she is known as the midwife of the body and soul, the one who tends to the wounded, accompanies birth and death or, metaphorically, the death of an old identity."

"Wow! How lovely... You know so much!" said Thomas. He looked at her with a new-found glow... a radiating aura borne out of that unexpected moment.

"It is... this whole story fascinated me too. Chariklo, as Chiron's partner, represents the feminine half of the wounded healer and wise teacher. How he surrenders to his wounded warrior nature, immersing his soul in love. Recognising his oneness with nature and all things."

"I'll never look at Chariklo the same way again," said Thomas, amazed.

"And I'd like to know what happened to her. Ever since I was little, I have loved getting to the bottom of stories, discovering the lost pieces of the puzzle. What happened to Chariklo when Chiron switched places with Prometheus? Did she go back to where she came from, becoming a water nymph again? Or did she join Chiron in his celestial home? I like posing questions to see where that gets me... given that we could never know for certain," said Helena.

"I can appreciate that same luminescence of the quest. I too travel the world looking for the best places to observe and uncover the secrets of space… I'm a born romantic, my choice would be for the lovers to have stayed together."

Helena laughed with a unique happiness.

"As lovers meet, they open the portal, the frontier to celestial power, the process of birth, the start and end of a cycle, unchanging truth and the passing of the initiated," said Helena.

"It sounds like poetry."

"The poetry of life," she said, teasing. "Have you ever considered that both diamonds and coal, seemingly opposite in appearance and value, are made from the same carbon? Sometimes you have to explore the depths of the earth to experience those luminous states," Helena reflected, lost for a few moments in contemplative silence. "I like to think of them together too, in that sacred union," she concluded finally.

"May they be together therefore... in the fire of love."

"You really are a romantic."

"I'm as Italian as they come in that sense," he agreed, laughing.

Thomas looked deeply into her eyes.

"I'm ravenous," deflected Helena. "I never eat on planes."

"Let's see if Ditirambo will still serve us," said Thomas.

Helena jumped to her feet.

"I'm up for running," said Helena.

"Now that's hungry. Let's get off then."

Thomas held out his hand and they made their way at a fast pace through the narrow streets until they reached the Piazza della Cancelleria. The feeling of freedom was overwhelming. As if the time between arriving at the airport and the moment of her racing through the streets of Rome hand-in-hand with Thomas had lasted a lifetime. The restaurant was closing, but Thomas quickly organised a special table for them.

"How did you manage that?"

"Easy. The owner is a childhood friend of mine," said Thomas.

"Ah..."

"I hope you don't mind, but I've already ordered for both of us."

"What did you choose?"

"Do you want to know now or be surprised by the flavours?" he asked.

"Oh my. So many surprises in just one day!"

"Ricotta pudding with marinated artichoke, pomegranate and Sicilian sheep's cheese and grilled octopus with celeriac puree with Gaeta olives and liquorice powder."

"Now that's poetry," said Helena, getting excited.

"The poetry of life," Thomas replied with a smile.

They both laughed while they were served a lustrous red wine.

"Okay, I won't ask anything else," said Helena.

Thomas raised his glass to make a toast.

"To life's happy surprises" said Thomas.

Helena held out her hand to touch glasses, looking him right in the eyes.

"By the looks of it, we have the same superstition," said Thomas, amused. "Nobody wants seven years of bad sex."

"It's worse than no sex, for me."

"I know what you mean," he said.

By the time the first course arrived at the table, Thomas and Helena were already lost in conversation, laughing about everything and nothing, intoxicated a little by the fragrance of the Carmignano, the Cinderella of the Chianti region, and also by the tenderness and warmth of that encounter.

It was a feast for the senses, experiencing joy with no need for meaning, poems on existence written in the lines of their lives, in an encounter that would change everything. Even they didn't know how much. When Adriana called Helena, they had both forgotten that they had been waiting for her. Adriana was back home. Their first night had an end in sight. When she finished the call, a kind of enigmatic silence fell over the table.

"Shall we ask for the bill?" proposed Helena.

Thomas asked for the bill, insisting on paying and they left. They walked back to the car in silence. They remained in silence until they reached Adriana's house. Thomas carried her luggage to the front door.

"Home, safe and sound."

"You've completed your mission with flying colours," said Helena, smiling.

"*Grazie.*"

" See you later?" asked Helena.

"Yes, I'll be in Italy for all of July and August. I'll text you. If you have time and if you want to see a little more of Italy, I can be your guide."

"I'd like that a lot. I'll be all yours," she said smiling, before opening her arms for a goodbye hug.

Thomas smiled back, hugging her tightly. A dizzying warmth spread over their skin, their breathing and heart as one, an urge to remain. Without thoughts, they would have. They struggled to pull apart.

"See you."

"See you," said Helena.

Having Adriana waiting for her at the entrance was a relief. Suddenly she began to wonder how a few hours could take up so much space in a life.

"I'm sorry I didn't tell you anything, it was just all so quick and Thomas asked if he could surprise you," said Adriana.

"He told me."

"When the situation came up, he was the only person I could think of. I felt that only he could be my replacement-host. Don't ask me why," said Adriana.

"I wasn't going to," Helena replied with a twinkle in her eyes.

"You already know, don't you?" asked Adriana.

Helena looked at her, saying nothing.

"He was up for it immediately," Adriana explained. "I had spent time with him the last few days and we'd been talking a lot about you, seeing as you were about to arrive."

"Talking about what?" asked Helena.

"About your incredible work. About our connection. That sort of stuff," said Adriana.

"And why didn't you tell me about him?"

"It never came up. I knew you were going to meet each other, but I never thought it would be in these circumstances."

"Life's funny," said Helena.

"Very."

"But what happened to you, Adriana?"

"Look, let's talk tomorrow. We both need our sleep."

"Too right," said Helena.

"Your room's ready. See you tomorrow."

"See you tomorrow."

Perhaps inspired by her first night, in the weeks following her arrival, Helena surrendered to the unpredictability of the days, putting aside any plans she may have had with regard to the documentary, research, interviews or even going to the Vatican Library. She hadn't felt so free and happy for ages. Adriana's home seemed to be the home of every family; despite not living for long in Rome, she had already created an impressive network of luminaries that made every encounter a treat, filled with music, dancing, laughter, excitement, pleasure, intense sharing, new ideas, joint creations.

Her house was one of many located on a small farm, converted by its owners into a small community of artists, with a large inner courtyard, where people could meet up, even during the time of Covid restrictions, and where they had a large terrace next to fruit trees, vegetable gardens, some farm animals, everything you wouldn't expect to find in the middle of Rome. It was a wonderful refuge, enhanced by Adriana's talent as a host. When she thought back to her childhood, she could recall joyful and lively moments like these in those Sunday get-togethers. Moments in which all barriers come crashing down and your body seems to open up entirely to the experience of being alive, without hesitation or doubt. A glowing soul in a body rapturous with the pleasure of living.

The trips, the events, the meals blessed by the skilled hand of talented chefs – which seemed to be ten a penny around there – the performances, the readings, the meditation, and always the music, the rolling rhythm of the body in the dances of the world. Something that brought to mind the idyllic scenarios of Mazunte, the *dolce far niente* engulfing the day, the days, every day, little sleep but a buzz of energy, and among the different faces adorning these encounters, the constant presence of Thomas. Their exchanged glances, the toasts, the poetry in his descriptions of the night sky and his many adventures in inhospitable places; bodies together dancing to Cape Verdian *mornas*, secretly burning; holding hands in the alleyways of Rome, in a sacred silence that they refused to defile. Helena lost count of the days. She had no idea of the day or the hour, carried along by the wave of events. Adriana was overjoyed to see her that way - bursting with light, free as a bird soaring through the skies, after years of working too hard. They barely spoke, to ensure the reflection-words didn't interrupt the flow.

"I'm going on a trip with Thomas," said Helena.

"When?" Adriana asked.

"Today."

"That's great. Where are you going?"

"No idea. I don't know when I'll be back, either. Maybe mid or late August, unless he manages to postpone his trip to the Atacama Desert," said Helena.

"No worries. Call me later."

"Thank you for everything, Adriana. Thank you so much," said Helena genuinely grateful.

"No need to thank me. It's a pleasure."

Italy

Helena set off. She got in Thomas' car as if ready to travel to the end of the world without looking back. Few people make you feel like that, but when it happens, it's as if you've been given your very own Garden of Eden, but without the forbidden fruit. A feeling of paradise, of great peace and confidence, where there is no less, because less is more, the silence is overflowing, words are muses, presence is connection, there is a mirthful joy in travelling along together. They had been alone a few times since that first night, but they had never before experienced this feeling of union that had a beginning, but which didn't seem to have an end.

Thomas had no itinerary in mind, but the country was in his veins, he knew paths less trodden by tourists, the back roads, lakes of crystal-clear waters surrounded by dense forests, so that they could immerse themselves in nature, have picnics where no soul could see them, stroll under the beech and oak trees, visit fishing villages named after women and, at the same time, travel back in time in historic towns, visit fairy-tale palaces, such as the Palazzo Farnese, which brought Helena to tears.

Nights were either spent in campsites in the middle of nowhere, or in magical boutique hotels in the green heart of Italy. It wasn't the price, rather the magic that called these two travellers who liked to hunt for mushrooms, visit medieval towns, such as Spoleto or Assis, eat Norcia cured ham, pizzas topped with truffle shavings and drink locally-produced wines, in those bucolic rural areas of rolling vineyards.

Just before they arrived in Siena, to pick up the SR 222 towards Florence, which Helen believed was a must, given its angelic number, formerly known as the Via Chiantigiana, Thomas turned off to a wonderful natural oasis, at the foot of a medieval village, not far from Arezzo and Cortona. Upon arriving at a stone house, encircled by vines and century-old olive trees, orchards, a herb garden and two lakes, Thomas was welcomed with open arms. Helena came to understand that Thomas had been the guide on many a stargazing evening held there. He had clearly earned a special place in that family's heart through his stories of the cosmos, as they offered him a suite with hot tub on its private balcony.

Until then, despite the magnetic attraction between them, the urge to delay their desire had prevailed, extending those experiences of intense union and wellbeing, which intimate entanglement might elevate or obstruct, provoking new expectations and thoughts. They had never discussed this, but it was among the many implied things connecting them. Their lips had been close to kissing on many occasions, their hearts had leapt from their chests, their bodies had already made love in different dances, there had already been furtive glances when they dressed or undressed, but they had never taken it any further. Here, there was a different feeling in the air. They were both aware of it, clearly. They could no longer tell if it was the intoxicating scent of the vines or if it was the shimmer of their bodies in bathing suits immersed in the hot tub, that took their breath away. When they stepped out of the hub tub, enchanted by the golden light of the setting sun on the horizon, they wrapped themselves up in their white robes as they entered their room and their eyes met, any modesty forgotten.

I'll pause here, to take a breath, as this is the gateway to a love story, which I would only be able to relate to you with words of an insufficient vocabulary to do justice to the love experienced there, in that house, in that room, in that moment, in Civitella in Val di Chiana.

Firstly, I'll revisit the invisible. The emotion of their souls in that intense look. That eternal moment of silence where Thomas and Helena were preparing their hearts for the moment that was about to erupt; flower and fruit of a seed sown in the earth from their very first encounter. They knew instinctively that the universe was preparing itself to witness the genesis of love, ripened in its bosom, in a slow-to-prepare alchemical process. A universe aware of the titanic plan that had led them there, eye to eye. This love gaining matter, form, expression, from which life can blossom, despite neither of them knowing in that instant its exact dimension.

The sensation that pervaded them was so transcendent, so complex and beautiful that the entire cosmos was held in their pupils. They didn't know whether to laugh or cry, because in this hymn to love they were both silently singing, their voices melted into the immense song of all creation. Their bodies aflame with the breath of the sublime, silent in space.

They earnestly wanted to kiss each other, this would be clear to anyone, but in response to this almost indomitable desire, they remained still, in a time that was theirs alone, anchored in the depths of their eyes, as if they were floating in outer space. Faced with the mystery that was unfolding, they could no longer tell who was he, who was she. To my eyes they seemed merged, despite the physical distance between them, which in that timelessness had also disappeared. They drew closer, although neither seemed to move. Their white robes on the ground, without anyone seemingly removing them. Filling the room: the sound of their breathing getting deeper. Helena breathing Thomas. Thomas breathing Helena. The sense of the divine bringing them together. As close as possible without still touching.

Sages of advanced civilizations, scientific experts, psychics or futurists: who on this earth could one day describe with exactitude the alchemical formula of these moments? How can you describe the glimmers of the infinite in the language of men? Everything I write is just a vain attempt at giving a name to something that appears unnameable to me. One more try. If Helena's feelings could be seen through words, maybe we would read:

I'm not thinking about you, because you're already in me, we are already something more than you and I. Everything and nothingness invade me in the breathless silence of this gaze. I understand everything I have ever wanted to feel, this powerful vibration of my heart resonating with the infinite. There is a rising fever in my body, a desire to experience this love that has no bounds. I yearn for this love to triumph over all the fears. But the word fear burns and contaminates. How can I live the everyday after this? I struggle against this question that has come to haunt me. A gloom looms in my gaze. I feel like running away. But I feel much more like staying.

When they finally kissed, space and time and everything that "the all" contains disappeared, as we know it on earth. Narrating this moment in which their lips and tongues started to merge, exchanging beams of heaven in those sacred chalices of theirs, is increasingly difficult for me. Hands brushing across their skin in that powerful desire and in full knowledge of their cosmic bodies.

They say that every dream man dreams, the world leaps and advances; I say that, every time man loves like this, every time love merges two beings, the cosmos is expanded, consciousness celebrates, reactions in the earthly world multiply and are like waves that know no end.

They undressed on the bed, lingeringly contemplating each other with their eyes, their mouths and the tips of their fingers. Their only words were in the strange language of lovers, sighs, moans, exclamations, murmurs, hands and mouths and skin in this timeless dance. I am so immersed in their story that I don't know when they intertwined in a deep embrace. Helena's legs wrapped around Thomas, her vagina feeling the hardness of his penis, their noses in communion breathing in each other's essence. Their eyes losing distance, blurred images in the depth of fusion. Thomas' hands on Helena's back, powerful, as if they knew how to penetrate her body.

Once again, in the middle of the whirlwind of sensations and pleasure, that thought of someone sat at its centre. Helena. Perhaps thinking: I want you inside me, but I hesitate. I want to slow it all down. To stop even, so that time cannot beat us. Ever.

And suddenly, quite unexpectedly, she recalls the weariness that flowed in her veins before she met Thomas, before that exact encounter. As if her soul had crossed the multiverse in fractions of a second in search of all the lines where she had striven to feel like this, in perfect union with everything, understanding all the pain, all the scars, all the instances, all the trajectories leading right here.

Their intimacy expanded in a slow process of continuous adjustments. From surrender to surrender, until feeling was all that remained. In the torrent of kisses of endless variations, they felt absurdly reborn, eager to endlessly laugh. In their own private garden, they skilfully harvested the nectar from their mouths, savoured the perfume of their skin and uttered the poetry of love, which gave them ground and dematerialised at the same time, which gave them direction and damnation, in the same note. The symphony was writing itself. Music reverberated in the depths, towards their centre.

When Thomas finally entered her, Helena opened herself to all the vibrations of the infinite, as if extending her arms towards ecstasy in that ball of fire that coursed through her, no longer aware of the limits of her body, water streaming from her eyes in an outpouring of love. A journey of joy, pleasure and love flowing through the veils of all dimensions. A body-fest-journey until dawn, leaving their souls singing a song of eternal gratitude.

When the first rays of sunlight bathed their bed, we could see two bodies wrapped around each other, their mouths and noses as one, as if they were still breathing and merging through the element of air. Thomas' eyes fluttered open slightly at the same time as Helena's. They smiled, before dropping their eyelids again, allowing themselves to remain in their love nest.

When they heard a knock on the bedroom door, and opened their eyes again, they realised that the sun was already high in the sky and they had fallen back to sleep for a few hours. They had brought a delicious meal to their room, seeing as they had been missing at dinner and breakfast. Thomas went to the door to accept and thanked them for such a lovely gesture. The light that emanated was so strong that the landlady melted into smiles, inspired by the light she was absorbing. Thomas returned to the bed with a tray that seemed to have been sent by the heavens, with delicacies that had surely invaded the dreams of their hungry bodies.

"Jesus! They were listening to my dreams," said Helena, throwing herself onto the tray of food.

"Yours and mine too! I think a genie of the lamp is watching us somewhere."

"But a genie with more than three wishes, no? Wasting one on breakfast would be a little daft of us, or maybe not," she said, laughing like a fool, licking the jam off her fingers that had fallen in her attempts to spread it on her toast in the midst of shaking with laughter.

"There's always that wish where you ask for all your wishes to come true, and then case closed."

"I don't know how I feel about being certain in advance that all my wishes will come true," sidestepped Helena, as she nibbled at a bunch of grapes.

"You're right. It would be strange to know in advance. Better to be surprised along the way."

"That's it. That's it," Helena remarked eyeing the banquet that had been presented to them, already deflated by hunger.

After happily licking the tray clean, they rolled back into bed, laying with a smile glued to their lips.

"You are a wish come true," said Thomas without looking at her after a few minutes of silence.

Helena looked in his direction, surprised.

"Sorry?"

Thomas turned to her, looking her in the eye.

"You are a wish come true."

Helena smiled spontaneously at the power of that phrase. She searched for words in the expanses of her mind, to no avail. She turned to her heart.

"You're a wish come true for me too. A gift from the universe. I must have done something really good to be given something like this."

"That's two of us thinking the same thing."

They kissed very lightly, perching their lips like a bee on a flower, in just the time it takes to gather the pollen, and then turned back around, eyes on the ceiling, the complicit silence of their teeming thoughts and emotions. Until Thomas leapt to his feet, as if someone had shouted fire, dressing quickly.

"I'll be back in a sec. Get yourself ready, we're going out!"

Helena laughed. She loved these outbursts from Thomas, how he embraced life and swept it along with him. She went to take a shower and, doing justice to the finest shower singers, belted out the few songs she could remember the lyrics to. When Thomas returned, she was finishing getting ready. He looked at her as if for the first time, dazzled by her radiance, her smile, her beauty.

Thomas had already noticed that Helena was a lover of dresses... linen, silk, cotton, embroidered, lacy, crocheted, printed, floral, tribal, daring, delicate, long, short, flowing or closely fitted, vintage, modern, casual, glamorous, dresses for girls, for women, for goddesses, for angels, in a dizzying diversity, covering every age of womanhood, goddess woman in her different guises, lunar cycles, ages, but always beautiful, always surprisingly beautiful. Often hats, scarves in her hair, necklaces, bracelets, earrings, many rings. Always a book and a small notebook in her shoulder bag.

After all those days, Thomas was no longer expecting to be surprised, he didn't suppose that a new dress could still emerge from that small travel bag, like doves or rabbits from a magician's hat. But in that white dress, with its bateau neckline and bare shoulders, in a statement of pure sensuality, with its flouncy, slightly transparent skirt and delicate macramé details, it was a new Helena-painting that revealed itself; he seemed to be looking at her for the first time, the first time after the merging of their bodies, the total surrender to the love that revealed her there in her deepest purity.

"I'm ready, Monsieur Thomas. Where are you taking me, sir?"

Thomas smoothed down his scruffy locks.

"You're making me look bad, like that. You're simply smouldering. A wonderful, Venusian, movie star. I have the feeling that even an astrophysicist could never match your sparkle," he said with a mischievous smile. "Wait a second! I'll have to put on my leather jacket if I'm going to be half-worthy to co-star in your film," he added, giggling, yet overwhelmed with love and admiration.

Helena looked out of the open window, out at the idyllic setting around them, inhaled deeply and when she turned around Thomas was already back, wearing his leather jacket over a white t-shirt, round glasses and a scarf around his neck. His hair was still unkempt, which gave him a rebellious look that Helena liked.

"Ah that was it, I've been wracking my brain for his name... you really look like that Greek model, Aristotelis something..."

"Like the philosopher! Never heard of him, but if he's a model I'll take it as a compliment."

"You might even be better looking!" said Helena.

Thomas laughed, a tad flustered, unsure what to say.

"Let's go," he said taking her hand and sidestepping the subject. "You'll need this!" he said, handing her a jacket.

When they got outside, Helena saw the Vespa waiting for them, with a huge picnic basket attached to the back, along with blankets and a few other neatly-wrapped items at the front that she couldn't quite make out. Her surprise was so perfectly packaged that it left her dumbfounded.

"How did you manage that?" asked Helena, amazed.

"Aren't you the one who likes solving enigmas?"

"Come on, tell me," said Helena.

"It's one of the experiences they do here. It was either a Vespa or horse-riding... both cinematographic, but I thought the Vespa was more intrinsically Italian. And then all I had to do was add a few little touches of my own," he explained with a cheeky smile. "They're the ones you should be thanking. You know production assistants in films? That's what they're like here. You ask and they find. You can even ask them for the stars," Thomas concluded proudly.

"Perfect. Where you taking me?"

"To the sky, Madame."

The wind in her face, the landscape, her arms wrapped around Thomas and her face resting on his back, that feeling of safety, of magic, of eternity, all this was just as she had imagined in who knows how many romantic films with scenes like this one. It was a moment of complete happiness, with no other thought than the desire to hold onto that overflowing source of emotion, to keep it firmly locked up in the back room of her memory, to pull out on rainy days.

When the moped stopped and she was pulled out of her reveries, it was as if time had stool still, but the landscape had definitely not, nor the hands of the clock. She had no idea how they'd got there, but they were now in a small clearing in the middle of an enchanted forest, close to a large lake and, on the other side of the lake, mountains rose up in the distance adding the final touch to the perfect canvas. She couldn't see a soul. It was the Italian *Blue Lagoon*. Words failed her. She looked at Thomas in awe, trying to bring words to the torrent of sensations she'd experienced in the last few days, but to no avail. Thomas could feel what she was feeling, leaving him enraptured and joyful to be part of that piece of life. He quickly set about removing everything packed on his Vespa, spreading the blankets out on the floor, sleeping bags, picnic basket packed with goodies and even two notepads and pens.

"Wow! A forewarned man is worth two! I'm not sure if I've translated it well into English, it's a popular expression in Portugal, I don't know if you have it here too," said Helena, her eyes widening as she watched him preparing everything as if by magic.

"Better than forewarned, is a passionate man," he said, almost between his lips, looking her in the eye.

That desire for their bodies to merge hadn't left them for a single moment since they'd woken. There was a longing to return to that place, to that feeling of union, to that expression of love, to that pleasure experienced that seemed to have been conceived in another dimension. They wildly embraced, kissing each other as if the world were about to end. In the midst of that daze, and already breathless, Helena pulled away a little, while slowly taking off her white dress, revealing her lacy white lingerie. She sat down on the rug, her eyes never leaving Thomas. Thomas followed her moves. He slowly undressed, his eyes still locked on her, and sat down before her, in nothing but his tight black boxers, giving her his hands. They stared at each other long enough to lose any sense of time: two souls in communion, then Thomas started to caress her, inviting her to lie down. The sun streamed down onto their bodies, creating the perfect cocoon for them. That place seemed to welcome their desire for fusion, fire and water, Divine Feminine and Divine masculine, to give form and expression to love. And Helena's skin welcomed all the majestic pleasure that Thomas' knowledgeable hands and warm lips were able to give her. Together with the sun's rays, these two finest of lovers worked in unison, transporting her to the heavens; a dazzling sky-blue canvas punctuated with white, which, from time to time, she could see when opening her eyes amidst throes of pleasure; her heart racing, uncontrollable moans coursing from her lips, and then tears, overflowing as she felt Thomas entering her slowly, in a perfect alchemy, carrying them onwards to a protracted explosion; a mystical experience of union with everything around them.

It took them a while until they returned to so-called normality. They felt like laughing, at nothing and at everything. At a sound, at a movement, at a thought. Joy was pulsing through their pores, the sun already lower on the horizon. The colours of the scenery as spectacular as the colours their hearts seemed to emanate.

By the time they got dressed, they were starving again. That picnic basket seemed to them to be the most beautiful gift, sent by the universe. They ate and drank in silence, taking in the enchantment of the place.

"You know the power of intention, Helena," he said, raising his glass of wine. "If I had a candle here, I would light it. You see, I didn't remember everything," he laughed. "May the intertwining of our two worlds, the baggage from our past, of our paths, may it be addition, multiplication, potentiation, even division can be present, but if there is to be subtraction... may that subtraction not be of joy, or lightness, or trust, and may it be borne only of our own volition. Like a sculptor, honing his work, perfecting it; or the urge to remove old garments, to deconstruct past walls, or to close cycles. I pray we will be able to give it all, while always having more - like a candle flame which ignites another. May we have the courage to let this love transform us, even when there are thorns, because there will be, all roses have them, and may we experience many moments like this one, complete, with this intense sensation of union, knowing that..."

"...there is no other place in the world where we would prefer to be in this moment," Helena concluded.

They smiled at each other, eternity quivering.

"How beautiful, Thomas! You even brought tears to my eyes. I have nothing to add. Your intention is mine," said Helena.

As they toasted, a ray of sunlight touched their glasses. They smiled, touched too. They sipped, fully engaged, as if performing some sacred ceremony.

"I've been going to Chile for ten years, because it is one of the best places in the world for stargazing, and whenever I go, I take some time to experience indigenous wisdom. When I was little, I used to find it hard to distinguish dream from reality. My nights were awash with dreams. I was, literally, a living dream lab. When I realised that some of them were prophetic, or better put, pre-cognitive, but back then I had no idea what name I should give them, I got scared. I was so scared that I must have somehow shut it all down, and for many years I would wake unable to remember a thing. It was if I wasn't dreaming at all. One day in Chile, someone told me about the Mapuche and their connection to dreams, and I felt a calling from my soul. The Mapuche were the first of many indigenous peoples I came across on my travels through the Americas. The Celtic culture, the wisdom of the Druids had already lifted many veils when I was studying in Wales, in my twenties, but then in Chile, in Peru, in Brazil, in Mexico, in the US, I met some shamans that made an impression on me... and it wasn't just what I could hear from them, learn from them, nor solely through the ceremonies I did, it was something bigger than that, something that you could only feel when you were there, with them. It's almost like a direct transfer of energy, of information," said Thomas.

"I understand perfectly."

"I'm talking too much, aren't I?"

"No. I love listening to you," said Helena.

"I mentioned shamans, but many of them don't like this expression. It was popularised, I believe, in the 17th century, through the travel journals of a Dutch explorer in Siberia, where he spoke of the Saman, people who were proficient in the ancestral practices of healing, ecstasy, devotion and connection with the transcendent. The word stuck. But we're talking about Shamanism and what does that entail? Practices tens of thousands of years old, and very much needed in today's world, don't you think? Recognising the sacred and the transcendent, respect for ecology, the relationship and interconnection of everything, the need for expanding human consciousness, communication with other worlds, dimensions and realities," said Thomas.

"I feel the same. But, as you're a scientist, don't you ever feel judged or looked down on by your colleagues for being interested in these things?" asked Helena.

"There's a little of everything, as in life. Some feel that spirituality undermines the credibility of science, whereas many of them focus on the importance played by religions, and there are others that don't think that way, but give into peer pressure. They think it's better to keep quiet so as not to affect their chances of getting funding. But this is changing too. Have you heard of the Templeton Prize? It honours people of science who are able to go beyond their own area of specialization and manage to make a contribution to the spiritual dimension of existence. There are already many scientists publicly rejecting the idea that only science can lead to definitive truths about the nature of reality. Many believe in God. As Marcelo Gleiser says, "The absence of evidence is not evidence of absence".

"That's true. So true," Helena agreed.

"I have long modelled myself on peacocks. It was a decision I took after my first ceremony," said Thomas.

"What do you mean?"

"Peacocks harbour a great mystery. They don't die from ingesting toxins. They can transform those poisons. And when I feel these stares, less friendly observations, criticism as threats, when they want to put me into their little box, I put all of this into my alchemical pot and transform. I use every perspective to my advantage. Like pieces of a puzzle that can bring me more information about the whole."

"Smart. Can you really stop it from affecting you?" asked Helena.

"It's a process. Everything is a path. For me it's very logical. Many of those who chose this path were children enraptured with creation, passionate about the starry sky, curious about what might lay beyond. The questions we keep on asking are older than science itself. For me it makes entire sense to recognise the wisdom of those who came before us, to honour a long human lineage. And this fusion of scientific methodology and ancestral knowledge has sharpened my imagination; it has opened my mind, my realm of possibilities, forcing me to ask more questions, which I may or may not be able to prove," he answered.

Thomas had been one of these children. He would escape to the terrace whenever his parents argued, that is, whenever his father returned from his travels. His mother couldn't stand the long absences and, when his father was finally around, his mother turned the space into a hell. This would hasten his departure and delay his arrival. During such absences, his mother's depressions hung heavy and that terrace was a place of wonderment, of escapism, and of peace. When, one day, he dreamt about the exact outcome of his parents' final argument, the last time the three of them would find themselves in the same house, and he saw it all play out in a distressing *dejá-vu*, all the details, where he was, where they were, how he reacted, he closed the door on dreaming, for fear of influencing reality. A small crack remained however. And that fragility of the system – those fragilities that are rather strengths in the light of a new perspective, pain and scars that might reveal themselves as a portal to evolution – allowed the light to flood back in.

"Can you remember the dreams now?" asked Helena.

"Yes, it was one of those gifts that came from one of those ceremonies I did," said Thomas.

"Ayahuasca?"

"Yes. I came back feeling connected, united to the forces of creation, part of the cosmic symphony."

"I'd really like you to tell me about it," said Helena.

"One day, Helena, today I would like to savour with you everything we see, hear, touch, anchor the magic of this moment in every cell of my body. I didn't even know it was possible to love a woman like this."

Helena lowered her eyes and face in a spontaneous gesture of shyness. She could feel her heart beating in her chest. Those words were still vibrating. Thomas lifted her face with two fingers on her chin, turning it towards the lake and the mountains, where someone was painting a myriad of colours in the sky, which were reflecting in the water, the trees, in the two of them... the beauty was so overwhelming that it hurt. Helena grabbed her notebook and began writing unabated, all in a single breath. Thomas smiled, looking at her with admiration, until she finally put down her pen. The landscape had already taken on other emotion-colours.

"My two favourite artists: you and nature," said Thomas smiling. "Are you going to read it out?"

Helena, after rereading her words in silence, looked at Thomas, stood up and began to read to him, as if dancing to the music of the words.

"We are like a poem in movement, always changing rhymes, without rhymes, changing words and meanings, concepts, with or without meaning, but always a poem, being processed, in evolution, in this magic of who we are, melding everything inside us, the sky and the earth, realms and dimensions, in a mysterious alchemy, mirror of the cosmos, stardust, sacred geometry, miracles of love bodies made of atoms that have travelled the world, that have travelled eras, that have been stream, stone, volcano, yew, olive tree, rose, water, horse, falcon, butterfly, gold, crystal, and now our body, living, seed forever, fruit forever, people that we are of the earth, maybe descendants of people from the stars, as the ancient ones tell us, learning with the trees the best way to live in Gaia, with deep roots in the soil, able to carry the light of the sun to the earth, and learn from the spirit of animals and plants, to recall, to bring back to the heart the knowledge gathered on the path of our souls.

"We are this mysterious ark, womb of life and of dream, able to see what is yet to exist and create the new; humans with consciousness, who think and observe what is thought, who feel and feel again what was though, recreating emotional memory, many times a cage, often rumination, others yearning, others wisdom, travelling beings of a thousand faces, heroes of our journey, with the power to transform everything through love. And I believe that some of us are already trying to be a bit like angels, but we can't quite flap our wings purely enough, we stumble in our earthly trappings or we don't stumble at all, we like them too much, we grow attached to them. There is a special magic in the voice that sings, in the music that we compose, we can call it celestial music, but I don't know if there is music in the kingdom of angels. There must be. All the cosmos sings. We like the embraces the body allows us, surrendering to pleasure in the river of love, sacred fusion of the bodies, rejuvenation in laughter, in joy, in dance. Do angels get emotional seeing us like this? With our emotions that are so intense, tears of joy, gratitude... It is so absolutely magical! And even so, there are some who see none of this, their eyes set on the robotization of their days, in the black holes of problems that suck everything in, hypnotized by fear..."

Helena looked at Thomas, suspended like a note of music, staring at her in rapture.

"It's not the end, but this is how far I got," said Helena.

"Words fail me. I feel overcome with emotion. Let's go down to the water... I think I need to bathe to allow your song-poem to swim within me," said Thomas.

"You go. I'll be there in a bit."

The last hues of the day swapped their garments for stars, while they made love in the water; knowing that there would be few days like this one, they surrendered intensely to the moment, without ifs, without subtracting anything.

When they came back, they wrapped themselves into the same blanket and started to laugh. About nothing. About contentment. About them being able to have the privilege of being so earthly and transcending.

"Do you want to stay? Spend the night? I've come prepared," said Thomas.

"I would love to."

Gathering up stones and twigs, Thomas lit a fire. It wasn't cold. Quite the contrary. It was of one of those summer nights you dream about, but contemplating the flames was a pleasure too difficult to resist. Helena took the bread, cheese and some tins out of the basket and, as they ate, they savoured the same sensation they might have enjoyed from a meal prepared by a Michelin-starred chef, so delicious was their simple repast.

They then lay down, side by side, to gaze at the stars.

"Sometimes as an antidote to the fear of death, I eat the stars," Thomas proclaimed to the air.

"That's lovely," said Helena with a smile.

"They're not my words, but they could have been. They're the first lines of a poem by Rebecca Elson."

"Are you afraid of dying?" asked Helena.

"I don't know much about death," said Thomas, laughing.

Helena laughed back.

"Do you think that death is the end?" asked Helena.

"What is the end? It's like saying the Big Bang was the beginning. Whenever we learn something new, we become more aware of how little we know. About the vastness of the unknown. That's why we need many eyes gazing up, increasingly powerful observation instruments and plenty of imagination. We always need to ask many questions; however absurd they might seem at first."

"It may seem absurd, but there's a side of me that enjoys dwelling in the melting pot of mystery. Does that sound contradictory to you?" asked Helena. "It's true that I'm insatiably curious, that I do research, I study, I interview, that I grab the end of a ball of thread in Portugal and end up on the other side of the world, always chasing new clues that interweave somewhere. I like to understand how everything interconnects, the origins, which then become lost in the weft of history. I like to uncover what has been hidden. But, at the same time, if you were to ask me: do you want to know what triggers love? I would immediately say no. I like not knowing, living the poem of feeling."

"I know just what you mean," he said. "But would you like to know what lies beyond death, if there is something?"

"I think I prefer the path of questioning. And to draw into myself everything that can enhance my experience of life. You see? I'm a scholar of near-death experiences, but more to take on board the richness of such experiences; how their lives are transformed once the fear of death is removed," she said.

"If you were to ask me, are you afraid of dying now?" Thomas began, half talking to himself.

"What would you say?" Helena immediately asked.

"What would I say? I don't know, I feel so serene and incredibly happy at the moment. If I were to go right now, I would go with a deep sense of peace, flying with glittering wings towards the cosmic embrace..."

"You're a poet," said Helena.

"But I can feel my heart beating harder at the idea. It's not at peace after all. I think it wants more time with you. Much more. And I would like to have children. A daughter, at least. I need to go through my Bucket List again," he said, chuckling.

"I'd like to see this list of yours," said Helena, without tearing her gaze from the stars.

"I ask my heart if I'm honouring the starlight resting in my chest. We're very demanding, don't you think? It seems we have to do something big to validate our life. I don't know if it's self-centred, but I'd like to make some discoveries, bring a little more of the sky down to earth, leave that legacy."

"When did you decide to become an astrophysicist?"

"I can't tell you precisely what my Big Bang was," Thomas said smiling. "I know that I used to love going out on the terrace to look up at the stars ever since I was a child. It was my refuge. My parents didn't get on. My father was always away, travelling. My mother couldn't accept this and when he was home, they fought. I have few memories of us happy, all together. I would take refuge in the world of the stars and of my dreams. It was better than TV. It was more emotional. I would imagine what I couldn't see. And, as I've told you, I would have such vivid dreams, as if I were living in another dimension... and with superpowers that enabled me to do practically anything. One day my father brought me back an incredible microscope from Germany..."

"Oh, how funny, mine too! What a coincidence," said Helena with enthusiasm.

"For me, it made me aware of the magnitude of the world that our eyes cannot see," Thomas continued. "After my microscope, I moved on to a telescope. I asked my father for one... much later, when my parents had separated, he got me one. I started to camp out on the terrace. I built my own observatory. As a teenager I was a bona fide nerd, devouring everything I could find about neutron stars, black holes, quasars, exoplanets dark matter, dark energy, cosmic microwave background radiation; all discoveries that had been spurred on by advances in technology. As you can see, I wasn't a particularly social kid," he added, laughing.

"But you were passionate."

"How could I not be? In a few decades, we were suddenly able to see what, for millennia, we'd only been able to imagine! Observation equipment, data processing, everything evolved exponentially. We have never had so many windows looking out over the universe, such as the Hubble... and now the James Webb, a veritable space Ferrari!" he continued, with growing excitement. "Just to give you an idea, it will be 1.5 billion kilometres from the earth. It's completely revolutionary! It's going to look at a part of space and time never before seen. Its infrared eyes should provide us with images that will take us back to the first stars and galaxies that formed more than 13.5 billion years ago. Many of my colleagues have already applied for time on the James Webb. Everyone wants a ride in the Ferrari, if only for a few hours" Thomas concluded, brimming with pride.

"Where did you do your studies?"

"I went to Cardiff. Pure chance. I can't even recall who told me about it. It might have been my father. They're both British, despite my mother having come to Italy when she was young. English was a constant in my childhood. It wasn't an obstacle."

"Did you like it there?" asked Helena.

"I loved it. I was a time of discovery, on many levels, including personal. I fell in love for the first time with a ravishing redhead, who was passionate about Celtic culture. Doors opened up onto a new world for me, one with sex, drugs and rock and roll in it," he joked.

"Hard drugs?"

"No. I was just kidding. Just to show you how I went from Billy-No-Mates, looking at the sky on his terrace at home, into a world of uni parties, concerts, alcohol, marijuana, and with Annie I even tried magic mushrooms once," said Thomas.

"So, her name was Annie, then?" Helena asked, curious.

"Are you jealous? You can be, I don't mind, as long as it's in homeopathic doses," he added, laughing.

"That's really funny..."

"I'm going to be really honest with you, Helena. Annie was a very important person in my life, no doubt about it. One of those people, how should I call them, portals-bridges-lighthouses-witches..." said Thomas.

"Now I'm really jealous."

"Don't be, it's all in the past, and a good thing too, because if she hadn't existed, I have a feeling that I wouldn't have been ready for you, even fifteen years later."

Thomas sat up, watching the moonlight reflecting on the water of the lake. He then turned to Helena.

"I was the kid with no friends, let alone girlfriends and, suddenly, I was going out with this gorgeous young redhead, who opened the doors onto sacred sexuality, and that alone would have changed my life, but it didn't stop there. Annie was passionate about Celtic culture, about the legends of Avalon, and so we use to spend a great deal of time in Glastonbury, at festivals, taking part in circles, ceremonies. This was when I started to intertwine spirituality with science. She was a wild woman, and I went along for the ride. We spent countless nights in Stonehenge and other stone shrines, many of them closed to the public; having somewhat mystical experiences, some even bizarre. She always found a way to get into these places. I could never work out how she managed it, but I actually got to experience the light piercing the heart of the tomb in Newgrange, at the exact moment of the winter solstice. Even now, my body shivers at the thought of it. Seventeen minutes of goosebumps, of divine presence, of living the mystery. The same sensation that I have felt at times when looking up at the skies. That I have felt today, loving you, here..."

The silence of words took over for a few minutes; they heard the crackling fire, a gentle breeze in the trees, their thoughts.

"Why did it end?" she asked.

"Between me and Annie? It was as spontaneous as how it started. I can't give you the whys and wherefores. It came to an end. It was its natural cycle."

"And you never saw her again?"

"Never. As I said before, from where I am now, with what I've experienced today, with you, I can see that it was like a rite of initiation, of opening horizons, of heightening consciousness, so that the pathways from that point on could one day lead me to you."

Helena sat up, embracing him from behind.

"Thank you for telling me this. For sharing yourself like that," Helena whispered in his ear.

"And you? Did you never want to marry? Have children?" Thomas asked.

"I've always wanted to marry and have kids."

"So, what happened? You could never have been short of suitors!"

"I don't know. I also had one great love, we were young, we went out for a few years, I fell pregnant, he didn't tell me to have an abortion, but he didn't say he wanted to keep the baby either, he just left the decision to me. And I had to deal with the situation on my own. From then on, it was never the same; something had broken and we were unable to put back the pieces," she said.

"Oh, that must have been a painful experience. I don't know, but I would imagine that an abortion is always a difficult experience for any woman, even miscarriages."

"Yes, the scar remains. You know, I never told my parents."

"Why not?" he asked.

"At the time I didn't have it in me, and then there seemed no point. Just now, when you were talking about your colleagues and what you would do when they criticised you, that you wouldn't allow it to affect you, that you would throw it all into your alchemical cauldron, well I wish I could be good at that too. Of course I know all the theory, I understand it, I try to live who I am to the full, my truth, to do only what I'm meant to do, say what I feel, even when it may seem a bit wacky to some, but in practice I allow myself to become affected when people make negative remarks, when they question my work, as if they were questioning my very being... and, between you and me, I really need my parents' approval. It's not even approval, it's really wanting recognition, appreciation... it is what it is! Back then I didn't want to be judged for the decisions I was making in taking away that life," said Helena, touched.

"Do you really think that they would have judged you? That they wouldn't have understood and accepted you?"

"I was the one that couldn't accept me, and that's why it hurt all the more. I was already making all the judgements, imagining my parents' voices inside of me. Of course, then it was easy for them to become the mirror of my reality... but I didn't even have the courage to risk it. I kept it all inside" she said, holding one hand on her heart the other on her belly. "Deep down, I wanted to have that child, but I felt alone, angry with Carlos, and I convinced myself that it wasn't the right time. I invented a heap of logical excuses for taking my decision of going ahead with the abortion, but it wasn't enough to get rid of the suffering."

"At least you are aware of this," said Thomas.

"Yes, I'm fully aware of my unconscious forces" she added, half laughing. "But I'm not always able to stop these forces from shaping my perception of reality."

"Who is? Don't go thinking that I'm always successful in that alchemical process! I'm a Leo," he added, puffing out his chest, while winking with a smile.

"Oh, it must be your birthday soon. When is it?"

"Today!"

"Are you kidding me? You never said anything... Why didn't you tell me? Happy birthday little lion," she said, planting a heartfelt kiss on his lips.

"It couldn't have been any better if I had told you. I will never forget this birthday of mine. My 37th," said Thomas, just centimetres from Helena's face.

"Oh, I'm older than you! I turn 38 in three months, on November 14," said Helena.

"Scorpio."

"Yup, with the moon in Pisces," Helena added.

"So much water..."

"Yes, lots of water, lots of sensitivity, but plenty of fire too!" she said with enthusiasm.

"I really like astrology, too. To think about the archetypes projected in the heavens," Thomas shared.

"You're really unique, an astrophysicist who likes astrology. I have the feeling that there are few astronomers who would admit to that."

"I don't know, we don't talk about astrology, maybe it's still a little taboo, you're right. But I'm a Jungian astrophysicist, I like to explore the soul of the world, the connection between the micro and macro, the material and spiritual. You know... I remember reading a letter from Jung to Freud, no idea in which book now, but he was reflecting on his astrological explorations and asking Freud not to worry about it. Jung wrote something wonderful like: *"Please don't worry about my wanderings in these infinitudes. I shall return laden with rich booty for our knowledge of the human psyche.... For a while longer I must intoxicate myself on magic perfumes in order to fathom the secrets that lie hidden in the abysses of the unconscious."* I also consider myself to be an explorer, and a true explorer cannot detract from his exploration with too many preconceptions. It is on the journey that you find the traveller."

"I can fully identify with what you're saying. I have never studied it, but as I have already told you, there are several astrologers in my parents' group of friends... I have been learning from them, informally, every Sunday," said Helena.

"Every Sunday?"

"Yes, one of the house rituals. Every Sunday, my mother makes lunch for a group of their friends, my parents' friends, the extended family. They don't even need to be invited. It's set in stone. Come rain or shine, friends always show up there. Sometimes a few, sometimes many. At times there have been dozens of them, plus partners and children. I grew up in this environment. Our house was like a place of pilgrimage on Sundays. Writers, musicians, actors, philosophers, you name it, a little of everything, and there were several astrologers, because my mother did actually study astrology for many years."

"How wonderful! It sounds just like the meetings at Adriana's house, doesn't it? Your Sundays full of people and mine full of imaginary people, because there was only my mother and I, except on rare occasions."

"What is your mother like?" she asked.

"A personality you could describe as being the archetypal bipolar, but not literally. She was so wrapped up in her own world, kind of depressed, as she seemed like a tornado, capable of sweeping up the world with her. Back then we would do the most random things; no rules could hold us back, and for a kid who was so often without a mother, these outings were magical. Crazy adventures! She is very talented, she's a painter, her paintings are on show in many galleries, and when she awoke with her creative juices flowing, the house was filled with happiness, with song," answered Thomas. "But when my father got home from long trips abroad, at times for months, everything was ruined, the house came tumbling down."

"I see what you're saying. Interesting... And your father, what's he like?"

"I don't know much about my father," he laughed. "Come to think about it, I said the same thing when you asked me about death" Thomas added, while still laughing. "But it's true, I know very little about what he likes, what he does, about his childhood, family, what he's done in his life. I really know very little."

"Don't you ever talk? Don't you ask him? What with you being so curious, and all?"

"In recent years we have been talking more than usual, because he travels, I travel, and sometimes we cross paths and have lunch, but our conversations are never personal. When I was a child, I got used to living without him, and so, when he was finally home, I wasn't particularly drawn to him either. Perhaps the opposite, even: I would get really anxious, shut myself up in my room with my toys, go to the terrace even more often, always anticipating the next argument. He would try to get close to me, bringing me things that he knew interested me, but I would only be interested in the things and not in him. Once they were separated though, I think I saw more of him. And when I went to Cardiff, whenever he was visiting his family in England, he would come and visit me too."

"Right, so you said. Your parents are British. My father is too, but like your mother, he moved to Portugal when he was young. For me though, he doesn't have a nationality, he's more a man of the world. But... do you like your father?" Helena asked.

"I do. He's an interesting man," said Thomas light-heartedly. "If he were a friend, I think I would actually like him a lot, but he's my father, an absent father, who I could never really count on, and it's difficult to be impartial, I don't really know what I feel."

"I can see that it saddens you a little. Let's not talk about it anymore. It's your birthday, unless the day is over already... is it past midnight yet?"

"No idea, I don't want to get my phone to see what time it is."

"Ah, that's right, you haven't look at your phone once today! You must have missed so many calls and happy birthday messages."

"I didn't want to have to share my attention. Today I'm only sharing you with the stars and, even so, as you've already noticed, you win hands down! My mother and my friends are used to me being shut off from the world during the night and sleeping during the day... they probably think I'm in the desert," said Thomas.

"Right..." stammered Helena, looking down. "When do you leave for Chile?"

"And to think, you didn't want to see me getting sad, and now you remind me that I won't be with you for two months."

"Two months?" she asked, surprised.

"Maybe a little longer. I'll try and get back for your birthday. And I shouldn't complain, because this is probably the first year that I've had July and August off work. I took a two-month sabbatical. I felt I needed it. Little did I know that I was getting ready to receive the most beautiful birthday present from the universe!"

Among kisses, Helena couldn't stop herself from asking the question: "But when are you going?"

"In September. I go from summer to spring," he said, a slight smile on his lips. "I reverse the seasons," he said, trying to lighten the moment. "But we still have many days before us, enough to travel all of Italy!"

Helena remained silent, watching the light reflected in the darkness of the lake.

"I'm being serious, Helena," Thomas said. "From now on let's act as if we have all the time in the world; then we won't have to think about it. Let's keep eternity on our side and, at the same time, pretend that we are living the last day before my departure, tomorrow the last, the day after tomorrow the last, every day the last, so that we can devour every minute, every little piece of this heaven on earth of ours, ok?"

"You're right. We have all the time in the world, on this, our last day. Let's go to sleep," she said seriously, joking.

Thomas hugged her. They fell asleep in each other's arms, feeling an open smile in their hearts as they slipped into the world of dreams, clinging to each other, their bodies tenderly entwined, Helena's head resting unconditionally on Thomas' heart, both of them determined not to allow time to constrain them, or the perception of time, or lack of it. And that's just what they did when they hit the road again, and just what they did on all the days thereafter, as they created memories in the places through which they passed, in every cell of their bodies, with every experience they had: when hearing the eternal song of the crickets on nights when they were wild camping, on the tips of their fingers, in everything they touched, in the fields full of grapes and olives, on lazy mornings, in their bare feet on the ground, in every sunrise and sunset, in the coffee rituals on seafront terraces, in every piece of paradise, in every deep conversation, in every glass of wine, in every breath, in every look.

In Forte dei Marmi they stocked up on sea breezes and summer scents. In the Gulf of La Spezia they wove endless poems, touched by its beauty; a feast for the eyes and for their souls. Someone told them Botticelli had met Simonetta Vespucci there, his inspiration for two of his most iconic masterpieces: the *Birth of Venus* and *Venus and Mars.* Mars being Giuliano de Médici, evoking one of those overpowering yet impossible love stories. They had both smiled at this because they shared a taste for delving into the memories of places, diving into history and into the stories hidden in the arms of every *Genii Loci*, the soul of the place, its protective spirit.

In the houses that had been lived in continuously throughout the centuries, they could feel the energy of a myriad of events, so entwined and fused in time, that they are now impossible to single out. They laughed at the possibility of coming across an Etruscan tomb in some backyard, and became lost in lengthy journeys back in time through their imaginings. "The whole landscape is a manuscript that we can learn to read again," they often told themselves, making their hearts swell.

They loved having an intimate connection with places. Every time they felt called to a particular place, building, environment, landscape, they would stop, close their eyes for a moment and allow themselves to feel. They would pose two questions, welcoming answers without judgement. "What events took place here?" and "Who am I in this place?". They thus allowed the *Genii Loci* to whisper in their ear and they would embroil themselves in the new stories that, to them, seemed to belong there.

We are never alone observing space. Space is observing us too. For, just as we can interpret the signs spread over it and uncover the stories woven into it over time, it also throws us into personal revelations, memories etched within us that we didn't even know existed. And the stories that Thomas and Helena would share afterwards, their eyes bright, their hearts impassioned, would transform the journey and the spaces, holding hands with past generations, ancestors whose blood could now flow in their veins.

In every town, every village along the way, every church, fountain, convent, on every green hill, rocky mountain, beside every lake, every towering chestnut tree, they would slip into the shoes of travellers and pilgrims, hunting out the invisible thread of narratives, at times taking on other identities, revelling in the creation of a new map of memories, theirs, and those of their love on this path of discovery.

The tangle of lives and stories of lovers that had preceded them, tucked into bends in the road, into the corners of houses, into fragments of the landscape, were now intertwined with theirs. Every place occupied them, just as they occupied the places.

They took everything at a slow pace... despite the urgency of love. With each day that passed, new poems were discovered as the pages slowly turned between the magical coastal towns of Riomaggiore and Corniglia. The pastel landscapes that welcomed them with a broad smile of serenity, were joined by the rich colours of villages clinging to the rocks above small harbours. So many embraces and kisses shared in cobbled alleys, so many new dreams dreamt in contemplation. So much fresh fish, fruit and vegetables, freshly-made pasta with pesto and focaccia. Thomas delighted in surprising Helena; like when he took her by canoe to a naturist beach in Corniglia, a stunning, untouched pebble beach lapped by turquoise waters. And when he taught her how to choose genuine *gelato*.

"If the banana ice cream is yellow, keep on walking. If it's a weird beige colour, like a banana when you leave it out, then stop where you are. This is the place we're looking for."

Helena would never forget it. Not this lesson, not anything of this trip. Her body was sacred ground to be inscribed in her core, her heart unprepared for so much immersion, juxtapositions and interpenetrations of so many feelings, so many profane experiences of the sacred, her heart surrendering time after time. At times, fears would flood into her mind, unspoken doubts, girlish insecurities, despite the power of that love, because of the power of that love.

Corsica

On a whim they caught a ferry to the 'mountain in the sea', Corsica, an island paradise, upon whose soil, many battles had been waged. The powerful, untamed nature of Corsica called to them, as did the lack of people in the inland forests. The assault on the senses was generous: their eyes amazed by the fortified towns, built high on the hilltops and anchored in crystal-clear waters; their mouths delighted by the sublime flavour of brocciu, the sheep's or goat's cheese with its explosive aroma; their ears captivated by the musicality of the Corsican language; their noses seduced by the resin-soaked scrubland or sweet-scented flowers; their skin touched by the hot sun and refreshing seawater. And, finally, their imagination moved by those cliffs, eroded by time, but still supporting so many lives.

After a while, the turquoise-blue bays were replaced by the wild beauty of the island's interior, wandering among flocks of goats and sheep, exploring the magical forest of Bonifatu and Monte Cinto, the island's highest peak. They stayed in Artemisia, a small refuge surrounded by nature, charmed by its simplicity.

On their return, they were left with the feeling that everything was powerful and striking there, from the people to the landscape, a wild heart that made them feel even more unrestrained in the expression of their love. Nothing, not even norms, rules or life's impositions could hold them back.

The dream

Back in Italy, destiny determined that they drive to the Fattorie Santo Pietro Farmhouse, another of those places Thomas knew well. If the idea was for them to a find a retreat in which to spend the last days of their trip, before Thomas' departure for Chile, they were instead surprised by a wedding celebration. The festive atmosphere, the joy shared by the happy couple, friends and family, the music, the dancing, that beauty and madness that permeates a summer wedding, all of this impacted their hearts in a unexpected way. The wedding was being held for the estate owner's nephew, and they were readily invited to join in. Thomas was like family, the owner said, and he wouldn't accept no for an answer. They stayed for the wedding, but were feeling ill at ease, so kept their distance. They exchanged glances in their confusion, silently deciding their next move. They didn't feel like hitting the road again either; for a certain weariness seemed to have fallen upon them. Indeed it was that party, that joy, the most improbable cause for sadness, but that was just what it caused. It was as if they could see their love from outside, their desires, and they were now able to touch the future, his departure, not their union, but the oceanic distance that was coming after having lived it all in a Dionysian intensity.

"It's all so strange. I'd never thought about the time we have or don't have. Here, now, I feel so sad... it feels like you're leaving forever," Helena said, a tear falling down her cheek.

"My love," Thomas whispered, wiping the tear from her face. "I feel it just as intensely. If someone were to ask what I would like to do right now, my heart would utter crazy, delusional things, such as that I would like to stay here, marry you, have children together, now..."

Helena raised her face, a broad smile etched on it, as if she had received the power of the gods in those words.

"You make me feel so happy! Come! Let's make the most of this party and celebrate love," she said, grabbing Thomas' hand and dragging him to the dance floor.

From then on, they drank and danced until their strength was sapped, and any possible sadness was replaced by a contagious happiness. To their intoxicated eyes, that happy couple was dazzling. For them, all people touched like this by love were bright and beautiful. That party was the best they had ever been to and they felt like they were the most blessed couple in the universe. As no rooms were available, they fell asleep in some chairs by the pool before sunrise, with a smile plastered on their faces, a huge sense of peace, security and joy in their hearts.

On the following day, still intoxicated by the same happiness, they decided to start the return journey back to Rome but, on their way, they were lured by the white waters of the Bagni San Filippo. Nature really does perform wonders, and the idea of bathing in those hot natural pools, that white sculptures formed by calcium deposits over the years, felt like the fairy tale their bodies needed after the excesses of the previous day. But there were too many people, and Thomas would rather give them one last night in the arms of nature, but far from the crowds, before getting back to Rome.

They arrived just before sunset and the golden magic descended naturally over everything. Helena felt like crying, overwhelmed by the intense feeling this place aroused in her; the beauty seemed to rise up from the depths and reach for the sky.

"How do you know these places?" asked Helena.

"During the night you'll understand," Thomas answered, smiling.

Sure enough, as night fell and the curtain rose on the stage of stars and the performance of the full moon proved as spectacular as the sky paintings of the setting sun, Helena took Thomas' hand, beaming a smile at him.

"I think that one of the things that I like most about my job is discovering the best places to examine the night sky. Of course, Italy is my country and so I know many interesting spots... but as a consequence of my research I have been taken to many remote and unlikely places."

"Taken?"

"Yes, by the very phenomena that I am studying. We have to determine, in advance, the exact location on the planet from where it would be best to view the occurrence of these phenomena. And, in these areas, when we don't have any colleagues, we go there ourselves. I recently had to go to a small mining town in the middle of the Australian desert, with kangaroos all around me, to observe the planet Venus. When we arrive with all our equipment in these end-of-the-world places, people look at us as if we are Indiana Jones. In the Azores, for example, I had to convince the management of the hotel in which I was staying to turn off all the nights for a night."

"You're so fortunate!"

"Well, you, too, have travelled the world, carried along by what excites you," he said.

"That's true."

"And what moves you the most at the moment? You haven't really told me what you're researching," said Thomas.

"Love," she said softly, looking Thomas in the eyes.

"The most researched subject of all time, is it not?" he replied, a huge smile on his face.

"The source is inexhaustible on that theme," she said, kissing him on the lips. "But... I was only joking with you! At the moment, I'm still on the hunt for the linchpin of this new documentary of mine. The operative word is Truth. I feel that I have to build something on top of this premise, but this subject is such a long drawn-out dance, that I had decided to be guided by the universe, to see where it would take me. But instead of the Vatican library, which I had in mind, it has taken me on a unique journey with a man called Thomas."

"The universe is intelligent," said Thomas with a huge smile.

"Ditto that."

"Do tell me more... love... truth... you don't mess around," he said, laughing.

Helena laughed with him, a little embarrassed.

"Oh... it's just somewhere to start. There are some things I've been mulling over for some time now, but now they've taken on greater importance. In the past, people who questioned official narratives could be burned at the stake or sent to the gallows. Today, they are called conspiracy theorists. Less dramatic, true, but it shuts people up all the same. By giving disparaging labels to anyone who question 'official truths', you end up halting any discussion on new points, perspectives, angles, because people don't want to feel discriminated, labelled, or outcast. Schools, which remain strangely unchanged, even within the massive changes of the last century, are based on just this: a group of quiet people, facing the front, receiving truths and you won't be welcome if you question them. I have already spoken to many young people about this. It's a straightjacket. Lower your head and question nothing. Who are you to question? If you want to get a good mark, write down what they tell you. This is the premise of the pupil, and this seems terrible to me, because it creates submissive followers and not exploring minds. And at times we have to wait millennia for these narratives to finally be questioned. You just have to look at the case of Mary Magdalene and the implications that the acceptance of a particular narrative has had over two millennia.

"Annie spoke a lot about her. In fact, Mary Magdalene was often referred to in Glastonbury," said Thomas.

"I imagine she was. I had a dream, many years ago, in which she appeared. I still don't know how to define what happened exactly, even today, but she took up a place in the back of my mind, in the books

I read and in the places I visited. However I wasn't always aware of her. She slowly occupied space within me without me hardly noticing," Helena said.

"Can you tell me more?" he asked with genuine interest.

"For example, in the 6th Century, a homily by Pope Gregory I, identified Mary Magdalene as a prostitute. And that's how it remained, for centuries and centuries. Only in 1969 did the Catholic Church officially revoke the label, but in a way that went almost unnoticed. Only since the discovery of the Gospel of Mary, the Dead Sea Scrolls and the Nag Hammadi library, new research has been made, new books have been written, several documentaries and films have been done on the subject; the assumptions are slowly changing, but there is a whole narrative that has remained deeply embedded in the collective unconscious.

"We're talking about something that has been passed on as truth from generation to generation for almost two millennia. Imagine how things would have been different in Western society, and beyond, if Mary Magdalene had been presented as being of royal blood, the Holy Bride of Jesus, the female apostle among apostles, the most important teacher, alongside Jesus, in the entire Christian movement, partners on an equal footing, the feminine counterpart of the Divine Masculine? What a huge difference this would have made to the archetypal Divine Feminine! How all of this has influenced the role of women and sexuality itself, in this case the disconnection of sexuality from the sacred. As all this was suppressed, obliterated. The Mother Goddess, Mother Mary, is portrayed as a virgin, whereas Mary Magdalene, the goddess of love, the erotic feminine, became the prostitute and sinner. And this wound is yet to heal. I really like listening to Betty Kovacs. She says that the mission of Jesus and Mary Magdalene was to restore the lost Love-Wisdom teachings and practices of the First Temple.

"Many authors talk about Jesus having learnt ancient tantric traditions on his travels to India and that Mary Magdalene studied tantric alchemy during her years of training as a priestess in the temples of Artemisia and Isis. So, there arises the possibility of a very pure and conscious union, from which a child, Sarah, may have been born.

"In this subject," Helena continued, "in a giant land of so many stories told, all that we have is our vision, our perception, opinion, what resonates or not. And within me, and through everything I have read and all the research I have done, this idea strikes me as true. Or is it a longing of my very soul; an urge to bring together these divided aspects within ourselves. There is a profound imbalance in the world. I believe it essential to reawaken the wisdom of the Divine Feminine; restoring balance with the Divine Masculine, so that, in full communion, they can ultimately bring harmony to this planet. For so much of the disharmony on the planet, at this time, is the result of narratives sown in the distant past, with less than good intentions, and which were have been passed off to us as truths. This is what I am interested in exploring: what makes someone have the capacity to question, to step out of the hypnosis and look for their own truth? Sorry, now it's me talking too much..."

"Not at all! I love seeing you this excited. But there are so many branches to this common trunk and the Catholic religion is just one of them. In all the major religions, women play an inferior, submissive role. I have no idea where this all started, but it has definitely greatly influenced the role of women in society, all around the world, in their exclusion from positions of power, in education, or lack of it," said Thomas.

"Of course!" Helena quickly replied. "I have given you just one example which I feel strongly about, but there are countless others all over the planet that compel us to question the origin of things. And it's not just in the world of religion, as you know, it's in all areas of life. Religion has clearly played a very important role in recent millennia and, even for people living in countries less influenced by religion, the archetypes formed over so many centuries have persisted in the collective unconscious, thereby, impacting societies. Have you ever heard of the Nag Hammadi library?"

"The collection of ancient books discovered in Egypt, right? I don't know much. I just recall having read something about it."

"The books were in a large, red sealed earthenware jar," she said, "found by an Arab peasant while he was digging for sabakh, a soft soil used for fertilizer. It was found in the village of Nag Hammadi, in 1945. Thirteen papyrus books bound in leather, composed of 52 texts. It is believed that were buried by monks from a nearby monastery. Possibly in the 4th century. Anything that didn't tell the official story was considered heresy. They contained secret gospels, poems and descriptions of the origin of the universe, myths, magic, instruction on mystical practice, a vast collection of gnostic writings, which became known as the Nag Hammadi Library. These ancient texts describe a God who is not only Father, but also Mother. Do you see? The illusions and veils are being torn down. We are starting to understand that many of the scripts to be found on this planet have been adulterated; they're missing key elements. In the case of the Divine Feminine, that energy, wisdom, which also exists in men, obviously, it's not exclusive to women, seems to be coming out of lockdown now. And in this case, it wasn't just a few months, but centuries and centuries... there is a protracted process of healing underway... and the world, Mother Earth, sorely needs this cure."

"I'm really interested in seeing where you'll go or where you'll be taken," he said.

"I'd like to let myself be carried away. I can't always manage to merge with the flow, but since I've been in Italy, I do nothing but!"

They laughed.

"Are we part of the documentary?" Thomas asked, with a searching look in his eyes.

"I'd never thought of it that way... We might be experimenting on the body this wonderful sensation of communion" she said, rolling on top of him, placing her hand on his heart "and in other dimensions, too. Maybe we are opening a path in our minds, and preparing within ourselves this new ground in which we can heal thousands of years of separation between spirit and sexuality," she concluded as she kissed him softly.

"Sounds great to me," Thomas replied, looking Helena in the eyes, their faces almost touching. "But Helena, although I've loved listening to you, when I asked you if you could tell me more, I meant more about your dream... I love dreams! What was the dream you had about Mary Magdalene that made such an impression on you?"

"Oh... the dream! You really are a Jungian astrophysicist, you weren't joking! You wanted to know about the dream and you let me go on waffling," she said, blushing slightly as she pulled herself off him and returned to her spot at Thomas' side. "The dream... I'm in France, somewhere in Provence or the Languedoc, I'm not entirely sure, maybe the Pyrenees. I'm in a house that has a large terrace, looking out over a vast expanse of vineyard. Hey, it looked like that place we stayed at in Civitella in Val di Chiana. I'm sitting on the terrace, and I have my daughter with me, in a cot next to me on the ground."

"A daughter?" he asked.

"Yes, a baby daughter. And I remember feeling this overwhelming sense of peace, she's sleeping in the cot and I'm writing and looking out at the landscape. Suddenly, Carl Jung appears before me, just imagine! I'm not joking... He appears quite clearly before me; he approaches and points to the sky, telling me something about the Dragon's Path, and leaves. I try to understand what he is telling me, but I look up to the sky and can't see anything. When I look back down, before me I see a man between the vines, coming in my direction... I can't see his features, but I know he is the father of the child and is coming in my direction with a rose in his hand.... and then suddenly he disappears, and Mary Magdalene is right there beside me, as if we were sisters but hadn't seen each other in a long time... and I begin to cry... out of longing, out of an incredibly powerful feeling that she is transmitting to me in such an earthly manner... and I wake up, still crying."

"Wow! What a dream! You see, Carl Jung never appeared in any of my dreams. You lucky thing! And, what did you make of it?"

"I have thought a great deal about that dream, about what it might be telling me," Helena replied. "And I spoke to some people too. I did some research on the dragon's path, which I'd never heard of before."

"And what did you discover?"

"You must have heard about ley lines before," she said.

"Yes, but ley lines remain a big mystery. And much has been written since Alfred Watkins introduced that concept," he said.

"Well, I see them almost like Mother Earth's veins: lines that carry enormous amounts of energy and, in the places where they intersect, energy vortices are created - higher vibrational points," said Helena. "In fact, prehistoric man must have been aware of these energy lines, as all megalithic structures were strategically built on top of them. Surely to explore its special properties."

"Where three or more ley lines cross, one can almost always find a place of pilgrimage, cathedral, temple, stone circle," Thomas said like he was beginning to tell a 'once upon a time' story.

"Yes! Stonehenge. Pyramids of Giza. Chichen Itza, you name it," said Helena, agreeing.

"I imagine them as straight lines, which intersect the planet much like the latitude and longitude lines on a globe," said Thomas. "Do they carry an altered form of the Earth's magnetic field? I don't think anyone has managed to define its real power even to this day. But it is certain that most ancient cultures around the world seem to have some understanding of ley lines."

"The Chinese call them Dragon Lines, while the Irish know them as Fairy Paths; different cultures, different words, but the same concept," she said.

"They call them Spirit Lines in Peru."

"And the Australian Aborigines call them Song Lines. I like that name best! But what they meant in the dream, I'm yet to find out. Perhaps a journey I need to take. But there are so many ley lines connecting prehistoric structures, natural and sacred ones!"

"As I recall, Glastonbury, Stonehenge and Avebury form a perfect right-angled triangle. It's astonishing to me to think that the first megalithic builders knew astronomy and geometry!" said Thomas with enthusiasm.

"It really is! But, getting back to the Dragon's Path, I found out that people who practise Feng-shui take 'dragon currents' into account when placing elements in the landscape, or in other words, the strength and direction of magnetic currents. But you know more about this than I do... about how the earth's magnetic field is influenced by the position of the sun, of the moon and of the closest planets," Helena said, a smile on her lips.

"Just for fun, the other day I read an article about some farmers who had discovered that plants placed within a magnetic field grew six times faster than in normal conditions," he replied, lightening the conversation.

"Right, also, people often forget about our magnetic field, that we are energy, and that our organs are electrosensitive! When I start to think about electromagnetic pollution nowadays, in all the high voltage lines, antennas, mobile phones and now even 5G," Helena said vigorously.

"Don't think about that now. Look at the beauty of nature all around us," he said to ease her mind.

"You're right."

"But what else did you think about the dream?" he asked, genuinely interested.

"I can't tell if Carl Jung's appearance has to do with the Dragon's Path, or with some route that he was trying to show me in that region I was in. An invisible path, such as the ley lines. There is so much that eyes will never be able to reach... but that the heart can."

"Now you sound like Exupéry's little prince, my princess," said Thomas, praising her, but Helena didn't react, looking, instead, at the sky for some minutes. She then embarked on a long speech, as if talking to herself.

"We have been conditioned to dismiss all signs of an inner reality and of a oneness with the universe. As if feeling had no wisdom and emotions just get in the way. As if what the eyes see is all that exists, and what the mind thinks is all that is credible. For millennia the feminine principle and energies have been rejected.

"I spoke to you of Betty Kovacs, who has a PhD in the Theory of Symbolic/Mythic Language. She often mentions that ancient wisdom, the first temple tradition, which was a shaman-mystic tradition, how it survived over time, through the Gnostics, the Sufis, the Cathars, many secret societies, but that they were all persecuted, many were killed, men, women, children, entire families ended up burnt at the stake, the texts burnt too, temples destroyed... Fortunately, there is always a crack through which the light manages to pass, even if it takes centuries... and the truth is that much of this hidden knowledge began resurfacing in the last century and is even more widely known today.

"When I was trying to decipher Jung's presence in the dream, I came across a letter he wrote to Eugene Rolfe a few months before he died, in which he said something like: *I am practically alone. There are a few who understand this and that but almost nobody sees the whole...* He was conveying that he had failed in his main task of opening people's eyes to the fact that man has a soul and there is treasure buried in the field. The missing key was his *The Red Book*, in which he fully reveals the experiential, Gnostic roots of his psychology."

"Gnosis, the direct knowledge of the divine mysteries," said Thomas in a whisper to the air.

"This all makes me think about a deep reconnection to the heart, as a bridge between the sky and the earth," Helena continued, "and about feminine energy, about being able to listen to and feel the invisible energies that surround us, which also connects with the shamanic paths. All of nature speaks the invisible language of the shaman. Everything is connected to everything else. There are many worlds, dimensions and levels in which you can operate."

"Yes, I agree, when you spend a good deal of time with shamans, you can clearly see that they consider the spiritual world to be as real as this one, and the idea of death gives way to the idea of transformation," Thomas added.

"Jung once said that the most important task of our time was to remember Sophia, and thus, emerge from amnesia. Sophia is the feminine cosmic consciousness and goes by many names: she can be Isis, she can be Mary, Mary Magdalene, she can be Shakti, but she has this power, wisdom and clarity that can help us escape from our sleep, from Plato's cave, and hence from the social conditioning which we obey unquestioningly. The key is to raise our awareness of the connection that exists between humans, nature and the universe," concluded Helena.

"I'm impressed. The power of one dream. I think you'll find it hard to sleep with all this adrenalin coursing through your veins, my sweet Shakti."

Helena looked at Thomas, as if emerging from a trance:

"Ah, you're the one who brought it up... when I start talking about this, I just can't shut up," she said.

"I don't want you to shut up. I'm going to miss this enthusiasm of yours, your fire. You can talk all night for all I care... well, maybe not all night, as you make me want you all the more when you're all passionate like this," he said.

"It makes me so happy to hear you say that; I can feel how sincere you are in my heart. I feel entirely accepted. Without any judgements. I feel loved. You know, my Shiva, I think you've balanced your feminine energy very well with your masculine energy, and this is something very precious, very rare indeed. Maybe because you have dedicated yourself to what remains hidden; so much of your time is spent beneath the light of the moon and the stars."

"It's funny you should say that, you've reminded me of something my mother has often said to me! When you see her paintings, you'll understand what an illuminated being is, despite her ups and downs," said Thomas.

" What would she say to you?" asked Helena.

"That each of us is like a thread of light for the world. She would say to me: wherever you go, whatever you do, don't forget that."

"How lovely!"

"She spoke so often about this, that there was a time when I thought of us as stars. Imagine that one of the stars were to think: there are so many other stars, so I can stop shining! And now imagine if they all had the same thought! We would be left in total darkness!" said Thomas.

"That's poetic and true. Sometimes people don't see the importance they have in the grand scheme of things. But we are all co-creators. Our thoughts, emotions and actions are like threads of light that create an eternal chain reaction... which will be seen, like starlight, long after it has been emitted."

"That's it!"

"Blessed be your mother, who brought you into the world. Never in all my 37 years of life, have I ever met someone with whom I feel so good, so in tune with," said Helena, embracing Thomas.

"Blessed be your mother and father too," he whispered into Helena's ear.

They made love as if they were huge windows letting in rays of sunlight in the middle of the night. The warmth spreading through their bodies, as they explored the magical possibilities of lighting each other up more and more. Paradoxically, at the same time, they felt a huge sensation of peace, through the profound experience of oneness. Them, the forest, the stars, the moonlight, all of them contributing to those paradise-emotions, molten fragrances sliding over their skin, warm waters preparing on their bodies to pour down in cascades, as if they were a river of love in the midst of the forest.

Even after this intense lovemaking, Helena did not fall asleep, as Thomas had predicted. Her mind appeared like a pure spring of thoughts, which overflowed endlessly. She looked up to the sky, and at Thomas who was already sleeping by her side, to the trees that surrounded them, and she imagined the wise women who, over so many generations, in the midst of the forests, at the peaks of mountains, along the banks of rivers and seas, in the temples and monasteries, bearers of ancient traditions, had gathered to perform sacred rites. Dancing in the moonlight, chant and prayer, conversing with countless forms of divinity through sacred gestures, they who were clairvoyants, priestesses, healers, oracles, agents of the Great Mother Goddess who gave birth to the universe.

What could Helena possibly be feeling now, as a woman who enjoyed these ancestral rites, knowing that millions of them had been killed during the Witch Hunts? Grandmothers, mothers, even children. She didn't know how to process what she was feeling, how those dark acts, perpetuated over centuries, could still permeate the collective unconscious and her feelings. She had spoken to Thomas about what she was seeking; the basis of her research, the ideas that swirled within her. It wasn´t about religions, politics, history, education, or any particular event, the question was to understand what constructs or truths still condition humanity today; what narratives had sculpted the lives of men and women, and how they subsisted over the centuries, at what cost, with how many deaths of dissonant voices; what energies continued to prevail on the planet, through competition, thirst for power, control, envy, hatred, wars and how much could be transformed with a new vision of oneself, with other "truths", or at least with other perspectives on some issues central to the human existence and the home where we all live, Earth.

Helena had seen how, over the last fifty years, so many scholars were now talking about neolithic villages as if they were mothers organising themselves around their needs and those of their descendants, practising matrilineal property. Social anthropologist Robert Briffault, for example, had written that women were the creators of the primordial elements of civilisation. Even after paternity had been recognised, and the hierarchies of kings began to appear in the Bronze Age, the connections with the Mother Goddess continued with primordial importance. The first kings of Sumer, Babylonia, Egypt, Phoenicia and other ancient lands were unable to govern unless they had a *Hieros Gamos*, a sacred marriage, with the Goddess embodied by the queen.

The *Hieros Gamos* ritual would have evolved into a highly developed spiritual activity, which allowed men to gain divine knowledge through ritualised sexual union with a woman trained as a priestess. Gnosis, physiologically speaking, would be the male orgasm or climax – a brief mental vacuum, a fraction of a second in which all thoughts are absent. In mythology, in that instant of ecstasy in which his mind was totally empty, he could see God.

But somewhere in time, she couldn't say when exactly, this communion and balance between the masculine and the feminine had been disconnected, disintegrated, disempowered, stripped of its importance; a whole feminine wisdom shunned from places of power, even within men and women, in their choices; the mind victorious over the heart, material prioritised over spirit, the focus on wealth, power, productivity, competition, control, success, and with that...

In the midst of the darkness shrouding her, everything seemed clear to her. If she were to dive into the heart of ancient civilisations, she would find the female body as a sacred alchemical vessel of creation; she would travel through the sacred mysteries of birth and death, sexuality and spiritual transformation; she would coexist with the sacred through dance, music, myth, geometry, art and architecture, attuning herself to the primordial rhythms, the cycles of nature and the cosmos, and she would bathe in the teachings of the female divinities. Perhaps the dream was a call to, one day, embark on that journey through time.

And there, among the trees, embracing Thomas, between darkness and starlight, not fully awake but not yet asleep, between dream and reality, she seemed to feel their presence. At first, she couldn't tell if it was the goddess Sekmet or Athena reminding her how the negative passions of anger, greed, jealousy, fear, can be transformed into the enlightened qualities of clarity, self-confidence, determination and fearlessness. Next it was Oshun, and Hathor, then Aphrodite, teachers of the sacred sexual mysteries, revealing to her the sacred nature of sensuality. In the end, bathed by an overwhelming sense of peace, she felt the presence of Tara, Isis and Kuan Yin, inviting her to look within, to delve deep into her heart.

Was she already dreaming? She wondered. But she was still there, feeling Thomas's heart in her right hand, her own with her left hand, thus attuned to the rhythm of the heart, remembering the man from her dream, who had come with the rose. Was it Thomas?

She hadn't told him, but she knew well that the rose is the symbol of love, of Aphrodite and Venus, of Mary, also the symbol of the secret and the feminine. The codes of the rose are like frequencies that remind the heart that it is safe to remain open, even in absolute vulnerability, and it is there that it finds its great and true power.

In that instant, it seemed to Helena that nothing would ever make her heart close again. There was no Shiva without Shakti, but neither was there Shakti without Shiva. It was in this communion between the masculine and the feminine, these two sacred energies, two systems of knowledge, two forms of expression, in a place of parity and complement, that the greatest potential resided. First within her, so that later, in harmony and completeness, they could both hold the sky and build on earth.

Without even knowing if she had fallen asleep, a vision of sunrise filled her eyes with tears and, rising in silence, she took her notebook and went to sit on a rock that seemed to be there for contemplation.

The love she felt at that moment for everything was transformed into water in the form of tears streaming down her face; before her, strands of colours heralded the arrival of a majestic sun, which rose sluggishly but full of pride. She looked at Thomas, asleep in that love nest, theirs, so very much theirs. And she began to write. Then she took the piece of paper from her notebook, folded it, and as she tucked it away in her pocket, Thomas appeared beside her, still sleepy, and sat down beside her, draping a blanket over Helena's shoulders.

"You didn't sleep, did you?" Thomas asked.

Helena shook her head and smiled.

"What were you writing?"

"Oh, just what came into my mind," she said, handing him the folded piece of paper. "Read it when you're on the plane. Then part of me will be travelling with you."

"We have to go. I still have a lot to sort out before I leave," he said.

"When is that?" asked Helena.

"They put me on a flight tonight."

Helena rested her head on Thomas' shoulder, and there they remained for a while, gazing at the beautiful sun as it offered itself to them, completely, fully, illuminating their tired yet happy faces.

When they got to Rome, Thomas dropped her off at Adriana's place.

"See you later," he said, softly kissing her.

"I'm not going with you to the airport, Thomas. I'd prefer to do our goodbyes here and now."

"I thought so. That was my 'see you later'."

They hugged each other tightly.

"See you later," replied Helena.

That night, on the plane, Thomas cried. It wasn't really sadness that brought on those tears, although he had a combination of sadness and joy inside him, but rather a strange feeling, as if he were travelling without a part of himself, without a part of his body. He had never felt such a thing before, and it even felt like a physical pain pressing against his chest. He remembered the piece of paper that Helena had given him and that he had placed in his backpack when packing. He wanted to feel closer to her. He read it savouring every word.

"You and I have so much that unites us. Our inner selves sing the same melody. Since we were children, we have sought out true silence and the mysteries that are still hidden, waiting for the right moment to be revealed, like the sword of Excalibur. We love trees more than anything else, their resilience, their trunks scarred by storms and their ability to bear fruit or grow crookedly towards the sky. Always skyward, no matter what the circumstances. We like people's smiles and their tears that carry the DNA of humanity. We can't help but wander into cemeteries, lost in the hills and near small villages, where time has seemingly stood still. We tell stories of the departed inside our heads, and of those left to cherish their memories. We keep all the letters and postcards they once sent us and we tend to re-read them on days of great sadness. We delve into old texts in search of wisdom, in the same way that we contemplate the horizon and intuitively envision the future. We love the sun and the smell of damp earth, books and dinners with friends. We follow what touches our hearts, without fear or with it. We believe in love. We believe in love, even when it feels like we don't. Today, as I feel it inside, so full, so great, so strong, so authentic, so naked, like the sun rising before me, I thank you because - wherever we go from here - I will never forget everything I feel: beside you, with you, in you, in me, in everything around me, the expression of love living in every element of nature, in everything that exists. In the memory of this feeling, we will live on forever."

Thomas drifted to sleep with these words, his tears silently sleeping on his cheeks.

In the Atacama Desert

Although he had slept for much of the journey, tiredness pervaded his body as he left Antofagasta airport. The journey had been long, with many stopovers and changes of plane. At the same time, he could already feel the desert and the stars calling to him. He sat behind the wheel of the rented car and looked forward to the journey, the same journey he had repeated so many times over the years, but which always brought something new to his soul.

He remembered the first time very well. The way the desert had made its presence felt, through its immensity, the clarity that blinded him, the cutting wind, a dramatically alternating hot and cold, a breathless rapture that had taken possession of his soul.

He always stopped halfway through the journey, letting the silence seep into him, taking over his senses, letting the desert flow through his hair, his eyes burning and, as he walked through its sands, he always felt closer to the stars and freer, freer than ever.

The first time he had wandered the sands, and without having asked for it, he had been confronted by all his pain and loss, by the bleeding of his heart, everything he had always run away from; the desert brought it all back to him, full-on, without meekly consoling him, forcing him to be whole, to be totally present, without distractions, melting him, disintegrating him, until he could no longer resist. And that's just what he did, after he had succumbed to the struggle. Thomas had let the desert in, pouring its silence and immensity into his heart, and when he had asked it what it wanted, the desert had replied, "For you to have the courage to feel everything."

That day, the feeling that occupied his heart was very different. Helena's voice joined that of the desert and he felt like the most blessed astrophysicist in the world. Love was present in the wind, in the kilometres of sand and burnt-ochre rocks, in the deep-blue sky and he could already sense the excitement of nightfall when he arrived at Cerro Paranal.

When, at the end of the winding road leading to the top of the mountain, he saw the Paranal facilities appear, with the telescopes hovering over the underground dome of La Residencia to the left and the squat, white buildings to the right, his heart began to beat faster, as if coming home after a long absence.

That unique sky to observe the cosmos, the lack of humidity preventing cloud formation, the positioning of the observatories at that altitude, the best terrestrial telescopes in the hemisphere, all that shone brighter than gold, for any astronomer eternally in love with the stars. And La Residencia was his "home on Mars" as he called it. A partially underground complex, built 2,400 metres above sea level, for those who worked there, technicians, engineers and astronomers, protecting them from the extreme conditions of that Martian landscape, from the dry wind, the blazing sun and the bitter cold of the night; offering them a soothing, humid interior, with a swimming pool and a thirty-five-metre dome, covering a huge indoor tropical garden, which let the sunlight in from above. Made of concrete, steel, glass and wood, hidden in the landscape, nestled comfortably in a depression in the Atacama Desert, La Residencia gave him a sense of home; with its canteen, music room, library, but also a feeling of a boutique hotel-house, with its fitness centre, cinema and sauna, as well as the countless rooms, with balconies strategically positioned to see as far as the eye would allow.

It was there, from his room, or the garden, that Thomas wrote to Helen in those months when they were apart. At night he would surrender to the cosmos, and in the daytime, after sleeping, he would surrender to that beautiful conversation flowing naturally between them, creating bonds even stronger with the distance.

Every day they would exchange good morning greetings, talk about themselves, their days, new discoveries, new ideas, how their work was going, but also about how they felt, and about their love. They would send photos, sometimes short, simple written messages, other times long, in-depth emails, often heartfelt voice messages. They would also talk on the phone, but rarely, only when they were really missing each other; and day by day the feeling of closeness, of living inside each other, increased. Helena devoted her time to research, to reading, to interviews, both face-to-face and on Zoom, very common since the pandemic. Thomas devoted his time to observations. Every fortnight he had a few days to rest or to travel, which he did, particularly to visit the families or communities he had come to know over the years, or ancient sites he still wanted to explore. As each day flew by, Thomas was filled with the giddiness of life, in a rollercoaster ride of feelings. There was a somewhat indefinable feeling of intensity, as if the Earth were in fast forward and, at the same time, in a profound process of transition, which led to this ambiguous and surprisingly complex sensation of experiencing days that seemed to have fewer hours, due to their accelerated speed, but which contained much more than ever, as if time and events were compressed.

One of the days, Helena wrote to Thomas, excited and in a whirlwind of thoughts, telling him about a conversation she had had with Martin Gray, an anthropologist and photographer specialising in the study of sacred sites and pilgrimage traditions around the world. Helena had filmed this same conversation, as she always did in all her research conversations, while she was looking for the mainstay for one of her documentaries.

She wrote to him:

"His story is very rich. His father was a diplomat, so Martin Gray spent many years of his childhood and adolescence living in different countries. When he was twelve, they moved to India, where they lived for four years. It was then that, with his mother, Martin started travelling around India and visiting sacred sites. After his return to the USA, it wasn't long before he had the urge to return to India, where he joined a monastic order. He started practising meditation, embarked on a decades-long study of the mythology and archaeology of Hinduism and Buddhism, and, enchanted by the beauty of sacred sites, envisioned producing a photobook on places of pilgrimage. But, after a few years, he left the monastic life and returned to the United States, where he set up a successful travel company.

However, and I have heard this same story time and again, despite his success, Martin felt an emptiness in his heart, he was not happy. On a trip to South America, whilst visiting the archaeological sites of Easter Island and Machu Picchu, he experienced a powerful awakening of his old interest in sacred sites. Old dreams came knocking at his door and, combining his scholarly studies, photographic skills and spiritual yearning, he decided to travel the world as a traditional pilgrim, and photograph these sites. It was a long journey, of forty years, which continues to this day! I think he is the man who has visited the most sacred sites in the entire world. More than a thousand. In more than one hundred and fifty countries. His photographs have been featured all over the world, especially by *National Geographic*.

It was a good, long talk - inspiring and thought-provoking. At one point, I was reminded of our trip through Italy; how we would talk and listen to the locals. So, I am sharing a video with you, of part of this conversation: I think you'll like it. In his work he talks a lot about an energy, concentrated in specific places on the planet, which catalyses and increases eco-spiritual consciousness. He explains that, before their prehistoric human use, and before appropriation by different religions, these places were simply places of power. They continue to radiate their powers, which anyone can access by visiting them. As you know, no rituals are required, no practice of a particular religion, no belief in a particular philosophy; all that is required is that an individual visits that place of power and is really present and open to receiving.

I like the image Martin uses: just as the flavour of herbal tea will permeate hot water, so the essence of these places of power will enter one's heart, mind and soul. As each of us awakens to a fuller understanding of the universality of life, we in turn further strengthen the global field of eco-spiritual consciousness. This is the deeper meaning and purpose of these magical sacred places: they are points of origin of the power of spiritual enlightenment.

I put it on Vimeo. I'll send you the link.

Love, Helena."

Sitting in the garden of La Residencia, Thomas put on his headphones and watched the interview, giving it his full attention.

"Do you know what I call a "truism"?" Martin asked Helena. "I find certain people saying certain things, yet they say that from the vantage point of their nice country, of a well-fed belly; however, if they travelled through Jakarta or Dhaka, in Bangladesh, or visited the refugee camps in Sudan or the prisons in Afghanistan, as I have, I think they wouldn't say some of the things that they say."

"The whole perception of good, bad, safe, unsafe, poor, rich, changes according to your history, which will condition your perception, right?" said Helena, agreeing. "If you have lived all your life in places of war or extreme poverty, you won't say that a certain neighbourhood in Rome is dangerous, but people who have always lived in safety can perceive it as dangerous. There are so many different ways of looking at the same situation, and it's so important to be aware of that, to embrace diversity and not get stuck in your own point of view, your own truth.

"You started going to India when you were twelve with your mother, didn't you? Since then you haven't stopped travelling! You could be said to be the person who has visited the most sacred places, of anyone in the world... What words would you bring to talk about your journey?" she asked.

"Oh gosh, sometimes I say it's a search for beauty and I use that term a lot," Martin answered. "Also, it's a search for Self. Let's see... I don't like so much the notion of self-development because, in my opinion, the self is already completely developed. I'm more into self-discovery, to discover that which is already perfectly developed inside of us.

"There is for me this long term yearning prayer to be of service here on the planet and, when I was a little boy, women would do dishes with these harsh detergents and it would make their skin very dry and so, back then, they had these playtex living gloves. I was six or seven years old and I had this prayer in my head: Great Spirit, God, I said, I would like to be a playtex living glove on the hand of God.

"The hand is doing whatever the hand does and the glove is just on the hand and I wanted to be on the hand of God. So there's a number of answers to your question, certainly a search for beauty, because if you think about what I've done, I've gone to photograph approximately fifteen hundred of the most beautiful structures that human beings have ever built with love. I go to the major art museums in the whole world and I like to stand in front of these beautiful paintings and see great beauty. I go to all these botanical gardens which contain the highest concentration of the world's most beautiful plants… so, for my whole life, I've been trying to stand in front of and see beauty!" said Martin, face beaming.

"A search for beauty!" Helena echoed, smiling back at him.

"If you go to pilgrimage sites, here's a very key thing for me: there's, essentially, two types of religious structures, there's the normal religious structures and then there's the pilgrimage ones. When you go to an Islamic mosque, people pray in a certain way. In Islam, every day there is a certain set of surahs that you're supposed to say, but when you go to the pilgrimage places of Islam, people aren't doing that, they dispense with normalcy and they pray in a very different way.

"Now, it took me a long time to notice this. I began to notice with Hindu and Buddhist and Christian and Jewish friends… But then, when I went to Mecca, which is the single most important Islamic pilgrimage place, I began to understand that at pilgrimage sites there's essentially two things that are happening: people are saying please and thank you. Please and thank you. There's prayer to Great Spirit, God, and there's praise. And so what I've been able to do in my life is go to those places on the planet with the highest concentration of that vibration, or that spirit, or that feeling of prayer and praise, of saying thank you and please."

"I had never thought of it like that," she shared.

"So, my life has been a search for beauty and a prayer that I might be able to help in the transformational consciousness on the planet. This thing of just going to places where a lot of love has been expressed... rambling and I get long answers!"

"Do you want to tell me one or two stories from those trips that particularly impressed you?" she asked.

"There's been some things that have happened to me, that, when they happened, I thought 'oh this is bad' or 'this is difficult', and then I reframe it, I look back on it days, weeks, months, years later and I go 'oh that was actually quite good'. As they say in America, sometimes there's a silver lining."

"Now you've reminded me of that Zen story that takes place in a village in China," said Helena. "For his fourteenth birthday, the boy's father bought him a horse, and everyone in the village said, "Isn't that wonderful, the boy got a horse?" and the Zen Master said, "We'll see." A couple of years later the boy fell from his horse, badly breaking his leg and everyone in the village said, "How awful, he won't be able to walk properly." The Zen Master said, "We'll see." Then, a war broke out and all the young men had to go and fight, but this young man couldn't because his leg was still messed up and everyone said, "How wonderful!" The Zen Master said, "We'll see." And so on..."

"Yes. There was this time I was living in Miami, Florida," Martin shared, "and I had a nice girlfriend and I had a lot of money and everything was going well, but my heart was empty. I didn't feel I was doing what I wanted to do, and I was in a state of real distress. One night I had this one vision that instructed me, basically, to go to Easter Island and then I would begin to find the answers to my prayers.

"I had lived as a monk for ten years, so I was already very proficient in different techniques of meditation and, since I was a young boy, I'd been having visionary experiences; seeing things inside my head, and so, when I started doing meditation more assiduously, I began having more visions.

"To cut a long story short, I went to Easter Island and I had this vision: I saw this five-story wooden pagoda, which I thought was, probably, Japanese, and I heard the words "follow the pilgrimage routes of the ancient religions" and that is what really began it for me."

"You were literally guided," Helena exclaimed.

"Yes, for several years, I had more of, what I call, visionary suggestions, or visionary directives, to do what I was doing. Along the way I became very knowledgeable about the subject, and hence, I now know a whole lot about the sociology of pilgrimage. I've read thousands of books and papers on pilgrimage sites and sacred sites, ad, in my opinion, and I'm not saying I'm right, often sociologists and anthropologists are almost missing the point. The pilgrims are going to say 'please' and 'thank you' and that's what I've done."

"What have you experienced in these places? What has it brought you on a personal level?"

"Oh Gosh, I mean, I've been to fifteen hundred of these sites over thirty-eight years and I had just tremendous experiences, some of which I don't talk about that much, because some people say they can't believe it!" said Martin.

"Yes, I understand you perfectly; there is still judgement and disbelief when it comes to unusual experiences."

"This becomes evident if you study medieval Christianity: many times there would be a man or a woman that they would see an apparition, they would see a vision, like those kids in Portugal, in Fátima, and they would see a vision of Christ, or Mary, or a saint, and they would talk about that… and that place would become a very important pilgrimage site over hundreds of years.

"I've had four of those apparitional experiences," Martin continued.

"The type of aboriginal experience that gave rise to some of the greatest of the European medieval pilgrimage traditions."

"Can you tell me one?" Helena asked.

"When I was in Machu Picchu, and after in Easter Island, I was told to go to Japan. So, then, I waited six months, because I couldn't leave the business I had at that point. I started studying Japanese and, then, I took one of my bicycles to Japan, to the northern island of Hokkaido. I was riding around... again I didn't understand what I was doing at that point, and I went to a certain area in South Western Hokkaido where there was a stone ring; not a stone circle, a stone ring! I didn't know what it meant, but somehow I'd gotten there and I decided to spend the night sleeping in the middle of the stone ring.

"In the middle of the night, something woke me up and there was this light… let's say it was about half our height, it was about a meter off the ground and it was about a meter in height itself… and I could see through it! It was this pulsating light and there was a light blue, a light yellow, white, a sort of silverish and a gold and it was just pulsating there in the middle of the stone ring!

"I had no idea what this was or what to do, but I felt extraordinarily peaceful while this was happening. I had already been doing meditation for many years and I just knew something very significant was happening. I felt great beauty and great peace, and then it faded and it passed away.

"Because I've studied so much about religion, I noticed that it was very common in Europe, for example, that people would see an apparitional experience like mine and they would say 'oh it's Mary', so it would became a Marian shrine. I have a great love of Mary and I've been, probably, to fifty Marian shrines around the world, but, in some of those places, people saw something very similar to what I'd seen. They just interpreted in a different way, according to their religious programming or the different ideas they had in their head," Martin said.

"What you're saying is very important to the subject of truth that's been brewing within me," said Helena. "What is real or not, what is true or not; the issue of subjectivity; of how events are interpreted according to each one's beliefs and that's how history is formed. And what about all that has been excluded? All the stories that have not been told for fear of the consequences. Even you, when you had those experiences, those apparitions, you thought that most people wouldn't believe you, that they might brand you as crazy."

"It's true."

"And it was just the beginning for you," she said.

"Some people think that's absurd, but this great planet, this living being that is maybe billions of years old, has different types of energy, lines, meridians, just like in the human body. And human beings, whether they know it or not, function somewhat like an acupuncture needle upon the living earth and, at the same time, there's some sort of energy, or spirit, or quality, whatever we call it, coming out of the place, which is beneficial to them.

"So, the service that was given to me was to go to all of these places and to take pictures of them," Martin continued. "I feel that the photographs that I take are like windows into these places; they allow a transfer, or transmission of what I'd call 'the visual homeopathic essence of the site'. If people say that's impossible, I go, well, maybe not; if you look at photographic film, it's a little itty bitty piece of earth and you expose it to a scene for a thousandth of a second, and that small piece of earth, that photographic emulsion made from the earth, remembers what it saw for a thousandth of a second. Or if you get magnetic tape and a tape recorder, it's this little itty-bitty piece of brownish tape, and it's going over these rollers and you sing and it remembers it. So, here's the earth remembering energy right?"

"I like those analogies of yours," she said smiling.

"So, if you take a larger sacred site, which is just a piece of earth, and then you have hundreds of thousands or millions of people coming there, and not being there just for a thousandth of a second, but spending hours or days making prayers, I feel the place remembers. And then, when other people go back there, they're in that field of remembrance. There's a trace of the expressions of love that all of these other pilgrims have made there, and, when we're there, that is transmitted to us!" he said firmly.

"What you say makes perfect sense to me," Helena agreed.

"When I'm at those places and I'm taking these photographs with my little camera, I'm making a prayer to the spirit of the place and I'm saying please help me create this photograph in such a way, that if someone else is looking at this photograph is looking through this window. I feel that not only have I been able to do a service of telling people where these power sites are, but because that website of mine has been so hugely visited, it's over a million visitors, that means a million have been looking through these windows at the places and the place is looking back at them," said Martin.

"It's funny you should mention that, because on a trip I took recently, here in Italy, my boyfriend and I always had that very much in mind, imagining the memories of those places, trying to get in touch with the 'spirit of the place', seeing how we looked at the space and how the space looked at us," she shared.

"Few people bear that in mind, it seems to me. In Hinduism, there's a word called *Darshan*. And *Darshan* means 'view of the deity'. Most people, they'll go: oh it means you're having the darshan of the deity. You're standing in front of the statue, or a guru, and you're having a view of the group, but it works the other way around also, the deity is having a view of you; it goes both ways. And because a lot of people are not going to be able to travel as widely as I have, I feel they can, in a sense, travel as widely as I have, just by looking at my photographs."

"Being present without being physically present, right?" said Helena. "I don't know if you've heard of it, but there were several experiments conducted by William A. Tiller Do you know him? Professor Emeritus of Stanford University's Department of Materials Science and Engineering. He did experiments with Tibetan monks meditating; getting them to place a certain intention on a physical object; for example, black boxes, or Intention Imprinted Electronic Devices (IIEDs), as he calls them. The monks would mentally hold a specific intention for the device for fifteen minutes, and then that black box would be sealed and sent to another laboratory over three thousand kilometres away. Say, for example, that the intention was to change the pH of the water. The IIEDs loaded with that same intention would then be opened in the distant laboratory, in order to check if they would have any real influence on their surroundings. The result was astonishing, as they were able to influence the pH of the water in this case. Human intention is really powerful... even when captured electronically."

"Very interesting! So much to discover. I have been very deconstructed by my experiences," shared Martin.

"As Rumi said, we just need to peel away the layers that keep us from love... and from our potential too. There are so many walls we build throughout our lives to protect ourselves from suffering that, before we realise it, we've spent years deconstructing them. Nobody can avoid suffering, but there are many choices that, out of a variety of fears, drive us away from ourselves and away from a more fulfilled and happier life," Helena added, smiling. "If we understand that we are the ocean in the drop, and not a drop in the ocean, and that everything and everyone is interconnected, cells of the same body, this will influence the way we relate to the earth, to all other beings, to the cosmos, to the divine, to ourselves, and thus how we see our role and purpose.

"In terms of your own experience, the life path you have undertaken, what do you think is most important to take into account? What is true for you in terms of our existence here? What would you like to bring into the light?" asked Helena.

"A lot of times people ask me how to live life, what they should do... and I say: 'get up each morning and put goodness and beauty into the world.' We're all equally embedded in the web of life and, so, looking at your part of the web, and what's around you, ask: how can I extend goodness and beauty into the world, here and now?

"Another question," she said. "You have mentioned certain geological and geophysical factors of certain points on the planet, where many of these sacred sites are located, as well as, the energy accumulated in those places, because they are centres of prayer, of compassion, or because of all the historical events that have taken place there! And even the masters who have inhabited them. I fully understand how this factor may enhance mystical experiences, since we are energy and since also, visitors to these sites may be more open and present. But thinking about the human body, the miraculous heart, the wisdom of nature, the connection with the web of life, and the quantum field itself, not to mention the unconditional love that exists in everything... can we not have that same connection with the divine next to the tree in our garden or wherever we are?"

"Yes, the closest sacred site, it's where you're sitting right now," said Martin without doubt. "Where's the most important holy tree? The Buddhists will say, well, it's in Bodh Gaya, in India, the Bodhi tree. But actually, that's not the original Bodhi tree. She was cut and taken to Sri Lanka, and after, the cutting of that was brought back to Bodh Gaya. But all trees are sacred. All places are sacred. How could you say some place isn't sacred? Even Auschwitz. That brings us back to the questions of good and evil...

"A little story here. I don't know if you know about this, but some years ago I fell off a cliff. I broke both wrists, both ankles, knocked out all these teeth, have a bunch of pieces of metal in my head and people say oh it was a horrible accident, I go no no no, it wasn't an accident, it was an incident. I have all these broken bones, and I have all these problems because of it, and yet my life is filled with such gratitude for that experience."

"What happened exactly?" she asked.

"I went out on this hill, not dangerous or anything, and I sat down and I said to the Great Spirit: oh Great Spirit, please, I want a big teaching! And it's not another sacred site, it's not another journey on a psychotropic plan, I have a huge amount of experience on all these different psychedelics, it's not another guru, I don't know what it is

Great Spirit, but, please, another big teaching please! Three weeks later, this thing happened. And if you heard the whole story, it's amazing, because I am an incredibly skilled rock climber and I was on this rock, it was almost impossible for this thing to happen!

"And then during the first four or five days in the hospital, I had two near-death experiences: the heart monitor stopped, effectively dead. I'm being taken out of this realm of darkness and I'm about to go into this realm of light and there's all these angels flying around, I can see it, and then this golden rope starts pulling me back; I knew that I was very badly injured, but I heard this sentence: 'there's two reasons you're coming back, the love of your friends around the world, and the work you came here to do that you haven't completed yet'; and so I was brought back."

"What a story! You really have to pay attention to what you wish for. What is the main lesson for you?" Helena asked.

"If you study traditional shamanism and the question is asked, how does a person become a shaman, in the traditional literature there's a number of ways that people become shamans, rarely are people born into it. And it's never that you go to a workshop in a hotel for a weekend and you become a shaman. One, for example, is you get hit by a lightning bolt; I don't have that and I don't want that one! Another one is you get clawed by a large mammal like a leopard or a bear; and then it's all over the literature, you fall off a cliff and you break multiple bones. I look at what happened to me as a shamanic initiation."

"You've had so many extreme experiences and remarkable journeys!" she said in awe.

"You ought to see how I travel. I go out for two years with two pairs of pants and two shirts, that's all."

"Oh, I can't even imagine a woman doing that!" said Helena, laughing. "But to finish, I was going to ask you about an experience you had in Mexico, I remember you talking about how it taught you to trust and surrender."

"I've always been kind of fearless, but there's deeper levels of fear.

That particular story happened in Labna. I was climbing a structure in order to photograph, from above, the only arch in the Mayan world. And, as I was climbing up, I spied a dark hole over on the side of the structure and something said to me: 'oh don't go in!' I've been to some sacred sites, some places of power, which carried an energy that wasn't good for me then, or I felt that I wasn't ready to handle it. Three weeks later, at another pilgrimage site in Mexico, another one of these apparition experiences happens, and I was told: go back and go into that hole. I went back.

"There are no words to describe this. You could put your finger this far in front of your eyes, you couldn't see. I'm completely moved; I'm very fragile and very sensitive in a complete dark. There aren't still words to describe this, but I'm falling into the void, and it's darker than the dark in there, I am darker than that. It was really frightening, so I pulled back. I didn't leave the chamber where I was, I just pulled back. I thought: 'I can't handle this', because the void felt also evil. And then I pulled back from it. I'm not moving. I'm still in this chamber and then this experience starts again. I thought, 'let's just surrender to it, let's just go with this'... and I started to let myself go into it, again and again. I thought: 'if I keep going into this, I could become evil forever', and so I pulled back again. Then a third time. I don't know how many minutes this lasted. And this time, I'm falling into it, and something just said 'let go, let go', and so it was the biggest let go of my life! I let go and I fell into this darkness that was this void, that was great evil; and then it transformed, because I had exhibited this tremendous courage to let go in the face of absolute darkness, in this great evil, and it transformed and it became extraordinary light and extraordinary love.

"So the teaching (one of them) for me was: there are times when something happens that we don't understand it and so we pull away from it. Well, sometimes, we shouldn't pull away from it; sometimes the only way over something is through it. I got over my fear of evil, and over my fear of darkness, and over my fear of the void, by that time, because of my willingness to cloak myself in love. I felt: 'I'm surrounding myself in love and I'm just going to pray to the Great Spirit and I'm going to dive in' and I dove in and I was transformed.

"I can now go into situations that would be terrifying to other people and they're not to me. I've gone into my deepest fears, the deepest dark, the deepest evil, and I've come out the other side with love in me so much stronger," said Martin proudly.

When he finished watching the interview, Thomas went to the balcony of his room and let his gaze linger on the horizon, reflecting on how he, too, had been deconstructed by life's experiences.

He wrote a long email to Helena:

"I know I'm not quite myself, I dither, trying to understand the melody of this universe, how it flogs us and tames us, how it is generous, gentle and tempestuous, but always so magical, so wise, so creative.

Thank you for sharing these conversations of yours with me, they're always so inspiring. They are like chinks of light that show us other feelings and senses, allow us to inhabit different perspectives, discovering which parts of us are illuminated.

I feel it more and more: our love ties us to all that is vaster than us. It fills our dreams with endlessness. Now and again, I catch myself thinking about men and women living their lives in a vacuum: without nurturing their dreams, without poetry or adventure, without love, without taking risks, without allowing themselves to explore or to be creative, without showing the world their gifts, believing they are unworthy, or that life blocks them, so they carry on half asleep, hidden below layers of apathy, hopelessness and disbelief. How many have closed their hearts to love, allowing themselves to vegetate their life away, like machines, switching on and off, simply functioning, satisfying basic needs, defending their actions with the old maxim of security, as if man were in no need of ecstasy, as if man were in no need of feeling his cheeks flush or his heart leap at the thought of being alive. As if man were in no need of experiencing transcendence in the union of two bodies. And what if the glimmer in their eye were to go out? We know that a man doesn't die when the glint in his eye fades... or is he, rather, the living dead?

And if so many slumberers live around us, right next door, in the building opposite, in the house across the road, scattered about the same old places, if so many have already allowed themselves to die inside, unceremoniously, what can we do if we aren't even aware of it? I like to think that, if we are present in every encounter, however fortuitous, we will give a little of ourselves to some, and we might be able to be these chinks of light that will be able to illuminate the dormant parts of the other person, reminding them of their beauty, the greatness that inhabits them.

Not everyone who starts a marathon reaches the finish line. Not everyone who opens their eyes, for an instant, keeps them open. Not every heart, which were once awoken, promises never to close again. And, along the journey, life serenely switches on lights, a bulb here, a beacon there, a candle further down the line, subtly calling to the sleeping hearts, as if sirens, singing. And, at other times, it opens no end of wide windows and doors, as if promising a new world on that journey.

It makes no difference how many awake, how many cross the familiar space of their habits, what matters is, if the few that were illuminated by love, the ones that felt more alive than ever before, what matters is knowing how these few will continue their journey. How much will they fight for the sustenance that keeps them alive. After life's revelations, we need to know how to keep the petals open, how to till the soil, how to water and care for it, so that the lost lustre remains alight; because the body that has rusted from having so much avoided movement, takes a while to find its bearings, takes a while to recognise the strength it has to forge ahead.

I'm not quite sure why all this is swirling within me at this time; why these thoughts have been rekindled. They say a new time is coming and with it, new challenges. And the greatest of these is renewal, the awakening of a new consciousness. Reinventing our lives, habits, our dreams, hopes and goals. It's not enough to want to do things differently. We need to find the courage to face our fears. We need to look within and delve deep into the darkness of the soul, lighting the way for a future of peace, love, health, happiness and abundance.

Plotinus said: "Go back inside yourself and look: if you do not yet see yourself as beautiful, then do as the sculptor does with a statue he wants to make beautiful; he chisels away one part, and levels off another, makes one spot smooth and another clear, until he shows forth a beautiful face on the statue. Like him, remove what is superfluous, straighten what is crooked, clean up what is dark and make it bright, and never stop sculpting your own statue, until the godlike splendor of virtue shines forth to you..."

In the Temple of Apollo, we find the inscription, "I warn you, whoever you are, Oh! You who want to probe the Arcana of Nature, that if you do not find within yourself that which you are looking for, you shall not find it outside either! If you ignore the excellences of your own house, how do you pretend to find other excellences? Within you is hidden the treasure of treasures! Know thyself and you will know the Universe and the Gods."

You awaken these thoughts within me, sculptor of lives. If there are any dormant parts within me, I am sure that your alchemical touch will awaken them. I surrender to you, and to myself, more and more, trusting that once awakened, I will not slip back; that together we will know how to care for this endless love in us, in acts and words, with each day that passes, in full awareness. I also want to be able to bring goodness and beauty to your life, I want to know how to intertwine the strands of light, give you hands, voice, body, blood and tears, warmth and comfort, words and sobbing, fire and air, books and dances and enchanting dreams, more than I could ever write or imagine.

You might even know why this is whirling within me. But it doesn't matter why. What matters is sharing.

Love,

Thomas."

A documentary filmmaker

Helena truly was a sculptor of lives, ideas, images and stories; in her work she would carve forms never before considered, by joining loose and distant pieces, in a magical concoction that effortlessly emerged. With each documentary she would transform huge blocks of shapeless stones into spaces of contemplation, resonance and reverberation. She was yet to have any children, but it was in her womb that she felt the creative process of every work. Lengthy gestations that transformed her greatly. With every discovery, every interview, every edit, the documentary would change, but so would she. Helena never remained unchanged. Her body, heart and mind, were, continually, being transformed with the passage of time; she was ever prepared to carry the light of a new life, which, she was well aware, would influence other lives, engender new waves of thought, feeling, and action.

With subjects that profoundly affected her, she would embark on cathartic processes in which she would purge herself of unconscious memories of pain, of abuse, recollections that she did not even know if they were hers or of the world. It was a hypnotic dance of surrender, to which she succumbed as if an act of love. In the unique melody of every documentary, she would dissolve herself and the world into intuitive gestures, combining dissimilar elements, merging materials never before melded, in a reinvention of reinventions of words, ideas and images, entirely indifferent to conventions, scandalously far from the predictable. Which was why her art provoked such moments of enchantment, surprise and insight. And this new substance built upon the convergence of elements never before connected, bonded by that love which danced in her choices, brought an almost blinding light to the fore, a light that defined her as a being and which gave her a powerful credibility despite her still being a young woman.

Although he was far away, on the other side of the ocean, for the first time Helena could feel that she was not undertaking this journey alone. She felt they were building something together, with each shared thought, each piece of feedback she received, there were new awakenings, ideas bursting into life, new paths gaining ground, not dissimilar to the exercises you do that awaken muscles you never knew you had. This excited her more than usual; the fire in her chest seemed to burn like an Olympic torch. Not that she knew where she was going, or that she had figured out what exactly she was going to do with the subject of truth, but the journey had the power of spring to it, burgeoning new forms in the space of her body. She felt strong, happy and highly creative.

They met up at Villa Celimontana, in Rome. Peter Engberg was passing through, on his way to catch a plane back to Copenhagen, after attending a retreat for Danish artists and scientists at the San Cataldo monastery, on the Amalfi coast.

Helena had met him a few years before, in the Netherlands, at one of those international forums where a large number of extraordinary people come together. For mysterious and rather peculiar reasons, they had both interviewed each other, in an uncomfortable experience for anyone who likes to remain behind the camera, but nonetheless challenging and unforgettable. Peter was a director and documentary filmmaker and, just like Helena, had travelled all over the globe. Just like Martin too, she realised now. Helena had a high regard for Peter's work, but more than anything else, she saw him as a box of surprises, because, no matter how many times they met up, she was always surprised by his latest adventures and wild stories, which she relished.

Having looked around this green oasis hidden in the heart of Rome, catching up on news, they sat down on a picnic blanket below one of those trees that looks like it has witnessed the history of humanity. With the camera running, Helena set the tone for the conversation.

"So many of the truths of yesteryear have been overtaken by new discoveries. Just think back over the last one hundred years. And we know this will continue to happen. There will be new discoveries, new perspectives, overturning what we take now for granted. So, for you, what is the truth?" she asked.

"To me, the truth as a word is a construction, like God. Truth is when I'm connected to something that I cannot define, but I know is true. And I know it on a cellular level, not on a mental level. And so truth to me is being consciously connected to that power that keeps us alive.

"Let's just start here. Here we are, we're breathing. The amount of processes going on right now for you to see, for you to hear, for you to feel... Millions of processes are happening, your cells are being renewed, you are able to perceive heat, light, feelings and even if somebody comes up behind you, you can feel it, even though you can't see it. Birds can fly from the North Pole to the South Pole without any GPS. It is a real miracle to be alive now. For me, this is such a message of hope, because it is easy to wake up in the morning and just do what you usually do, without appreciating the gift of being alive.

"Once, I went to Colorado," Peter continued. "There was a group of young Japanese people, between 17 and 25 years-old, who had come to learn more about nature, about sustainable living, about sustainable architecture, ecological gardening and so on, as part of a training program called 'Earth Restoration Core'. For three weeks they were given a basic introduction to these things. And then, in the last week, we went up high in the mountains, it was called 'Wilderness solo'. On the first evening, we were sitting around a fire up by a mountain lake, at a height of about three thousand metres. And then Chief Red Cloud's grandson, an American-Indian chief, he came and began talking to the young people about "all relations", their flying relations, four-legged relations, swimming relations... Because the whole area was full of mountain lions and pumas, eagles, bears, snakes, serious environment. I saw two pumas.

"The young people were given an instruction to take their sleeping bags and go and find a place to sleep alone, far from anybody else. And, not one of them, had ever spent a night under the stars. So, everybody went out, and next morning they came back and met by the lake and I interviewed them. One by one, by one, they each said: "I have learned more during this one night, than in all my years at school.

"So, for me when I feel alive, when I feel that breath coming in and the breath coming out, it is a gift, it is the ultimate gift. And it's so simple that we take it for granted. We're not alone, you know? It is the same energy that is keeping you alive which is keeping me alive. But I'm straying from the subject, without being. For thousands of years, people have tried to define the truth and I think we're not here to define it. We are here to experience it," he finished, eyes shining with pleasure.

"I think we're not here to define the truth. We are here to experience it," Helena repeated. "I like that!"

"And many lifetimes can go by in trying to understand truth, and in my own life I've been trying that, but there comes a point where you've had enough of defining it, you just have to experience it. Like right now. Recognizing that I am an instrument of something that is speaking to. Something that is looking out through your eyes and listening through your ears, that power… And when I'm tuning into that, just like a radio frequency, you know that there's no extra thing around the corner that's missing. But only you, as an individual, will know. Nobody can tell you what the truth is, only you will know."

"What is true for you?" she asked.

"Well, for example, what we call 'love'. To me, it's also a construction, but the feeling of love for the Earth, and the sky, and the sun and the moon, and for your children… that brings you a certain taste of truth to me. If you really want to explain truth, it's like a diamond. Is it blue?

Turquoise? Yellow? Green? It's all that. But more. You have to go to the diamond heart."

"Are you saying that from the outside there will always be many facets of the same truth? That it is necessary to go to the heart of things, and of people, to get close to the truth?"

"To feel what is beyond the transitory. Have you ever been present at someone's death?" asked Peter. "I remember sitting there while my father was dying. It was clear that something left the body. And the room was actually filled with light. I think it should be mandatory for every human being to participate in, at minimum, one birth and one death. Just to understand the framework of this picture, just to get a sense of it: the first breath and the last breath, and what happens in between. Yes. So I know, I know in my cells, that there is something that cannot be born and cannot die."

"Do you consider that it is this something that brings us closer to the truth?"

"Did I ever share with you that experience in Malibu? About the fire..." asked Peter.

"You have already told me so many amazing stories!"

"There were these wildfires that happened while I was living there. This one, it came one hundred miles an hour, and suddenly it was there. We just jumped into the car just as the flames surrounded the car. So I'm driving into the fire... it's not a movie. I'm driving into the fire with a full gas tank and two other people.

"And, at that moment, my consciousness entered that place where I go when I meditate, like a drop landing in the ocean… and I just felt such deep peace... going, driving through the fire. We came out unharmed. And many other events like that have shown me again and again that there is something that is real, but it's not physical. It creates the physical."

"What an overwhelming experience!" she said, feeling the miracle of all of it.

"I have some of those," he said, laughing jovially, from the fullness of his seventy five years. "What we call 'the truth' exists, but it's not physical and it's not outside us and continues even when we die..."

"And what name do you give to this something that is inside of us and never dies?"

"I don't have a word for it because it's an experience. And as soon as I try to find a label for it, I know that I'm limiting it. It's just a habit of the mind, this labelling factory."

"Good expression! We really are a big labelling factory!" said Helena, laughing.

"One day I was in Louisiana, a beautiful art museum in Denmark.... I was living with a woman who worked there. So, I was sitting there and people were coming in and, beside every painting, there was a little sign with the name of the artist and the title of the picture. At one point, I decided to sit on the side and look at people's eyes. What did they look at first: the label or the picture? Oh, is it a famous painter? So I decided to sit in front of the label."

"You had fun!"

"I even put a little piece of white paper on top of some other labels, and I just watched... some people went into a kind of panic. You mean, there's no label? I don't know if it's a famous painter? Do I have to experience it all without a label?" he replied, laughing like a child. "Yes, it was fantastic. And you can move that into life on Earth, this mind that insists upon having labels. That's also the whole point of Zen practice, right? To dismantle the labelling machine," said Peter.

"A thought provoking story. It's as if we need prior information to dictate how to live each experience. Like when Joshua Bell went busking in the subway, and no-one noticed. And he's one of the finest talents in the classical music world. It was a social experiment organized by the Washington Post. Did you see the article or the YouTube video?" asked Helena with enthusiasm.

Peter shook his head, no.

"It was a cold January morning. A man started to play the violin just inside L'Enfant Plaza Metro entrance, in the busy centre of Washington DC. He played two Bach pieces, one Massenet, one Schubert, one Ponce, one Mendelssohn, for about 45 minutes. During that time, since it was rush hour, it was calculated that one thousand people went through the station, most of them on their way to work, yet only seven people stopped and stayed for a while. Only seven, astonishingly! About twenty gave him money, but continued to walk at their normal pace. He collected thirty-two dollars. No one knew this, he was playing incognito, but the violinist was Joshua Bell himself. He played one of the most intricate pieces ever written with a Stradivarius violin from 1713 worth 3.5 million dollars. Three days before, he had played a sold-out concert in Boston and the seats averaged a hundred dollars.

"If people had known that it was Joshua Bell, such a famous virtuoso, they would have stopped immediately, in amazement, they would have filmed it... it's like the plaque with the name of the famous painter on it, next to the painting. So, do we really know how to appreciate beauty or talent or does this depend on preconceptions we may harbour? If we don't take a moment to stop and listen to one of the world's finest musicians playing one of the greatest musical compositions, how many other things are we missing out on?"

"No doubt about it... it's food for thought!" he agreed.

"What about you? How have you stayed connected with what is true for you?"

"I've been listening to my intuition since I was very little," said Peter.

"What do you call intuition? How does it communicate with you?"

"As you know, there's only one voice from here," he said putting his hand on his heart. "Up here, ten thousand voices," he continued, pointing to his head. "One voice. And it's quiet. In some cases, it's immediate, I focus and I know. But if I'm constantly surfing around the Internet, then I'm not able to concentrate on the *Innernet*."

"Good expression, *innernet*," reflected Helena with a smile. "I feel the same as you. Some days I am hyper-connected and I know immediately. Other days, I need to stop, to get away from the external hubbub and chaos, in order to access my *innernet*."

"What I see on the planet right now is that a lot of people are beginning to see the *Innernet*, not the Internet, but the *Innernet*; that everything is connected without computers and without satellites; this has been understood for thousands of years. So, to answer your question: when I was eleven, my father, my mother and I were driving through Yucatan, in Mexico. I was sitting on the backseat, when suddenly, I had these goose bumps and I said 'stop the car'; so my father stopped the car and I got out. And I went into this dense jungle, which was just one hundred meters from the road, because something within me told me to. I felt that nothing could stop me... and sure enough, I saw this step pyramid, it grown over with a lot of plants, and which was not visible from the road, not excavated. No signs.

"You cannot explain logically how an eleven year old boy that's driving, you know, eighty kilometers an hour through a piece of jungle in Mexico knows, with this one hundred percent precision, that there is this step pyramid, one hundred meters into the jungle, that cannot be seen from the road!" said Peter, smiling.

"You're a box full of surprises. And your life is a myriad of tales that writers would find hard to imagine," she said.

"Reality always beats fiction. The perspective of my life changed dimension. Seriously and immediately. I started to trust my intuition immensely. It's the same thing that happened with the Dogon tribe in Mali, I think I told you, right?" he asked.

"You've told me just a little. But I'd love to know more."

"It's another turning point in my life. Many years before, I had seen a National Geographic magazine where there were pictures of a tribe in South Sahara in Mali. The Dogon tribe! They had never had any contact with the modern world, but had measurements of Sirius, the stellar constellation, that were more accurate than NASA's have today. So, they had a very advanced cosmology. And when I saw the pictures of this, these dwellings at the foot of a cliff, I decided one day I must go there. Cut to, about 15 years passed, I was starting the film "NOW, a moment on Earth", where I went around the world to ask people: what is most important in your life? Do you remember?" asked Peter.

"Of course!"

"We had been to Japan, and Mexico and America, a lot of places, but then I remembered the Dogon Tribe, and I thought 'I have to go'."

"No reason, just fifteen years on, now is the time," said Helena, smiling.

"Yes! And so, a friend of mine said, but if you're going to be filming in Mali, you have to have permission from the government to make the film. You must deposit the cash value of the film equipment with the customs, because they're afraid you are going to sell the equipment. And the cash value of the equipment was over a hundred thousand dollars. And you must have somebody from the local Film Institute to follow you around. And when I heard it, I thought, well, I'll just go, I trust life. So I didn't contact anyone in Mali. Not a soul."

"A full-on adventure," said Helena, amused and curious.

"So, I arrive at a little airport in Bamako – all this is before Tourism in Mali - there's this black woman standing there with the biggest smile you can imagine and just looking directly at me. So, I go over and I explain in French, and she also spoke French, that I've just come, because I heard about the Dogon people, and I want to make a film there; but I've also heard that I must have permission from the government to make this film. I must deposit a lot of money, cash with customs. And I have to have somebody from the local Film Institute to follow us around. And in Mali, when you speak to people, you stand 20 centimeters apart, so we're standing like this.

"And then she says with an even bigger smile: '*pas de problème*. It's not a problem. My father works for the president of Mali. My uncle is the customs' chief. My brother is head of the Film Institute.' I can just feel the synchronicity, the truth of the moment, if you want to call it anything. So we go into the uncle's customs office at the airport. There is the uncle, just next door. And she talks with him, and about five minutes later, we have it fixed, we don't have to deposit anything. Then she calls her father who works for the president of Mali and I get a personal permission. I still have this permission from the president of Mali to make the film. As if that wasn't enough, then she calls her brother, Head of the Film Institute in Mali and he says: 'No, you don't have to have anybody following you around. On the contrary, if you need any equipment, or if we need help, we're at your disposal.' As if that wasn't enough, then she says: 'if you need a four wheel drive, a chauffeur, a guide and an interpreter, I work for the Red Cross, and I'm going north of Bamako,' and when you go north of Bamako, you go into the Sahara. Sahara is bigger than Spain, France and Germany put together, but she was heading the same direction I was going. And so, I don't have to think, I don't have to say anything, we just go directly to the Land Rover. And we take off," said Peter with passion.

"Unbelievable. I am speechless... if we wrote that in a film script they would say it was unrealistic," said Helena, completely surrendered to the story.

"So, for about three days, we were driving and now we're in the sand; and it's a serious place, no margin for mistakes. So, we finally arrive at this cliff and I remember, because I remember the pictures of the cliff from the National Geographic magazine! I tell her: 'Thank you so much. I have to go out. Thank you for everything.' And then she drives off. And there I am, alone, with my little backpack. I sit down, I just close my eyes… and I can sense the incredible silence of the desert, which is not absence of sound, it's the presence of the universe.

"About 20 minutes later, I see this silhouette coming towards me; a black man with white hair who looks like a medicine man. He comes right up to me, stopping 20 centimeters apart, in front of me. There's nobody else except us. We look at each other for a very, very long time without a word. And then he says: '*Bonjour.*' It's like, oh, my God, he speaks a little French. And then I explain that I've come, because I heard about the Dogon Tribe 15 years ago, and all I know is that they had no contact with the modern world, except there was a person who had met the journalist from National Geographic magazine who had written the article. Then again, we just look at each other. And then he leans forward and says: '*C'etait moi!*' It was him of all the people in the world."

"Tremendous! I'm trying to find words to do justice to this sequence of events. Haunting? Fascinating? Extraordinary? The universe couldn't have been friendlier," Helena said, astonished.

"I was speechless, too. What were the odds? He was the one who had met the journalists 15 or 20 years ago! So, for the next ten days I followed him around and went from one village to another. I met all these incredible people. And I just felt that the only thing I had done to get there was what? I had let go. Well, not in theory. I had really let go. The Sahara is a dangerous place and I was alone… but I trusted life."

"You said they have accurate information about the Sirius constellation," Helena remembered.

"Well, you should read a book by Robert Temple, called '*The Sirius Mystery*'. He talks about all that. I can just briefly tell you one little thing about Sirius. Once every 20 or 30 years, they have a ritual festival among the Dogon Tribe, where they wear masks with long antennas, two, three or four meters long - I can send you the pictures afterwards. And these are antennas to Sirius. The purpose of the ritual dance is to tune into Sirius; you would love it!" said Peter.

"I imagine."

"So, I didn't know about these dances. I just had heard that it happened very rarely. And when I was there, there were no white people, no tourists, just me alone. So, after three days or so, I suddenly heard drumming. Standing right in front of me. I'll send you the picture. Right in front me these dancers with wild Dogon masks and antennas!"

"That's incredible. I've seen videos. I can imagine what it would be like to be there! I think I'd go into a trance," she said enthusiastically.

"I can still feel it right now. The frequency changes. There's a point where everything vanishes, where you just go into another realm… you have probably experienced this with Trance Dance or whatever, right?" he asked.

"With dancing? Yes, but not only. I've recently experienced what you are describing, but it's not just about that - everything in this story of yours is surprising. What were the odds that you happened to be there at the exact moment of the festival?"

"It's just another indicator of the potential that lies in letting go on a real level! I just thought that if we, as a species, could learn to let go on that level every day, we would have a totally different world."

This conversation with Peter resonated in Helena's heart. She was aware of the power of trusting and leaps of faith. Yet, despite having already experienced many of these wonderful synchronicities when surrendering to the arms of life, and following her heart without any "what ifs", most of the time she would flip back to control mode: planning alternative scenarios, making calculations and strategies, everything that might give her a sense of control or security with regard to the future, even when she knew it was an illusion. Just as life could reward her when she surrendered to it, life could also pull the rug from beneath her feet, dashing any of the plans she had made, if she needed to learn certain lessons.

Before saying their goodbyes, Peter reached out to Jim Garrison. He felt that they should meet and that Helena would really like to interview him, which she did. Jim was an American living in Paris at that time, with a long and impressive career, heaps of knowhow and an abundance of remarkable stories. Starting with his birth. Born to missionary parents in China at a time of great violence, in a walled village with no running water or electricity, where there were no doctors or even anyone to help with the birth. Seven days after his mother had given birth, alone, pushing him out of her belly, they had been placed under house arrest and, at gunpoint, his mother had watched her breasts dry up, in a place where baby formula was impossible to obtain.

Jim imparted all of this with the skill of a seasoned storyteller. These were the first signs of a highly unusual life. Helena readily became lost in the moment as he talked; as if absorbed in the words of a compelling book. After graduating from Harvard and earning a PhD in Cambridge, Jim had travelled throughout the Soviet Union, meeting its leaders before witnessing, first-hand, the collapse of major modern empire.

His was a life brimming with social and political activism, kicked off in the 1960s with anti-war and antinuclear movements, citizen and environmental diplomacy. Arranging historic meetings of great minds and hearts was in his blood. In the Cold War period he arranged them between astronauts and cosmonauts, as chairman of the Esalen Institute US-Soviet Exchange Programme. From 1995 onwards, through the State of the World Forum, he brought together luminaries such as Desmond Tutu, Jane Goodall, Elie Wiesel, Nelson Mandela, Ted Turner, Vandana Shiva, under the banner of transforming conversations that matter into actions that make a difference. During the pandemic, as president of Ubiquity University, he created a daily online programme, called Humanity Rising, inviting creative geniuses on a quest for solving major challenges.

In one of their conversations, Jim asked Helena if she believed in the truth pursued or truth possessed. Jim believed that this was a fundamental distinction between how people approach the truth.

"My father believed in truth possessed. He believed he had 'The' truth," said Jim aflame. "I believe in truth pursued, I'm Socratic, I believe that it's much more important to live in the question, than to live in the answer, because, if I'm living in the answer, I'm trying to convince you of my truth. However, if I'm living in the question, I want to hear what your heart believes, because I'm interested in your perspective, and it may shed some light…

"Yet in order for hearts to commune around truth, they have to be open to higher truth. That is bigger than all of us. We are all like blind men looking at the elephant," he continued. "Everybody holds the truth, but not the whole truth. And everybody holds some falsehood, but not all the falsehood. And as the Buddha said, when two disciples meet on the road, let them discuss noble truth or keep noble silence."

Jim would pause in the right places, his silences, which varied in intensity, seemed to open up doors to us for a few seconds, inviting us to enter his thoughts.

"You know the contradictions in my youth," Jim added, "being the son of a missionary but not a Christian, being an American white growing up in Asia, with the oriental races speaking a foreign language; so from the very first episodes of my life, I was always a stranger in a strange land. Always having to explore the opposite which was not me. And how do you both appreciate that opposite and maintain your own sense of authenticity without judgment of the opposite? That's what is so difficult and, yet, absolutely necessary. It's a discipline to be able to hold your truth with a conviction that another truth can be held, which is equally true, as a partial part of a larger whole. That's really, I think, a high art form that the world is yet to learn."

Jim was contagiously inspiring and his words always left Helena with something new to reflect upon. She reiterated his words: to be able to hold your truth with a conviction that another truth can be held, as a partial part of a larger whole. And how do you do that? Through the heart. Acceptance. Love. The recollection that connects us. Which is much larger than what separates us. She recalled that experiment filmed on video where they had brought together, two by two, people who lived in opposite poles, often divided by long-standing hostilities, caused by their country of origin, by religion, gender, age, culture, skin colour or beliefs. They were only asked to remain in silence, facing each other, for four minutes. And what was the result? The participants in the experiment formed bonds that scaled the walls that seemed to exist beforehand. Eye to eye, the windows to the soul.

Between Sandra Cisneros, a Chicana writer, and Helena, it had taken less than four minutes for their hearts to celebrate their encounter and to feel great empathy.

"Sandra, how do you perceive the truth?" Helena asked her at one point.

"That's a big question, like asking me what's the secret of the universe or why are we on the planet?" she replied, smiling with her eyes. "I think everybody's here on Earth, and I'm still figuring it out, but I think everybody's task is to discover our truth. To discover who we are and to somehow express that truth in whatever life work we have. That's what I think my truth is. That I was put on the planet to discover who I am, and I'm still just becoming and I'm still discovering who I am in my writing… and my writing takes me to the truth. That's how I know truth, you know, from my writing.

"For other people it might be through their children or through their garden or through their profession. For me it's through my art. And I never know what that truth is until I feel it… It may sounds strange, but the answer comes first. Then I discover the question and so that takes me to my truth… like my writing is a question, but I don't know the question until I get to the answer. And the answer is a truth that you know it's a truth, not "the" truth, one truth; and every piece of writing I do is a question, but I don't know the question until I get to the answer."

"How do you know it's really true? Body, mind, heart?

"Because it tells me something that I didn't know I already knew... that's how I know," explained Sandra.

Helena was unable to explain to anyone precisely how she chose the people she interviewed. The idea that all of existence is a vast network of interconnected and interdependent phenomena seemed applicable in this intuitive and, at the same time, domino-like process. It was as if those people were calling to her, inexplicably. When she tried to understand what connected them, it wasn't a puzzle she could immediately solve, given they were from such disparate areas. She noted that, without knowing it beforehand, many of them had had boundary-pushing experiences in their lives, they had travelled the globe, they were great scholars and they all had life stories that were so rich and complex that they would fill a book of various volumes; they were also pioneers and activists, speaking out on controversial topics and most of them had gone through life-changing mystical experiences.

For a while she thought that, from an academic point of view, two of the hallmarks of mystical experiences were their ineffability and their noetic quality: two words that made her think of angels and poetry, she didn't know why, but which she also associated with the best experiences she had had in her life. Ineffability, because it called to mind those moments for which there are no words equal to them, even in the largest dictionaries. There are things that you just can't express. And the noetic quality, by bringing to light the sensation that many men and women have already experienced, when they receive within themselves, without any processing, the direct knowledge of things; they know that's it's true without any logical explanation, revelations of profound significance that change their entire existence and perception of reality.

That's how it had been with Jude Currivan: an intuitive calling. Again, Helena couldn't explain why. But after getting to know her work more deeply, she clearly understood. With a master's degree in physics from Oxford University, specialising in Cosmology and Quantum Physics, and a PhD in Archaeology, Jude herself was an admirable meeting point of science and spirituality. Sensitive, since she was a child, she had experienced multidimensional realities and recognised openly that she was working with higher guidance.

As Jude said "science and spirituality are just two different ways of understanding the nature of reality. I mean, when we go back thousands of years, what is often called the 'sacred science' was exactly that; it was trying to understand the nature of reality. And science is a great tool, but so is experiential understanding and that deeper perspective of more than just the physical reality, but of multidimensional realities, which of course is the journey of the seeker of truth through spiritual practice.

"And so I studied science, I studied ancient wisdom, I went to university and did a master's degree in physics and specialized in quantum physics and cosmology. And then I went into the world of business for a whole raft of reasons, but I think that, when I now look back, I have a very strong sense that, for all of us, nothing's wasted. I studied for a Ph.D. in archeology because I wanted to have the credibility to explain ancient wisdom, ancient cosmologies, ancient ways of looking at the world, universal wisdom, perennial wisdom. And somehow bring that all together with the leading edge science that was really beginning to go beyond what I feel had been a limiting perspective of the world for a long time".

Her journey and vision resonated deeply in Helena's heart. Jude had experienced multidimensional realities since childhood, received guidance many times since the age of four and, in adult life, had been able to scientifically confirm much of the information she had received. Not forgetting that she had previously been a highly respected businesswoman in the United Kingdom, which had endowed her with vast experience and knowhow of world events, international politics, and global economic and financial systems.

She was, in the purest of terms, a woman conversant in a wide variety of fields of knowledge, as Helena, herself, aspired to. Over the last two decades, she had travelled to more than eighty countries in support of planetary and collective healing, and was awarded a Circle Award by "WON Buddhism International", citing her "notable contribution to planetary healing and to the expansion of new forms of consciousness".

When they spoke for the first time, Jude was finishing her second book of a trilogy, entitled "Gaia: Her-Story".

"It's called Gaia, the story of our planet, our universe and our evolutionary journey. Conscious cosmology. To heal our relationship with Gaia is such a vital part of healing our relationship with ourselves and with each other.

"Actually, I was looking back and some of the research papers that I had in a pile, that high! Yet most of what I share in the book comes from incredibly recent discoveries, you know? It's beautiful to watch the researchers wake up and really understand this deep intelligence, this deep sentience that she is!" said Jude, smiling.

"What is your experience? Do you feel that, normally, when people read your books, it changes the way they see the world? Do you feel they are open to go beyond what they know? Because it's very difficult to learn about what you think you already know, isn't it?" asked Helena.

"Absolutely. We've all got cognitive biases, you know? So, in that sense, we're more open to what we think we know, rather than something that disagrees with what we think we know. But I'm never trying to convince anyone of anything. What I am doing is: I'm inviting and I'm sharing. Just inviting people into an adventure of themselves; if they felt able to be part of that adventure to open themselves. But it's always an invitation.

"I interwove information from chemistry, meteorology biology, cosmology - lots of logies - and physics; but I, also, combine a lot of evidence showing that the same patterns that underlie ecosystems and earthquakes, or how atoms behave at face transitions, or how galaxies behave, underlie our human collective behaviours! The patterns we play out are the same relational harmonic fractal patterns that play out in those so-called natural systems. So, I wanted to really show the evidence.

"And when we look at the interconnections throughout the internet, they're the same patterns as the interconnections through an ecosystem. They're dynamic and on the edge of criticality, which gives them flexibility and resilience, but it means that they are deeply intelligent, deeply informed.

"We are entering this golden age, a golden era, and we are really moving from fear-based and separation-based perception towards a more loving and also unified view of the world; but this is not what we are seeing right now! Right now, we are in the middle of more fear and more separation," said Jude.

"What example could you share that would give hope to people who have to stay aligned and really trust the process? Deep down, how can one trust a birth without knowing that it is a birth that is taking place?" asked Helena, in her eternal search for solutions.

"This is like a collective right of passage, and with any right of passage, whether it's a birthing, whether it's going through puberty, whether it's, what they call, the little death of spiritual awakening, we're going through this, and we're going through it individually, personally, and we're going through it collectively. And with any right of passage, with any initiation, as any indigenous wisdom keeper will tell you, there's no guarantee of survival. But there's something that, when we go into a right of passage, whether we're conscious of making that choice or not, we're in it. It's like when you're giving birth to a child. There comes a point where the birth is happening, you can't go back; all you can do is literally breathe and push, breathe, push… And I haven't given birth in that way myself, but sometimes giving birth to books feels a bit like that. That profound simplicity when there is no other choice, because we're already going through this.

"I learned many years ago, through many rites of passage, that it is infinitely better to go with the flow and, literally, align with our universe's evolutionary impulse," Jude added with simplicity.

"I agree," Helena replied with a smile. "But assuming that we are microcosmic co-creators, but we are in a collective… So, from your point of view, what influence and power does each one have in their own reality and in the reality of this world?"

"In my experience, our expectations limit the possibilities of what can flow through. What I've found, over many years, is when, not just myself, but many people feel called into service in some way, and they actually get out of the way of what will flow from that, miracles happen," replied Jude.

"When you say 'get out of the way', do you mean get out of our own way? Not letting our mind, and the limited perspective we may have, end up restricting the field of possibilities of our action? Is that it?"

"The path is guided by synchronicities, it's guided by intuitive insights, and then it's just serving whatever is flowing through us. When you say: what effect can I have? You don't know. I've had people call me ten years after a conversation and say "you changed my life", and I couldn't recall at all what was said… I'm sure you've had numerous conversations where you've changed people's lives and you have no idea. And that's good. So life is non-linear. A tiny change can have a massive effect. So, it seems to me that, the more we're willing to just go with the flow of what's flowing through us, if we put aside our fears, because fear just closes us down... We have so much biological research that shows that when we become fearful - occasional fear is absolutely right, of course, if a tiger coming at us, we're not going to stand there and wave, we're going to run - but it's when we move into chronic fear, we literally shut ourselves down from fully experiencing life, we shut ourselves down from possibilities, we shut ourselves down from openings, we shut ourselves down from love, because if we fear, we're not loving."

"And how do you maintain close contact with your true voice, and then just surrender and trust?" asked Helena, aware that she had questioned herself on this several times.

"To really surrender is one of the most difficult things to do. Even when you understand that it's really important to do it. The illusion of control is like the illusion of separation, it's an illusion; because we're not in control and yet we cling on to it. And yet, again, it stops us from opening up and flowing with this wonderment that is the universe."

"How to we free ourselves from fear?"

"I suggest having an inner practice, whatever it may be," said Jude. "It could be meditation, it could be yoga, it could be dance, it could be being in nature, whatever supports you. And if you love singing, sing. If you love dancing, dance. If you love running, run. If you love baking, bake. If you love dancing on a table to Abba, dance on a table to Abba... whatever it is, find it, and welcome it into your life.

"And do that daily: ensure that what brings you joy is part of the way you live your life, obviously not hurting anyone else... because sometimes we get so tied up with "we must do that", "we should do that", that we forget to be joyful, we forget what brings us joy and we forget to welcome that into our lives, every day.

"Joy is always creative. And when we are in a joyful, creative space, that's when we are living. It's like when you see a three-year-old child, there's nothing else, just that moment. We spend so much time looking ahead and looking back, either regretting the past or fearing the future, but when we find our joy, we find our creativity and we find how to be present. And, in my experience, with creativity and joy, there's no space for fear.

"My mom used to say - and this was such good advice: what you can do, do. And what you can't do, don't worry about it. My mom was the most practical person in the world and she knew the futility of worry."

"You were talking about your mom and your childhood and I know that you experienced a psychic phenomenon that influenced your path. Could you share a little about it?" asked Helena.

"It hasn't just influenced my path, it's been an intrinsic part of my life. When I was about four years old and I was in my bedroom, a discarnate light just arrived in the bedroom and I started to hear a message clearly. So, within two or three years, I was finding that I was, you know, clairaudient: I could hear messages. Also clairvoyant: I could see things. And precognitive: I was able to start getting a sense of what might be. I was becoming a clairsentience: I could touch and feel and remote viewing... These are all innate to all of us; it was just that I never, in a way, lost those capacities."

"Did you tell your parents?"

"It never occurred to me to share any of this with any human being for a very long time," said Jude. "And it wasn't because I was fearful, I was just having so much fun! I know my mom would have been accepting and encouraging. I'm pretty sure she knew what was going on, she was highly intuitive, but she never imposed herself upon me; if I wanted to share, she was there for me.

"When she passed, she came to me a few hours after she had passed. She passed with dementia and she came to me and, literally, the whole room that I was in lit up. And she was there in her glory, and it was so wonderful, it was just so wonderful to have her presence there as she truly is!"

Helena recalled what Peter had told her about being present at his father's parting. She also recalled what Sandra Cisneros had shared about her mother's death. Both similar experiences. Sandra's mother was in the hospital, hooked up to machines. Sandra was in the room, holding her hand. And, the moment when her mother passed, she felt a light, a butterfly of light in space, and an emotion of absolute tenderness and love. Used to a harsh mother, destroyed by unfulfilled dreams, Sandra told Helena that this experience had enabled her to know the loving and beautiful essence of her mother. And make peace with her.

"In adult life, what other experiences have marked your ability to communicate on a multidimensional level?" asked Helena.

"Do you know Abydos in Egypt?" Jude asked back.

Jude was referring to the temple which the Greeks called Memnonium, at Abydos, now dedicated to Seti I, Osiris and Isis together with Ptah, Ptah-Sokar, Nefertem, Re-Horakhty, Amun-Ra and Horus.

"It's a place called the Osirian and it's very, very ancient. Archaeologists don't even know how ancient it is; and it's very difficult to fit it into their dynastic timeframe. And in the temple of Seti the First, there are three small chapels and one of them is dedicated to Osiris," Jude continued. "I asked for an initiation by Osiris and I received a pretty interesting response. It was as though a veil had come over my eyes. I started to sob, I was absolutely racked by sobs; and I walked through the temple – I had never been there before – I went to the outside of the temple, at the back, and I just knew the way, even though I had never been there before. I started to walk down in the sunshine to the Osirian. I sat down, pulled my jeans up, took two steps, and fell into a 35-foot deep cave, or well, that was filled with water. And as I'm going down – and the water by this time is over my head – I'm not panicking, I'm just realizing: this is the initiation! And it was the initiation by water, which was the ancient Osirian path.

"The next moment, after I had the thought that this was the initiation, I found myself sitting on the steps absolutely wet-through, dripping wet, having somehow levitated out of that well. So that was pretty interesting. Within about 5 minutes of sitting on the steps I felt that I was on fire, as my kundalini was raising... and that lasted for 3 days!"

"What an incredible initiation!" said Helena in awe.

"For me it was incredibly opening, it just took me to a whole new level of my spiritual path and my spiritual awareness. And that journey literally opened the way, by the new millennium, to a major download of information about undertaking what I thought was going to be 12 journeys, but it ended up being 13 journeys around the world to particular powerful spots; to basically be a conduit for consciousness to come through and help activate the planetary grid for whatever shift of consciousness humanity was preparing for, and is preparing for, or is undergoing."

Helena thought for a moment about what Martin had told her. Their paths were interconnected, even without knowing each other.

"I imagine those journeys have impacted on your work," said Helena.

"I told the true stories of those journeys in a book called "*The Thirteenth Step*", which is also very much an inner journey, as well as an outer journey, because it deepened my own spiritual awareness; it broadened my own ability to communicate multidimensionally."

"As a cosmologist, and based on your understanding of the cosmos, what knowledge, or insights that have emerged, have been most important to you, and may be useful for the collective journey?" asked Helena.

"For me cosmology is a curiosity about the nature of reality itself at a much grander scale and a multi-dimensional scale. And for me it's about consciousness. So the cosmos is the infinite eternal mind of Great Spirit, of God, whatever we might want to call it.

"And ultimately, consciousness isn't something we have; it's what we and the whole world are. All the scientific evidence is pointing to this being the case; that consciousness is the deeper fundamental nature of all that we call reality. Physicists have known, for a very long time, just how truly ephemeral physical reality is. When we drill down to subatomic levels, however solid it appears to be, everything is something like 99.9999999999999999% no-thing-ness. And subatomic entities themselves are the tiniest excitations, they're not tiny billiard balls, they are excitations in a field of what is now being understood as being an informational field rather than anything we've previously termed 'physical.'

"We're really having to restate our understanding of what we understand by "physical." The only reason you can sit on a chair or I can stand on a floor is the way that those excitations relate to each other; but that is an appearance; it is not the fundamental nature of reality.

"The same bits of information that are allowing us to have this conversation over Zoom, that are the workings of our computers, that make up how we create holograms and our virtual realities, those digitized bits of ones and zeroes – that digitized information – is exactly, exactly the same as the universal information that makes up physical reality.

"So information – not random data but patterned information – is more fundamental than energy, matter and space-time. As a result, is taking us beyond this appearance of duality and the appearance of materiality. And it's taking us into the recognition – as the ancient spiritual understanding and all spiritual understanding is – that reality is essentially unified. It plays out on many, many different levels but it is essentially unified. And this is incredibly empowering, because it show us that material duality perspective, that you and I are separate, that we're separate from our beautiful planetary home, that everything is random and meaningless ... is nonsense. That just isn't the way that reality is!"

"Incorporating this new perspective changes everything," Helena said thoughtfully.

"Yes! We pollute our planet, we're causing environmental mayhem, we fight and kill each other, and all this is really coming from this duality-based perception which of itself is wrong. So if we can heal our fragmented perspectives into what I'm calling the 'Whole World-View', then perhaps that will play its part in helping us heal our behaviors."

"To be the microcosmic co-creators, but in the recognition that we are a cell of the body of our universe, that when we fight against the other, we harm the whole that includes us," said Helena.

"For me the deepest importance is understanding the integral, unified nature of reality, and that we're not separate and we are empowered. We have meaning, we have purpose. It is very crucial that we show up at this time as you say, we don't have the luxury of being able to go on acting irresponsibly – whether it's to each other, to ourselves, or to our planet, because we're at a point of global emergency.

"What I call an 'octave of eight co-creative principles,' which I've gleaned from many, many different traditions and in my own experience in life, and it is that when we become more aware, we become more attuned to that innate intelligence. And therefore, when we are open to this, we experience more and more synchronicities, which essentially are our way-showers, that we are in attunement with that highest flow. And life becomes progressively effortless. And I don't mean that it won't have its challenges, but it's about showing up and flowing with this higher flow of the universe's evolutionary impulse. It is rather like being a surfer catching the wave and going with it, rather than trying to fight it or second-guess it.

"That's what I've heard all my life: that our universe, our universe soul, finite thought form in the infinity of the cosmos, is evolving! We are all learning, we're all moving, so yes, work in progress," Jude concluded with enthusiasm.

When she was just fifteen years old, Helena, already a huge fan of maths, physics and the mysteries of the world, had gone to the *Science and the Primacy of Consciousness* symposium at the NOVA University of Lisbon, and had attended a presentation given by neurosurgeon and university professor Francisco Di Biase, a major researcher of consciousness, who, when quizzed by an Australian scientist, had spoken brilliantly about the universe as a vast and immense informational quantum holographic network, harmonically organised on all levels of cosmic complexity.

Helena recalled how that had ignited a host of ideas, and how she had travelled in deep enchantment as she visualised that universal holographic principle harmonically interpenetrating every scale of the universe, and are present in systems far removed from each other, such as in: the distribution of matter in the universe, neural networks, cosmic background radiation, climate patterns, the formation of galaxies, the frequency of earthquakes, social, economic and business systems, conflicts and wars, traffic flow in cities, the stock exchange...

Jude reminded her of this knowledge present in the cosmos, in Gaia, and within each of us, when calling to mind this great thought of the cosmic mind that was the universe, manifesting itself as a cosmic hologram of meaningful information, which vitally exists to evolve. Jude Currivan drew on cutting-edge scientific developments, but liked to play around with words and with the wisdom she poetically interwove, leaving, between the lines of these thoughts, deep reflections on the cosmos, Gaia and our place on earth.

If Helena were to draw her thoughts at that instant, the image of spaghetti would have looked about right to her. Her mind went to Dennis Gabor, Nobel Prize laureate for Physics, who had argued that, in holographic systems, each part of the system contains the information of the whole. She thought about the wonderful Buddhist metaphor of Indra's Net, illustrated in the Avatamsaka Sutra, thousands of years earlier, already evoking a holographic system of the Universe. Described by Francis Harold Cook in his book *Hua Yen Buddhism: The Jewel Net of Indra*: "Far away, in the celestial mansion of the great god Indra, there is a fabulous net which was woven and hung by a cunning craftsman in such away that it extends infinitely in every direction. To appease the extravagant tastes of the deity, the craftsman placed a shining jewel in every one of the net's holes. Because the net is infinite, the jewels are infinite. The jewels hang in the net like shining stars: a fantastic image to behold. If one were to arbitrarily pick one of these jewels and closely inspect it, they would discover that, upon its shining surface, are reflected all of the other jewels hanging on the net; infinite in number. Each of the reflected jewels then reflecting each of the other jewels, and so there appears an infinite number of reflected reflections."

She thought about Hermes, scribe to the gods, inventor of the arts and sciences, father of alchemy, the god Mercury, and his well-known axiom written on the legendary emerald tablet "As below, so above. As above, so below". In the schools of mysteries, for a long time this tablet had been considered one of the oldest and most profound revelations of spiritual alchemy.

She was reminded of the mathematician Benoit Mandelbrot and of fractal geometry, which emphasised that the observable universe is derived from the integration and interconnectivity of all its parts. She thought about the Fibonacci sequence, found throughout nature, the so-called golden ratio that inspired her so much, and which was part of the signature of a harmonic and holographic universe full of self-similarities on all scales of complexity of the universe. She thought of Leonardo da Vinci already recognising that the branches of a tree, in all the phases of its height, when put together are equal to the thickness of its trunk. All the branches of a watercourse in every stage of its course, if of equal speed, are equal to the body of the main current.

She thought, like Jude, that the laws governing the evolution of the universe, and this on all scales, are neither random or absurd. On the contrary, they are the result of a process of organisation and very precise interactions. From micro to macro. From quantum to cosmic. From inside to outside. In part as in whole. As above so below. As on earth so in heaven. All full of meaning. A quantum field linking everything. A unifying structure stretching to infinity. A unifying field of consciousness. A quantum vacuum full of intelligence, love and life, from which all the matter filling space and time emerges, and through which it continues to interact.

She thought about David Hawkins when he wrote that chaos is just a limited perception. Everything is part of a larger whole; everyone is involved in the evolution of an all-inclusive, all-attracting field of consciousness itself. It is this evolution, innate to the general field of consciousness that guarantees the salvation of humanity, and with it, of all life.

"As my friend Ervin Laszlo said, we're the first generation to both have the ability to destroy life on earth but also the ability to consciously evolve," Jude had said. "We have this amazing point of bifurcation it seems to me, at the moment: either we breakdown or we breakthrough.

So, the message of The Cosmic Hologram is that everyone can make a difference. We are all microcosmic creators of our realities and we are all fundamentally interconnected as part of a unified and coherent and intelligent universe."

All the new discoveries, new ways of perceiving reality, what is true, fuelled her creativity. Helena was used to opening the windows of her mind whenever she was doing research for new documentaries, but this time the feeling of going with the flow was even greater. She didn't force herself to know the path before she reached it. It was if she were collecting loose parts, without knowing how they would fit together, while believing that this is what would happen and, very probably, in an unexpected way. She put her faith in the process. She herself was part of this work in progress, this evolving dance. The conversation with Jude Currivan had underpinned that faith in her intuition and openness to the path and, reflecting on it now, none of it required effort. Despite the distance from Thomas, time has mysteriously disappeared, the two months has passed in this immersion in suppositions, in interviews, in reading and in Adriana's house, in any house of Adriana in the world, she had the feeling that the magic of Mazunte would remain, that magic where time has everything and nothing wrapped in life.

Where the light is brightest, the shadows are deepest

It was the beginning of November and Thomas was on his way back. His heart was already racing in anticipation of their reunion. This time it was Helena greeting Thomas at the airport, her turn to surprise him.

The sun was shining brightly that day, as if autumn had forgotten who it was when Saint Martin's Day comes around. Helena had put on her most sensual dress and put on lipstick, adding to the beauty of her smile, moored to her face by the closeness of the embrace. When Helena spotted Thomas in the airport terminal, half hidden behind a wave of people, standing looking at his mobile, she went round behind him to catch him by surprise and hug him from behind. When she reached his side, her heart already bursting at the seams of her chest, she gently leaned against his back so that he could feel her heart beating before anything else. A shiver ran through Thomas' body the second before feeling this warm body against his back. He wasn't expecting her, hoping or wishing she would be there, not knowing if she would come, but he was in no doubt that it was Helena; he knew her energy, her scent, her presence in the midst of any crowd. He allowed himself to stay there for a few moments, in that tender embrace, feeling Helena's chest on his back, her hands on his pounding heart. On an impulse, he turned around to lift her off the ground with the lightness of a dancer,

Helena also caught by surprise, laughed in the air like a child, before allowing herself to slide down next to him until their mouths met and the world came to a halt.

When they finally moved apart, Helena seemed like a young woman, rejuvenated with joy.

"Thomas Gatti?" Helena asked, in jest.

"Yes, Thomas Gatti, astrophysicist, pleasure to meet you," Thomas replied, with a huge grin, holding out his hand to shake hers.

"I'm Helena, Adriana's friend. She asked me to come and pick you up," she said, reciprocating his handshake.

Thomas looked at his phone.

"Oh, she never messaged me about it."

"Yeah, but she asked me to come and get you," Helena continued. "Where am I taking you? "

"To Rome," Thomas replied, giggling.

"Wherever you like. I'm all yours..."

"Oh, you're all mine? Let's go to my place, then!"

They both laughed as they headed off towards the car.

Once on their way, a heavy silence fell over the car until they reached Rome, a pervading sensation oscillating between serenity and exaltation.

"You know, I never actually got to go to your place... What's your address? Can you show me the way?"

"Ah, that's right. I'd entirely forgotten that. We were always at Adriana's and then we spent all our time travelling."

"We've had so many homes!" said Helena, remembering.

" Today you'll see mine, my refuge."

"How lovely!" she said, happily. "And in the boot, there are shopping bags full of treats, so that we won't have to leave the house for the next few days," she added, laughing.

"Woman forewarned..."

"A woman in love is better than a woman forewarned," she reminded him, with a smile.

"But you'll have to let me sleep, I'm so exhausted I won't be able to keep up with you!"

"Oh, I'll make use of you sleeping, don't you worry," she replied with a laugh.

Thomas' luggage was parked alongside the shopping bags in the entrance to the house, while in the bathtub, their naked bodies were reunited, in the bed they fell asleep and woke and made love and fell asleep and woke and made love until hunger struck.

Helena made some Italian recipes that she'd been experimenting with at Adriana's house and at the kitchen table they indulged their senses, firstly with a delicious meal, then with the magical flavours of love, savouring them as they passed from kitchen to living room, before collapsing into sleep again on the rug. Their clocks were not tied to the yoke of duty, rather they navigated between pleasures, at times reversing with the sun with the moon the order of waking and falling asleep.

No longer aware if those faint, golden rays where from dusk or dawn, Helena got up to head towards the kitchen. Deep within, there was a feeling so full of love that it seemed to cleanse her of any disappointments of the past. Feeling that union of souls, while drinking from the fountain of love, was one of the most beautiful experiences on earth, the kind to which names such as paradise, Eden, happiness, nirvana, ecstasy, transcendence have been given, but which in that moment, she would describe as the possibility of living the infinite in the finite, heaven on earth, the extra in the ordinary.

Goethe said 'where the light is brightest, the shadows are deepest'. It all depends on where you're looking, what you feed, what you grow and, inevitably, what you need to evolve. She looked over at the photos stood next to books, on a corner shelf in the living room. In one of the photos, her father alongside a woman and a child. She stumbled over to the photo, grabbing the frame in disbelief, and stood there, getting her mind straight. She turned around, livid, the frame still in her hand. Thomas looked at her.

"That's us. My parents and I. I must have been about six," Thomas said.

Suspended in time, Helena remained motionless, until she let the frame fall to her feet. Thomas got up, to join her.

"You okay?"

Helena was startled by Thomas' hands on her arms. She pulled away as tears sprang from her eyes.

"What is it, Helena? You're scaring me."

Helena hastily grabbed her clothes, pulling them on she stumbled to the door, Thomas trying to stop her.

"Helena? Where are you going?"

"Your father, the man in the photo, that's my father... Julian."

Thomas froze, while trying to make sense of what was happening. Helena leaving, running out into the street. Running to the car. The car driving off to who knows where, him sobbing like Helena. Thomas running to his phone, his trembling hands calling his father.

"Thomas! You never call me... Has something happened?"

Thomas trying to ask something. Trying to form the words in his mouth.

"Dad... Helena..." he uttered with difficulty.

"Thomas, I don't know what you're telling me. Helena?" his father asked, becoming nervous.

"I'm in Italy. I met Helena."

"Which Helena?"

"Helena, dad. My love, dad..." he stammered.

"Which Helena?"

"She uses her mother's surname. Helena Santiago."

An icy silence.

"What happened?" his father asked.

"What happened? You tell me what happened!!!"

His heart pounding, thousands of thoughts raced through Julian's head, his mind used to hiding, to covering up secrets, to creating escape strategies, but now caught by surprise, drowning in his own deep well.

"What happened, Thomas?" he asked again, already beside himself.

"We fell in love. We fell deeply in love. Today, at my house. She saw our photo..."

"How is Helena, Thomas?" Julian shouted.

"I don't know... she ran off."

"Go after her, Thomas, before she does something stupid. It's not what you think..."

"It's not what we think? What else can we think?"

"Thomas, do as I tell you, call her, go after her. I know my daughter, she might do something stupid, impulsively!"

"Your daughter..."

"It's not what you think. I said daughter, but... I'll tell you about it when we have more time. Now I need to find her."

He called Helena a thousand times until Helena answered his video call. When she answered, Helena was already on a hilltop, outside Rome. She was still rocking between sobs and moaning, lost in a sea of tears almost unable to see.

"Dad..." she said, making an effort to control the emotional outpouring, leaving her in a state of total disarray.

Despite the instability of her phone in her hand, you could make out where she was and what state she was in.

"Helena, it's not what you think... Calm down."

"Calm down??" Helena screamed, losing control again.

"Give me five minutes," her father said, his voice trembling.

"You have five minutes, and then I'm hanging up."

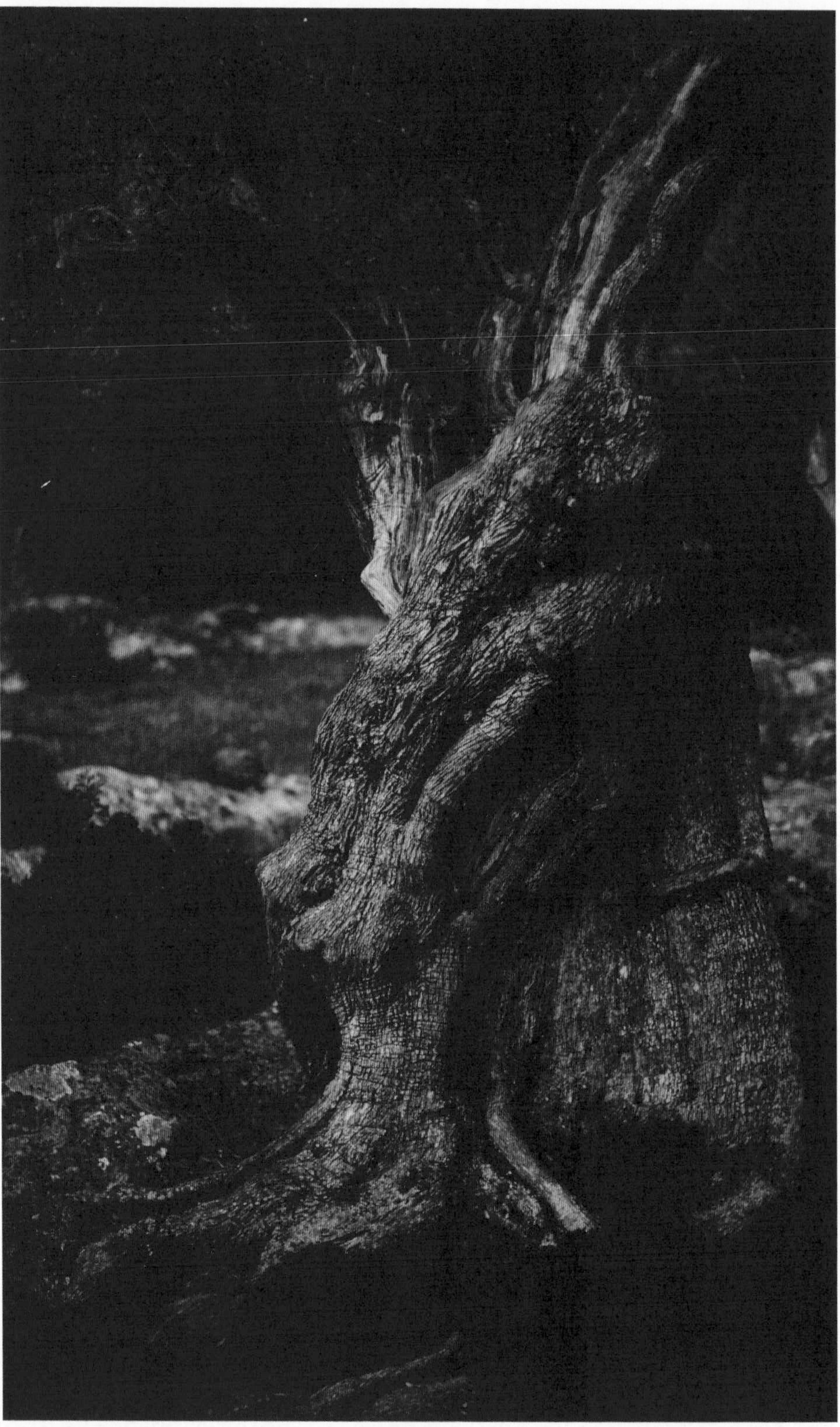

On the 2nd day of the Dark Night of the Soul

Adriana is in the car with Helena. They're both sat in the back. One of the doors open towards the boats in the harbour. Helena is calm. Her voice is unrecognisable. It has a trace of bitterness and irony, but, more than anything else, an ice-blue chill to it, as if the North Pole had sunk south.

"Oh, Adriana," Helena said, with sarcasm in her voice. "I've been told that I'm unique in the universe. Ironic, don't you think?! Right now, I feel just the same as the millions that have gone through this story, this despair, who have felt their guts churn, their hearts ripped apart, who have been faced with the same lies and who unwittingly have become part of a cheap soap opera! I'm just the same as anyone who has spent nights on end, sifting through their memories, trying to fit the pieces together. The same as anyone who has had the same conversations as we are having now, who has repeated the exact same words, who has felt exhausted from insomnia or unlocked secrets that have almost destroyed them; the same as anyone who has fallen hopelessly in love and found themselves between a rock and a hard place... do you see, Adriana? I feel the same as everyone who has wanted to experience the end, for lack of light at the end of the tunnel."

"You know how much I get you and, just like them, there are no shortcuts to being truly healed; you'll have make it through the dark night in order to show your face to the sun on the other side," said Adriana.

"You say 'make it through the night' and in my mind all I feel is a sense of exhaustion at the thought of what seems endless."

"Seems. Just seems. There's no way around the weariness of pain, until it stops being weariness and stops being pain. There aren't even any precise formulas for the process. Each of us has their own path, I had mine too and it took me a long time to get to the other side. Now, on this side of the shore, everything seems different, even the memory of it isn't the same; everything seems to be so much brighter, so full of light, everything that, before, was darker than pitch.

"At the end of it all, you feel like you've travelled the globe just to make it back home, to come back to yourself, as if you haven't been there for a long trip. But what's the point of telling you this now, apart from sounding like empty words? But I'll say it anyway: this too shall pass," Adriana said, trying to bring hope to her heartache.

"*Passará, não passará, algum deles ficará... se não for a mãe da frente é o filho lá de trás,*" Helena sang in Portuguese.

"I don't get you," said Adriana, confused.

"*Linda Falua* is a children's song we used to sing and play: 'It will pass, it won't pass, one of them will stay, if it's not the mother in front, it's the child in the back.' I was just being ironic," Helena said sadly. "I'm not sure you understand, Adriana. There are memories inside me that aren't mine. They aren't true. I, who love truth, who seek truth, am made of lies. I have heard my mother telling me, again and again, the story of my birth. In a way, this story has been imprinted within me, has become mine, you see? It has shaped who I am, or who I thought I was."

"How does the story go?"

"Following the birth, my mother was in a coma for 33 days."

"You never told me."

"I think I've heard that story so many times, that I have never dared repeat it. In a way, I'm not really sure how or why, but I've always felt responsible for this."

"What do you mean?" asked Adriana.

"For having endangered my mother's life... But I'm going to tell you the story, as it was told to me."

"Don't tell me, if it's going to hurt you."

"I want to tell it for the first time, now that I know that none of this story belongs to me," she said sternly. "My parents had gone to a restaurant, I can't remember which one, but my mother would always mention the name when she told me the story. I say mother... it doesn't matter. Her waters broke in the middle of the restaurant; her evening gown soaked. Dinner was over. My father played ambulance driver and they headed to the hospital, but as he wasn't qualified to do so, they were stopped for speeding by the police who, scared that they would be left with a baby in their arms, decided to escort them. Flashing lights, siren wailing, and my father following them at 120 kilometres an hour down the Avenida da República. This was the funny part... a majestic entrance into the world, worthy of kings and presidents. But that's where the joke ends, because when they got to the entrance doors of the hospital, my mother fainted. From then on it all got more complicated. When she regained consciousness, the pain was awful; there were blue scrubs all around her, nervous and assertive, doing things to her, which she struggled to comprehend. She tried to ask what was happening, but despite them all being around her, nobody seemed to be aware that she was there. She screamed out in pain, in fear, caught in the turmoil and the unknown. It was such a piercing scream that, in that instant, she had the sensation that the entire room came to a halt, and all eyes turned to her, but only for brief moments, before they went back to what they were doing before. They didn't put her to sleep, because it was important to keep her awake, but she fainted again and only returned to reality thirty-three days later. Since we were both in mortal danger, they asked my father if they were only able to save one of us, who should they save and he said my mother. At this point in the story, despite understanding his choice, there was always something inside me, in my stomach, in my heart, that would contract and react... I didn't want to, because I understood perfectly, but only with my head. And my mother wouldn't emphasise this point, but neither would she leave it out. In truth I never understood what she felt about this, whether she saw it as an act of love, or of bad judgement, on my father's part; and I never plucked up the courage to ask, probably out of fear of what she might answer. Fear that she might say that he'd made the right choice, as it would mean that neither of my parents placed any value on my life. And, as I said, despite understanding with my head, that hole in my chest would grow, that sense of emptiness, that soul pain."

Up until that point, Helena had spoken in a voice free of emotion, her eyes dry, but suddenly tears welled up and her voice cracked with the pain that was now plain to see.

"My father hadn't chosen me, this was the only explanation for my feelings, for how I have always felt. The image I have is of a being within me, carved out between the flesh, blood and organs; bent and hunched over its knees, in a posture of abandonment. I always thought that being born as a second choice, and having endangered my mother's life, had produced in me a mixture of guilt and inferiority, which was expressed in a sense of inadequacy, of nostalgia, a deep pain in my soul, that feeling of emptiness.

"Now I know that none of that was part of my story; I never put my mother's life in danger, but isn't that part of my story now? My brain can't tell the difference, can it? And how many times have I thought about it? How many times have I imagined this situation? It has, truly, lived within me."

"I feel you. I feel your pain," Adriana said, holding out her hand to Helena's.

"Now imagine applying this to everything that I have been told throughout my life! How can I tell if something is true or not? Everything that seemed set in stone has lost its foundations. Everything is as fragile as..." Helena looked down trying to compose herself. "It's obviously not a coincidence that this subject has been on my mind, in my body, as if there were a part of me that wanted to go deeper, to question what we take for granted. And lo and behold, that's just what happens in my own life. This time my father outdid himself. He got me the most interesting game for my birthday. The most challenging. Discover how it all happened. How I happened."

"You're really upset, resentful. It's only normal, but you don't need to question everything. These parents of yours will always be your parents. You still don't really know what happened."

"I don't know, but I will know. I had asked the universe to guide me in this documentary and here it is! What makes the truth true? Now I understand clearly why I have always felt attracted to secrets. I am a secret," Helena continued, her voice steeped in irony, in outrage, in contempt for everything. "I am the protagonist, the subject and the reason for the journey I have to make."

"What are looking for?"

"For me. For truth. How can I deconstruct the beliefs that are etched into me, when I discover that the foundations of my life are not true, that they are false stories constructed by others? And how does that change how I feel? What I think? How does this change my path? Is my life just an example of so many other false truths upon which we build our lives?

"You're questioning everything."

"Shouldn't we question everything?" Helena shot back.

"The important thing is for you to know the higher purpose that exists in your heart. What are you really looking for?" asked Adriana.

"To find myself again. At the moment I see fragments all over the place and I don't really know how to find them all, let alone stick them back together. And maybe I don't even want to put them back, because who I thought I was, isn't real."

"What is real?"

"I thought I had found the love of my life, after having been through so much, as you know; and suddenly I think he is my brother, as if I were in some Mexican soap opera repeated a gazillion times, because if there's a repeated story, this is it... and the feeling of love changes abruptly, as if a wave of disgust washes over me, kicking me in the gut; and I lose my footing, and I let myself sink, while at the same time vomiting; and I discover that actually he's not my brother, because I am not who I thought I was... but is it possible to go back to the moment that he felt like the love of my life? This man, the son of whom I thought was my father? Just saying this out loud makes me feel sick."

"Does being the son of someone call into question everything you experienced?"

"At the moment, I don't know what I feel about anything. I just feel pain and revulsion. I have to get to the bottom of this story. The enigma is me."

" Do you know who they are?" Adriana asked, slightly afraid.

"My real parents? I have the name of my mother. I pressed him to tell me. He knew where I was from WhatsApp and got scared. It was possibly the first time that I had seen that man look scared. He told me that my father had died, but now I question everything he says. He didn't really explain what had happened. He spoke about an accident and little more... Then he asked me not to talk to my mother... not my biological one, the one I thought was my mother! He said that she knows nothing about it and really thinks that I am her daughter. Can you believe it? That he made sure she never knew their daughter died in childbirth and that I was like a gift from the universe, appearing at that exact moment... during the time she was in a coma. I don't know. With my dad anything is possible! By dad... I mean Julian! He says he'll tell me all about it in person, but I don't want to see him. I need time. And I want to talk to my mother... my biological mother. I need to see her, to ask her what happened. Before, I thought that I was second choice! Now, I know that my mother chose to give me away. I'm not even second choice."

"You can always look at it from many perspectives. It was your father's choice to keep you."

"He didn't choose me, for me, but for my mother's sake. I had no idea, but apparently, she had already lost another baby in the final term, two years before me. He thought that she wouldn't be able to get over another loss like that. I was the possible fix-all."

"You're seeing everything through the lens of pain," Adriana said softly, stroking Helena's hand.

"The lens of truth."

Adriana pulled her close for a hug, but Helena's body was stiff, constricted, as if the waters of this small body had been swollen in biblical fury. In the midst of the collapse, in the fall, Helena wanted to remain upright, ready to counterattack, but her body buckled, she spewed hatred in her words in disbelief of such a lie; the logic of everything that she was had vanished, as if the planet she inhabited had been exiled to another galaxy. She wanted to rediscover the path of who she was, now that she had been ripped away from her usual orbit. With the secret of her existence so brutally unleashed, she felt all her senses shut down, as if an all-powerful virus had taken her over, annihilating all the information accumulated in years of life: toppling and robbing her of her identity, forcing her to embark on a new process of consciousness about herself and the world, with her eyes closed, in the middle of the darkness.

And, as this disgust sat deep within her body, and layers of memories ripped apart in a flash, Helen abruptly pulled out of the embrace and jumped out of the car, because she couldn't stand still after the shipwreck.

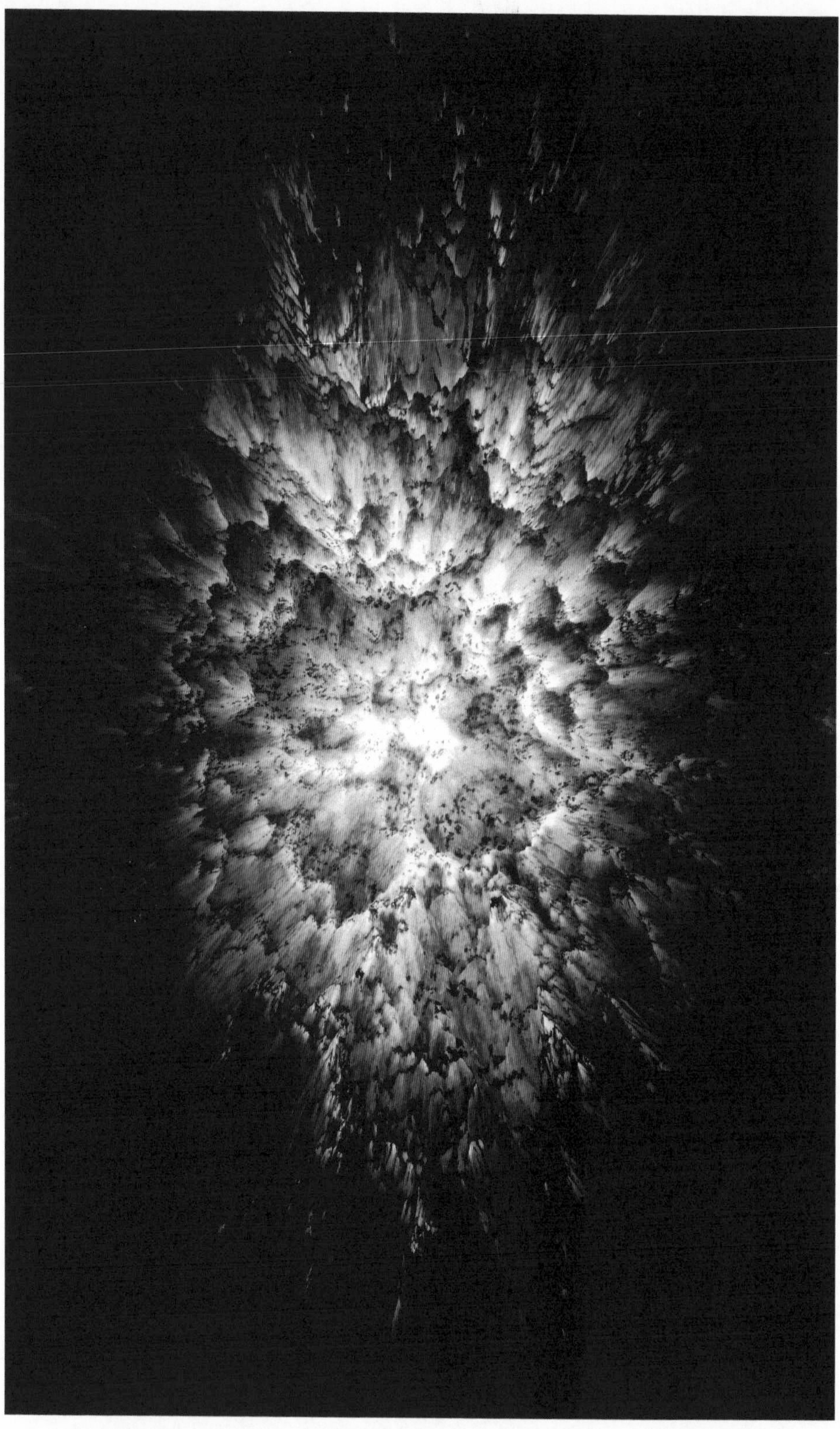

Helena's Heart was on Fire

Before the pain, hearing Helena talk of her love for Thomas touched Adriana to the core, sent shivers through her body, brought to mind moments of intense connection to life. It was one of those loves that reaches out to all of nature, that unites all that is, that invisibly awakens other hearts to the sound of their music; loves of a rare beauty and unique purpose to which no-one is left indifferent. Prior to the shipwreck they would have said: a love that will endure any catastrophe, like the love that remains in the heart of those who help, those who withstand, those who replenish, those who replant, those who are reborn, those who grow wings after the fire, the earthquake, the implosion, the tsunami.

But in that moment, it wasn't possible to predict if it would be like that. The realm of possibilities was arranged like a prison-labyrinth. Adriana saw Helena's heart burning, imploded, drifting, like a shipwreck in the middle of the sea. They say that, when you are shipwrecked, you spend half your time fearing death, and the other half wanting it. That's how Helena felt, her love wounded, stripped and torn, with nothing to hold on to that would give her real hope.

Adriana knew, through her own experience, that nothing she could say in that moment, would make her rediscover the healing powers of her heart. Being there with her was all that counted. Helena's heart was on fire and, in flames, she was still in her desperate, angry monologue, in her own resentful and tragic apocalypse. Adriana knew it would take time, but didn't know how much. She knew that she couldn't cross the dark night of her soul for her, or transform the pain with magic words. It was going to take time, whatever time was needed and, during that time, no one could predict whether Helena would come out the other side enlightened or if she would remain engulfed in darkness, slowly sinking.

Helena had to undertake this inevitable journey on her own, even if she had to follow a map drawn in invisible ink. She had to cross unknown territory with her thread of fire, close to the abyss and the shores, even when cruelly ironic and given to angry outbursts, surviving the passage of time of pain, until she was able to see the same landscapes through different eyes and from there, who knows, usher in a new world.

The hero's journey

Since she was a young girl, Helena had been interested in what could be found beyond the visible; beyond the earth and beyond death. Her mind had been born eclectic and holistic, open to multiple dimensions and possibilities, however improbable they might seem. While she opened the doors to the poetry of the cosmos and of limitless and infinite existence, she closed the doors on everything that might smack of control, confinement, lack of freedom, fundamentalism, sects, cults, manipulation, or exercising power over others. Her eyes effortlessly sought out anyone who could bring her news on the less than obvious, open new horizons, shine the light on knowledge that made her reflect on the greater meaning of our existence in the world and on herself; she would always lean toward the realm of the invisible: that which can be found at the bottom of things, in the heart and in the mind, emotions, feelings, thoughts and dreams - in the vibration and essence at the heart of each being - in consciousness, magic, miracles, in ecstasy and in enchantment.

She watched documentaries, interviews and books about people who had had near-death experiences, storing the interconnections between the different experiences in one of the drawers of her mind. She read up on quantum physics theories that delved into matter down to its most microscopic constituent, addressing on the existence of all that there is, including the so-called void that was actually a plenum. She listened to people channelling beings from other dimensions, just as she had always liked to listen to the viewpoints of astronauts, who, once again, literally had a unique point of view of the earth and its affairs. She took an interest in every researcher of ancient civilisations and the knowledge they had, which seemed to have been lost or erased over the course of time. She was interested, too, in people who knew how to look up the skies and draw conclusions on the cosmos and our place in it; whether astronomers or astrologers. As above, so below. This and so many other so-called universal laws fascinated her too; they were like beacons in the desert she now found herself traversing, beacons in the jungle that her life often resembled, guiding lights helping her understand the doubts, the pain or the worries tormenting here, guiding hands to help her co-create reality. Like Campbell, a mastermind for Helena, she let herself be seduced by the language of myths, which allowed her to gain an insight into what so many others had gone through before us. And, obviously, she was interested in the words of great spiritual masters and their time on earth. Despite always putting into perspective what had actually made its way to us, because "a tale never loses in the telling", she imagined the parts that had been added by the person who had put it down in writing; and by the people who passed down knowledge over the centuries and down through countless generations.

If she was being entirely honest, she, too, edited her own experiences without realising; for whatever she wrote or spoke about her experiences was already a screened version, a conscious or unconscious selection, but a selection of what she considered to be important. Even when she attempted to remain as impartial as possible, when she transcribed or edited an interview, she would find herself distilling it according to her own understanding and bias about what she believed to be essential. In not being able to put it all in, the part she chose was, in a way, a construction of her own making. So, how could you believe that people, many of them who had no direct contact with the masters, could have been entirely faithful to the message, when they were writing on the basis of their consciousness and wisdom, and perhaps some of them on the basis on their own intentions?

That's why, throughout her life, she had trained the exceptional detector of her heart to help her separate the wheat from the chaff, whatever the source. A reliable detector, in which she had placed great faith, until, that is, the foundations of her existence had been rocked to the core.

When a person dedicates their life to secrets, it shouldn't seem especially strange to discover that their own life contains one that causes the foundations of their existence to crumble. From another angle or perspective, she would have been the first person to say that such an adversity was part of a greater plan for her soul to carry out its mission, or to achieve true mastery, but, as things stood, she couldn't bring herself to acknowledge this, because the pain that been inflicted on her was just too great and had blinded her.

Journeys are often synonymous with searching and finding. Man comes to know himself through the world. Helena had a few trips on her bucket list: similar journeys to those undertaken before by other human beings in search of revelations, in search of answers through certain experiences, allowing the light to enter through their wounds; but now it was almost a matter of survival. There was nothing else she could do. She had to take this journey in order to not die.

It was the hero's journey, pushed by pain down the path, where she would have to step away from comfort, from the familiar, to embrace her greater purpose. Along the way, she would have to sit down with the shadows that had taken hold of her heart, until she could look into the light again; and she would have to fight her inner demons, until she could find the divine within and, from that place, return home, reborn.

Mexico

We know that everything that we think and feel goes with us, even if the journey is long. But there's nothing like trying! Helena flew to the other side of the world. Adriana had convinced her that now wasn't the time to run off looking for her biological mother. She could even undertake this journey, if she felt called to do so, but she should answer this question first: did she really want to meet her mother at a time in which she was in pieces, pieces scattered in a sea of pain and defiance? Helena knew the answer, but the words were Adriana's. She would first have to get through the pain; care for the wound without allowing it to get infected; find the fragmented pieces of herself and understand which pieces she should leave behind, which would take her forward. She knew she had to get some distance from the situation, in order to find clarity, and for this she would need time: 'Mazunte time'.

Mazunte possessed that magic of the tales of Adriana's childhood, which gave Helena the feeling she was heading outside the world without leaving the planet. Adriana had a good friend there, Jojo, and the promise that she would take good care of Helena at a time in which she was more fragile than crystal.

Jojo intuitively knew the silent hug Helena needed when she opened her front door. There was no small talk, she didn't ask how she was or why she had come. She showed her the neighbour across the way, the turquoise-blue sea-scented giant, the fridge full of food, the colourful market nearby, the room where she could fall asleep with the soothing sound of the waves, the courtyard surrounded by palm trees, full of exotic plants, two rocking chairs and a hammock from which she could watch the sun set on the horizon. And, with a gentle nod, she indicated a pot of Mexican tea that Helena could and should drink whenever she wanted.

"Pretend you're at home. If you need anything, and I'm not about, just call. I'm going to be busy in the coming days, but I'm always nearby," she said with an open smile.

For several days, that nobody counted, Helena barely left the house, spending most of her time in the courtyard, between the rocking chair and the hammock, mulling over whatever came up, and always with a mug of tea that never seemed to end or go cold, despite rarely seeing Jojo actually make it or fill the pot. Sometimes she would walk along the beach at sunset, occasionally at night, but she would immediately feel the need to retreat to her room or the courtyard. One night, Jojo sat in the rocking chair next to Helena, with a mug of tea too.

"Have you known Adriana for long?" Helena asked Jojo.

"Since we were kids. We didn't see each other for many, many years, but when we were reunited it was magical. Magnetic. It was here in Mazunte. We saw each other from afar, in the market, we stared at each other for a moment, synchronising our adult image with our childhood memories, before bursting out laughing. It was quite a hug. All I can tell you is that the adventures we had enjoyed together were tattooed on our hearts; they weren't the kind of memories or feelings that fade with time or wash away in warm water," she laughed. "Deep friendships go beyond space-time, don't you think? Now, whenever she comes here, she stays with me and whenever I go travelling, I check where my gypsy-Adriana is and if we can meet up."

"I really love your house."

"Me too."

A silence curled around the sound of the moonlit waves.

"You know," began Jojo, breaking the silence, "this house was very important for me when I was ill with dengue fever."

"Oh, what happened?"

"It took weeks of suffering before I recovered. I had never imagined that it could be so hard... and dangerous. There were times when I feared for my life. The fever, the pain, the lack of energy, I can't really explain, but it was really hard. At a certain point I realised that I just had to sit with the pain, experience it, and it was only then, when I surrendered, that I started to get better."

"Sit with the pain..." Helena mumbled.

"That and papaya leaf juice all the time," she said, laughing.

"Is this what we're drinking?"

"No!!! This tea is made from a plant that came to me when I thought of you," Jojo explained.

"What plant? What did Adriana say?"

"Nothing specific. She just said that there had been a tsunami in your life."

"Ah!" Helena let out between thoughts.

"But what do you think of the tea?" Jojo asked.

"It's hard to put into words what it's been like drinking it. It's as if part of my left hemisphere has been switched off and I feel merged with the sea, with the sky, with everything around me... It brings me comfort and lightness. It takes away a lot of these heavy feelings that are drowning me in sadness... And I don't know if it was because I interviewed an amazing cosmologist, just before I came here, who left me very inspired, but I have felt in the womb of the universe, being cradled..."

"How wonderful, cradled in the universal womb... that exceeds any expectation I could have had. There is always something in the natural world that responds to your needs. It's impressive! The other day I read about a naturopath who discovered that if you spit on a seed when you plant it, this plant will produce what your body is lacking. Isn't that astonishingly clever?" asked Jojo, joyfully.

"Absolutely! The intelligence in our body, in nature, in the universe is astonishing! If you were to look at me through a powerful microscope you would see a community of trillions of cells in a magical dance; it you went deeper, you would see octillions of atoms, and if you looked at these atoms really closely, everything would disappear, you would see energy. I am a very complex energy pattern and, even when I'm not moving, I am moving at the speed of light and I am as old as the universe," said Helena, inspired.

"Wow, that's poetic."

"It's the poetry of life," she said, immediately reminded of Thomas, allowing a dark shadow to fall over her face.

"What happened?"

"I wish I could sing beauty again," Helena said, lowering her head towards the ground. But she immediately lifted it again, as if she had caught a ride on an invisible wave. "All of creation is expressed through numbers and numbers are frequency; they are manifested as colour, sound, shape, and even as emotion and states of consciousness. Each of us is a living symphony of frequencies... some of our notes are sung in harmony, and some are entirely out of tune; normally because of stress, trauma, these things that happen in life! I am totally out of tune, now!"

"When I see and hear you, that's not what I feel," Jojo said softly.

"This tea of yours has been a great tuner; the other day it even got me dancing. I started to twirl, twirling like Sufi dancers, and there was a moment in which I seemed to be in every proton, in all of them at the same time. It's really hard to describe, but there was this feeling of expansion, but very much grounded in the movement, at the same time. It was as if I wasn't moving myself, rather I was being moved, being danced. It was truly incredible. The feeling of expansiveness of the universe, and I was every particle of the universe. There was no separation between me and these palm trees, between me and these chairs, I was just flowing energy," Helena shared.

"I've had a similar experience in an Ayahuasca ceremony," Jojo said.

Once again Helena recalled Thomas. Whenever this happened, the deadly sensation of the poison within her seemed to spread through her body. It hurt all the way to her soul.

"If we were able to visibly see the pain we are going through, what would we see" Helena asked Jojo.

Silently, for a long time, they both crossed their places of pain, their bodies contracted, curled up a little over their knees, rocking back and forth, trying to find comfort on the crossing. Then, in an unforeseen gesture, Helena unwrapped the words and poured them into the notebook by her side, writing continuously for some time. She thought about Thomas once again, about how he had inspired her to this 'freewriting'. Everything seemed to remind her of him.

"You know? Some people see me as a lighthouse, can you imagine? It seems like a joke! Maybe because I have collected so much light from other people, through the interviews I've done, or maybe because I have witnessed their stories and dreams coming true. Imagine how it would be if they were to look at me now... they would see nothing but darkness. And do you know the worst thing about it? It is being aware that these people that I interviewed, full of light, were not people without pain or sadness. They had many scars, shadows, nightmares, but they had made it through the night, fought their demons, risen from the ashes. That was what gave them a unique light. A music that was theirs alone...

"Now I am in this crossing place and feeling worse that someone shipwrecked on the high seas, with the hallucinations brought on by deprivation... close to death, but without any belief of that rebirth. I am very far from seeing any light at the end of the tunnel."

"It's all very fresh... and yet you're already being cradled by the womb of the universe," Jojo said, smiling.

"It's true, the tea is good, but the glasses I am wearing are too dark! Even dancing momentarily with countless galaxies and billions of stars, mysterious black holes and celestial bodies, all interconnected by this dark matter, a kind of invisible fluid that seeps throughout space and creates a cradle for me to swing in, to float, I only think about how all this is ironic and that I don't feel prepared for any crossing at all!"

"Nothing should be rushed," Jojo reminded. "Everything in nature has its cycle. Even if the moon wanted to retire early, it would wait for the sun to arrive. Do you hear it? It's the sound of the tides; after they ebb, they will rise again. Trees grow every day before our eyes without anyone noticing. The sun will come... just stay here as long as you need, there's no hurry for anything."

And so she did. The days in Mazunte flowed by without anyone noticing, the weeks became a month, and then two.

"It's great having you here," Jojo said in passing.

"It's great being here. Lifesaving, even," Helena assured her with a smile.

Helena perfectly understood now what Adriana had meant when she talked about Mazunte, about the quality of time effortlessly passing by, about her parents, who had turned up for a few days and ended up staying for a few years. Life seemed simple, but it wouldn't be simple to explain what she had been doing, because she was not aware of doing anything. She would essentially cross paths with Jojo in the courtyard, which they liked to share as much in silence as in deep conversation, perhaps sparked by the magical teas that the hostess continued to make daily. Jojo organised retreats for women and, one day, she invited Helena to join her.

"It's very nurturing. It'll do you good to be among sisters," she said simply.

After hesitating and not being able to dispel her doubts, she let Jojo take her on the journey, regretting it in the final long miles of dirt tracks, but allowing herself to be won over when they arrived, in awe of the beauty of that place hidden from the world. The lush vegetation harboured little thatched huts in a circle, with a natural pool of salted water heated to 32ºC, which welcomed the goddess-women as in a baptism. An initiation through water. All floating in the water, surrendered to the vibrations of the words that could be heard, repeatedly, one by one: "You are beautiful. You are powerful. You are pure, radiant and Divine Feminine power. If you don't feel it yet, may you remember the strength and grace that is within you."

Each woman was given a floating hammock so that she could surrender effortlessly. Curled up in the foetal position or laying on their backs, eyes closed, there in that liquid space, they would begin their journey to the sound of the shamanic drum, in search of their power animal that would bring messages to those ready to hear them.

Despite remaining closed and a little distant, little by little Helena was experiencing "the froth of days". There was even a wave of love permeating that circle of women and, with each day, she drifted through new sensations.

On the last day of the retreat, they all sat in a circle and the shaman invited each of the women to sit down in front of her. For each in turn, she looked into their eyes, in silence, for four minutes. Then, as if in a trance-like state, she would pass on a message. When it was Helena's turn, to ensure that she grasped everything, as she usually did, she sat down in front of her with a pen and notebook, but whenever she tried to write, a powerful energy hindered her movements, forcing her to surrender entirely to the moment. With no apparent choice, she welcomed the shaman's words with all her senses. And, if she had been worried she wouldn't be able to remember the entire message, those words seemed to her as if engraved in her very core and, even if she had wanted to, she would not have been able to erase them.

"You cannot return to yesterday," the shaman began. "The nature of life is governed by cycles; there is no avoiding the tides. When we experience great chaos in life, we also experience great tension; it is the force of opposition within us: What is truth and what is a lie? Who is worthy of trust and who isn't? We search for reasons for what is happening to us. But the chaos always wants to bring to the surface patterns of life that need to change, so that we can evolve to a new level of consciousness. Do not resist. Resistance does not stop change; it only makes it more painful.

"I see you. You are a deeply-wounded healer in this life, but your wounds serve your gift to the world and the power to heal others. But first, that wounds need to be healed, for you to be free and use your greatest gifts.

"The world is waiting for you.

"It's hard for you to imagine now, but if you walk the path, you will come back dancing the dance of love. Before, your mission is for you to enter into the phrases "who am I" and "what is my truth". And for you to access your identity, you have to access each of the sacred chambers of your heart. And to access this sacred place of your heart, you need to go deeper into the pain.

"Have faith in the process. Like a warrior-hero who takes off his armour in the middle of the arena, even though he is injured and thinks he might die. Realizing that his true power lies within, not in his armour.

"Accept the path.

"Love is waiting for you.

"Self-knowledge and self-confidence are powerful inner graces.

"True freedom lies in finding the courage to trust your inner guidance, no matter what challenges you face in this world. True freedom is the ability to transcend fears, limitations and interferences of your mind. Especially the fear of being happy. There's something inside of you that feels like you don't deserve it.

"You are being called to regain the power of the Divine Feminine within you. Let feminine energy be your compass now - your heart, your Venus. On this part of the journey, let the world of doing, doing, doing. Turn inwards. Trust your intuition. Listen to what comes to you naturally, softly, like a whisper. And go with the flow."

Helena listened to her without blinking. She too in a trance-like state. She said nothing, she asked nothing, even in the final sharing. If before she already knew she was tied up by threads, she now felt that she would fall apart as soon as she tried to articulate and put into words the sea of pain that now flowed in her blood. She hadn't cried anymore, since in Adriana's arms, in Italy. But the words of the shaman had been spot-on, arrows planted in strategic points of her body. She had asked the universe to guide her. But where had it taken her? How could she believe that it was for the greater good? An acid-fuelled scream was lodged in her throat. There was a great deal of pent-up revulsion in her chest, and many other things that she couldn't even name. Go with the flow? Was she capable of going with the flow, whilst being carried adrift by this dark current of pain?

When leaving Mazunte, Jojo told Helena to listen to the Narayan Kriya mantra.

"The Narayan sound is associated with the element of water and to surrendering, going with the flow. The water cleanses, it flows and it can carry you if you allow yourself to float, to relax."

"I'll do just that on this journey. It will be my mantra."

"Water was our primordial home in the belly of our mother, where we felt safe and protected," Jojo continued.

"I see, but for me, perhaps as I know nothing about my gestation or about my mother, it gives me a strange feeling to think about that," Helena replied, a little tense.

"Everything that has happened to this day is what allows you to be who you are."

"I know that, intellectually... but I don't feel it yet," Helena cut in.

"I understand... We are all on a journey!"

"That's true. Thank you, Jojo, for everything! Your hospitality was everything I needed to set me off on this journey of mine," said Helena, stressing the word 'mine'.

"Where are you going?"

"I'm not exactly rudderless, as I know that I'm heading towards Tabasco, Campeche and Mérida. But I'm just going to take it as it comes, no plans. This is my first time in Mexico, so I am going to play at being a tourist and walk along white, sandy beaches, through tropical forests, bathe in waterfalls, walk amongst parrots and monkeys, visit mountain villages and, of course, explore Mayan ruins. I sound almost like a tourist brochure for Mexico," she added, laughing.

"Sounds to me like a great plan," Jojo confirmed. "Can I give you another tip that has just come to me?

"Of course!"

"Look up Ariel Spilsbury, the author of the book *The Mayan Oracle: A Galactic Language of Light*. She is also the founder of the *13 Moon Mystery School* where I studied... I think you'll really like talking to her."

"Okay, thanks!"

By giving herself to the journey, the journey gave itself to her, packed with encounters and synchronicities that could hardly go unnoticed. In a hotel stood in the middle of the jungle, in Tabasco, she met a group of three women, each of them from a different nation, but friends for more than a decade. Mary, Esperanza and Aurora, were experimenting with remote viewing, following a course they had taken. Helena found them fun and insightful, and she just clicked with them, so they invited her to join them and try out her extrasensory perception. Helena took the invitation as a joke, coming as it did in the midst of a conversation between tequilas, but she accepted to take part in the experiment as an onlooker, that is to say, the person who actually does the remote viewing.

The following day, the four of them were ready to start the experiment. Mary had chosen different places in total secrecy, and written them down on small cards before placing them in sealed envelopes. Esperanza, who was going to be the sender, had chosen one of the envelopes at random and then, headed off there by car, on her own. At an agreed time, Esperanza transmitted, by thought, detailed impressions of the place where she was to Helena. Shapes, structures, textures, colours, sounds and even smells. She also took a few Polaroid shots, which she insisted on transmitting in particular. Helena, as the viewer, connected with Esperanza during the same thirty minute period, wrote down and drew everything that was going through her head. During this process, Aurora would simply make sure that the person who had chosen the places, in this case Mary, had had no communication with the viewer and would ask Helena some questions so as to keep the process flowing.

When the four of them met up again, they were utterly amazed by what Helena had been able to capture. When they compared one of the Polaroids with one of the drawings Helena had done, they were rendered speechless at the similarities, as was Helena.

"I suspect it was beginner's luck, if you can call it that," Helena commented, laughing. "You know what I think? The fact that I know next to nothing about remote viewing, and that I wasn't at all concerned about the outcome, made all the difference! If I'd received nothing at all, I would have thought it normal. So I just played along and judged none of the thoughts that came to me. Now I'm impressed! Really impressed," she said, slumping back in her chair. "If we were to do it a second time, though, with that inner pressure to get the same results, I think that it would be very different... I'm even afraid that it could be a total disaster, now that I've experienced it. Not that I doubt telepathic transmission per se, but I clearly would doubt my abilities. I don't know... all this reminds me, I'm not sure why, of some stories I've been told about people who had a highly developed sixth sense during their childhood, who could see what others could not, or who knew things before they happened, but, when they were ridiculed or labelled as mad, they lost these powers. Gifts that are possibly innate are often shut down throughout life!"

"You're so right," said Mary. "That's why I enjoyed taking this course so much. To remember that 'knowing' that once lived in me, but that was lost in the back of a drawer somewhere."

"I never thought I had it in me, I have to confess," said Esperanza. "But one of the incredible things about remote viewing is we can get immediate feedback, like you did Helena."

"That's true. I hadn't thought about that."

"It's been important for me to develop my ability to discern sensations within the field," Esperanza continued, throwing out her arms to encompass the invisible space around her. "It is a field in which there is a nonlinear language, a little like the soundwaves that dolphins send out. Dolphins read the returning interference pattern, creating a map of the environment around them. The wave forms that come back to them have textured geometric patterns, whereby they not only see what is underwater, but also feel it. They are touching it. They feel how large it is. They can even detect fish hidden in the sand!"

"Dolphins are from another world," Helena said excitedly.

"Like us, human beings, if we don't diminish ourselves," said Aurora. "Have you ever thought about that? There are studies that reveal that four out of five people have low self-esteem. And, in my work, I have had the misfortune of experiencing that statistic; I see on a daily basis the way in which people belittle themselves with what they say, and think, about themselves. It can be relentless and very distressing for anyone caught in the web of self-doubt: I'm not capable; I'm not good enough; I can't cope; I can't do. These are the phrases that most often inhabit people's minds. Change this way of thinking, change the world. Imagine a world of people that believe in themselves, who love who they are, who trust their voice, what they have to bring to the world. Just imagine! It would be like changing the music of the world! It would be an entirely different radio station!"

"I believe I've been living in that other bubble: I have interviewed so many brilliant people, passionate about what they do, who are already at that different frequency," Helena added.

"There are some incredible people," Aurora continued. "They say that we share 98.7% of our DNA with the chimpanzee Bonobo! But have you ever seen a Bonobo compose a symphony like Beethoven or painting the Sistine Chapel? Making a film or going to the moon? Inventing something like the Internet? Discovering secrets of the universe? Building the Golden Gate Bridge? What an extraordinary difference 1.3% can make, eh?" she concluded, laughing.

"Little big differences that change the world. Some changes for the better, others not so much. There is also no known Bonobo responsible for polluting the oceans or clearing huge forests," Helena added.

"That's true too. So much depends on how the great power contained in the small differences is used. You can build a cathedral with stone and you can kill with stone," Aurora reflected.

"And it's also a small yet huge difference that makes me feel as if I'm in the midst of so much noise and shadow, without light, in a lower frequency, I can't even explain it," Helena confessed.

"From where I see it, I don't feel that; I can see your light really present! But I also don't doubt what you say. There are things that that only one feels," Mary replied. "Have you ever been seen by a shaman? When they look at you... it's like a dolphin when it scans you. They can see far beyond the physical."

"Before I came here, I was at a women's retreat, where I met with a shaman. She looked at me, as if she could see right through me and perceived what I was unable to see, beyond space-time," said Helena.

"Ah, we've come full circle-back to remote viewing again," commented Esperanza. "The ability to access information that is, non-linearly, in the field. What you talked about, also happened to me at the start of the course; scared of getting it wrong, I wasn't able to receive anything! Once I stopped worrying about the results and about what other people would think or say, everything changed," she added, smiling pointedly at Helena's bridge drawing. "I really enjoyed being the sender in this experiment; I also felt freer when transmitting to someone with no prior knowledge. I didn't think about protocol, I did what I felt. I went with the flow, allowing myself to focus on that suspension bridge, whilst I was already by the water, and trying to pass on the odour of the sulphurous waters and that waterfall..."

"It was so funny... the suspension bridge thing," Helena confirmed. "I was filled with the idea of a bridge I had crossed a few years ago in Portugal, in Passadiços do Paiva, and well, they're similar. And I felt the urge to be in water, though I had no idea why."

"Ah, and that detail about the ape was marvellous!"

"As it turned out, one of the messages to me from the shaman was to trust in my intuition," Helena said, laughing. "Thank you all for this experiment! It has given me a newfound confidence in myself!"

That night, Helena emailed Ariel, to say that she would love to talk to her. Later, Ariel replied saying that, when she returned from Mexico, she would be happy to do a Zoom call. When Helena realised that they were, in fact, both in Mexico, she laughed to herself, then wrote back to set up a meeting for a few days later in Campeche.

"I'll just say that one thing again, I am a great listener, I've learned to empty and listen," said Ariel looking at Helena, sitting across from her on the wooden porch, which contrasted pleasingly with the petrol blue façades of the boutique hotel where they had met for tea. "The Maya, that gave us the Mayan Oracle, everything that's in their frequency, it isn't so much the words, they're beautiful, but it's the frequency imbued in the words... that really is impactful and what I ask you is: have you read the 'Mythic Call' in the *Mayan Oracle*?"

"Don't think so."

"I want to call your attention back to that now."

"I will."

And later she did so, underlining three paragraphs that seemed to sing in her ear a very old song that said:

"So it is that you, the children of the sun, are now being bathed in the waters of remembrance, prepared as rainbow warriors to fulfill the new and ancient myth; by simply anchoring love's presence on earth, you lovingly draw down the mantle of the gods, sending waves of healing and love throughout Gaia's eagerly receptive body.

As you emerge in this time, your gifts awaken and empower others, utilizing the tools of laughter, song, dance, humor, joy, trust, and love. You are creating the powerful surge of transformation that will transmute the limitations of the old myth of duality and separation, birthing the miracle of unity and peace on earth. Utilize your gifts on behalf of Gaia, in a supernova of consciousness. Gaia and her children will ascend in robes of light, forming a luminous light body of love to be reborn among the stars.

The mythic call has been sounded, the great quest has begun".

"What you said is so beautiful... the frequency imbued in the words," Helena observed as she took in that ageless woman before her; made of flesh and bone, yet who had a touch of fairy to her. "I'm certain that we are able to recognize the various frequencies within every aspect of life. We can feel it when we meet someone, in the places we go, in what we do, we can feel and connect with the frequency of that... So, how did you learn or remembered how to be such a good listener? How did you know, for example, you could hear and understand that Galactic Language of Light of the Mayan Oracle?" asked Helena.

"Well I think you hit upon the word right there: remember. I feel like I am a Mayan, albeit a cleverly disguised one, no less. It is just remembering. It's like being able to speak in my native language, you know? So it's easy, it's not like a struggle," replied Ariel in a simple way, with a hint of playfulness.

"And how was this moment of remembrance for you? How did you know? How did you connect to that inner knowing?" asked Helena.

"The first thing that came along, the kind of trigger point, was that a friend gave me a handmade set of the Mayan glyphs and the minute I laid eyes on those things, I went, oh my God, you know? I just had this rush of electricity and feelings! I knew there was some major part of my soul journey that was carried in those glyphs. So, I started playing with them, because this is my way in life, not to be serious about anything, but play with it. And, as I was playing with them, I started to hear what it was that each glyph was trying to communicate to me. That's how the oracle started."

"Wow. And going back in time, how was the beginning of your journey?"

"You know, I didn't think I was going to survive it," Ariel said viscerally. "I really didn't. I had a hard time in childhood, and in my teenage years, just trying to make sense of being here at all. There was so much cruelty. I remember being, maybe two years old, watching a man hitting a dog with a stick and his mouth bleeding and I just was in a state of horror. I said why am I here? Why? Why have you done this to me? Why am I in hell and nobody just knows they're in hell? I mean, I was really asking some big questions in my early years, you know?

"If it weren't for the exquisite beauty of Gaia, that's what kept me here. I feel like it was Gaia that called me to be here during this particular section of the road we're in right now. So I'm glad I lasted. That's all I can say, I'm glad I lasted out the density and said okay, this is it and I'm here and I'm going to serve while I'm here."

"I hear you. Much of what is still happening on this planet lies in the realm of the incomprehensible," Helena said, "and is causing immense suffering."

"Later I understood: all I can do is be loving here and open my heart compassionately to the suffering that I see, but not to buy into it, as to say. Because if you really go into that, you'll end up in despair; which I have had, in my life, and I know that's not the way, because, if I'm in despair, I can't really be in service."

"True," said Helena.

"We are living in a time of fulminating chaos and everything seems to be falling apart, but I feel, and the Mayans feel, that we are moving towards a much higher level of coherence and order. I know from the Entropy Theory Nobel laureate Ilya Prigogine, and his dissipative structures theory, which states that when a system is ready to move to a higher frequency, it disintegrates into a chaotic state. Out of chaos comes a new order, an order that would not have been possible had the previous order not devolved into chaos. What looks like chaos at one level, looks like a birthing in the new dispensation," said Ariel.

"But when you are in the middle of that dark and chaotic tunnel, and you cannot see with your eyes as you are used to, you have to use another guidance," commented Helena.

"Exactly, that's what this is all about: you have to use another form of guidance, from inside. You have to navigate with your feelings."

Helena thought for some time about the experience of navigating through feeling, something that had been happening since Italy.

"I don't know whether you know about random number generators," Ariel continued, "but when enough people are focused on the same thing, the computers go into coherent numbers, they start putting out coherent numbers instead of random incoherent numbers. Now that says it all to me, that means we can, with enough of us focusing at the same time on this transformation occurring, we can change things!"

Ariel was talking about the Global Consciousness Project, an international, multidisciplinary, collaborative project of scientists and engineers, created at Princeton University. Using a global network of random number generating computers (RNGs), located in different parts of the world, they are continually gathering data which is then transmitted to a central archive, which currently holds more than fifteen years of data. What have they discovered? That when a major event synchronises the feelings of millions of people, the network of RNGs becomes subtly structured. They have calculated a probability of one in a trillion that the effect is due to chance. The evidence suggests an emerging noosphere, or the unifying field of consciousness described by sages in every culture. When human consciousness becomes coherent, the behaviour of random systems can change.

"So, just imagine for a moment, that there is a mass of people who are still not awake, but that there is a crack into which you, Ariel, can whisper something, for one minute, and you know that you will be carefully listen by all these people... what would you say?"

"What a great question. Let me feel that," Ariel said closing her eyes for a few moments. "I think I would just say, "you are love, you emanate love, you come from love, you are embedded in love and, as you act from that place of full knowledge that you are love, this reality will transform." And then I would ask people to use, as a standard, the question: what would love do now? I would ask people to use this standard for every action they take in this world; always be asking as the highest possible outcome: what would love do right now?

"And if you're living in that standard, then a lot of things just naturally dissolve away. It was the only message that Christ had: love one another as you love yourself. There's really no more important message than that. But to begin living from that place is another thing."

Helena and Ariel remained in silence, a silence that lasted eight minutes, each of them in their thoughts, drinking tea and contemplating their surroundings. For Helena, these were the words that made sense. Even in a place of pain, she knew that this was the message, the only message, but as Ariel said, knowing it was one thing, bringing it into your life was another.

What eight minutes of thinking can do for a person... Like John Milton wrote in the poem *Lost Paradise*, the mind can make hell of any heaven, but it can also transform a hell into heaven. Helena was well aware that the totality of human experience, as well as the satisfaction with that experience, depends on the filters of the mind, and on the spectacles of perception. Someone who is perpetually angry and without love, cannot enjoy life, no matter how successful he is.

She the began reflecting on television and the entertainment industry and how much they contributed to the lens of perception of so many men and women. And what did it show? Why weren't there any films or series with characters inspired by people like Francis Collins, for so many years director of the Human Genome Project, talking about his faith in God? Or like Sam Harris, neuroscientist, describing his experience with Ecstasy as a return to truth, to love without limits, and to love as a state of being, as described by the mystics? An unforgettable experience that percolated throughout his subsequent work. Or like neurosurgeon Eben Alexander, on his near-death experience and the sensation of oneness with the whole, of full consciousness, and how it changed his view of life and science?

Why not create more series inspired by these people who don't believe in separating science and spirituality? How can we talk about this love and about experiences of transcendence, and about the sensation of oneness, in a way that is free of dogma, when we know that there is a growing body of scientific research that substantiates age-old knowledge? How can we talk repeatedly about the law of love, which Tolstoy brought so beautifully to his letters to Gandhi, without being labelled as utopian or coming from people without their feet on the ground? As Tolstoy wrote, we need to free our minds of what has suffocated this truth: that love is the only way to save humanity; the renunciation of all opposition by force. Love, or according to him, the struggle of men's souls for oneness.

But as Tolstoy also said, men can only recognise this truth in all of its breadth, when they have fully freed themselves from all religious and scientific superstitions and from all the consequent misrepresentations and sophistical distortions by which its recognition has been hindered for centuries. To save a sinking ship you need to throw overboard the ballast that had previously prevented it from sinking.

In the final minute, before returning to the conversation, Helena thought about how precious it was to be touched by people, such as Ariel whispering love through the chinks of light, such as Jude, such as Martin, such as Peter, reminding her of the essential; as the physicist Alan Lightman described in that meeting with an osprey, a look of connection, of mutual respect, of recognition that they shared the same earth; a brief encounter that left him trembling and in tears and that affected him so much. Experiences of love. With himself, with others, with all kingdoms of nature, with the cosmos.

"I've seen in maybe an article this question… It was many years ago, but it's the same core, it's the same idea… If someone asked you on your deathbed: how much did you love? How much did you learn? I think that's a great question to understand, if you are on a good path," said Ariel, interrupting the silence, as if she had been listening to Helena the whole time.

"How would you answer that right now? How much did you love? And how did you love? How it was your love in action?" replied Helena.

"Just holding love in my heart all the time. Just being love. I mean, I'm not separate from it, I am that and thus I'm always emanating love. I love Carlos Castaneda saying "follow any path you like, for as long as you like, but if it does not have heart, it is not the right path". Being that love... that is the path. If I perceive myself as love itself, then how would I make an action that was not that, you see? Instead of looking at love as a concept, that you do or don't do. It's a very different way of holding it and that's what I would really ask people, to recognize that, independent of what people are doing."

"Some actions are so dark, making it very difficult for people to hold that in the same content of being love. It's extremely difficult," said Helena.

"Love doesn't have to have an action, it just is. And if you can recognize that and look at every human being through the lens of understanding that they're acting out of their hurt, or they wouldn't be doing the things that are so hurtful... I don't have to do anything about that other than love that person. I don't have to like what they're doing or condone it, but my only responsibility is to love them regardless."

"I understand the idea, but loving a person who is responsible for genocide is immensely difficult, not to say impossible!"

"There's no question that that's a difficult stretch, but if you've ever had a transcendent experience where you experienced yourself totally as love itself, then it makes it a lot easier. Most people have just not had such a spiritual experience, that direct gnosis and that direct experience of that kind of love. If you've had a near-death experience and you've gone over the veil and you felt this just overwhelming love, everyone who has that experience comes back and changes their lives absolutely. I said one time, recently, to God, why don't you just give everyone a near-death experience and have everybody come back here and be much more loving toward each other? It would be so simple, but obviously that's not the way it's meant to be. It's not being dreamed that way."

"Wow, I'm speechless," Helena said in utter amazement. "A great friend of mine wrote the very same thing in her novel *Tomorrow is Another Day*, some years ago, because she had interviewed many people who had had near-death experiences, and understood how these experiences were life-changing. When she interviewed Gregg Braden, this was her first question, because he had two near-death experiences when he was five years old, but most people are unaware of this.

"But look, thinking once again about people who experience great suffering," Helena continued, feeling the presence of pain in her heart, "one of the things that is most difficult for them is loving themselves in these places of fragility, of incapacity, wrongdoing, doubt, sadness, pain, lack of confidence. I see so many people struggling to love themselves. What do you think is the most important thing in this journey of self-love?"

"Wow, I don't know... all I can say is... in the context of the Mayan five wheels of evolution, that I put in the Mayan Oracle, the first wheel of evolution is self-love and there's no way around it; that is the initiatory gateway that leads you to self-empowerment and leads you to self-consciousness, awareness, it leads you to the other areas. But it's the gateway and so, to learn to love the self is the most important thing we will ever do. And that requires our willingness to do shadow work, to clear up the wounding that happened to us in childhood, so that we can love ourselves. And that, for most people, it takes a lifetime; others they don't ever even look at it, they just go on stumbling along with this wound and don't heal it and, thus, are incapable of loving others fully, because they don't love themselves fully.

"So, I would say: do your inner work, do look at your wounds, look at the things that have hurt you and heal those. Look at them with love and forgiveness that would be the basic thing, because it is that first wheel, I would say, that it's the seminal thing people do in a lifetime curriculum of work here on earth. And there are plenty of opportunities, because almost everyone has been wounded in some way or the other in passage here. It's brutal!"

"So how did you make it through that time when you didn't want to live anymore, when you were struggling to cope with this reality, what really helped you at that time?" asked Helena.

"Oh this is a really juicy story, because I got so depressed that I just couldn't get out of bed, I almost didn't move and I wasn't eating much either. In some point of that process, I was taken out of my body and shown how my depression affected this person, that person, and all the way out; how my consciousness was impacting other people's consciousness, how my choices were impacting their choice. I went, oh my God, I am so done with this, I will never do this again; it was so impactful to me... that was it for depression for me.

"People think that their own suffering is only their own suffering, but because we're all one, as the Maya say *In Lak'esh*, we're all one, it's everybody's suffering. So I had to really own that and stop doing it. That's what changed everything for me. I just said, from this moment forward, I am going to do nothing but love, and that is what I am doing."

For a while, tears welled up in Helena's eyes. It was like Ariel had said, it wasn't the words, rather the energy they carried, this ancient wisdom they liberated and which, in that exact moment of her journey, on her dark night of the soul, allowed her to step out of herself into the whole. To see with the eyes of the world, of stones, of rivers, of trees, of eagles, of oceans, a vision without boundaries.

For the Mayans, the universe is a great oneness, where everything is interrelated. Individuals, the community, plants, animals, wind and the spirits are united and nothing exists without the relationship with the other; everything is alive and everything is connected. That's why any action by one affects the other. *In lak'ech*. I do not exist without you and you do not exist without me. If I respect you, I am respecting myself, and if I attack you, I am attacking myself.

In lak'ech, Hala ken, I am you, as you are me; I am the other you, as you are the other me. Just like *Ubuntu*, the Zulu word that Nelson Mandela and archbishop Desmond Tutu used as a mantra. I am in you and you are in me. A single co-understanding that has no place or time.

"People say all the time, 'to be true to who you are', or 'live in your truth', but sometimes people cannot even know what does it mean, because they don't really know themselves! What is your perception of truth, what is the truth and the difference between what is true and what is real?" enquired Helena.

"I don't perceive that there is any ultimate truth. Everyone has their truth, their own experience, the looking through their hologram, through their eyes has its truth. The way that it's perceiving, and the way it's been hardwired, and the way that it's been imprinted over life. But there's no ultimate truth and that's very disconcerting to most people to hear, because they want there to be a one and final truth, and I don't perceive that there is one. I think it's a multi-faceted universe and it's all being looked at through a particular lens by each of us... and so there's no ultimate truth.

"Now as to what is real," Ariel continued, "that one is a really interesting question. I always love to entertain the how do we tell what is real or not... and for me, I think it's important to be able to tell what is real, before you're navigating the Bardos. To do that, one has to learn, to have developed an inner knowing that you'll call intuition, or gnosis, or feeling navigation; and when you start developing that sense, you start paying attention, you start asking the question all the time: what is real here? What is really happening? Not what's being said on the surface, but what is really happening underneath.

"And people get in there social media or see the news… I'm always stopping and saying: okay, what is real here, what's really going on here? So, thank you for asking that, because I really do think if we would all start doing that more often, not accepting what's on the surface bubbling along, and asking the question what is real here, we would be so much more of an awakened state. Thank you, that was a great question."

"Even for those who believe in reincarnation, if you knew that you would never return to this planet, what would you encourage your present self to do? How would you like to live your days? How could you make the most of this experience?" asked Helena.

"The answer for me has resoundingly been being love in every moment, whatever that looks like," said Ariel. "My loving service right now is in the Sanctuary of the Open Heart, a virtual temple, with planetary priests and priestesses over the whole planet, to gather together the beings who want to hold this alchemical frequency of transformation on the planet. My service is there. I work seven days a week but I don't call it work, because I deeply enjoy what I do."

"I understand perfectly," empathized Helena. "Yesterday I picked an oracle card as I was entering the Sanctuary of the Open Heart. I said to myself, okay, I'm talking with Ariel tomorrow, let's pick a card today."

"And what did you choose?"

"The Goddess of Love."

"Well then... I rest my case! The whole thing is being unconditionally loving."

"Going back. You said you don't think there is one truth. So you don't believe there's an eternal truth? An immutable truth?"

"Here, there are different truths, depending on the lands or the conduit that you are."

"So how do you perceive God? What is your perception of God and the divine?" asked Helena.

"You don't start with the small questions! Let's see how would I respond to that... I perceive the divine as being imbued in all things, so it isn't separate from the very fabric of creation; existence itself is the divine, so we're divine rocks, divine roses, it's all divine and so I don't perceive it as being separate from ourselves; it's a powerful emanation that exists in everything, in every molecule of space, in atoms and galaxies... now how that manifests is the mystery that no one will ever understand; the complexity of whatever that energy is that imbues everything. But, to me, it's not something separate that you can point to and say that's God. That's far too limiting and anthropomorphizing, to say that God would be like us, you know? I mean, that's just like crazy to think that small. Anything that could have created what we are existing in has to be so vastly beyond our comprehension, or our ability to define, that it's ridiculous to try to. That's how I feel about it. So that's as close as I can get to an answer."

"Oh, I fully understand what you mean. Just thinking about this little blue dot that is Earth, just a part of our solar system, that is just a small part of the Milky Way Galaxy, that is just a galaxy between other 100 or 200 billion galaxies in the observable universe, galaxies that we really don't know, adding to everything we don't even know that we don't know… And, then, just thinking about how difficult is for human beings to even know themselves, let alone everything in the universe and how it works," replied Helena, also thinking about what Carl Sagan had said 'if we ever get to the point where we think we completely understand who we are and where we come from, we will have failed.' "Apart from that, don't you think we all feed off each other in terms of energy?" asked Helena.

"Yes, I mean, there's no separation, that's what I was saying; it's all the same fabric. Everything. So for example now, with the things that we are living now, all the division... And we've gotten now fractured into so many seemingly separate parts, that all we can see is the fracturing; all we can see is the brokenness of it. But what's required is shining that light through the piece of whatever the fracturing is. Right now, we're all having to do our own homework on that what is fractured in us, what is still broken and perceiving reality is separate, how am I perceiving myself as still separate from this unified whole! And when we really address that, then we'll move into that higher order of reality, because that is unity consciousness.

"The transformation that's coming is happening from the inside out and each of us must be a part of that mitosis process! We live, sometimes, the most difficult of circumstances, but we can come back to unity through conscious choice... to transmute it all from the inside out and become unconditional love."

Helena was dumbfounded. Ariel seemed to be speaking to her, to her wound, to what she was feeling at that moment. She seemed to be reading her.

"Thank you for that wonderful answer. But sometimes it's so difficult to embrace that suffering, to loose the foundations of the known and return to a sense of unity," said Helena.

"Yeah exactly! That's the main thing; our initiation as a planetary collective right now is walking into the unknown together, because nobody knows the outcomes, right? We have to learn to navigate in the unknown and to be okay with it, not only okay, but actually become adept at navigating in the unknown, and being able to feeling navigate, like I was saying; telling what's real in the moment, in the unknown, knowing how to navigate without having to have everything figured out… that's part of the whole collective initiation for the planet right now.

"Nobody knows, not even the people who think they've got it all figured out and their foundations set! Everything's illusory! In one moment the whole thing could be pulled out from under us. We're in a massive process of surrender and to me it's surrendering to the Divine Feminine, it's surrendering to the Mother, surrendering into her arms and saying, okay, I trust that wherever my life is carrying me right now, it's okay, I trust you, I trust the divine that I am, I trust the divine in life."

Everything Ariel was saying, without her realising it, rung true with what had been happening in Helena's life - making her feel like sharing. She told her, without going into too much detail, that a little over two months ago she had discovered that her parents weren't her biological parents and that the way she had found out had been particularly devastating, because it had also shattered another great love.

"From one moment to the next, I felt every foundation my life was built on disappear, just as you mentioned. My world changed," said Helena.

She told her that so much of what she had thought was true about herself, now seemed to be mere illusion. She felt lost. That she was going to look for her birth mother.

"Don't feel obliged in any way, but is there something that you feel might be good for me to hear at this time?" Helena asked after sharing about herself.

"Oh my goodness," Ariel said before falling silent for a moment. "You can't be defined by your parents, by your country, by your this and that. So I would start looking within."

"What would I start looking for?"

"Answering the question who am I. That'll take you down some trails. If you start looking galactically and spiritually at who am I, that will take you more toward the truth of who you actually are.

"All of our mothers do the best that they can, as physical human mothers, but it's the Divine Mother's unconditional love that you're actually seeking; because that's the only mother that can ever really hold you, and not abandon you in some way or the other. Go to the source. That's all I can say."

The shaman's words intertwined with Ariel's. At the start of her journey, she was asking 'who am I?' and 'what is my truth?'. After bidding farewell to Ariel, and a long embrace, Helena immediately felt the urge to finally book a trip with Miguel Angel, a good friend of Adriana's and an expert in the cosmovision of the Mayans, with whom Helena had been exchanging messages since she had arrived in Mexico.

Miguel Angel, or Maestro Nazul, had studied for seventeen years with an elder guardian of Mayan wisdom, and as such had extensive knowledge about ceremonies, Mayan shamanism, astronomy, calendars, symbols, glyphs... He was the best guide to take her on a trip to these sacred places on the Yucatan Peninsula, bringing her into contact with the masters of light that are still in the sacred sites waiting to teach and guide whoever arrives there now, as they did in ancient times.

Miguel Angel had previously spoken to her about Oxkintok and its mysterious inner maze of tunnels, which, in former times, had been used for the process of "living resurrection"; Oxkintok was a gateway to Egypt through sacred geometry and mathematics used in the Mayan calendars.

Miguel had told her about Uxmal, 'City of Kindness of the Mother Moon', a place where women received sacred knowledge and were educated to be priestesses, and how this powerful feminine energy could still be felt.

Miguel Angel had told her about Kabah, where the 'Powerful Hands of God' prevailed, to transform the life and destiny of pilgrims.

Miguel Angel had told her about the glorious Cenote Santa Cruz, with its purifying waters, as a sacred gateway to Mother Earth herself.

And, lastly, he had told her about the cosmic university Chichen Itza, where there was also the circular observatory known as El Caracol.

This all seemed to take on a greater meaning after her conversation with Ariel. Helena was the pilgrim in search of answers within herself, and she was intending on making the most from the light from the masters present at those sacred places, as well as the powerful energy there. She was also looking forward to 'drink' from the wisdom of Miguel Angel, with whom she had just arranged a trip.

During the first week, in Oxkintok, Uxmal and Kabah, Helena felt like a canvas of intense experiences, on which a series of paintings were being overlaid, still somewhat maze-like in her mind and heavy in her body. After the turquoise-blue waters of the Cenote Santa Cruz, she felt everything diluting, preparing her vision, in a deep connection with Mother Earth; but it was only in Chichen Itza, days later, that she realized that the pilgrim's journey does not reveal itself immediately, and that instead it prepares you, as on a path of initiation, for crucial moments of profound discovery.

Helena wanted to see the stars from the observatory and with Miguel Angel she was able to enter at night. It wasn't allowed, but he had his ways and means forged from his many years of experience. After climbing the pyramid, and crossing the observatory, Miguel invited her to climb an old crumbling staircase, which was half hidden and a little dangerous. Helena accepted without hesitation. At the top of that place, Miguel sat down, Helena sat down beside him and looked upwards. The sensation of being within the stars swept over her in a whirl of giddiness. She had no idea that you could feel such fellowship with the sky. Miguel Angel smiled beside her, without saying a word, understanding the magnitude of the moment. A little later he moved away, leaving Helena alone with the stars.

She remained there for some time, looking up at that infinite sky, feeling connected to hundreds of generations of people who had witnessed the circumpolar movement of the stars and the changing course of the bright moon from that exact spot where she was sitting.

Overwhelmed, she lost track of time and space. She felt like a star herself, looking down on herself, able to understand in seconds every phase of her life, stories within stories within stories, lived across the cyclical rhythm of the four seasons.

The Flower of Life seemed to draw itself in that sky, to which she belonged too, all part of this same living web, connected, animated by the spirit. Everything infused with divinity. The air was sacred, the stones were sacred, the stars, the moon, her, every atom of the manifest world was sacred. What dream of the universe was revealing itself here through her consciousness? What was the splendour of her evolutionary journey?

There she was, breathing to the rhythm of the world, reconnecting with the timeless wisdom of the soul, the eternal terrain of her own consciousness, and she said she knew. She knew that she had no idea what she knew, she just knew that she knew. Something inside her was saying she knew.

In that instant she could feel Thomas' presence, along with all the pieces of that trip of hers through Mexico, of every conversation, every message, every sensation. And, as she wept for the love she felt within herself, linking her to the whole universe, her right hand instinctively searched for her belly and, if her voice had said before that she knew, without knowing for sure what she knew, now she was certain that she was pregnant and a flood of tears poured out.

That night, she dreamt about Mary Magdalene again, who was hugging her and congratulating her on the birth of Thaís, a name that means the one that is beholden in admiration. There was a calling there, in that dream, someone singing in her ear again about where to go. And, when she woke, she felt it was time to follow her, starting with Egypt, where Mary Magdalene had fled and had possibly had her daughter, Sarah.

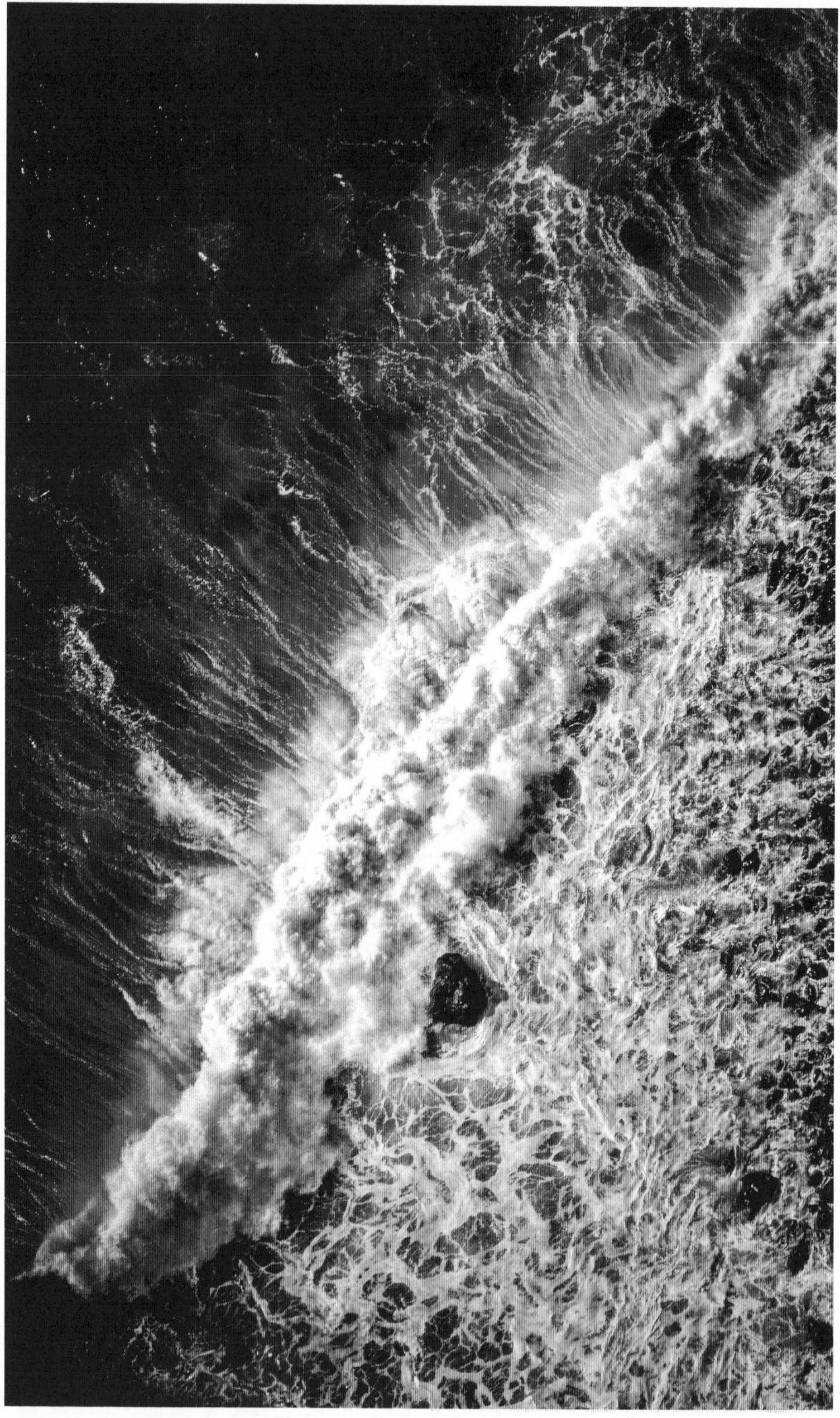

Thomas

Thomas flew to Portugal immediately after the revelation, to speak to his father eye to eye and in the hope of finding Helena there. He needed to know more. Adriana hadn't told him anything, despite confirming that they weren't brother and sister. She had promised Helena not to talk about her whereabouts and, when he called, Helena didn't pick up or reply, ever. Thomas had no idea where she might have gone, but as she lived in Portugal, like his father, he got on the very first plane. With his anger restrained in his solar plexus by the weakest of cords, Thomas let rip as soon as he met his father, in the apartment he had assumed was his father's home, but actually was just an apartment his father owned.

To the untrained eye, it could almost seem that all of Thomas' anger was focused on that situation, but the truth is that, at that moment, all the rage pent up for his entire existence, for the absences in his childhood and arguments with his mother, came together in a single, tragic mass, which he launched at his father's face with shrieks of fury. His father took that ball of fire made of words without saying anything. He knew that if he were to try to defend himself, it would only provoke more attacks. So, he remained passive until Thomas had calmed down, after saying everything he had trapped in his body for far too long.

When he finally stopped shouting, he collapsed on the sofa, broken and sapped of strength, totally drained, as if a train had railroaded him.

Silence fell over the room for enough time to regain some strength.

"Can you explain it to me, please?" Thomas asked, sounding as normal as he could manage.

"I'll try," his father said, his face stricken, his eyes brimming with tears, something Thomas had never witnessed before.

"And don't go trying to invent anything. I know you're an expert at that. But, if I find out you've made up any of it, that'll be the end of us."

"Stories that sound like they've been invented are the ones that haven't. This is one of them. Tragic yet true."

"No more bullshit," said Thomas, impatiently.

"Ingrid, my wife, well... Helena's mother... well, you know she isn't her biological mother, before Helena, before your mother, you, many years before then, I met Ingrid at a party and fell in love. I fell madly in love! Whenever she entered a room, heads turned, she was beautiful, clever, with an incredible energy! We got together. We grew together professionally, her family was quite well-off, but we wanted to conquer are own world and that's what we did.

"When Ingrid fell pregnant for the first time, years before Helena, she miscarried the child at four months. It was sad for us both, but we got over it, convinced that we would have more chances. And we did. Ingrid fell pregnant for the second time. But then she lost the baby again, at five months this time, another miscarriage. The joy of announcing the pregnancy ended in sadness and depression.

"Nobody could tell us why she was miscarrying, but this time Ingrid didn't get over it. Something had broken with those two losses, her sparkle, confidence, her *je ne sais quoi*. She thought that motherhood wasn't part of her destiny! She lost her light, her enthusiasm. And I had lost my Ingrid, until she fell pregnant again. We were ecstatic, but scared too. We did all we could to ensure an entirely healthy pregnancy; she spent the first seven months in bed, with every care. It was a mammoth effort for us both. On that day, at almost 40 weeks, we'd gone out for dinner, when her waters broke, and we urgently went to the hospital. We were even given a police escort. It was real adventure. Everything seemed fine. But when we got to the hospital the complications started. Out of nowhere. Once again nobody could really understand what was wrong with her... Ingrid went into a coma and they asked me if I had to choose, who did I want to save and I said Ingrid..."

He stopped for a while, a tear running down his face.

"Go on, dad, don't stop," Thomas said, his voice steely and to-the-point.

"The baby, our daughter, didn't survive," he added, a lump in his throat.

"What do you mean?"

"Just that. She didn't survive. Ingrid was in a coma; the baby had died and I was devastated. Who can say how the universe works and why? In my work, I have often been caught up in situations that are so tragic that they seem comical, with coincidences that seem almost like miracles, and this was the situation of my life.

"In those days, while Ingrid was in a coma, I was called by a woman, her name is irrelevant, a close client of mine, who was in the hospital following a terrible car accident and wanted me to give her baby a home. Her husband had died too, it had been an accident just after leaving the hospital, on the motorway, on the way home, only the baby had survived; and her, of course. She had had twins, two girls, and one had died in the accident... The mother was emotionally destroyed, in danger of becoming crippled, and in a really dark place... She wanted me to make the baby disappear, as if she had died too, to arrange another home for it. She thought that it would be better for her, than staying in that hellhole of death and disability, where nobody would be able to grow up happy," he said, looking Thomas in the eyes. "I don't know if you understand the irony of destiny, Thomas? They were handing me a baby, a little girl, just days old, the same age as mine who had died, while I knew that Ingrid, even if she came out of her coma, would never survive another loss. I did what I felt was right. I kept her. Without saying a word to Ingrid. I did what I needed to do so that the nobody at the hospital revealed what had happened and, when she woke up, all

I said was that our daughter was waiting for us, at home.

"As you can imagine, this news brought Ingrid back to life, to her sparkle, back to her enthusiastic, naturally joyful self. Even when she couldn't have any more children, she had Helena. And I took her in as mine too. That's how I feel about her, how I always have; I have always loved her, even knowing that she wasn't our daughter by blood. I was the only one who knew... and it's true that I had always wanted to have children!"

"So, my mother was the solution to your problem," he said aggressively.

"It was never planned, Thomas. I met your mother at a painting exhibition, in Italy, and I felt hugely attracted to her. We were together for days, nothing more. But your mother fell pregnant. And I wanted to have this child. And I really glad I did. I'm so glad you're here..."

"So, you thought that living a life of lies was the best you could do!?"

"Where's the lie? Helena is my daughter, my dear daughter, even if she's not of my blood. Ingrid is the love of my life, and I tried to be a little present with your mother for your sake, but I could do no more. I didn't love her, she could feel that, the arguments were endless... And it's true that my job has always involved so much travelling, I never stopped for long in any place, with the exception of Portugal. This is all true. Now, has it been a life with many omissions? Without a doubt. It's as I told you. I know that I've made a ton of mistakes, but they were to protect or serve the people I love. Let him who has never done the same, cast the first stone... In your case, my son, I tried to be more present in your life, but I couldn't."

"That doesn't matter now. Did you tell Helena all of this?" asked Thomas.

"Well, not absolutely everything... It wasn't possible. She was on the verge of doing something stupid. But I did tell her that she wasn't my daughter and I told her the name of her mother."

"Where does her mother live?"

"In France."

"And have you spoken to her? Have you stayed in contact over the years?"

"I spoke to her. I had to tell her. To prepare her for the possibility that Helena would go and see her," said Julian.

"And has she?"

"No so far."

"Do you think she will?" asked Thomas.

"Probably, I don't know. At the moment I don't know anything..."

"There's a first time for everything," Thomas said sarcastically.

"Or a second, following the same tragic and ironic pattern. In all of Italy, among sixty million, you had to meet each other."

"Meet? It wasn't simply that we met. We fell hopelessly in love," Thomas said, clasping his hands together.

"Yes, my God... I should have known better. When two people have to meet, they will meet each other. Even at the end of the world."

"You should know that, yes. Does Helena already know about her twin sister?"

"No. It wasn't the right context to tell her that either."

"And have you told Ingrid in the meantime?"

"No," his father said, his voice cracking. "And I beg you not to tell her either, under any circumstance. This is not her fault and, for her, Helena is her daughter. Have you thought what that would be like for her?"

"Yes, I won't tell her. For her. Not for you," Thomas insisted.

"Thank you. What are you planning to do?"

"Go to France without knowing if she's going? Keep my distance until she decides to reply to one of my messages? I don't know... We wanted to marry and have children, you know? We had waited all our lives for an encounter like this... and, out of nowhere, lightning strikes, burning us to the ground," he said, overcome with emotion. "I have to think. I need time too!"

"Maybe I can help... Find out where Helena is."

"No, you keep out of it! You've done enough already. Just leave it now! Leave us to follow the path we need to. This all happened like this for a reason."

The path

Between Mexico and Egypt, Helena decided to stop off in Portugal and managed to talk with Freddy Silva on Zoom. Miguel Angel had told her about him; together they were leading tours of the Mayan temples in Yucatan, and Freddy Silva did them of Egyptian temples too and other sacred places. Since Helena had decided to go to Egypt, following the ancient paths that others had walked before her, it would be interesting to talk with him. Helena knew his work as an important researcher on ancient civilisations, and had already seen him on the Gaia platform, The History Channel, the BBC, and she was especially conversant with his research work on the Templar Knights, through the book "*First Templar Nation: How Eleven Knights Created a New Country and a Refuge for the Holy Grail*", but she knew that he had then gone on to produce thirteen documentaries in addition to publishing seven books. "*The Lost Art of Resurrection: Initiation, Secret Chambers, and the Quest for the Otherworld*" grabbed her attention. She knew he was Portuguese, which, even unconsciously, gave her a sense of kinship. Despite the fact that Freddy had moved to London at the age of eight, lived in the US and spoke little Portuguese now, the fact that they shared the same heritage prompted her to contact him.

Even though it was virtual, their conversation was immediately open and relaxed, as is typical between Portuguese people when they meet abroad.

"Much of what you have researched was secret knowledge, passed on in Mystery Schools to a chosen few; or through the arts! But, once again, only those who had this understanding or wisdom could see and understand the symbolic messages! The majority, even if they saw, didn't see, or even if they heard, they didn't understand," Helena began.

"No matter what year we're in, I share some material, and the process is still the same: ninety per cent of the people in the room think it's just a funny story, and forget it straight away! Only ten per cent read between the lines, realise that there's knowledge there that's being passed on to them," Freddy agreed. "Still people go to Egypt and, most of them, go there to take selfies and photos for Facebook; because it's more about them, and being on the picture, in front of the statue. It's not about the temples. But then you get those few people that actually take the time to understand what Egypt is all about; they're the ones that get changed."

"Yes... you have to be awake," she said. "I've been thinking about this! If you know how to look for it, today you can have access to knowledge that comes from so many sources! From the Mystery Schools of Ancient Egypt, Persia, Greece, India, China, Tibet, and from the Mayan and Inca civilizations. You can read ancient books on Sacred Geometry, Sacred Architecture, Alchemy, Astrology, the writings of great masters. You can drink from ancient wisdom that is still alive in ancient temples, as well as from the Gnostic movement and from the Occult Sciences whose knowledge, in the past, was only passed on to people that had been tested morally and physically at length, and had to stay hidden, because most people would not accept it."

"And the people chosen had to undergo years of training to understand the symbols," added Freddy. "And once you understood that, then they would observe your ability to be responsible, to have integrity with the information, because this stuff is actually very dangerous in the wrong hands. So you'd spend years learning the symbols, and the symbol behind the symbol, the metaphor, the allegory; everything was dressed up in such a way to protect the information, because once you apply these things, the idea is that you became a better person!"

At that moment Helena remembered when she had first heard Robert Gilbert speak, saying that the possibility of accessing esoteric information from an incredible variety of traditions all over the planet was both a blessing and a curse. A blessing because people could be more independent in their spiritual quest, and cross-fertilise knowledge and different perspectives, but also a curse because everything was scattered, fragmented, and to bring these fragments together into a coherent whole that was applicable in life required a contextual basis, discernment, proactivity and awareness, which was often lacking.

"I now have many years of personal experience in these things and I still don't know everything, by the way I'm still scratching the surface," Freddy continued, as if listening to Helena's thoughts. "I usually get invited to speak in places you've never heard of, even I haven't heard of, places very conservative, but you'd be surprised how many people are doing what we're doing, and what we're talking about! I'm very encouraged by it! Because, you know, even in Europe, if we were having this conversation not so long ago, we could be burnt alive! We've made a lot of progress!"

They laughed.

"And the way to see that we're having a profound effect," said Freddy, "is to look at how the world is right now. There's an old system that is fighting to hold on, kind of like the dinosaurs looking at the comet that's coming. They know they're going to die, and so they try to take power from the mammals one last time. And that's usually a sign that they know that their time is up. We're in the middle of a great change, a lot of chaos; but the more chaos, the greater the potential jump to a new level of order. So, the more chaos we're seeing right now, means that people like you and I are having a positive effect on waking people up to get them to be responsible, or to get them to initiate new ideas, or change their way of doing things, like during Covid.

"Sometimes humans need to be driven to the edge of a cliff, because we are complacent as animals and we have to go and face the fire to realize 'oh perhaps we should put the fire out!' We're at the edge of the cliff now! And sometimes when that happens, earth or nature makes us face the problem in a very difficult way."

Helena had often thought about this. What humanity? Although there were a growing number of people serving a better world, where were we still? So many seemed not to be waking up, unable to recognise the symptoms of a planet out of balance. When some friend couldn't understand why she felt a deep sadness within her, for no apparent or logical reason, Helena would reply: 'unfortunately, for any sensitive person, connected invisibly to everything, there are so many reasons for sadness'.

Despite being a heartfelt optimist, and believing that most of humanity is good and has the same hopes for peace and love, Helena could not help but see the reality that still persisted. She found it hard to name the feeling that revolted in her gut as she watched the continuous devastation and pollution of the earth; or at the women that were still being oppressed, belittled and raped; at the children who were victims of sexual abuse, neglect, mistreatment; at all those still being discriminated for the colour of their skin, physical disability, gender, sexual orientation, political conviction or religious beliefs; at the wars instigated by economic interests, dictatorships, murders; at millions going hungry while billions were invested in weapons; at the acidification of the oceans, forest chopped down, burnt down, mountains dug up, vast areas of land destroyed to extract raw materials for different businesses; at a patriarchal civilisation glorifying power, conquest and the domination of nature; at seeing that money was still having the last word, and the female voice was still so often silenced. All that showed an absurd distance from the feeling of the sacredness of life and the relationship with the cosmos, in this forgetfulness of the divine wisdom that lies in the human heart. For her, humanity should rather be the guardian of creation, beauty, love and truth.

"It's a very lonely job," Freddy continued, between conversation and reflection. "You don't have a normal life. You have to accept that most of your life would be spent alone. Because, I mean, it goes back to what we were saying before about learning the mysteries, learning the teachings, a lot of it has to be done alone. And you have to remove a lot of layers of your ego!

"When I was writing the material for the Templars, I was growing at the same time. The more you perceive, the more you become expanded. You begin to realize that there's a soul in the body. You begin to see things in the invisible world. By the way, it's not because I'm special. Anybody can do this. You just have to give yourself time, and time to these places. And before you realize, the site is telling you something, either through an image or a voice, a song or you just take a piece of paper, you sit down, you have a *pastel de nata*, or maybe two, and you start writing a lot," he ended up laughing, for being able to introduce the pleasure of Portuguese custard tarts into the conversation.

Helena remembered Jude's and Martin's words, in tune with Freddy's.

"The hardest part is knowing how can I back up the information that I'm getting from the Local Spirit, so that people don't think I'm completely out of my mind. So, then, you have to do the research! That's where libraries come in, that's where books come in, that's where the understanding of symbols come in, which is a fundamental language, and then you put this all together! To write a really good book, something with depth and meaning, takes time!"

"Yes, I also recognise this process in my documentaries," said Helena.

"When I go to Egypt, and I've been going there at least twice or three times a year with people, with a group, and I have five minutes to myself... It's really important to leave people alone as much as possible, because I can sit there and talk for hours about the temple, but it's not good for you, because it's just me doing 'yak yak', you won't remember anything; what you'll remember is your interaction with the place. So, I leave you alone and, in those five minutes when I'm alone, I just sit there and take a deep breath..."

Thinking back, Helena recalled for a moment what Martin had told her about his experience in sacred places; how it could be amplified through a conscious connection with them through knowledge, intention and meditation. Helena had already experienced it and, without managing to restrain the memory, remembered all the experiences she and Thomas had had on their trip. Wonderful experiences that were imprinted at a cellular level. Martin had also said that, by knowing about the existence of energy fields, and by practising meditation in sacred places with the intention of connecting, we could establish a psychic connection with the power of the place. Such a connection would help us to benefit more fully from the powers of the sacred sites.

In essence, it was about experiencing sacred sites through knowledge and feeling, uniting mind and heart. It was just like Freddy said: knowing how to deepen the knowledge associated with the sacred site and then feeling, having that capacity expanded, tuning into the energy present in that place. Being silent. It was no coincidence that there were so many stories of extraordinary phenomena associated with sacred sites.

"Every single culture I've looked at around the world talks about exactly the same thing: you're here to have an experience as a soul; the idea is to become better," Freddy went on after reflection. "You're having your experience, but you're also influencing the people on your left and you're on your right. Actually Gandhi had the best quotes, just be the change you wish to see... and that's the best you can do. If you can leave the planet one percent better than when you found it, you've made real progress! You've improved yourself and the state of things around you, and you become a source of inspiration for others to do the same, right? It really comes down to very simple human elements. I mean, when I first started, I used to think there was a big mystery to all of this; actually the mystery is very simple. The hard part is to follow the guidelines and put them into practice. I mean, I get in my car and I still get angry in the first seconds when some idiot in front of me does something stupid on the road," Freddy added with a smile, "and I have to go, all right, I can do better than this... so it's a constant process of improvement."

"A work in process and in progress," Helena exclaimed, smiling too. "But back to your research and what you were saying..."

"Yes, after connecting to my intuition, I begin to write and, then, I begin to research. I want to be a bridge builder between people that are really septic and need proofs through a more modern scientific model. I don't know what the full truth is. I'm just sort of adding a few more pieces of information, and someone else will do the same thing tomorrow; and that's how we keep spreading the work around to a point where we understand what the truth really is.

"When you hear the most incredible music, you don't think where did that come from, no one questions musicians if they channel the piece of music," said Freddy.

"Yes, we call it genius, inspiration, pure creation!"

"Exactly. You just bought the record and you still play it years later... We're doing the same thing; somehow we get inspired by sitting in a temple in Egypt."

"Music is a very good analogy. I can't quite remember the story! But I think it was Prince who, when he woke up at 3 a.m. with a song, woke everyone up for work straight away. And why not wait until the next morning? Because he thought that, if it wasn't for him, Michael Jackson would get it. Or vice versa," she said.

Freddy laughed.

"There's a musician in the sky who says: 'hey, I want to share my idea with all these musicians on earth'," continued Freddy playing with the idea, "and at three in the morning all the musicians will go 'hey, I've got a great idea for a song' and then, when it comes out, five thousand musicians will say 'hey, you plagiarized that from me'. Of course, the first person gets the credit. Some people have greater antennas, and are more inspired."

Helena thought: inspired. In spirit. More connected with the spirit.

"I always encourage people to go to sacred places because, actually, the laws of physics are slightly different in sacred spaces. Mosteiro de

Alcobaça, in Portugal, it's a good example. It's one of the most perfect and unspoilt Gothic cathedrals in the whole of Europe! I mean, the connection you can have there," said Freddy with a sigh. "If you wait until people have gone to lunch, because there's always a bus full of very noisy people... you sit there in the nave, in silence, and if you hum softly, your sounds will fill the whole building... suddenly it feels like you're on drugs!

"All it takes is... a little hum and the building is alive! Because the laws of where these buildings are placed are different! That's what helps you connect to another level of reality where you get that inspiration."

After a few seconds, Freddy went on.

"In essence, these places were built, so that we can connect with ourselves easily! And the more you do it, becomes second nature. But here's the fun part, after a while you recognize that you can do this anywhere. You are a temple and you can access this information at any single time. I wish someone had told me this many years ago...

"Well, Jesus said you are the temple, but most did not understand. I think we're going to keep building temples until we fully recognise that we are the temple. Because when we forget who we are, we travel to these temples. Of course, everyone has to discover the truth for themselves, because my truth is my truth, it's not the same as your truth... And if I woke up tomorrow morning with my compass pointing south instead of north, where would that take you if you were following me? So everyone has to find their own truth.

"So, that's kind of where my barometer is: if it makes me feel happy, and I'm doing things through which everyone is benefiting, I'd say that's pretty close to natural law, which is, in essence, what truth is. If everyone understands their frequency, they'll know where to go. You just have to understand the frequency: do you feel good? Do you feel bad? Do you feel good with this person? Do you feel good in this place? And based on that, you choose.

"That's where the disease comes from, you're no longer at ease with your environment. You're not feeling well," Freddy continued in his reflection. "We have to be very aware of these moments in life when the spiritual world tells us: look at the people around you... or the ideas! For example, right now the Internet is full of ridiculous conspiracy theories about everything, see if that uplifts you, if it makes you feel good. That's when you realise if you're in that stream of consciousness... uh, you can't go wrong with that! If you're surrounded by negativity, doubt and fear, that's not the right way to do things, really.

"And I'm not saying it has to be easy, I mean, life on earth is never supposed to be easy, you're supposed to have obstacles and the more obstacles that you can climb over, and do it elegantly, the better you become as a person."

"I understand what you're saying," said Helena. "And did you need to have great adversity, or some dark nights of the soul, to really redirect and realign and connect with your inner knowing?"

"I had a pretty hard life growing up. I had parents who didn't understand who I was, well, I had my share of problems dealing with severe depression, suicidal tendencies, a lot of heavy drinking which did not do my body any good... And there was one moment I ended up in hospital. I had just lost my fiancé, who was not a very good person at all, thinking back on it. I had literally two days to live! I had a hole in my stomach, literally... the anxiety, the drinking, and everything, eaten away at my stomach. I was eating myself alive with my own acid! It was horrible and the doctor just said "look, I don't know why, at your age, you are so anxious, but whatever it is you're doing, you've got a choice now: do you want to live or do you want to die?. And, at that moment, things become very clear. I think, that's where you discover your character... at those moments where you're at the edge of the cliff. I was so angry at the world and people around me, how they had mistreated me... and I said, at that moment, I can do better! I channeled my anger into something creative. I stopped drinking. I stopped smoking. I stopped dating the wrong women, that's for sure, and I started doing all the things I really needed to do... and I'm very happy. I'm not perfect, that's okay, but I'm much better than I was!"

"Now, that was a turning point in your life," Helena said with admiration.

"I was talking to a friend of mine the other day about this, about practicing what you preach... and so much of what I do, in terms of taking people on tours to sacred temples, it really comes down to teaching about fear, if I strip away all the other stuff. Fear it's one of the greatest problems here on earth and, in Egypt, there's a temple at Kom Ombo that has two entrances. No one understands why there are two entrances, you should have one. I said, 'well, there's a reason behind it: now, I'm not going to tell you which entrance to go through. I will meet you at the other end and don't follow me! I want you to follow whatever entrance you want to go. I'll tell you why you went into each entrance'.

"One entrance has to do with the dark side of the soul and the other one to the light side of the soul. And two people walked in between the two and it's absolutely right. It's not about the dark or the light, it's the bit in between you want to be... in balance! That's the whole purpose. And you'll know if you've conquered both extremes of yourself, when you jump into that water full of crocodiles! I'm not making this up! They actually did that in Egypt, at one point, for you to overcome your fear! You had to take an earring and put it on the crocodile!"

"Oh, I believe you!"

"Michael Bajin, who died a few years ago, was an excellent theological researcher, marvellous! He helped me understand a lot! From his reading of restricted Vatican material and other sources that he was able to access as a theologian, he told me: "I was very disturbed by the fact that we have two completely different versions of Christianity fighting each other." Fundamentalists absolutely believe that all the stories of Jesus were literal. The Gnostics say: No, no, no, these are mysterious teachings, they're symbols, they're metaphors! We're not going to tell you what's behind the story, we need to know that you have integrity and only then will we teach you what's behind the story. Then you'll find it's about self-improvement, highly spiritual teachings to the advancement of the self, to learn how the self communicates with a God within, not outside, and also the fact that there's a complete honoring of the masculine and the feminine.

"In ancient times, women were, in fact, the central key to everything. You couldn't do an initiation without women being involved. They were the highest level, which brings us to Mary Magdalene, because when you reached the highest level of initiation, you would take a drug or a poison to induce a near-death experience where you could leave the body and go to the other world for several days. As real as I'm talking to you right now. Not a dream, but a real ability for the soul to leave the body, travel and return with a complete memory of where it was, of what it did. That's what raises us as human beings, realising that there is more to this world and being able to say: I know exactly what I need to do with my life, because I've seen what my soul is. I can live my life fully awake!

"Now, the only way you could know that, was when the women, at the very end of the experience, would give you the antidotes to get rid of the poison from your body. You would be described as raised from the dead, because you had, to all intents and purposes, died and come back from the dead."

"Wow," Helena exclaimed without any further words.

"Women had the highest level of clearance in the temple. They knew the poisons and antidotes and how to administer them; because at the end of your initiation, when you had learn all these stories and truths, you were then ready to marry the divine bride. It could be Isis, Mary Magdalene, Inanna and so on, but you always marry the divine woman. Why? Because a woman defined all the knowledge that exists in the entire universe and she always had black skin, because it identified her as the source of all knowledge which resides in the dark, before light, before sound, before matter, there was nothing but darkness. Therefore, when you see images of the Black Madonna in Europe, that's the woman who represents the source of wisdom. Wisdom is expansive, it has to be a woman, a man is not usually defined as expansive, he's procreative, the woman is expansive, because she gives birth. That's the symbol behind the Black Madonna and the symbol of the divine feminine to which the initiates always married," Freddy said.

"Oh, I didn't know that!" she said.

"Back in the day, it was the women that had the power, but, with the patriarchal system, we've been in a in a three-thousand-year fight. In 1200 B.C., and especially around the Mediterranean, there were a lot of problems, a lot of solar storms coming out of the sun, which set fire to half of the Middle East and it precipitated the end of the Bronze Age. People had no food, they had lost everything, there was a lot of fighting over resources, and that's when the patriarchal system comes in, that's where the warring culture really steps up. And we've been in this for three thousand years! We've gone too far the other way, and the patriarchal system it's now falling apart, we have to find the middle ground."

This was the issue that had been on Helena's mind for a long time and, now that she was going to be the mother of a little girl, even more so. There was work to be done, to balance out these two energies, starting with her, within her. In the darkness of her womb a new being was being formed, heart, mind, body, like a miracle, a new life being generated inside her belly, without requiring any instruction. This divine wisdom lived inside her. And, just as in the birth of a planet, Helena knew that it was time for women to come out their confinement of thousands of years. To bring the Divine Feminine into the light.

It was just that to embody this ascension she would first have to thoroughly heal the wounds etched on a cellular level, and forgive the abuses inflicted by the masculine throughout the ages; a healing that could only work on a heart level. Layer upon layer. It was the same wisdom that had been eroded in thousands of ways, which they now needed to summon, so that the fathers, brothers, uncles and grandfathers of the world could also open up to their feminine sides, uniting mind and heart. Helena knew: when the mother creates the space for healing, the divine father is also awakened to the sacred marriage on earth. Not the masculine that is or was abusive, but the Divine Masculine.

'I live in the silence. I shine in the darkness'. This was how she saw Thaís. And so that she could be free, Helena was being invited to bring love to all the areas blocked by pain. Her dark night of the soul was walking hand in hand with Gaia and its inhabitants, who were also going though the *nigredo*, with too many wounds caused by this age-old culture of war, competition and material gain. A society that taught people to look outwards to find answers.

Close your eyes. Go inwards. To make more conscious the sacred current of light that flows through time and space, the Divine Feminine light. Maybe the essential role of women was to keep this pure light of divinity in their hearts, Helena thought, to keep the lamp of inner freedom burning in the darkness, to nurture and protect this light, whatever the cost, and to transmit its radiance, its loving beauty to men and children. Knowing that each thought, each gesture, would have a profound impact on the fabric of life itself.

First, within herself. In her heart, in her body, the Divine Feminine in ascension, earning its rightful place, despite the pain, despite the darkness, despite the resentment, despite the uncertainty, despite the lies at the foundation of her own existence, despite having lived more in doing that in being, more on the outside than on the inside, could she possibly then, along with the Divine Masculine, rebalance the (her) world.

"I have to ask. What it's your perception of the Holy Grail?" asked Helena.

"I actually looked at that, when I was writing the book on the Knights Templar in Portugal and I didn't want to go there… It's a very problematic subject, but I finally came down to the point that the Holy Grail is essentially the embodiment of what we just described, which is the wisdom that resides within the universe. It's a cup. The cup symbolizes the foundation of all wisdom into which everything is poured; and when you drink from that cup, or that chalice, you're drinking the knowledge, you're ingesting the wisdom. And when you're filled with that wisdom, you become one within yourself, you've married the divine bride. You are the man and the woman. You are the two, that have become one. So, the Holy Grail is about the quest of yourself, it's about the search for universal truth, knowledge, which you then imbibe through reading, experience, practical application, you learn to master the light in the dark, and you become one within yourself. So, that's what it comes down to, but at the same time it's also a womb, because the divine bride also encompasses the blood of the Gods from very old times; she is also the repository of the knowledge that is conceived to be the Grail. So when you're searching for the Holy Grail, you're also searching for the bloodline from where all this information came from. So it's the ultimate quest of the individual, and depending on how you phrase it, it's the same thing. It comes down to drinking the knowledge of the Gods and becoming godlike. But when you say "Tomar" (to take, in Portuguese, and the name of the Portuguese city connected with the Knights Templar) that universal wisdom, you're talking about the universal truth… and then you have to accept that there is this universal truth, the immortal, immutable and eternal truth, isn't it? You have to accept it as a framework, a guideline for living, and then you can choose to either follow the right way, to apply it or not, and this is why it was secret… Can this person be trusted with the deeper teachings? First, they would teach just the simple things, to test your integrity. Second, you would go into the deeper layer of the meanings. And then, you would have a practical understanding, control of fear, and eventually taking the poison to have the out-of-body experience. In fact, one of the wells at Quinta da Regaleira had to do with the soul travelling to the other world. Most of them are sealed off because of all the earthquakes in Sintra, they're actually in very unstable condition, but the idea of building all those tunnels was for us to enter the well, into ourselves, to enter the dark night of the soul and eventually, if we followed the right path, return to the light."

"It reminds me of the interviews I've done with people who have had near-death experiences," she said.

"Yes, and even then… nothing will give you the absolute truth. You have to be part of the work, otherwise... A great example is *Star Wars*, the moment where Luke Skywalker ditches his ship into a swamp, and little Yoda raises the ship from the swamp and Luke comes out and says 'I don't believe it' and what does Yoda says? 'That's why you fail, you don't believe!'.

"You've got to believe in yourself. And *Star Wars* is a great example of the Grail story written for modern audience; *King Arthur* is a variation of the story of Isis and Osiris, which is a variation of *Jason and the Argonauts*. It's the same story about self-development in the search for truth, with all the obstacles you have to go through for the hero to meet the divine bride."

"Yes, the Hero's journey."

"Written for a different audience, we have *Alice in Wonderland*, *Star Wars*, *Lord of the Rings* to a certain extent is the same thing, the search for divine enlightenment, the search of the light over the dark... So yes, you have to make the effort, you have to want to be better in order for the doors to open. When you say, okay, I'm ready for this, I want to know more about the meaning of this, *boom*, the doors just miraculously open in front of you! So be careful what you asked for, because you might get it," he said.

"Before you go, and thinking about what I ask for, I'm in the middle of one of those deep journeys, hoping to return home, to the light, but I'm still in the tunnel... So, as a simple guideline, do you have any suggestions for temples in Egypt that I should visit?" she asked.

"Each temple is designed and encoded with a different piece of information. If you look at all the temples in the world like a library, each one has its own book. You just have to follow the gut feeling, you just follow that voice, your voice, and suddenly there's this picture that comes in your head, you suddenly feel the need to go somewhere, probably because the site has what you need and what you're looking for. Because you're sending out a packet of information, when you have a thought or a feeling! It's like an envelope of electromagnetic energy and it gets sent out immediately. And all these sites in the world, because they're all on the earth's electromagnetic grid, they're listening to you, and they're going 'oh I have exactly what you need', and suddenly you get this image, you feel 'I need to go to'… and you go there, and you don't ask why, and you walk around quietly... before you know it, there's your answer!"

"Thank you very much, Freddy."

"Just stay there for a long time and meditate… to receive all that life force, to connect with what is really true. It's not difficult. It just takes you a long time to work it out."

To the sound of her heart

Despite dreading some unwanted encounter, Helen dashed around Portugal, stopping off at her house in Guincho, to drop off some things and get some others that she needed, and more importantly to attend a consultation she has booked online with her gynaecologist.

She was used to spending long periods abroad and had a friend, Sofia, who looked after her house while she was away. She found out, from her, that her father and her mother, separately, had stopped by the house several times in the hope of finding her there, as had an Italian called Thomas. Knowing this made her all the more anxious and, after packing her bags again, she asked Sofia not to say a word. On those days passing through Portugal, she decided to stay with her good friend Júlia, who was older than her, a journalist for whom she had a great deal of respect and who she had met many years beforehand while working abroad.

She had been introduced to her by John Vicente, during a World Forum in Sweden which the three of them were attending. He had described her as the women who revealed stories of *Wabi-Sabi* people. People who had come through traumatic situations, hardships, imperfections, shortcomings, scars, personal circumstances, and who found, through the pain and challenges, opportunities and ideas to help others in similar situations, contributing to a better world. His description had piqued Helena's interest. Later on, Júlia had gone into more detail about the work of *IM Magazine* and, through the empathy she felt for her, they had developed a deep bond of friendship over the years.

Sat in her house, Júlia told Helena that her father, Julian, had called her, asking if she had spoken to her, without elaborating too much, but saying that he'd be unable to get hold of his daughter for some time. Júlia had found this odd, because everyone was used to Helena's prolonged absences, when she was working, often in places without phone or Internet.

"What's up, Helena?" she asked.

"I'm going through a difficult time. Sorry for not telling you more, but the time isn't right yet. We'll leave the discussion for later, okay? I just want to be far from home, I really don't want to meet anyone."

"But have you called your folks yet? Your mum in particular? From what your father says, reading between the lines, she's been fretting about you."

"I'm going to send them a message saying I'm fine, I promise. But nothing more. Don't let them know I was here in Portugal, ok?"

"You know I don't like lying. If they ask me..."

"I know, I don't want to put you in a difficult position. So, the less you know the better. Besides, I heading off again in two days. I don't know when I'll be back."

"Because of the new documentary?"

"That too. But there are other pursuits that weigh on me now."

"I can see that you can't talk about it. I won't ask anything more. How about we order a pizza and watch a comedy series?"

"You've got a deal!"

On the following day, Helena confirmed that she was pregnant, had her first scan and was deeply moved on hearing Thaís' heartbeat. Seeing and hearing that new life she carried inside her brought on a flood of emotions. Fourteen weeks had passed since her conception, where the miracle of love had joined hands with fate. A time of such intense and unbridled changed that she had become another Helena, even if in the mirror didn't reveal this yet.

Egypt

She stopped over in Cairo, before taking a plane to Aswan. She wanted to end the trip with the pyramids, after the initiation journey along the Nile. She had booked a trip on the *Dahabeya Abundance*, a traditional boat shaped like a bird that seemed to carry with it, carved into its timber, the feeling of timelessness and many stories from past centuries. She had also found a guide to take her to Abu Simbel first. He hadn't been recommended by anybody, because she hadn't asked anyone, as she hadn't wanted to tell anyone where she going. But searching online she had come across this man and intuitively arranged it all with him.

The experience of being driven, at dawn, by this guide she had only just met, across the Sahara to get to Abu Simbel, her first temple in Egypt, already had something inexplicable and inexpressible about it. Helena could feel her heart flutter and shivers in her body, as if preparing her for what was coming next. Everything on earth prepares you for the experience of heaven on earth, but nothing really prepares you more than experiencing it in full, in the here and now. Helena had taken some sand from these ancient lands and said a silent prayer to awaken the goddess and open the doors of the Divine Feminine but, at sunrise, on arriving at the gate to the main temple, in that moment in which night and day touch, understand each other, subtly merging, in a temple in which the parity between queen and king could be felt in all its incredible magnificence, Helena found herself in a completely altered state.

That night she had seen two shooting stars, and it was as if Ramses II and Queen Nefertari had made themselves present, bringing their love story to life. Helena thought about Thomas, felt him in her body, it was impossible not to and, for seconds, she believed that all the chaos that had been poured over their lives, at the greatest moment of that love, was just the path for them to reach something greater. Ma'at was revered in this temple, the goddess that rose from chaos to create order in the human world. It was a sign.

Suddi, her driver and guide, had impressed Helena from the get-go, for his appearance and a certain something that she associated with the image of the prophets. Tall, upright, well-built, in a white turban and tunic, dark-complexioned, and with long dark hair down to his shoulders, a broad powerful forehead hinting at a sharp intellect, a face weathered by time, but not too greatly, eyes as keen as a hawk's yet at the same time kind and friendly.

She hadn't been afraid for a second, despite the cautionary voices in her head, which surely belonged to more prudent family members of countless generations, having asked questions and made observations: but are you really going to go on this car trip at night with a man you know nothing about? This could be your last journey. Helena had left word at the hotel where she was going and with whom. She wasn't entirely daft, but she was learning to let herself be guided by her intuition, to trust this inner awareness. And, out of her own painful experience, she also knew that there was little in life you can control. When you think you know it all, and that you've got everything in control, that's when the known and apparently secure falls apart the quickest and you're left with no foothold.

When Suddi spoke, it touched her heart; he seemed to impart his great wisdom with unbearable lightness. At a certain point, he said to her that despite much of academic literature stating that Abu Simbel had been built to celebrate victory in battle, the purpose of the symbol of Abu Simbel seemed to him rather to exemplify a temple, with all its many crypts and dark passages, which described the first stage of the Mysteries - rebirth.

It made entire sense to her. She had already heard Matias de Stefano talk about Abu Simbel as the Chakra of the Root of the River Nile, the first place of the initiation path, which together with Philae and Kom Ombo, represented the first three temples of the path, where travellers would learn to deal with their emotions, the deepest, strongest ones, as in a healing process of their own history, creating neutrality, understanding them as energy, learning to use this energy of the body to illuminate their heart and their mind. On this part of the journey, you had to liberate your fears. Only after this could they move on to Edfu, Luxor, Karnak, Abydos, Dendera, already engaged in the challenges and learning of the solar plexus and the heart chakra.

Just as in Oxkintok, in México, she had already felt the presence of Egypt, now, having arrived in those lands, Helena was breathing the air of countless generations who had searched for themselves and for the divine there.

"The Temples of Abu Simbel have a particular wisdom for each of us on how to live in the world at the moment," Suddi explained.

At the entrance to the sanctuary of Nefertari, expressed in her temple as the Goddess Hathor, the energy was palpable and a deep silence could be felt. Suddi fell back a few steps to allow Helena feel more at ease. Both of them knew that this was a place to liberate fears and illusions, to receive courage for the rest of the journey, and to fall in love with your own beautiful essence.

In tune with the vibration of the place, Helena asked herself: what are my true fears? Not being what I thought I was? Not being ready to become a mother? Not finding my truth? Not knowing how to be happy? Losing my way and never finding myself?

She entered cautiously, closing her eyes and, in a protracted silence, felt the unconditional love of Ramsees II and Nefertari filling her heart. In this place, there was no fear, there was only the calming sensation of being part of this greater love. She looked at Suddi and, with a simple gesture, asked him if he would like to pray with her within the temple. He silently nodded yes and came towards her, coming to a halt by her side. Without thinking, Helena held out her hand to him and, curiously, Suddi didn't find the gesture strange. There they stood, hand in hand, their eyes closed, sending up their prayers. What was happening was truly profound. They had put aside any judgement, and thus witnessed how the energy of love, when allowed to flow freely, dispelled any fear.

On the following day, Suddi also took Helena to the Temple of Philae, this time by water. Along the way he fed her a few details. That the Temple of Philae, completed in around 690 BC, had been built to honour the goddess Isis. It was an example of the important cult regarding the story of Isis, Osiris and Horus. Osiris, symbol of justice, resurrection and source of royalty, Isis, symbol of endless love, compassion and motherhood, and Horus, symbol of victory.

"The Philae temple is now located here, on the island of Aglika, downstream from the Aswan High Dam and Lake Nasser. But this wasn't where it started out. It was originally located close to the first cataract of the Nile in Upper Egypt, but in order to save the temple from the rising dam waters, a huge operation was undertaken to physically move the temple to higher ground."

"It's staggering to think that this entire complex was moved from one place to another," Helena said in awe.

"For many Egyptians and Nubians, the Temple of Philae was the most sacred temple of all, as the god Osiris was buried on the island where the temple stood. In fact, only priests were allowed to live there; legend has it that no birds ever flew over it, and that even fish and other water creatures never approached the island's shores."

"How poetic," Helena replied, her eyes fixed on the horizon where the temple could already be seen.

Then, shifting tone, Suddi told her the entire story. Osiris ruled Egypt alongside his wife Isis, goddess of motherhood and healing. He was responsible for everything, from creating law, religious instruction, culture and everything to do with agriculture. He was highly respected by the people, and kept everything in a harmonious balance in accordance with the Ma'at principles. But his brother Seth, "god of the desert", jealous of his power and glory, hatched a plan to kill him. He organised a huge celebration with seventy-two loyal friends and, at the event, he held a competition in which the person who could fit inside a solid gold sarcophagus would get to keep it. Everyone tried to lie inside it, but only Osiris fit into it perfectly, as the sarcophagus had been secretly customised to his measurements. So, when Osiris was lying down inside the sarcophagus, Seth and his friends shut it and threw it in the Nile, where Osiris suffocated to death.

Osiris was swept northwards by the current and lost. Finally, the currents carried him to the shores of Biblos, where a great tree sprang up around him, encasing him in its trunk. The king of Biblos, astonished by the sheer size of the tree, ordered it be felled to make a column for his palace. The column-trunk emitted lights and sounds and anyone who approached it was mysteriously healed.

Seth then seized control of Egypt, ushering in a new era of chaos, terror and darkness.

Isis started to look for her husband and vowed to bring him back to the world of the living. When she heard tell of the Biblos miracles, she worked out what had happened. She managed to find and release the body of Osiris from the king's palace, and began preparing the magic potions needed to breathe life back into him, leaving his body under the protection of her sister Nephthys. But Seth, having been warned, discovered her location and cut Osiris's body into 14 pieces, throwing them to far-flung parts of Egypt and the Nile, where temples later sprung up.

Isis was aghast, but she didn't give in; she collected all the pieces of the body and was able to bring him back from the world of the dead; but Osiris was no longer complete, so he could no longer rule the living and thus became the lord of the underworld.

Just before Osiris descended to the underworld, he and Isis gave birth to Horus, the god of the sky. Horus was raised in absolute secrecy because of his uncle, Seth. When Horus came of age and became a powerful warrior, he challenged his uncle to a battle, which went on for eight years. In the end, he was the victor and banished Seth to the desert. The other gods recognized Horus as the legitimate heir of Egypt and a new era of peace, prosperity and harmony began.

"You see, Helena, it's important to know these stories, but the main thing is to discover the inner meaning of the myth, to understand how it applies to your own life. And to do so, you need to delve deep inside yourself and discover the hidden truths that are being conveyed to you."

Helena remained silent, looking towards the temple, gradually gaining form; that story rippled within her, like the boat, coursing through the water, and she knew that its full meaning would only be revealed later.

At the entrance to the Temple of Philae, after passing through the first large portico, on the western side of the courtyard, Helena found the Birth House, which was dedicated to the goddess Hathor and Isis in honour of the birth of her son, Horus. And there, for the first time, she felt her baby move. She stood still, giggling, her hands on her belly.

"Is everything okay?" Suddi asked, surprised.

"Yes. My daughter Thaís decided to talk to me for the first time!"

"Ah, I had a feeling you were pregnant," he said, smiling.

The second pylon is an extraordinary gateway, thirty-two metres wide and twelve metres high. The foundations of a small chapel stand before it. There are also some faded Christian paintings. After a series of antechambers, they reached the Sanctuary of Isis.

"The Divine Mother Isis is known as The Lady of Ten Thousand Names and therefore, within her capacious wings she could hold all people, all animals, all plants, all insects, all reptiles. She is the embodiment of Mother Nature " Suddi said, as naturally as possible. "This is her sanctuary. Here reign virtue, gratitude, peace, truth, respect, joy, harmony, kindness, acceptance, laughter, compassion, respect, conscience, openness, forgiveness, love, purity, humility, integrity, goodness, acceptance of the whole, and everything that is part of the 42 Ideals of Ma'at, in their positive affirmation."

Helena looked at Suddi with amazement and admiration, at his boundless wisdom and humility. The way he shared things was as if he were talking about someone in his family, from his mother's house, perhaps.

"Would you like me to say a short prayer here?"

Helena nodded in the affirmative.

"The Divine Mother has been ignored for thousands of years, causing a huge imbalance on the planet. This is her time!"

Suddi placed one hand on his chest and the other on one of the walls of the sanctuary, and invited Helena to do the same.

"Divine Isis, Goddess of Ten Thousand Names, I call upon Your Grace " he began, quietly. " Make of our hearts Your altar and Your home. Bring us vision and healing. Give us wisdom, reveal the truth and protect us with your feathered wings. Breathe into us the breath of life, health and strength!"

At the sound of Suddi's voice, those words melted into her bones. Suddi himself was deeply moved. Without thinking, Helena rested her forehead on the stone wall and it was as if the memory of her own wholeness and her connection to all of life was reawakened in her. She knelt down and something burst in her; an ocean broke loose. She wept, but it was more than this; it was as if she were being wept over. She was not alone. She was crying and being cried over by all the stories of the world like hers.

Suddi remained where he was, by her side, in a silent presence, without disturbing the moment. He was used to moments like this, of awakening through tears.

When her tears finally stopped flowing, Helena got up, and tried to find a tissue to dry her face.

"I'm sorry," she said to Suddi.

"Sorry for what?"

Helena regained her composure and felt a lightness that she hadn't before, as if she could fly.

"Now, if we had a mirror, we would allow it to reflect our face, so that that we could reflect back what we wish for ourselves and for the world on this day. As we don't have a mirror, we can use our hands and our imagination," Suddi added with a slight smile, placing both hands in front of his face.

What could she wish for herself and for the world on that day? Lasting peace and the radiant joy of love. That would change everything.

"And now, as has been done in many cultures throughout eternity, we will honour the sacred directions. Let's turn first towards the East," Suddi revealed, getting into position. "Then we move clockwise towards the next sacred direction, which is South. And so on."

Helena followed him, holding out her arms towards the East.

"Let Us Honour The East, Element Of Air, With The Winds Ever Blowing."

They turned towards the South.

"We Honour The South, Element Of Fire, With The Flames Ever Glowing."

They turned towards the West.

"We Honour The West, Element Of Water, With The Rivers Ever Flowing."

They turned towards the North.

"We Honour The North, Element Of Earth, With The Seeds Ever Growing."

They moved their arms up and down.

"We Honour The Spirits Both Above And Below, With The Wisdom Ever Knowing."

They opened their arms and lifted their hands to their chests.

"And we Honour Our Bodies Both Without And Within, With The Love Forever Showing."

They stopped for a moment, their eyes closed, with their hands still on their hearts. Helena felt the incredible flow of energy within her, she felt embraced by Isis, a broad smile blooming in her heart. Everything's fine, she heard. Everything is fine. Later on, next to the water, Helena shared with Suddi what she had felt, not without some embarrassment and coyness.

"Do you doubt any of what you felt?" Suddi asked her.

"No," she said emphatically.

"Well then?"

Helena thought about it for a while.

In Western culture there was, in a certain way, a downplaying of knowledge through direct physical experience, emotions and feelings, of the sensory relationship with the environment, to ensure the capacity for reasoning wasn't compromised. Even the educational system still separated reason, logic, understanding, and knowledge from the senses and from feeling, from the non-spatial and non-temporal world of being. There was a certain subliminal mental sectarianism, as if we should only trust the rational mind; and that all other forms of perception, of cognition, of knowing, of seeing, were inferior or couldn't be trusted.

Helena thought about all of this in a heartbeat, looking deep into Suddi's eyes, as if looking into the eyes of a shaman, and felt that she didn't need to say a word, that he saw her. He saw the shame of her intellect that still wanted to prevail, despite a life spent searching for answers to great questions amongst the invisible.

There, in those two temples and even before, in Mexico, and with Thomas, she knew facets of a greater truth, that lived inside and outside her, in the web of life... A cradle that held her, but which she couldn't see or corroborate, which she had to feel and trust. That she had to live.

"I'm so glad I found you at the start of this trip through Egypt. I was looking for a guide and found a true guide. Only the North Star could have been better, and even then..." she added, laughing.

Suddi smiled serenely, as if in slow motion, but illuminating everything around him.

"The funny thing is that I'm still surprised by these coincidences," she continued.

"Carry on that way. Being surprised is what keeps us young!"

"So true," she agreed, looking at Suddi with the admiration of a little girl for her father, as he gives her pearls of wisdom.

On the following day, Suddi's taxi passed between the final buildings of Aswan and the huge cruise ships that littered the shores of the Nile. It then continued along a quiet, deserted road, along the green banks of the river. When it stopped, Helena could immediately see the dahabiya, an inconspicuous white bird with elegant lines, bobbing on the calm waters, ready to set sail.

Tears were already welling up in her eyes even before Helena turned to Suddi to bid farewell.

"I know that this isn't goodbye," Helena said, managing to control her sobbing.

"Nothing is lost, everything is transformed, isn't that so?" Suddi asked, also moved.

"I would like to thank you from the bottom of my heart. You have given me something that money could never buy," Helena confided with sincerity.

"When Thaís is born, send me a picture."

Shimmering tears full of emotion sprung from her eyes. Before they could hug, two smiling young men grabbed her luggage and rushed away to take it to the dahabiya.

"Go! They're already waiting for you."

Helena still held out her hand and in those clasped hands they bid their farewell for seconds.

"I'll write to you," Helena shouted as she got on the boat.

She looked around and saw the smiling crew, a beautiful boat that looked as if it had sailed right out of *A Thousand and One Nights*. A floating palace, beautifully decorated, yet empty.

"Aren't there any more passengers?" she asked, surprised.

"Yes, they're coming up."

Helena looked back at the road, but Suddi and his taxi had already disappeared. She felt a tightness in her stomach. One of the crew took her to her cabin, the large suite, a large room with four windows with white shutters, a comfy seating area in the corner, and exclusive access to a round balcony, with a sofa, at the stern of the boat.

Helena felt like the Queen of the Nile, in that suite, on that slender, gracious boat with its two large sails, ready to glide gently along its waters, as in a dream.

Returning to the deck, Helena met the cordial Captain Mohammed, the owner, Johanna, who she'd dealt with when booking the trip, and her two only companions on the trip. An elderly gentleman, wearing a huge smile on his face, with long white hair and a very healthy glow, and a dark-skinned woman in her fifties with a delicate face, piercing dark-green eyes, long curly hair and a mysterious air, who was travelling with a small harp.

"Pleasure to meet you! I'm Finbarr."

During the trip, Helena would discover, not without some astonishment, despite feeling that this was a journey of synchronicities, that Finbarr was a mystic, connected to Celtic spirituality, legends of the Grail, the Divine Feminine, Mary Magdalena and emotional healing workshops.

"Glad to meet you. I'm Helena."

"Ada," the woman said, subtly smiling.

"I don't know if there's been some sort of misunderstanding, but they've put me in the suite," Helena said to Johanna. "I don't think I booked it, despite it being a dream room!"

"You have this gentleman to thank! This was all his doing," Johanna replied, gesturing towards Finbarr.

"Oh!" Helena exclaimed, without understanding, looking at Finbarr in search of an explanation.

"There's no need for an explanation! It's fine the way it is! That's just how I wanted it," he said, glancing quickly at Helena's belly, which was starting to show, before depositing himself in a hammock.

"Thank you so much! What else can I say?!"

With a sharp heave, and the sails fixed by the crew, their fabric flapping in the wind, the dahabiya departed. With no motor, gliding along slowly, at the mercy of the wind and the current. A blessing for anyone who, like Helena, wanted to avoid the crowds, and to slowly and silently soak up the Egyptian landscape, beside the water, dropping anchor anywhere along the banks of the Nile.

Helena had thought about saying to her fellow passengers to not pay heed to her prolonged silences, but, seeing how quickly each of them settled into their different position, she realised there was no need. Everything was in place for them to be able to sail down the Nile as they had hundreds of years ago. More majestically even, with fresh mango and guava juice, fresh food every day prepared by the cook, Saber, from ingredients bought at the market by the captain every morning.

Each of the members of the crew was attentive and cheerful, but Helena missed having Suddi by her side. Over those two intense days, Suddi had been a pivotal presence, a deep friendship, of the kind deemed unlikely but which, without a doubt, has been forged in former lifetimes. She knew though that she was now one of the daughters of the majestic Nile and, to experience it, to be able to allow that landscape of palm trees, herons, ibises, wild ducks and banana trees to truly enter her, she would need to let Suddi drift from her memory. She smiled at him as he parted.

Ancient Egypt, the silent country, was stretched out before her, under the calm breeze of the Nile. The tassels hanging from the canopy protecting them from the sun danced discreetly. The crew bowed silently before the majesty of the landscape that whispered ancient stories into their ears.

Little by little, with all that uninterrupted silence, beyond an occasional creak of the rudder ropes, the emerald-green water at full sail, the reeds, the lush rural scenery, Helena felt herself regaining her breath. Before stopping in Daraw, mango, fig and lemon trees lined the banks, interspersed by reed beds, fewer houses and villages, more steep ochre rockfaces; the desert experienced from within, even with her eyes closed, swinging in a hammock. Memories that couldn't be hers came to her as if in a dream.

At the market in Daraw, the thrum of life was noisy, contrasting with the silence of the boat. Throngs of children and women covered head to toe in black, buying fruit and vegetables, herbs and spices, beans and lentils, as well as everyday utensils. In front of the tea house, men of all ages sat cross-legged on well-worn benches, drinking *karkade* tea while smoking shishas from their extravagantly coloured glass hookahs. Wide-eyed, Helena, Finbarr and Ada wandered the streets, occasionally dodging tuk-tuks and weighed-down donkeys. In a stable, Helena saw a toothless man sawing half a camel and felt the first nausea attack of her pregnancy. From then on, she would avert her eyes when passing the meat stalls, where live chickens where packed into cages awaiting their final moment, before being slaughtered and plucked in front of customers. Powerful images that shook her, despite recognising the importance of honouring what would be their food.

Everyone was cordial. You continually heard *salaam alaykum*. Peace be with you. But even though she enjoyed the experience, Helena felt relieved to return to the peaceful intimacy of the dahabiya, anchored before the extensive green plains.

At the end of the day, they arrived in Kom Ombo, where the Nile forms a u-shaped loop and the current is slower. Freddy had told her. Kom Ombo is a double temple, dedicated to two divinities, the crocodile god Sobek, associated with the merciless Seth, and the falcon god Horus. Despite the late hour, the temple was still packed with tourists. Helen didn't feel well and immediately returned to the dahabiya. As an antidote to the hubbub of sightseers, Captain Mohammed chose an idyllic, peaceful spot to rest for the night.

Helena didn't feel like dining and was still feeling uneasy without understanding why. Finbarr and Ada suggested a different evening to her, of music, meditation and healing. She hesitated before answering, the evening was very inviting, but she felt more inclined to withdraw. However, when she felt Thaís move once again, she accepted. Ada brought her harp to the deck and her crystals. Helena lay down. Finbarr placed a green fluorite octahedron on her heart and asked her to close her eyes. Ada began to play angelic music. With her eyes closed, Helena could hear Finbarr talk to her about the octahedron, about its connection to the heart chakra, the centre of love and compassion.

"And now relax... Breathe in the green colour of the octahedron through your heart. In and out. Listen to your breathing. Allow the thoughts and feelings that emerge to rise slowly to the surface. Allow them to flow as if they were carried by the gentle current of the River Nile. Maintain the flow in movement without analysing what is happening to you. All the repressed feelings and emotions that surface will be addressed and cleansed in a gentle and loving way."

In that moment, Helen saw herself as a Russian doll, even without knowing how many layers she still had to shed to understand every part of herself. It was funny to think that, the deeper she delved inside of her herself, the more she felt in an apparent inversion of the process. It was in these deep dimensions, in the sacred space of herself, that she felt closer to the truth and to the whole.

On that journey again and again she had been invited to delve deeply into the invisible mystery of her inner self and, now, she became aware that, with the inner cosmic intelligence, she had connected to an expanding field of possibilities. Possibilities that she contacted when she closed her eyes and let herself flow with the current, willingly and without judgement. These were the thoughts that rose to the surface.

On that journey, she was abandoning the model she herself had made, of what she had to be, to achieve, to do, of the strange idea that she would only be loved and admired if she were perfect or if she did something extraordinary. There, even when lost, she was finding herself, even though she was wounded, she was opening up to the beauty of the moment, even though she had been betrayed, she was letting go of the pain so that it could washed away and she could return to a purer vision, as pure as the being growing inside of her.

She recalled that Thomas's mother had told her about us being a thread of light. She imagined a sea of awakened people carrying their thread of light, millions of threads, which, intertwined, creating a cosmic web of light around the planet.

"Place your left hand on your heart and over your fluorite octahedron," Finbarr continued. "Commune with the wisdom of the earth through this sacred crystal. Immerse yourself within it and listen to what it has to say to you. A powerful sense of freedom comes from forgiveness; this is a great moment to forgive yourself and release whatever is blocking you and tying you to the past..."

An image popped into her head of taking off her shoes, her socks, and starting to dance, feeling the touch of the earth on the soles of her feet. The music and the vibrations of the harp even made her cells dance. She was surrounded by the children she had seen on her trip, all of them dancing with her, joyous, carefree, unquestioning. As she was dancing, she let go of trapped feelings, frustration, anger, fear, judgement, guilt, shame; she could clearly see the suffering flowing like water through her body, seeping from her feet into the earth, which welcomed and purified it.

"Now, raise your arms; picture yourself as a chalice, an eternal vessel of light, being filled with the fire and sustenance of the spirit. See how everything you have emptied can now be filled with the fruits of your desire and unconditional love. You are the grail, the chalice of the expanded self, the alchemist who transforms everything. Rejoice in the generous gifts showered down from heaven."

A golden-green light danced in her chalice. Her hands vibrated. Her body seemed to lose its physical contours, merging with the Nile, with the sky, with the boat, with all the people around her; she felt the ecstatic union with all of her potential as a human being.

"You are the wisdom you are searching for. You are the seed that has within it the wisdom to achieve your full potential. This power and intelligence of the seed is firmly pushing you towards becoming what you are here to be. Feel it. Breathe deeply and say out loud: I am full of truth and clarity."

"I am full of truth and clarity," Helena said softly. "I am full of truth and clarity," she said a little louder. "I am full of truth and clarity," she said loudly, while her body seemed to emanate a warmth beyond measure, merged as she was with the world.

Once again that feeling of greater love coursing through her blood. The crystal-clear notion that, even in the depths of trauma and suffering, she was able to open up to life and joy. This wasn't escaping, rather a gargantuan power that was given back to her in that sacred choice. When her heart was opened in the midst of hell, a primordial force emerged. She was the only master of her path. The architect, the master alchemist.

She felt an overwhelming urge to laugh and laughed without stopping for some time. Albeit with a certain feeling of impropriety, but she just couldn't stop herself. Then laughter mixed with tears. Finbarr and Ada, one either side of her, sat on the floor of the boat, with their hands on her shoulders, as present as her own arms.

After that night, Helena felt renewed, open to the world. Like an opening without ifs and buts, and focused on the present moment. She seemed to relish everything, walking along the trails between the mango trees and the fields of sugarcane, surprising the various birds, discovering the sabils, which offered fresh water out of large pitchers to passers-by and to people working in the fields, having a closer look at small farms surrounded by earthen walls, meeting farmers on their donkeys.

Helena particularly liked the sabils. Unlike Cairo, the water systems in rural Egypt are limited or barely functional, with many disruptions to supply and, at times, there are alarming levels of pollution and sewage mixed into the tap water. And the sabils are public water supply stations, for offering drinking water or irrigation water to those who don't have access to it, based on Islamic teachings on the importance of sharing water. In religious texts there are many references suggesting that supplying water to humans and animals is something virtuous to do. Water isn't seen as a commodity. Water comes from God. For anyone hoping to be rewarded by God through charity, they build sabils, because they accumulate good actions for every human, plant, or animal that benefits from that water. I help you; you help me, we are all connected.

All those details, the generosity of people, every prayer said by the crew in the morning, the blessed shores of the Nile, the reflections of dazzling daybreaks in the waters of the river, reminding her just how beautiful the world is and how there was peace in her heart. A sensation that seemed to herald the next temples, Edfu, Luxor, Karnak, Dendera and Abydos, the temples that according to Matias prepared the solar plexus and the heart chakra on this path of initiation, learning to channel the information of plants, of minerals, animals, other people, civilisations, to recognise who we are, where we have come from and how we can transcend all that we think we are. Ultimately, it was the possibility of being every being, living within you the different levels of consciousness of the divine. Sea, rain, lakes, rivers, different kinds of water and of expressing this divine intelligence, as well as fire, earth, mountains, hills, the air, breezes, winds, trees, flowers, animals and birds, fish, the underwater world, different aspects and levels of consciousness.

After this, they would learn about love; love through sexuality, love in the path of creation, about how to become the mother, the feminine aspect of reality.

In all these temples, Helena willingly shared the path with Finbarr and Ada. Something very special had connected them on that night after Kom Ombo, a bridge between the light and darkness that she had crossed with their help; even without having visited it, that double temple had forced her to delve deep, and maybe it was no coincidence that so many temples of Ancient Egypt revealed successive dwellings, each darker and smaller than the next, in a symbolic progression towards the sacred sanctuary. The sanctuary in Edfu was an unlit space too, located at the end of the temple's axis. This was perhaps a good symbol for each person's path, from the light from the outside to the inside and, within oneself, in the dark, to rediscover the greater light.

In Edfu, the three of them wandered through the twelve rooms surrounding the sanctuary with no particular agenda in mind, following their intuition and aware of what they were experiencing. Finbarr had waxed poetic about the twelve houses of the zodiac and their constellations, the twelve chakras, which, in perfect vibration, are portals in the body to contact with the twelve faces of the universe, twelve shades of the colour scale, about Thoth's book of the twelve pyramids, and about how the twelve pyramids of light came through the dark void to enter into the physical world and create a reality that souls could experience.

As each of them was in the centre of the twelve rooms, in the unifying vibration of the thirteen, Finbarr suggested to them that they spend some time in each room, while returning each time to the sanctuary, at its centre, to the granite pillar where the boat of Horus was resting.

Back on the dahabiya, they spent hours sharing their experiences.

"It was magical," Helena began. "To start with I was still very much in my head, thinking about the results I hoped to achieve, but I found an inner litany that neutralised this. I sat myself down, very quietly, closing my eyes and said to myself, over and over, 'I see what I receive. I hear what I receive. I speak what I receive. I feel what I receive. I translate and I am true to what I receive.' Then I stopped and remained quietly where I was, intent on connecting and receiving the wisdom that each room had for my path. I asked for my heart to beat to the rhythm of that place and the experiences I had are difficult to relate. It got to the point where I could no longer tell if it was the rooms that were magic or if it was me doing the magic! I actually travelled through certain elements. The experience of being able to alter consciousness to other states of being was really impactful!"

"How amazing, Helena! Tell us more..."

"At the start, mixed a little with that mantra of mine, I can't recall which room exactly, I began to hear 'Wake up, darling, wake up! It makes no sense to sleep all the time'," Helena recounted, still a little bewildered.

"Sounds crazy, doesn't it?" asked Ada.

"It does!! I even thought that it was one of you saying it in one of the other rooms, messing with me, until I understood that the sound wasn't coming from outside my head, rather inside. Something happened there. I can't explain it, it was if someone had pushed me into another dimension, through a tunnel, and suddenly I found myself in water, in the dark depths of the sea; it was really confusing to begin with, I couldn't tell if I was dreaming, but the feeling was entirely real, as real as here now, I remember trying to swim up to the surface, but it was strange, because I didn't feel like I was separate from the water, I felt I was part of it, and I felt everything, every emotion of my mother, of joy and sadness, anger and frustration, I was in her womb after all, connected to her and, at the same time, connected to all of life in every dimension; I was floating in the dark, but I felt bathed in the calming light of the cosmos. The strange thing was that I wasn't alone, someone was embracing me in that place, someone travelling and growing with me."

"Did you have a twin?" Finbarr asked.

Helena froze, feeling a lump in her throat. She had never asked herself that question. In truth, that was the first time that Helena had ever raised the possibility of my existence. I smiled. Helena thought for a few seconds about everything she didn't know.

"Maybe... I don't know. I've never thought about that possibility!"

"Sorry, do carry on..."

"It was all so powerful, and then I felt I was being pulled towards a light, I felt pain, something blinded me, but I did nothing to stop it. I simply asked my Higher Self to lift me to the level of light consciousness and... bam!... I felt a golden light penetrating the entire space, all around, in every direction, to infinity. There was nothing else but light. Light that was endless love.

"After some time, I started making out threads of light, ethereal fibres of energies that are the fabric of the universe and that make up all of creation. I could perfectly see the tapestry and the small holes of that structure. I let myself fall through one of those holes and I passed through dimensions. I know, within myself, after this experience, that these are the passageways that shamans use to travel to other realms. Them and Alice in Wonderland," she added, smiling. "I remember being in the air, falling, and I was so entirely at peace with it all, so confident of being safe that I entered the vortex of energy of the temple as if I were being carried in the arms of angels. It was incredible. I came back to myself full of confidence in life."

"What do you feel now about what happened?" asked Ada.

"I'm still processing it. At that moment it was so exhilarating that, in the other rooms, I spent the time trying to absorb the experience, my body was in ecstasy and so charged with energy. It was like in a dream, or better put, it was a mystic experience without the use of psychedelics. I was awake the entire time, of this I am certain. What I felt in my mother's belly, if it was a flashback or simply my imagination, I don't know, all I know is that it was the first time in my life in which I didn't feel emptiness, the painful hole that I have always felt."

"You are allowing yourself to be loved, and to understand that it is these "holes" in our existence that allow us to go further," Ada said softly.

"At least it's good to think about it that way," she said, lowering her eyes and remaining silent for a moment. "And you? Tell me... How was it?"

"Ada?" said Finbarr, looking into the green eyes of the catlike Ada.

"For me it was a musical experience. Sometimes I have feeling that my entire life is a musical experience," she added, laughing. "I'm very attached to the footprints of the forefathers who sang of creation. As I know that these sacred places unite us to all the other energy vortices of the planet through the ley lines, I placed a crystal on my third eye, tied it there with a scarf, and requested opening and passage to other places, where I could travel along the song lines until I found my original song, of my soul, at my beginning.

"What a wonderful idea," Helena marvelled.

Ada spoke about Australian Aboriginal people and about Dream-time, and how for them the earth had to be sung to be manifested.

From there, tracing the footsteps of their ancestors and singing the verses in their original form, without changing a single word or note, they can recreate the creation and connect with the past.

"I began with a buzzing between my lips. As if I were a bee. Then guttural, primitive sounds started to come out of me, similar to shamans or Buddhist monks. I didn't force anything, it all happened naturally, as if I were being guided by some inner conductor. I saw how tenuous the veil between worlds is. I seemed to have a spherical consciousness, as I could see everything around me, in front of me, to the left, to the right, behind, above, below, from every angle, even within me. There was an energy that was being awakened coming from the first chakra and which rose up my spine. My crystal became hot and seemed to be radiating light. I strengthened my resolve to travel the song lines, and I began to make contact with everything through their sound vibration, with people in my life, objects, clouds, stones, crystals... I felt the vibration and rhythm of everything, and I started to hum. My song was wind, it was waves in the sea, it was everything at the same time in a language that was new to me, but which made by soul dance. I heard: 'Through all of nature, I hear your music, my beloved!'

"Oh, what a wonderful feeling to be in tune with all of creation. Nature was the great composer, and I accepted everything without exception, without judgement, just singing its song. It filled me with happiness. At the same time, I realised that I was being asked to add my own identity to the lines of the song, to help heal the earth. I remembered that the look of each of us is important, that simply by looking we can affect creation positively or negatively. And my look was of unbridled admiration for everything. It was love. I embarked on a deep silence, sat with the first inhabitants of this earth."

Ada looked at Helena and Finbarr with tears in her eyes.

"In the silence I could hear Sophia singing the Infinite Melody of love with more clarity. It was there I discovered the musical lines of my heart, and how they are connected to those of the earth in this infinite melody of love."

Helena, Finbarr and Ada also fell silent for some time, listening to the music of these words vibrating, the music of everything around them, as if they were moving without moving and were able to peer into everything with the eye of their mind, as much in water as on earth. They took a deep breath in unison.

"How beautiful, Ada. And you, Finbarr?"

"Different from you. Many thoughts came to me, in fact, it was more of a conversation that I had with the Divine Weaver. I would ask him things that crossed my mind and I was given answers."

"Seems like a great place to have these important conversations. What did you ask?"

"What will I find if I allow myself to fall into the great pool of collective unconsciousness? That was my first question."

"That question has never crossed my mind," Helena marvelled. "You guys are really special... And?"

"Something like... You will find potentials waiting to be used by anyone who dares to enter their realm. But you need to be ready, because you will also find demons. Everything you find is a reflection of your own self, and they are all forms of energy. You can call them good or bad, for being pleasant or not, but when you turn the unconscious conscious, you should take the energies for what they are. Nothing in the universe is good or bad; these terms only apply to your experiences."

"Nothing in the universe is good or bad; these terms only apply to your experiences..." Helena repeated, recording in her mind.

"Obviously I then asked: how do we transform those experiences that we consider to be bad, the ones we endlessly repeat since the birth of humanity? How do we break this cycle of repetition? And what I'm telling you is only the way in which I remember the answers. These might not be the words, but this is the meaning I took from them."

Helena and Ada didn't move a muscle, frozen in anticipation of the answer.

"Recognise the energy behind it; of this bad experience. Ask it why it introduced itself to you. Don't turn your back on it. Sit down with it.

It's part of getting to know yourself. Whatever meaning you give it, or even if you find it impossible to give it meaning, you have four powerful weapons to disarm any oppressive energy. Love, forgiveness, acceptance and gratitude."

"Love, forgiveness, acceptance and gratitude," Ada echoed.

"With love for yourself, and for the world you influence in that frequency, you can choose to free yourself of that energy consuming you, whenever you repeat these experiences in your memory. You need to consciously defuse those memory bombs; take away their strength by cutting their wires loaded with hatred, hurt, guilt, and other painful feelings. Remembering your sacred power of transforming your reality by the light of a new consciousness."

"To change the landscape, all you need is to change how you feel," Helena recalled.

"By forgiving yourself, and others, you can free yourself of the pain of the trauma," Finbarr continued, "and cutting the ropes binding you to the prison of the past."

"Forgiveness is a superpower!" said Ada.

"By accepting and appreciating yourself and everything that happens," Finbarr continued, "you can release the fears that lurk beneath the surface and constantly influence your choices: fear of disapproval, fear of being hurt, fear of losing, fear of not being enough, fear of not being loved, fear of not having..."

"Fear of failure, of the future, of rejection, of being unqualified, fear of getting old, of becoming ill, fear of commitment, fear of being alone, of being abandoned, of suffering, fear of ridicule, of madness, of death, fear of fear... How many fears do we suffer? How many fears control our life?" said Helena, in a tone of catharsis.

"Acceptance dispels it all. And with heartfelt gratitude for what you've been through, for what you've survived, for what you are, you enter in harmonious resonance with everything that vibrates in these higher frequencies. With this, everything in your life transforms, transforming everything around you.

"That's how you can heal your history, as much for the past as for the future. This was the answer I was given! Well, that was the idea... from what I can remember. Obviously 'it's easier said than done'. But Rome wasn't built in a day. One step at a time and we reach the other side of the world. One brushstroke at a time and we have a Sistine Chapel. One stone at a time and we have the Great Pyramid of Giza. Drop by drop and you have an ocean. One change at a time and we can be master alchemists... transforming the lead of our experiences into gold," Finbarr concluded.

"You should be recording this," Helena reminded him.

I am recording this. Here," Finbarr said, pointing to his heart.

"Did you ask another question?"

"The one that Gregg Braden highlighted as a priority and I agree with him. So, how can I best serve?"

"How did they reply?"

"By healing your wounds, which unconsciously shape your actions in the world, you find a neutrality that will allow you to be the mountain that you are going to climb, the stone that you are going to carve, the plant with which you will make the medicine, the person you are going to help... An awakened dreamer has great powers to manifest what he wants in life and can help many others, through the darkness, back to their own light," said Finbarr.

"How lovely! One thread of light at a time we weave a cosmic poem!" she said.

Helena thought of the words of Paracelsus "There is in each person, in every animal, bird and plant a star which mirrors, matches or is in some sense the same as a star in the heavens", but she didn't say it out loud.

Instead, the idea just sailed about there, in silence. And because there is a star within, man can find his counterpart in the universe; and because he has that star in his own soul, man can understand and merge his rational and emotional energies with the most distant ones in the heavens. There can be no understanding between the different ones. Man can only understand what he himself is. It is because he is everything, that he can finally understand everything. That was perhaps the great mystery that they taught in those temples: that was the reason for them advocating that human beings have limitless potential and contain within them the possibility to grow and know everything.

They gazed into each other's eyes, embraced for a long time and, without expressly announcing it, they spent the following days in silence, at times singing, dancing to the sound of Ada's harp, contemplating the landscape as the dahabiya slowly drifted along, quietly enjoying the sumptuous meals that the crew served them, meditating in the Chapel of Isis, in Luxor, in the Great Temple of Amon, in Karnak, wandering through villages and smiling at everyone, just like they say fools do, swinging sweetly in hammocks, spellbound before the zodiac of Dendera, in the Temple of Seti I, in Abydos, the "mecca" of ancient Egypt, in Osireion, swimming in the waters of the river that marked the end of the voyage.

On that last day, the sun set, leaving in its wake a blend of colours that drew sighs at their excessive beauty. The said their goodbyes to the crew, with immense gratitude and, without much discussion, spontaneously decided that together they would go by camel towards the pyramids, after having flown back to Cairo. Despite not being recommended for pregnant women, Helena felt that was what Thaís wanted and that nothing bad would happen by riding on a camel.

They had no high expectations, as they had experienced so much thus far that it was already overflowing from their pores. They were as full as a chalice can possibly be, but Helena had come with this idea of ending her initiation path of the River Nile at the pyramids, just as she had heard Matias de Stefano say, and she didn't want to leave that part out. Finbarr and Ada wanted to accompany her.

Obviously, often the difficulty for us to adapt to what happens in heartfelt contentment, bound to our original plans, spoils the beauty of life and its natural course, but this wisdom takes it time to take root in the human mind.

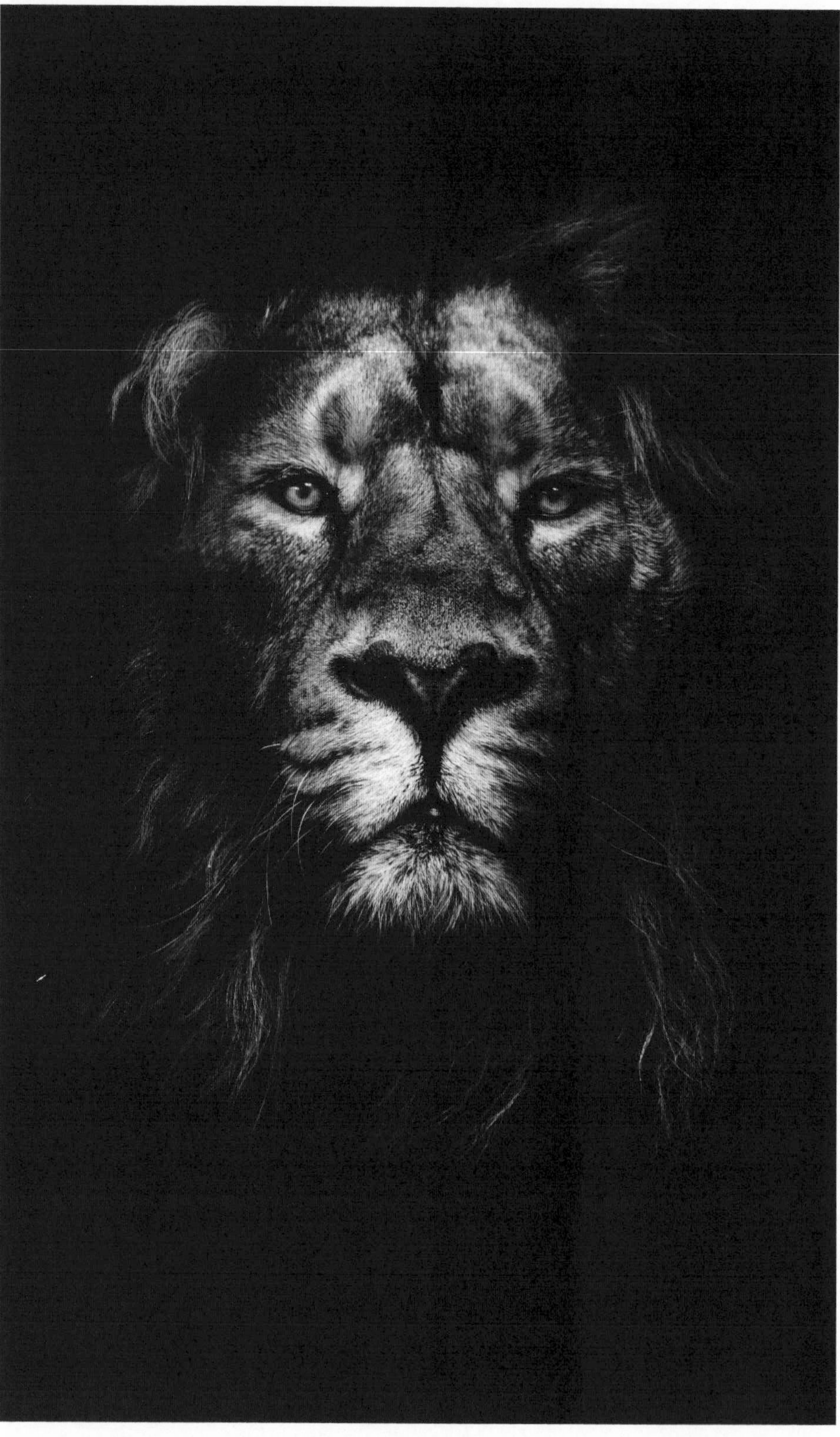

The lion heart

The chaotic airport and bus ride through Cairo to the hotel took forever, but nothing bothered their smile, and when they reached the rooms, the pyramids smiled back at them.

"We're destined to go an adventure among the stars... We've seen it," said Adam, sitting next to Helena, who was looking at the starry sky, sitting in the hotel's garden, facing the pyramids. "It's why all these movies, it's why Gene Roddenberry's work with Star Trek, it's why all of these things resonate with so many people... because we know that's our future, because it's also our ancient past."

Helena looked at the man who had just sat next to her and said that.

"People often think of the Universe as a machine, a dead device entropically destroying itself over time; this is really just the lingering of Descartes' philosophy. The Universe is alive, formed from a quantum light lattice that interconnects all things, informing the evolution and development of living organisms, planetary systems, and galactic structures through feedback," he said.

Helena laughed and gestured with the glass of juice in her hand as if making a toast to this. It was Adam, they had dined at the same table. One of those coincidences that have nothing to do with chance. He was visiting Egypt and in the hotel bar had come across Finbar and Ada, whom he had known for some years.

"Adam Apollo has been a physicist, systems architect, designer and developer for nearly twenty years, founding several education and technology oriented companies and organizations" Ada had said right at the beginning of dinner, introducing Adam to Helena. "It's hard for me to remember everything you've done," continued Ada turning to Adam with a smile. "I remember that you organized two 'Prayer Runs for World Peace' with Indigenous elders and youth from around the North American Continent. I thought that was amazing. And that you offered insights on global transitions and physics and technology at the White House and in a summit at the United Nations, isn't it? Maybe it's best if you share," said Ada to Adam. Turning to Helena. "Oh, and as founder and CEO of Superluminal Systems, he built the Resonance Academy for Unified Physics, writing the college level Modern Physics module exploring physics history from Descartes to Planck."

Later, even over dinner, Helena realized that the curriculum was even more extensive and varied, but mostly that, as a child, he had several encounters with extraterrestrial starships. Which for some would be a reason for scepticism, for her it was fascinating. And after having a vision of the Universe as a fractal hologram at the age of 15, he had studied a wide variety of branches in theoretical astrophysics, completing major research papers on the potential interface between consciousness and the physics of space-time by the time he graduated High School.

But it wasn't just the work carried out in the field of physics, and astrophysics, at such a young age, that had caught her attention. Since his awakening at age 15, Adam had studied symbolic geometry, past-life recall, Taoist alchemy, martial arts, energy therapies, and many diverse ancient and modern spiritual traditions and practices. And people who delved into different sources of knowledge, wisely interweaving this diverse knowledge, attracted her greatly. Thomas came to her mind; he was a good example of that.

There was a peculiar, unexplained familiarity. Helena didn't know if it was Adam's blue shining eyes, his smile, the way he spoke or the things he said, but she knew that even in sensitive, non-consensual matters, and incredible life stories, he seemed to carry an impetuous honesty. One could feel. And that was that.

"Some years ago, I took people on a journey here and Peru," he told at one point. "And then kind of led it into a Jedi training where I had them actually working with energy and experiencing first hand uh, you know, the discovery of something that a lot of people don't even realize exists, that they have a human energy body, a vibratory field that's responsive to their consciousness. And that's a big deal, right? The biggest gap in our education system is the fact that we have no framework to even teach people about their own life force."

They laughed. That night, everyone was in high spirits. They all had stories about the world to tell, some of them outlandish, and there, at that table, all together, they felt open and happy, which allowed them to talk animatedly, even when what they were sharing was profound and forced them to pause, reflect, take a sip of wine and then continue in the same happy vein.

Before sitting next to her in the garden, while still at the table, Adam had said something that she had cherished and taken with her in her thoughts to the garden, after dining.

"We've all heard the Golden Rule, 'Do unto others, as you would have them do unto you', but few of us have embraced it's deeper meaning and wisdom," commented Adam glowingly. "What is it that we need most? We need to feel supported, loved, and honoured. We need to feel like there are people behind us, cheering us on, and people in front of us, clearing the way for our work to thrive. We can try to be everything we need for ourselves, yet we often only fully appreciate our own work when it's appreciated by others. So how do we get all that help? We give it.

"We come to understand that the things we need the most are also the most valuable gifts we can give. We cherish these gifts, and develop a practice of giving them to others at every opportunity. We uphold the principles that allow these gifts to shine and grow, and we protect them. We become Guardians of the deepest gifts of Life, as we come to know them and share them, and in doing so we become Guardians of each other."

The entire conversation had been inspiring, illuminating, entertaining, the type that fills your heart with hope about humanity, while at the same time reinstating her bug for documentaries, of the inquisitive young lady, full of curiosity and desire to explore new perspectives. And so, when Adam sat next to her, in the garden, Helena the interviewer, who had travelled to Italy to dance with the truth was present there, awakened, along with the stars.

"What helped you break paradigms, deconstruct an entire belief system, or indoctrination you received? What helped you to open up, to question, to reassess your origins, to look for other possibilities and things that resonated more with you, that felt more true to yourself?" she asked him spontaneously. "In other words, what helped you to go into your bias mind and really hack what was true or not?"

Adam smiled, that very vivid blue in his eyes.

"Well it started with asking the right questions. It started with not being afraid to ask the big questions, the questions that people didn't have answers to, you know, what is energy, what is life, how did we get here, what is the universe, is this the only universe?

"These kinds of questions, I think, lead us to that sort of edge of the mystery; they lead us to the space where we can't necessarily have proof. Like can you have proof that there's more than one universe? If you're inside of a universe and there's other universes outside of this universe, and all of space-time that we witness is within this universe, like not directly, right? Because we would not have the power of instrumentation to get past the event horizon of our own universe... So there's innately a mystery there. You can postulate, you can explore by looking at logically, looking at patterns and systems and how other aspects of our reality unfold. So, what you start to realize, when you open up to the right questions, and you start really looking at things with fresh eyes and exploring nature with fresh eyes and looking at synchronicities, patterns and connections, you begin to realize that there are patterns, that there is connectivity between layers of scale, things that are small holding the same patterns as things that are extremely large, whether that's a nautilus shell to a hurricane, to a galaxy or the structure of graphene to the structure of a honeycomb that bees make, to the structural lattice of space-time and equilibrium. So, there are all of these interconnections that we begin to witness and, for myself, I think that's the first stage: questioning. The first stage is actually getting in touch with what is true and what is not. There's a deeper vibrational sense to that, that I think is worth cultivating; the vibrational sense of what's true versus what's not."

"How did you do that?" asked Helena.

"For me it's something that we can deeply get in touch with through the experience of the shadow, of having lied to someone. When we've lied to someone, we actually have to create a field of energy to carry along the weight of that lie; we have to keep it up, we have to add additional lies to make it work; we have to constantly build a story around it and make other people believe that story. And this is something that everybody has had an experience with. We've all done it, as kids we lied, you tell a little falsehood you think it's harmless, you're like... well they won't know any different, I'll just say this because… I just moved to this new place, or whatever, and then you realize how difficult and how much energy it takes to keep up a lie. There's an incredibly horrible feeling of fear that you're going to be seen, that you're going to be found out and that lie is going to be broken.

"It can make people so opposed to ever revealing the truth, ever facing that shame, that they may hold it for years, before they can actually relinquish it. And when it's done, when it's released, the feeling is a very different experience. It's as if you drop carrying sandbags, like you've had all this weight on you and you drop it all. And, suddenly, you can breathe again and it's like whoa!"

Adam's entire body accompanied his words. Helena laughed at his physical eloquence.

"There's this rush and all the energy that you had created, this false timeline, this fake branch that doesn't lead anywhere, it can't lead anywhere, because it doesn't connect to the truth of who you are; all that energy slams back in and suddenly is now being reintegrated… Now, that doesn't mean it's not going to create some massive waves in your life, because now, yes, you have to deal with the fact that you've been dishonest, that you have broken trust, that you have, you know, whatever has happened, right? But I articulate this journey, because we all know it very well and it's exactly the journey that we're on as a collective human species.

"So you can bring great light and, at the same time, bring great shadow," he continued. "That is the nature of reality, that's how life moves, that's how life grows and it's the places where we've made mistakes, the places where we've lied, the places where we've been ashamed, those are also the crucibles of our greatest growth, those are the things that help us to actually sort out the energetic connections and lineages of what is actual truth in the stream of the true reality, and what is not.

"When you get to know that by getting to know yourself, and getting to know your own trauma, your own shadows and your own falsehood, then you start to be able to see through other people's a lot easier. So, when you have this truth campaign coming out saying this is the truth, it's when you've started out just kind of questioning! And you've realized there's big holes in education, that there's definitely something weird going on behind the scenes, you can tell that people have been lying in so many areas," he said assertively.

"But let us be honest, it's difficult for a lot of people to accept that many sources of information, they've always seen as truthful, aren't," Helena intervened. "Afraid to imagine that many foundations they have in their own life aren't reliable, they're rotten inside, they have to fall down, and they will have to go through a lot of suffering and change in the midst of chaos; it's not easy for people to accept some 'new' truths that will dethrone the old ones, and will force them to recognize that they've been blind all their lives, or didn't want to see;

not to mention the painful stuff and changes and stormy tunnels they'll have to go through when facing the truth! Pain and suffering that they don't want to feel anymore, scars that are deeply carved inside, open wounds from this or other lifetimes... So, what do you think it could help?" asked Helena.

"Well there's a simple way to approach this great quandary of pain and suffering, and why and what is all this about. And I'm not going to take the Buddha's approach that, if you just sit still in the middle, it all goes away. Because to one extent, yes, you can walk a middle path and stay centered and suffer a lot less, but you may also grow a lot less as well, right?

"So there's different ways to approach the path of evolution and the nature of soul growth; and when I look at this shadow, when I look at that, which is the pain and the challenge and the suffering, what I generally see is that these shadows, these places of darkness, the stuff that we're scared of, that we don't want to face, death, the experiences of dishonour, of oppression, of conflict, of dominance, to use different words, these kinds of experiences and their repressive faculties... We've all had this experience, you go so deeply into an emotional well, it's almost like everything else goes away, but that current of emotion. And that's terrifying: Am I going to lose myself to this? To this horrible thing? To this evil? And so people try to put it away, push it back, put it in a shell, ignore it, don't feel it, right? These are all defence mechanisms, because we're terrified that we're going to die, if we go through that portal. And, yet, what's really interesting is, we get pulled back to it over and over again. Somehow life brings it up again. How does this happen to me again? No, I can't deal, right? We fight it every time until, one day, we surrender to it. We actually let ourselves go into it, and we rage and we cry and we let it flow, and suddenly something moves; it's like the core of the knot, the core of the black hole, the core of this vortex that they would call a Samskara…

"You get into the core of that knot and suddenly something happens; the emotions of pain, of fear, of anger, all that cross over into something else, because we're surrendering to the current of the whole field of emotion. As they would say, the sort of divine feminine current reveals that all the emotion is, in fact, love. That there is only goodness inside all of that pain, but we can't actually experience that goodness, until we fully surrender to it. Until we fully allow ourselves to experience all of what it is; because once we do that, it's like a seed and that seed suddenly opens up, because we've put our consciousness inside that singularity, inside that point of darkness.

"And, suddenly, there's space. We start to put together how we've been in this pattern of pain. We start to see why we did it, what happened, how did we get led to this moment, what was the past life experience that started this whole track and this whole pattern.

"You might realize that part of your entire soul's existence was connected to this horrible evil thing, or perception of yourself, and you don't have to see it that way anymore, you don't have to hold it as something to be afraid of. You recognize that it's part of the living unfolding pattern of life, and that seed of shadow blooms itself into this incredible lotus and consciousness evolves… In that moment, you've literally just unlocked one of the keys to the entire universe! You've opened up more information and more energy and more possibilities for what can be. And that is a huge gift!"

Adam expounded these ideas as if he were playing a long piece of music; the words, phrases, ideas, were all intertwined, like music notes in a symphony that was being unleashed there. There was passion in what he shared, and Helena took it all in a silence of someone who sees and feels, listening, a fixed smile on her face.

"If we wonder where is all of this going, well, inevitably, when you have deep spiritual experiences, you come to realize that part of this whole thing is the self realizing the self, it's God realizing God, it's consciousness realizing consciousness and awakening to more consciousness... so it's got to grow, it has to evolve, it has to change, it's got to move, that's just the nature of space time, that's the nature of the universe, that's the nature of galaxies and planets and stars," Adam continued looking at the stars, "and so when you face your shadow, and you unfold its seed, you experience its fruit and the gift of life, and consciousness that arises when you face those dark places. You're participating in the evolution of the universe itself!"

The stars seemed to come closer, also taking part in the conversation. They remained there watching them twinkle above the pyramids.

"There's a huge amount that comes with simply remembering... to remember more of who you are, and access more of your gifts, and reconnect with the lineage of your being," Adam said.

"Did you talk about it during your interview on Gaia Channel?" she asked.

"Yes. When I was in high school I had a dream where I flew into the sky and then went through a stargate in the Big Dipper and I ended up on a planet that had two suns. I arrived to a two sun star system, and flew down to a planet, and found a place there that was my home… that I knew was my home, and an observatory and… I woke up from the dream, like… what is a dual sun system like??? Where is a dual star system? And I'm searching on the internet, and I came across the Dogon tribe telling a story about beings from this other planet that had two suns, you know, coming down and teaching them about their star system and it was Sirius A and B... and so that was like a little hint."

"Wow! In Italy, I was with a friend that stayed with the Dogon tribe!" shared Helena.

The moon now appeared next to the pyramids, dazzling to the eye. A silence filled with thoughts.

"If this were yours, mine, last life on this wonderful planet, what do you think is most important to enjoy life, have the best experience possible, and provide the best service to future generations and Gaia?" asked Helena touching her belly, each day more protruding. "Since I'm pregnant, this question is more and more present."

"For a species to actually get to a point where we can become a part of a larger interplanetary society, I mean, it's a huge arc and it's at the heart of major transitions that we see on the planet... It's like, how do we unlock just that one next step in technology, in science, in understanding, that frees us from our fear of lack of resources? And that unlocks our ability to be stewards of our planet, instead of constantly taking, extracting, and needing, needing, needing? Why don't we realize that consciousness and space-time are connected and we can generate what we need?! And we can actually produce what we need in a lot more efficient ways!

"But coming to your question... When you get to the kind of higher perspective of looking at your life, and what's really valuable in each lifetime, what I always come back to it's relationships, it's experiences, it's actually letting yourself do things and have experiences! Try novel things, try something different, something you've never done before, I don't care what it is like, just try it... and be okay with it. It could be perceived as good or bad by society, like who cares, give it a shot, feel into what serves you, feel into what moves you, where does your consciousness expand or contract, you know? What brings you joy, what brings you pain, like, are either of those things good or bad in the long run?

"Well, I mean, pain is growth in some ways, and so there's good in there, and good is good and that's great too! And joy is amazing, bliss is wonderful, and there's many ways for us to experience that. So I'd say connecting with new kinds of people, exploring your being, exploring your body, its powers and abilities, exploring your sexuality and all of the different interesting amazing fruits and dynamics of how you can experience your sexuality in life!

"You're educating your mind, getting to know how you can look and perceive connections and patterns; you're developing your heart and your communion with people, and really getting to know what love is and support is... and learning how to let go really painful and difficult relationships that don't seem to let things evolve, because they're just too full of fear, and dropping it, and moving on, and creating new relationships that do enable you to grow, and to feel like you can be yourself; you're learning how to express your gifts, your truth!

Helena nodded.

"Every kind of experience is a gift and it's worth opening ourselves up to it," continued Adam. "Now, of course, certain kinds of experiences, if we choose them, are going to cause us, and other people, a great deal of pain, and I don't recommend doing that. Go back to the Wiccan Rede 'An ye harm none, do what ye will'. Because you don't want to do something, that's actually directly creating harm in somebody else. You want to do our best to avoid that, and as the golden rule says, do unto others as you would have them do unto you. And recognize also that, when you intentionally hurt somebody, the power of the impact of that choice comes back at you usually by the power of three times."

"Three..." Helena echoed.

"Which means it's going to be three times harder when it comes back! So that's a very simple groundwork of ethics for living an incredibly diverse, amazing and exploratory life, and causing as little pain as possible for others, while facing pain as it arises, and growing, and becoming an amazing soul and an amazing being!"

"I remember a story Donna Eden told on her Energy Medicine course," said Helena. "She saw energy all her life, and she was saying that, as a child, she thought everybody could see the same… So, one time, a little boy was passing by with a beautiful and colorful aura and then some girls just started to make fun of him, like many children do, and his aura instantly transformed, contracted and darkened. Donna just didn't understand how people could do that to others, seeing what happened… and yes, if people saw auras, they would know how their words could harm people.

"When I think that we have experiences that mirror what's inside us, or that we are like an antenna that attracts whatever is on the same frequency, I think of people who don't love themselves. Who are very hard and demanding with themselves in thoughts, emotions and actions. I've been talking about this, and I'd like to know what you think," she said.

"Well it goes back to that journey of self-acceptance, I mean, in terms of will I be loved, or I will be loved just if I do or be or achieve this or that. So, this conditional thinking of love really shapes the future, your relationships, your things, and your way to relate... and you really condition your love for yourself, because you don't like yourself this part and the other and whatever…

"Sometimes when I think about the collective, it's like the truth: you have so many pieces of the puzzle that you have to connect and it's also the same with each one of us, isn't it? We have to do the work, because it's very difficult for you to really understand the whole, and all these things, if you are still not accepting yourself.

"When we're deeply honest with ourselves and really connected to self-acceptance, then we communicate, in our relationships, who we are and what we need; what we want and how we want to live our lives."

Helena looked at Adam. Adam looked at Helena with a beaming smile.

"It's funny, because we don't actually get what we want until we accept in ourselves! Accept all the parts of you! And the more deeply you do that, the more empowered you will feel in communicating that truth to others. And the more you will align yourself, the more you'll find people that enjoy life the same way that you do," said Adam.

And there they remained, side by side, in silence, each lost in their thoughts and memories, until Helena decided to retire to her room, saying her thanks for the conversation, the meal, the inspiration, already a little excited about the following day and the intimate conversations she might have with the pyramids.

On the following day, with the love potion vibrating with a youthful joy in their bodies, Helena, Finbar and Ada crossed the Giza plateau, approaching the pyramids in the footsteps of the gods.

Almost the entire universe is invisible to the eyes, Helena thought as she looked around her, on that approach to the pyramids on camelback. She recalled Thomas talking to her enthusiastically about how 4% of the universe is composed of baryonic material, protons, neutrons, electrons, everything making up the Periodic Table and which forms the stars, the galaxies, the clouds of intergalactic gases, the planets, our bodies, everything that is visible... The question was: could our philosophical comprehension of the world be based solely on 4% of everything that exists in the universe? The baryonic matter interacts with electromagnetic radiation, light, radio waves, microwaves, ultraviolet radiation, gamma rays, infrared radiation, and so our biological bodies interact with radiation... and our science and technology has evolved in this direction, but if 96% of the universe is made of Dark Matter and Dark Energy, invisible to our eyes, how much do we have to learn about with our eyes shut?

This was also the question that Helena took to the pyramids, a true interface between the civilisations of the past and those of the future. Like a continuous access point to certain ancient aspects of the consciousness of the planet and, at the same time, future civilisations that are yet to come into being. She was no longer searching for "The" truth, but for truth, truths that would enlighten her as a mother, as a daughter, as a woman, as a creator.

Inside one of the pyramids they experienced the real path once walked by the initiates, wandering with no expectations or particular direction, absorbing the energy of the place in a magical synchronicity. They meditated together within the Chamber of the King and the Queen, joining hands, minds and hearts; they asked for memories to be unblocked, becoming very emotional, with many tears and much laughter and, in this expansion of consciousness, they imagined and envisioned the best possible future.

They felt that state of love that they had experienced every day since Edfu was the great portal of the spirit. It was also the best playground to imagine the preferred version of future reality, embodying it and infusing it with the vibration of gratitude, of love, of joy and excitement. The mind's imagination established the GPS coordinates, the body was the vehicle, love and passion were the fuel to propel them in that direction.

Helena clearly felt that the moment of meeting her mother had arrived, the one who had loaded her with love for nine months and had literally been her entry portal in this life. Many of the feelings of resentment, betrayal, anger, seemed to have diluted in the waters of the Nile, buried in those sands, and there was clarity and joy gaining ground within her.

Before returning to Cairo, they had spoken about exploring what the eyes couldn't see; the underground world of Giza, the Tomb of Osiris. It hadn't been easy to get permission in such little time, but Finbar had already taken groups to the pyramids, knew the right people and was able to get special permission to explore the hidden underworld of the Egyptian Plateau of Giza. At the day's end they were then driven to an iron entrance under the walkway between the pyramids. The inspector handed the key to Helena and gave her the honour of opening the secret door to the Tomb of Osiris.

A few steps beyond the heavy gate they came to a square opening in the ground. The inspector pointed to an iron stairway leading down to a first shaft. From what Helena could make out, the stairway didn't look too sturdy, but she went down without saying a word, her heart racing. They were told that there were three lower levels, the lowest leading to the water tunnels more than 38 metres below the ground.

The first level opened up into a spacious, yet empty, room. The air was heavy with dust, the temperature high. They continued on their descent to the second level, the longest, barely lit, when they found a room with six or seven niches for large sarcophagi. Only two black basalt and granite sarcophagi remained, both empty with their heavy lids slightly ajar. They wandered around, feeling. According to Herodotus, the ancient Egyptian priests spoke of a long tradition of creating underground chambers by the original builders of ancient Memphis.

Looking below, they saw the steps leading down to the third underground chamber where the sarcophagus was to be found, the one they said had never been opened; Ada recalled Kathy J. Forti mentioning just this. And that she had managed to analyse the waters to be found on this third level.

"She discovered that the water was salty. And the only saltwater lake known of in Egypt is Lake Moeris, which is 80 kilometres southwest of Cairo. Today it is called Lake Qarun."

"Ah! I remember Matias talking about that lake," Helena said excitedly. "That after passing all 33 tests through the temples and pyramids, after facing death and being reborn, the ceremony to become a true Arsayian, the one who would speak to the world, was to make a lone crossing of the Habbadabtra, the 'mirror of the beyond', which is now Lake Qarun, exactly. They had to cross this great lake, in a boat, at night, when the stars were reflected in the water; they had to lie down in the dark waters, naked, and float with the stars reflected there... It was like swimming with the gods! Only they knew that that water was full of crocodiles... If you did this you would be part of the divine on earth."

"I could never swim with crocodiles! I wouldn't pass that test," Ada replied, laughing a little.

"That lake is also the site of the Hawara pyramid complex," Finbarr added. "Greek legend tells of the labyrinth, hidden above and below the ground, that contained Twelve Great Halls, twelve large chambers, larger than football pitches."

"Twelve Great Halls... this reminds me of our experience... in the twelve small rooms," Helena said, a smile on her lips.

"So much information that overlaps," Ada mused.

"And we're only just starting to piece together the puzzle that has eluded us for centuries!"

"Yes. When Herodotus wrote about the paths between the Hawara Labyrinth and the Giza Plateau he certainly knew what he was talking about," Finbar remarked.

They smiled at each other, embarking on another descent. The hairs on Helena's arms stood on end when she reached the last step.

"Oh, I can't tell if I just shivered or something else," she said, showing her arm.

"Kathy J. Forti also mentioned this, that her magnetometer had a very high reading. Maybe they're right. It's not a tomb, but a portal between dimensions."

"Wow, now that really gives me the chills... these have been some truly intense days, but I'm not sure if I'm up to travelling between dimensions," Helena joked.

"Don't worry. Only those who have the right DNA can ever hope to open the sarcophagus. It has been hermetically sealed using some kind of ancient technological process," said Finbarr.

"Like King Arthur's sword... And how do you know that I don't have the right DNA?" she answered, laughing.

They laughed for a while and then fell silent, navigating for some minutes through the sensation of mystery filling that underworld, before then deciding to go back up. It was time to end the day next to the Sphinx, now that they were all alone in the complex given that it had long been closed to the general public.

When Helena sat in front of the Sphinx, a crystal hanging over her chest, she closed her eyes, put the sound of shamanic drums in her headphones and let herself be carried away. The lion came to her, that powerful animal, with the invincible radiance of Grandfather Sun, bringing self-confidence and courage to face up to all of earthly life's adversities.

Helena knew that, if the spirit of the lion was presenting itself to her, this was the right moment to face any challenge, to roar at her fears and conquer the internal conflict that was standing in her way. In the hero's journey she was travelling, the lion heart brought her personal power to the surface, where love was the invincible light brightening any darkness. It was time to go to France, where her mother was.

France

The moment it became clear to her that she should go to France, Helena starting making plans. She felt that she needed a break from so much travelling, so many emotions, that Thaís needed this too, and so, inspired once again by Mary Magdalene's journey, she decided to spend some time in that area around the Pyrenees, Languedoc, Provence, as it had appeared in her dream.

Searching along the Cathar Trail for a place to stay, totally intuitively she discovered the magic of Les Contes and its owner Anaiya, and made an open-ended booking for an apartment there.

But her arrival at Bed & Breakfast Les Contes proved even more magical than she could have imagined. The energy of the place could already be felt from the road, from where she could see the white building, with its light-blue shutters, its windows to the sky. The greenery of the mountains behind it, the huge expanse of lawn before it, and the narrow tree-lined drive crowning that entrance, which she could tell, deep within, was fascinating.

Anaiya and Pete's warmth went hand in hand with the wisdom rooted in that place. In the walks accompanied by goats along the stream, in the stories Anaiya Sophia told by candlelight, her powerful transmissions, sat alone in the chapel dedicated to Notre Dame de Sophia, Our Lady of Wisdom, in the birdsong in the early hours of the morning, when the colours of the rising sun touched everything around her, in the blessings and natural beauties of the place that welcomed her into that state of grace in which she felt.

There she could feel her belly growing with each day, with a joy and liveliness that she was unable to explain, while at the same time wrapped in a calm like no other, gradually taking in everything that had happened to her in the last months of her life.

There she felt it was the moment to turn her mobile phone back on, which she had left switched off ever since she had left Italy. She had even bought another one so she could make the calls she needed to make; not because she wanted to stay "connected" there, but because it seemed the right moment to her to receive the messages that she had avoided until then. It was also time to open all the emails that her parents had sent during those months, as well as those from Thomas.

She now had different eyes, different ears, a different body, another heart to receive whatever was awaiting her. There was also a profound wisdom, coming to her from her belly, from Thaís, from that chalice that she was, memory from other eras too, that was awakening and continually expanding in that ancient and sacred land. She felt strong again, inside, and invisibly supported by an entire sisterhood of very wise and compassionate women.

There she wrote long letters to Thaís, in a notebook for her alone, that she would like to give her one day. She spoke to her about Mary Magdalene and that she was feeling her presence again. MM, her initials, are also the Roman numerals for this Millennium, and Helena liked to take note of these signs.

She wrote:

"In the silence of night, if you listen closely, you can hear echoes of the songs that many troubadours sang here about the fruit of her womb, the Sangraal, the living mysteries of the Grail and the Sang Raal, royal blood, the lineage of Jesus.

I am a woman and, when you read this, you will also be a woman. I cannot know what you will be thinking at that time, but in my view, Mary Magdalene is one of the manifestations of Sophia, bringing this wisdom to earth and reminding us about it two thousand years later.

Much has been written in recent decades, and I wonder what will be discovered in the next 30 years. For some authors, Mary herself is the Grail, or her uterus is the Grail as the bearer of the lineage, or her very body is considered a sacred vessel. Whereby each one of us is a potential bearer of the Grail. With you, in me, growing, this is what I feel. You are a secret revelation. You carry in you a wisdom that embraces the world, the whole cosmos, and in me you make the sacred in my life more conscious.

With you I perform daily rituals of connection with the spirit of the earth, and with the stars and our guides. I feel keenly attuned to the external forces of nature, but also to the inner world of the spirit. I see my body transforming every day. I feel you growing stronger and more present inside me. I look at myself in the mirror, naked, and I only see myself as a sacred alchemical vessel of creation and transformation, a true Guardian of the Sacred Mysteries.

We are in desperate need of a new culture of love and wisdom, harmonising the spiritual plane with the material one, communing each day with nature, remembering the storyteller that lives within us, the singer, the dancer, the creative self, developing the sage that lives in our heart... This is what I have been trying to do, here with you, on the Cathar Trail.

For many eras, to open themselves up to other realities, to explore other states of consciousness, humans would use chanting circles, the sound of drums, rattles, bones and stones, the pipe and the sacred fire, plant medicine, power animals, totems, crystals, pilgrimages, sacred directions, rituals, meditation, contact with spiritual masters, rhythms, music, dance and body movements, connection with the elements of nature, and so many other paths... Here, in Montségur, so close to nature embracing Les Contes, in the church of the village of Rennes-le-Château, perched atop a steep mountain, in the glow of the planet Venus, which here at night seems to shine a light on my lap, I connect with the legacy of Magdalene every day.

She has invited me to fully embrace my fragile and luminous reality, to be left with what really matters, to dig the depths of my being, while I search for what seems the most authentic, now, in this exact moment. She has invited me to be gentle with my limitations and to honour my intuition and to feel.

With her, I have also recovered my sensual and passionate nature, which had been fractured and damaged when I was separated from your father. Your conception, Thaís, never forget, is imbued with divine love and earthly passion, in a sacred marriage. When the knight finds the Grail a being is created. This in the encounter of the masculine and the feminine in our own interior. Pregnant with you, I feel the world, life, strength and unconditional love.

I remember hearing Satish Kumar say that, in his next incarnation, he would like to be a woman. Because, he said, the next transformation and change that we need in our world is the resurgence or resurrection of feminine values. He insisted that we need the masculine as much as the feminine, but that, at the moment, we need the feminine more, because there is a kind of exaggerated and overwhelming masculine principle at work in the world today.

At the moment, what seems clear and important to me, is that each of us, men and women, can harmonise this masculine and feminine within ourselves, to then go on to reflect this harmony to the world. And perhaps because of that imbalance that had lasted thousands of years, of focusing on the material, on the outside, on doing, on unbridled competitiveness, on success, we need many men like Satish Kumar, who want to increase these feminine values, to work on them within themselves, with us, to give that harmony back to the world."

When Helena at last got round to reading the emails and messages from her parents and Thomas, she let the tears flow, without trying to stop them for a moment, as if they were a huge river she needed to forge. She wept for two whole days almost unceasingly, interspersing her tears with moments of profound silence. She then took to the trails, with their words in her heart, and walked a long distance, soaking up nature.

Beneath a tree, it was if she heard 'I am reconciled with myself and all of humanity' and this phrase stuck, echoing within her like a song-prayer.

In her mother's messages and emails, she recognised this maternal preoccupation after months of silence and distance, a little incomprehension too, despite her father having explained that there had been a disagreement between them, without wanting to tell her why. Father-daughter stuff, he had said. Reading between the lines, she drank up the deep love that never fades, not even in the throes of disagreement, distance and upheaval. But also, the plea of "I'm your mother. Whatever happened with your father, I just can't accept this estrangement from me. At least tell me that you're alright".

The email letters her father had sent were longer, somewhere between a deposition and a confession. At the beginning, he repeated many times that "he would do it all the same again". Then he started sending shorter, but daily, emails, in the format of a tale, very well written, full of emotion, in which he would recount a different memory every day, something they had experienced together and that had affected him or that he kept in his heart. Memories that Helena recognised as vivid and true too.

Thomas' emails were spaced out, like the space he wanted to give her, but in them he condensed his intense feelings, overflowing like a torrent. Helena reread one of them many times.

"I know that I am unable to give you a true account of the endless jumble of feelings that jostle inside of me with each day that I receive no news from you. It reminds me of prisoners, marking the passing of days on the wall. I too am making hash marks on the walls of my body, making a tally of the passing time. And all I can write is little more than the visible tip of an iceberg.

I've been left in the dark without you. I read Khalil Gibran's poem on love, and I feel its words in me, because I have felt pruned, trimmed, shaken at my deepest roots.

I go back in time with the precision of a man from the future, because, to know the seed of this love of ours, I need to travel back to its origins. I think of its birth somewhere along this time line, because this gives me the strength to endure this emptiness. To accept that it couldn't have happened any other way.

Our story is coloured by transcendence. When we contemplated each other, we suspended time. Every gesture seemed to take on the essence of what dreams are made of. When we touched, we expanded. We lost the boundaries of our bodies. Under your gaze, which you offered to me with a smile, you brought me a childish cloud of admiration, an enamoured, child-like gaze that made me believe that I am, that I could be what your eyes were seeing. My heart then played the most perfect melodies that only the most sensitive of maestros would know how to conduct.

I know that this place that we make clings to eternity, but despite making the concept of time disappear, I'm afraid in this waiting, my whole body aches in this distance, my chest has splintered under the weight of this doubt to whether we can ever feel pure and light again. I have to tell you. Over-inflated, I feel like a balloon about to burst. I no longer know what to do. What you expect me to do.

I know that you are walking your path and I accept this, but I want to believe that, if you were to allow me to come to you, we could continue on that path together, getting through whatever we need to get through, enabling our great love to become even stronger."

She felt the urge to reply to him, so she did, saying nothing more than "our love lives in me". She didn't feel the time was right yet to reply to her parents. She needed to talk to her biological mother before this and, now that it was almost May, she booked her train ticket for a week's time. And, that same week, gently immersed in feminine knowledge, she had the rare opportunity to talk to four women that she really wanted to listen to, in a conversation about truth.

Pam Gregory was one of them. Helena had been following her work for years. Pam had stumbled across astrology 47 years ago and, ever since, it had become a lifelong journey of study. She was passionate about helping people through astrology, which, in recent years, she has done primarily through her book and YouTube channel, which has reached hundreds of thousands of people. For Pam, that profound language, of sacred geometry and meaning, helps us to see the overall picture in the context of our spiritual journey and evolution of life on earth.

Another of those four women was the South African Judith Kusel. An inspiring writer and Soul Coach, who gave Soul Readings to people all over the world, helping them to reconnect with their own souls, and with their highest purpose and vocation.

Sarita Cameron was the third. Helena has already done various meditations with her. A shamanic practitioner trained in the ancient forms of the "The Lyceum", a feminine tradition rooted in healing and clairvoyance, her vocation was to enlighten others about how true healing and empowerment come from a sovereign and authentic connection to the self, to the earth, and to the awareness of origin. Sarita also lived in France, in Aquitaine, running a retreat centre called SolHenge and, recently, had also brought her teachings to the world through YouTube.

Marin Bach-Antonson was the fourth. Mystic, quantum healer, Priestess of Mary Magdalene, she has been working for more than 20 years with women, contributing to the awakening of the sacred feminine, also as the founder of the Priestess Rising Mystery School, in the US.

"It's so great that you're here, with me. It's a pleasure and a great honour. You have no idea," Helena said with warmth, placing her hands over her heart. "About eight months ago, I embarked on a journey; I went to Italy at the time, to do research on the subject that was stirring deep within me, and which will form the basis of my next documentary: the truth."

"I mean that's literally my favourite subject," said Sarita enthusiastically. "My whole life I wanted to know where I've come from, why I'm here and where I'm going. I just want to know that, it's what sparks me!"

"How wonderful," Helena continued, excitedly. "I didn't have any particular direction; all I knew was that I just had to let myself go, get out there, keep that focus, keep the light of truth lit, stay tuned in, to see what came up... And, honestly, never in my wildest dreams could I have predicted what happened. In pictures, I imagine Portuguese explorers, out on the high seas, thirsty and hungry, and the skies turn black, the waves crashing down and them having to sail through the storm, masts breaking off, holes in the hull and, as Tolstoy said so well, to save a sinking ship you have to throw out the ballast that had previously prevented it from sinking.

"Basically, this is saying that men can only recognise the truth in its entirety when they have fully freed themselves from all religious and scientific superstitions and all the ensuing sophistic misrepresentations and distortions, by which its recognition has been hampered for centuries

"I think that's a little like what happened to me," Helena continued, "my ship almost went under when I realised that my life has been built on fake foundations... what I mean here is that I was thrown into the water, carried overboard by a giant wave, and I sank down in the dark waters, where I have been swimming underwater for months... It was an incredible journey through the darkness, until I could make it back to the boat, throw that ballast overboard, which, for me, represents the eyes of the past, celebrate my rebirth, set sail once again, but with a different perspective, a different knowledge, a different direction...

"I had many messengers during the journey. After Italy, I went to Mexico, Egypt, and now here in France, along the Cathar Way. So many things have happened! Thaís, my daughter, guiding me from within," Helena said, touching her belly, "and now you, incredible women doing such important work for humanity and so full of love... open and willing to have this conversation with me. Thank you so much, from the bottom of my heart! And here we return to the truth. How to find our own truth and what is the truth?"

"I've always wanted to know the truth, since I can remember," said

Judith. "And I wanted to search the truth... but I wanted to know the truth deep inside me, because I always felt that there was more to life than I can see, you know, more than we were told."

"I was so lucky that I actually ended up being librarian! That was to me the most amazing thing, because I would ask questions and then the books would fall off the shelves, and I would literally open them up at random, and then the answers would jump out at me! So, I always had these invisible helpers who were teaching me… And it also taught me to seek the truth in ways that you would not normally do.

"What a beautiful image of books falling into your lap... And, Sarita, what was your life like? Your story? How did it guide you?" asked Helena.

Sarita let out a short laugh.

"I think from a very young age, I didn't live quite in the same reality that everybody else appeared to live in," she said, chuckling some more. "So I had some gifts. The main gift that I had was that I could read people's minds and it just seemed very normal to me. I was really good at it. I could read verbatim word for word what they were thinking. When I got to my teenage years, I think, with that whole thing of trying to fit in, I lost it a bit, I never quite lost it completely, but then it sort of started to cut and then I had a lot of things that went wrong in those teenage adolescent years.

"I levitated once when I was a very little girl. I was in my garden, I was looking up into a tree, and I just literally came off the earth for a few seconds and then came down! My brother saw me. We never spoke about it, but years later, he came up to me and he said: I saw you that day in the garden! And I knew exactly what he was talking about! So, there was always…

"I saw my grandmother die, a week before she died, and exactly the way she died," Sarita said, remembering. "There were always funny things going on that got me thinking about the nature of reality and time. For example, I didn't realize that I was reading people's thoughts until I was about twelve or thirteen. I was watching these two people have an argument and I suddenly realized that what was coming out of people's mouths was not what they were saying in their heads! I was watching two different conversations, one of them was in the head! So I just had all this stuff going on and so it was always sparking my curiosity, you know?"

Helena nodded her head in agreement.

"My mum divorced my dad when I was like six and I had a very strange life, because I was living two really weird lives," Sarita continued. "My dad was like super rich living in a hacienda in Mexico; and my mum was super poor living in a council house in England. And I was going between these two lives! So, about once a year or once every few years, I would go back and forth…

"So, I was just never normal and then had a series of difficult things that happened to me from teenager to adult. My mum married a violent alcoholic, beyond usual teenage stuff. And then I got ill, because I was very energetically sensitive. I now realized that I was picking up everybody else's illnesses. So I got glandular fever, then I got Amy, then I got cancer, then I had kids, you know, it was all kind of like busy in there. And then, somehow, after all of that, I landed up at a retreat teaching shamanism, I had no idea what I was going to, I hadn't even read about this retreat when I turned up.

"It was the first time I'd left my kids to do something for myself for a week… and I sort of landed in this place! And, you know, the lights went down and I could see and feel they were calling all the spirits into the room. I could see and feel everything! I was like oh I get it now! All of the light bulbs went on! And then I did this training for like seven years. It was a real journey into the self and into authenticity. A journey into giving up pretending to be what I was not! And that's a very difficult journey, because when you make a journey like that, it affects all of your relationships, everything in your life; and you have to let go of everything that is not authentic and those are things that you've been clinging to, because they seem familiar and safe. And, so, you let go of that. It's quite a huge journey, but then when you come out the other side, you're much clearer.

"I came out the other side and started teaching meditation, started doing ceremonies, in my barn, with a few people, and the rest is all an organic coincidence! I don't really know what happened, but I really feel that I'm very clearly doing what I'm supposed to be doing now," said Sarita assertively. "I'm a healer, I give people mentoring, I teach and run ceremony, obviously I do my meditations and they seem to really help people heal themselves, and step into that authenticity, and so that's really what I'm about. I'm about getting to the truth of who you are and letting go of all of the constructs and the restrictions, the mind control, the indoctrination, the matrix that we live in, which is all false, but which we've clung to, because it's what we've known, and it's what we thought we are. I use a myriad methodologies to go there. And that's ever evolving, because as I arrive at one truth, it's like awakening, you know, as you arrive at one truth, you realize that there's a deeper truth underneath that, and it just never stops."

"I was very lucky in that regard," said Judith, "because I worked with banned books and when people complained about books I would have to read them; books beyond my scope that I normally would never have read. And what it did is… it opened my mind first of all! It also made me understand that I'm not there to judge in whatever way. I am just there to seek the truth in the highest way that resonates with me, and to live my truth. Because, in the end, you've got to be able to look yourself in the face."

After some silence, Judith continued along the same line of thought.

"We all - at one stage or another - will be faced with ourselves in so many ways. It's a matter of keeping your path clear! You might not be ready for some truth in the beginning, but, as you grow at soul level, you become ready for truth in a higher level… and then you can also understand that you need to bring out the truth in your own way!

"When I started off on my journey, when I first asked myself why I was born in Africa, my life was caving in. I learned to keep a journal. Whenever information came to me intuitively, I would write that down, put the date and if I couldn't write it in words, then I would sketch it! That has stood the test of time… and it's something that I always teach my students, especially in the beginning, when they need to trust that voice. Because most of them have got such great difficulty trusting their own intuition, what their own gut feeling is telling them.

"I say to them: listen, write that down even if it's one word, even if it is a sentence, you know, just write it down, eventually you will see that gets confirmed. Then, as you see your journey unfold, you look back and you can see how you've been guided, how that inner voice has actually kept you in the right direction, and has helped you so that you can trust it! You will trust it more and more, and then you will actually be able to take those leaps of faith and start living it with all that you are.

"So, I always wrote down what was given, even if I didn't understand it… because with my awakening I was suddenly seeing energy fields, I was asked to take a map of Africa and draw energy lines. I didn't know what they were and also I grew up in a very strict religious background, where you never were told about psychic abilities, or even trusting that, you know? Except for having that connection with God, so to speak.

"I needed to trust that, what was given to me, was not my imagination! And what I learned to do is write it down. I always asked for confirmation and, interestingly, that confirmation would always come from different forms, and then I knew it was okay. Somebody might say something, or I would switch on the radio, a music or a phrase would come in, and it would just be what I needed to hear, so that started my trusting journey!" said Judith.

"Lovely!" Helena remarked. "I would have liked to have done this on my journey; well, I recorded and wrote down some things, but for most of the time I was so deep underwater... And you Marin?" asked Helena.

"My story of becoming? Yeah, I can tell you that there is one specific event that absolutely opened my awareness and got me on this path of awakening and revelation and it starts when I was 25 years old and experienced my very first really intense tragedy. My younger brother, who was two years younger than myself, committed suicide and it was an absolute shock to our family. There were no signs that my brother was troubled in any way, shape or form; he was a great looking athlete, a wonderful kid, just really vibrant and healthy, said Marin with emotion. "However, when that happened, looking back, I learned that I was at a very important place in my life and that I was broken, but I was also open. And what I understand now about that combination is that is an exact crossroad where divine mother or the divine intelligence can reach us.

"I had been pursuing acting and dance as a passion, as a career and as a pathway. I had gone to performing arts high school, I went to college, and was very much pulled in that direction until this happened and I assessed my own inner truth. I recognized: it's not what I want to do anymore; it was a passion, but I had almost outgrown it… and my brother's death gave me permission to stop being the good girl, and playing that good girl archetype, in pursuing that path, because my parents had invested all the money that they did, and my dad wanted a star in the family. For the first time as an adult, I began to really follow my own impulses, and that led me to spiritual teachers, it led me to different ashrams, it led me to yoga - like many of us find our way on the path through the gateway of yoga - and I began volunteering at different spiritual centres at that time.

"The moment that my life opened, I was at the New York Open Centre. I lived in New York City at the time. As a thank you, they gave us a workshop every month. It was my day to pick my workshop and I had two that I could choose from: I could either go to a Feng Shui workshop or I could go to a Women's Autumn Equinox Ceremony and I was weighing both of them… oh I want to do both! Looking back, I have no clear idea what made me choose the Autumn Equinox Ceremony except that I remember thinking well, I love the fall in New York City, so I'm gonna go to that one.

"I had no idea what equinox even meant! I had no idea what a woman's ceremony was, but I chose that one… and, on the night that it was being held, my subway was late, and so I got to the event just a couple minutes later than it had started. When I opened the door and I walked in, the best way that I can describe this is that I had a visceral biological memory… there was a scene in that room where the lights were low, and the women were in a circle, and the candles were lit and the priestess was drumming a beat that was dropping everybody into their body, and when I saw this for the first time in this lifetime, something in me remembered, in my blood, in my bones, in my soul, I remembered this thing that was sisterhood, ceremony, sacred space, ritual and the appropriateness of it all was overpowering to me!!

"And I went through the evening unable to control the buzzing in my body. I felt so aligned, excited, at home, and I went right up to the priestess who facilitated afterwards; she was an older woman and I practically grabbed her by the shoulders and I said: I have to do what you do! And she took a liking to me and was sort of, you know, overcome by my energy and my clarity and, after several talks and teas, she invited me to be an apprentice to a woman that was walking the path of the priestess. I was young, I was only twenty-five years old, and what happened for me was I got to be re-womaned!

"My relationship with my womanhood, the rightness of my body, the power of my blood, the wisdom of my womb, the magic that was lying dormant inside of my cells, it all came online! And I know that, on that day that I hit that door frame for that autumn equinox ceremony, although I could never have understood it at the time, what I understand now is that my priestess codes got activated that evening and that was the beginning of the unfolding of the rose of my heart, the rebirth of Marin in this lifetime. And that began my story of becoming," said Marin.

"Oh my goodness… Beautifully put," Helena said, with a large smile. "And you, Pam?"

Pam stopped for a moment, looking down at the ground.

"You made me think very deeply today," said Pam. "Actually, I think the story really began when I was tiny. I've never talked about this publicly, but I had an extremely dysfunctional childhood. I won't go into that, it doesn't matter anymore, but really from the age of three I was thrown back on my own resources, and I was very aware that there was only me that could support myself emotionally as it were! And then there was another very big kind of crisis point at the age of seven, and I remember that crystal clear, I can see myself… and I made a very mature decision: I am never going to live like this, I'm never going to live in this level of chaos and destruction! I'm going to work hard, I'm going to university, I'm going to immigrate to Canada and I'm going to have a great life!

"And I did all those things! I absolutely delivered on those strong intentions at the age of seven. I think that I did all those things, because of those childhood experiences! And it really continued almost in my social life, because I was there, it was a tiny village, way up in Northern England, very rural, very beautiful, but no other child of my age in the village. Even when I went to school, many miles away, because of my home background, I was very isolated essentially. So, I always had this sense of isolation growing up, and that can kind of go either way, you know, it can make you or break you. But looking back now, that was very difficult, but I actually am thankful for what it taught me, because it constantly threw me back on my own resources, it made me go on deeper pathways, it made me think very deeply, it made me think very independently, because I was never on the same page as anyone else!

"I think those have been great assets actually in my life, that sense of self-determination, self-sufficiency and just being able to cope whatever the external circumstances. In today's world, that's actually quite useful skill!

"But the real epiphany with astrology is when I emigrated to Canada. First week joined a yoga class, met this amazing big man from Jamaica, the astrologer, and then spent seven hours with him… and that was my epiphany… how could it be, that there was this entire realm of meaning, that I'd been completely unaware of until then, that was so precise and so accurate? This man didn't know me, he didn't even know my surname, I just arrived in the country two weeks beforehand, so how was it possible to know so much? And that really took me on a deep dive... and actually I'm still on it all these decades later! I'm still kind of holding my nose on that deep dive... I haven't come up yet. Because I don't think you ever get to the end of that exploration with astrology! There are so many layers to it, you know?" said Pam.

"With all you all went through, I wonder," said Helena, touched by Pam's words. "Do we really have to have traumatic experiences, pain and suffering, and go through dark nights of the soul, to wake up and really connect to our inner truth?" she asked.

It was Marin who answered.

"I can't speak of that as a divine truth for everyone. What I can speak of is that was absolutely the case for me, that there is a dance between the paradox of light and dark. Although we often think of the dark, like the dark night of the soul, as something bad, wrong, challenging or hard, we often feel like we're in an encased tomb, when parts of us feel like they're being squeezed and are even dying... What I recognize now, looking back, was that darkness was the womb that I was gestating in and I didn't even realize it! So, yes, in my opinion and from my personal understanding, there's absolutely an interplay between pain and purpose, light and dark, death and birth, and it's perfect divine intelligence."

"Humans seem to need adversity to wake them up, which is lucky, you know, because we have a lot of it on this planet," said Sarita. "If you really wanted to get down to it, I think it's because we're programmed to be heads down: do what you're told, nine to five! We're basically contained and constrained, but when you have something like the death of a loved one, you can't put that in a box, you just can't put it in a box like your nine to five job, or eating three times a day, or watching... you can't put it in a box, it does something to that infinite spark of your quantum consciousness that reminds you of who you are. It wakes you up... yeah, it's normally adversity... and some people will not even wake up through adversity!"

Helena immediately recalled Arkan Lushwala's book, *Black Jaguar*, which she had already read, but now, when picking it up again and reading it with different eyes, with a different consciousness, it had taken on a greater meaning. He said that, no matter how difficult times had been for the survivors of a wave of destruction, they always have the opportunity to recover their happiness, using the power of ceremony, connection with the spirit and the simple truth of the heart.

In his book he related that in indigenous cultures and in all the ancient cultures of the earth, there is the practice of studying the changes of the main cycles of life. The cycles that intensely affect our life and our collective destiny. So, when we don't listen to the cosmic rhythm, we trip and fall. He said that it was time to change and that if we don't change something stronger than us will do it for us. Which, with the events of recent years, especially the pandemic, was now very clear to everyone.

Helena reread that "sages of many Indigenous nations and other ancestral nations of the world say that we are now at the end of a very long cycle. There are small cycles, like the 500 year cycles; there are bigger cycles that last around 2,000 years; and there are even longer cycles, always containing smaller cycles within them. These longer cycles are the time of a complete humanity that lasts almost 26,000 years. According to the memory kept by some Indigenous nations, there were three other humanities before ours, so we are part of the fourth humanity. Now we are not only at the end of one long cycle of around 26,000 years, but we are also at the end of four of these cycles that amounts to 104,000 years of human experience. Many endings are happening at the same time, which means that a big change is ready to happen. These 104,000 years are the longest cycle we have ever completed. After this, the fifth humanity will begin."

In Arkan Lushwala's words, he too sharing the knowledge he had received from various elders, the complete cycle of a humanity involves three movements. First comes the time of creation, next comes the time of conservation, and last is the time of renewal.

The time of creation is that magical time that is spoken of today in myths, legends and stories. This is the moment in which the creative capacity of humans, bolstered by powerful cosmic forces, knows no impossibility. It is the time of conceiving and constructing the forms that will become vehicles and recipients for the essences that are to be developed. A moment of great power and happiness, driven by an extraordinary possibility of expanding consciousness to places never before visited by the heart and by the human mind. This is a moment in which divine beings guide men and women.

After a few thousand years in that place of creation, we reach the time of conservation. The creative forces start to dwindle and now the darkness is needed to temper what has been created. In this time, humans are tested and learn how to become stronger by dealing with difficulties. To connect with creative forces requires effort or an infinite grace.

In Arkan's view, some people pass through that period in the best way – singing, dancing, laughing – while others find it really hard to deal with their suffering. Scared of losing the light from the beginning, some humans of this era tend to become more conservative than creative, more educated than spontaneous. Others become more rigid and authoritarian, creating rules and upholding traditions that are zealously passed down from generation to generation.

Helena recognised this, not only collectively, but also individually, in every life story.

Of the three, the time of conservation is the longest. And it always ends when the essence of the beginning is forgotten, when the magic can only be found in certain stories, and young people rebel against formalities that have no relevance or explanation. Helena recalled Joe Cocker singing, *I heard my father say, Every generation has its way, A need to disobey, N'oubliez jamais, It's in your destiny, A need to disagree, When rules get in the way, N'oubliez jamais.*

At the end of this time of conservation, corruption among those who have held positions of power for a long time is also evident. The tension continues to rise until humanity becomes like a bomb, ready to explode, or a woman, ready to give birth. This is when the third movement arrives: the time of renewal. This is the shortest and most intense of the three, the time when purification is required for life to be able to continue.

For Arkan Lushwala, we live in this time of renewal. Helena agreed. The time of a purifying chaos in which lies are seen for what they are, and there is a collective desire to the return to the simplest truth. Arkan described it perfectly. In this confused era, ancient groups and ethnic identities lose their strength and millions of humans are unsure about their future and their true place in the world. The social pillars and belief systems of the conservative past have crumbled and new pillars are yet to be built.

The collective state – which is similar to being in labour – is laced with a mixture of pain, fear and great hopes. This moment is the hardest and also offers more opportunities for anyone striving to free themselves of the old mental prisons. But it is also the most dangerous time for anyone who resists it, because its energy is iron-fisted and incontestable. It also has the potential to quickly return all those who act in favour of real change to the light.

"I'm coming from an astrological perspective and I'm just going to do the best job I can, with as much love in my heart as I can, to help people through this transition. Because humanity's on a big ride right now!" said Pam.

This is where the great change takes place, so that a new time of creation can arrive and find cleansed, open hearts to see and support the blossoming of a new, uncharted world. But this is also where many people experience great losses in their lives; some are brutally ripped from their comfort zones. Many see their old life is no longer working, or live in fear of seeing the destruction happening to the rest of the world. It can only mean one thing: it's time to change.

"I'm reading again the book *The Time of the Black Jaguar: An Offering of Indigenous Wisdom for the Continuity of Life,*" Helena said. "And from my point of view, everything Arkan writes is truly a great gift to any of us, in this moment in time. For him, real change happens in three different ways.

"The first way is a gift from the Spirit, a huge blessing that comes to us unexpectedly through a dream, an extraordinary meeting with someone, a transformative encounter, or an event that awakens our mind. He says that this gift is like a loan from the Spirit, so that we have the spiritual capital we need to start doing our own work. I think this is so poetic...

"The second path is the path of the Black Jaguar, who comes and says 'Enough!' and destroys the prisons in which we feel safe and comfortable so that we can wake up. The so-called adversities...

"The third way is the will of the heart. This path of the will of the heart allows us to constantly reach out to sacred sources that support our awakening.

"Only that in times of renewal, such as the one we're going through now," Helena continued, "the most predominant way, because it is the quickest and we have so little time, is indeed that of adversity. And after having been pushed into the storm myself, I believe, that if we are deeply connected to our inner awareness, we can always choose the path of our heart's will. Avoiding the path of suffering. I want to at least believe in that. That I can walk the rest of the path with new eyes, the kind that are always open to transformation.

"I also feel that our lives will always fluctuate, from happiness to pain and back again. It's all part of it. But the fluctuations might become less frequent if we can develop our own will, if we put in the work to understand ourselves, if the choice is to awaken, more and more, right? That way we're not at the mercy of major upheavals. We take responsibility for our own life, we choose how to look at it, past, present and future. To change the landscape, you just have to change what you feel, I never tire of telling myself this. And there are certain ways of looking, of thinking, of feeling, that help us so much in this dance, don't you think?" asked Helena.

"When I began to really live by the tenet that life is always happening for me, it was very important for me!" Marin shared. "And recognize that, even in the most challenging or frustrating or uncomfortable moments, if I could keep my heart open lean towards the back of my body and trust, give myself over to the mother and trust that everything is happening for me... the perception, the frequency that I was holding, that experience or that circumstance ultimately would open up in a way that served me, as opposed to being detrimental for me!

"I heard a metaphor that was really important for me to understand. Imagine that you're in a busy city, on a really hot sticky humid day. You go to your friend's apartment that's on the very first floor of a building in that city, and she doesn't have air conditioning, it's loud outside, the windows are open and the garbage is stinky, that's one experience at that address!

"Now imagine that you have a friend that lives up on the 33rd floor of that same building, you go up the elevator on the 33rd floor, that friend has got her air conditioning on, she's got cool lemonade for you, she has a deck that overlooks the beautiful river that's right near the city... and your experience on that day, at the exact same address, is different than it was on the first floor. And it's a metaphor for the different dimensional possibilities that are always available to us within the same experience, within the same circumstance, at the same address.

"I really recognize that, at any given moment, it is within my power as a great creator of life - as I don't always have power over the circumstances that are coming to me, or conscious power anyway - but I do have the power of how I'm going to interface with it. And that one tenant, that pillar that is really like embedded within me now 'life is always happening for me', if I can stay there, trust that, live in that frequency, then it's inevitable that it always will open up, that it does happen for me!

"I have one quick example that happened not long ago," Marin continued, remembering. "My car broke down on the side of the road and I was waiting, because there's a flat tire and I thought, oh my god, this is terrible, I was going to miss an appointment, you know? It was such an inconvenience and I sat in my car waiting for the tow and I was just breathing 'life is always happening for me, life is always happening for me'. I have no idea how this is happening for me, but it has to be happening for me in some way shape or form!

"I really tried to just relax and soften into that experience. Well the tow truck guy came and he helped me. We started talking, and he was so lovely, and I was so much more open to that exchange, as opposed to being so frustrated, because I had done that little bit of work of getting back into my heart. And he looked at me afterwards and said," Marin paused, already feeling tears welling up, 'miss, you've totally made my day, my daughter recently passed away and you remind me of her… and I just want to thank you so much!' Life asked me to play an angel for somebody… yeah there was a flat tire, yeah there was an inconvenience, but what a privilege to be able to be somebody's angel that day! And that's when I recognize like, no matter what, I can trust this and that's just a small example."

At that moment, Helena thought that each of us is a library of experiences. These experiences are like stories, they are like books to which we give a title, with which we associate certain emotions, which we label and arrange by subject in the library of our memory. Of course, at any given time, the archive is made according to the perception of the moment, of the feelings experienced, of the consciousness and the possible distance. When we are children, these memories are engraved in stone, they are old books that will greatly influence us, for the most part unwittingly. That's why it's so important to revisit certain memories with different eyes, through different lenses, to be able to change the labels we put on certain books in our library and which ensure that certain wounds remain unhealed.

Helena smiled at the thought that we need to rewrite everything we know, all the labels, all the words of anger, pain, we have new eyes to reimagine everything through our heart. And at how it was so important to look at events of the day through a positive lens.

"The work of getting back into your heart," said Helena, "and how this simple magnificent gesture can change life, all lives, through the guidance of the heart, through love…"

Helena looked at Pam.

"I'd like to think I have a lot of empathy and compassion, because of my background," Pam revealed. "I think sometimes people think oh she's had it so easy, you know, she's had a glorious life and that isn't true. But, the fact that I had that challenging childhood, makes me empathetic and compassionate for whatever people are going through and that brings up a lot of love. I mean, particularly in these extreme times that we're in right now, I have huge love and compassion for people. None of it's easy for any of us. Even if you've got a clear path, it's still challenging on a practical day-to-day level. So, that just brings up immense love and I think many of us have chosen, because of our soul contract, to be here to help people in whatever modality we're operating at this time."

Helena smiled at Judith.

"We just need to understand that every single thought that we think, and every single word we speak, and every action we take is broadcasting out into a certain frequency!" assured Judith. "So I ask every morning that every word that I speak, whether I write it or speak, it will speak directly into the heart, and it will cleave the heart open to the soul, so that they recognize themselves at the soul level. You cannot give anything oddly into the world without being in the state of love.

"Now, I am not aware of what I write or speak most of the time, but I trust that the seeds that I'm sowing will actually go right into the soul, and into the heart. And when I get the reaction back, I think to myself how wonderful, I have let go of my own ego in this respect. It's not about me, it's about what is broadcast through me… I am the instrument, and I'm busy playing the music. It's like a beautiful music. You will always touch the heart strings, and even the most hardened person will start wiping away tears, if the music speaks to them…

"And we've got to remember that sound is something of a divine feminine that's now being brought back. And I have been given lightly the terms that we've forgotten about. Those sounds, I've been told, were always chanted in the ancient mystery schools to open the heart centre and the soul. You didn't need to speak a word, because that sound would immediately go into them at a very deep soul level.

"My father always said to me: the Zulus do not need to speak your language, because they read your heart... they read you, and they give you a name which fits you exactly! And it's the same with animals: will read your energy. Don't ever show fear to animals, because animals will bite you, if you show fear. So, as a child even, I learned that I had to watch out for my own energy and what am I projecting outwards. Often we need to just sit quietly and open our hearts, and then allow the energy from our heart centre to move into their heart centre, which will have far more effect than if we speak too many words," said Judith.

Helena's smile seemed to grow.

"Oh that reminds me the first time I heard you talk about Chariklo, Pam," said Helena. "I was walking with my headphones in nature, and I was like, oh My God, it touched me so deeply... and I saw in your next video, saying that you've received hundreds of emails about it. For me, it was like connecting with the divine feminine wisdom that was repressed and restricted until a few decades ago! It was incredible, and so much connected to the truth: you just can't see, even if it's there, until you can see..."

"Yes indeed! It's so interesting you say that, Helena, because the archetype of Chariklo touched so many people in the same way that it touched you! There was something profound and exquisite and fine and feminine," said Pam. "What was remarkable, was that I heard about her for the first time from Melanie Reinhardt, a wonderful woman who'd done research on Chariklo, and the day I heard about it was the day that the solar eclipse was exactly to the degree, in minute, on my natal Chariklo!"

"Wow!"

"It was a new beginning!" continued Pam. "It's shining a light on something I've been utterly unaware of. It was just a dumb note in my horoscope until then. That was another down the rabbit hole journey! And because she's so exquisite in terms of the Buddha state of being, this permanent state of stillness, that we can drop into in meditation, that she can guide us through states of consciousness, life to death or evolution of consciousness...

"She's coming into our consciousness now and the comment you've made about, you can't see until you can see, that appears to be the case. These new discoveries are made when our consciousness is ready to integrate that archetype and take another step as it were. She has an incredible discovery chart with an almost exact six-pointed star, which feels so auspicious. And, yeah, she's brought in something I think really fine and beautiful into astrology!

"And boy, with these new kind of Kuiper belt dwarf planets being discovered now, there's a whole new level which I think is running parallel to the evolution of consciousness. I need another several hundred years to study that... but that's only one of the amazing things about astrology, that, in some way, it's either leading our consciousness or echoing our consciousness! Or that there's this synchronicity, this melody between the stars! And that, to me, is the harmony of the spheres that Pythagoras talked about!"

Helena thought about Thomas, about their conversation at the Spanish Steps in Rome.

"It's happening to me a lot," said Helena. "It's like opening a veil and boom, everything takes place... and I see what I couldn't see before! And then, for example, I read a book that I had read years before, and say, oh my god, how didn't I see this? It's like revisiting with another understanding and consciousness. You see 'the same' differently, as it happened with *Black Jaguar*."

"It's really interesting," said Sarita. "I started my channel some years ago, I just started it by accident, and when I listened to some of my videos I don't even remember thinking that, I don't even know where some of them have come from. When you're really aligned to your source consciousness, you're in the now, in flow, and source is just moving through you… consciousness, which is love!

"So I think we don't really understand love, the power of it, but we're getting there. I think it's this incredibly potent mixed serum that makes things… that can do anything! And I think that our romantic idea of love is, again, an indoctrinated set up, so we consider it to be airyfairy and wishy-washy, but it's the one thing that everybody wants. And what happens when you fall in love? Bruce Lipton talks about this: you fall in love and it's like nothing is impossible! You can leave your job, you suddenly feel sexier than you've ever felt in your life, just nothing is impossible, because what you've really done is fallen in love with yourself through the eyes of another! You suddenly realize that anything is possible! You're completely amazing and that's like one tiny glimpse of the power of love!" said Sarita.

"Just makes me think about the power of relationships in terms of our own evolution," said Helena, making the connection.

"Because everybody is a mirror unto you, and nobody is more mirrored to you than the ones you love the most!" Judith replied. "Isn't it funny? We sometimes think we can say what we like to those that we love the most! We're nice to other people, but we can be very horrible to the ones that are nearest to ourselves. We're all kind and cruel, nice and terrible, we can't deny our shadow, we are both. We can be kind and we can be cruel, and the thing is that we need to love ourselves from the deepest shadow to the highest light. To be genuine with ourselves! Now, with every relationship, the ones that challenge you the most is showing your own face back to you… all that you have not loved within yourself and you have not owned within yourself!

"Because people will not push your buttons, unless you have buttons to push! So, if somebody starts pushing your buttons, it's very good to sit down and say: why is this pushing my buttons? What do I have inside myself that this is triggering? It might be a childhood memory, that might have come somewhere along the line where somebody shouted at you or used that word, and it's triggering, but it's actually not the person in front of you, but that emotional charge within you.

Once you start asking why, then you also say, okay, where do I have this inside me? Have I done this to other people?

"It's essential to dissolve your charges inside and to love yourself unconditionally, because now you understand that, actually, what you project out in life is what you choose to project out in life! If I choose to be love, then that is what I will radiate out! But if I choose to be angry, then that is what I will go radiate out and what I will also attract… Once you start taking responsibility for your own inner well-being, and for the love that is inside of you, you'll live it within yourself. We cannot teach anybody love, we can only be it ourselves! And we're going in that direction!" said Judith.

"So, imagining we are on the birth canal, but not knowing that" began Helena, "just seeing all the confusion, all the chaos, all the doubts, all the pain, all the suffering, and all the separation also, because there's a lot of separation right now, and people having real trouble to accept the diversity or the difference of positions…"

"I think the divide that you're talking about is really clear," Pam confirmed, "and so many people I know are exactly in those circumstances, like having a dear loved member of the family who has a very different view; so, people are in agony about this, they're struggling, and I've struggled with it too, with people very close to me in my life. But, ultimately, I've come to the decision that if you try and persuade them of your point of view, what happens is you both lower your frequency, because you get into a battle. So, what I've now done is bless them for who they are, because they're good-hearted loving people who just have a very different view to me!

"I think through the coming months, if I look at it astrologically, that division is going to intensify, but with the intensification is going to come more awakening, because it's also the year of truth, and disclosure, we are going to get a lot of truth coming out, and with that truth spilling out which will be utterly shocking for many people, it will also awaken more people...

"And because the world is very complicated right now," Pam continued, "and we're getting a lot of information coming at us every day, most of it very fearful, what do you do? Particularly, if you don't necessarily have a lot of spiritual knowledge, or you don't practice meditation or any of that… I mean, as a child, when I didn't have any of that, my saviour was nature and, luckily, I lived in a very rural area, so I would just disappear from all the chaos with my dog, and I'd be gone for days. Sometimes, my parents didn't notice, because they had lots going on. I just lived in the woods and, in that sense, it was idyllic, the simplicity of nature and the reliability and the silence of the trees, and just dropping into that kind of simplicity that nature could hold, you know, whatever hell and fury was happening around you, that was just a container that could just warmly decompress your energy.

"And I've learned how to hug trees with a wonderful spiritual friend. Apparently, trees are very polite, so you have to ask if you can approach them first of all, then you thank them and you, ideally, you put your heart against the tree, in connection; then you ask the tree to take everything from you that you do not need, and let that run for a few minutes until you feel some energy shifting. Then you say to the tree 'please give me everything I need' and, again, you may feel energy coming back to you. The trees always give me stillness, they give me absolute calm, solidity, you know? Being the calm in the storm as it were, so that's one big simple thing that all of us can do," said Pam.

"When we talk about division," said Judith, "for me, it doesn't matter what other people do, if they want to go and fight each other, I just choose not to engage. Okay, let them go and fight each other, it's their choice, but it's not my choice. I don't want to get involved with that. Because if you are lifted up to a higher frequency band, and you have this absolute oneness with the divine within you, and you embrace your definition in the deepest sense, you cannot live duality anymore… It's impossible, because that's the minute that you get out of sync.

"Every time you actually have a new birth, there will be chaos and destruction, quantum physics tells you that! Within the whole of creation there is a constant rebirth, but with every rebirth comes chaos and destruction. So, the trick is not to get involved.

"I have people telling me 'there's something about you which, immediately, brings calm and love.' I always wanted to know what is the book of love, but when I started working with Mary Magdalena, I understood that we cannot live love, unless we allow ourselves to become a vessel of love; unless we allow ourselves to have a power of love sweeping through us. You cannot be that, if you've got the ego saying I'm on this side and you on that side. It creates separation. But if I come from the heart of love, I cannot see you as opposition.

"Let me tell you, in South Africa, we have violence which nobody else has and this is a daily living thing. We have poverty as people don't know about poverty in Europe. It's daily life in Africa. We have been on the brink of civil war during the apartheid years and you must remember, that apartheid was separation! I remember working in the library, they had books for the white people, books for the black people, books for the Indian people. We went through all of that, and I have to say thank you for my country, because we've literally got everything under the sun.

"When you live in South Africa, you can choose what you see. Are you going to choose the violence? And say the world is so bad, that you make yourself bad? Because with everyone that's violent, there are also the ones that have a big heart… And whenever something happens, they will always come and stick together and help each other. It doesn't matter who's who, but that community will come together, and they will help each other, because the Ubuntu is so much ingrained in the African people, that they cannot not do it; they will always feed each other, and help each other!

"I have learned so much from the African people. Now, if a man called Nelson Mandela had not come and became our president, this country would have been in civil war; and what Nelson Mandela taught me and everybody else, and I remember how people were divided, I mean we had soldiers with machine guns patrolling the streets, that's how near we were to a civil war, but Nelson Mandela was loved by every single South African… and I always felt that he had to sit years in prison to find his inner peace, and to find the deepest forgiveness within himself, so that he could stand in that leadership role!

"It doesn't mean that he didn't have a shadow, of course he had, it doesn't mean he didn't have sins, of course he had, he was not a saint, we all are saints and sinners, but if one Nelson Mandela can change the whole country, it takes one person to change the world. Don't ever think that you cannot make a difference… It's got nothing to do with ego, it's got to do with your purpose, and your calling, and if you have a purpose and a calling to bring a certain message out into the world, it's none of your business who hears it or not! I'm always told: sow the seeds! What happens to those seed is none of your business, but throw the seed anyway!" said Judith.

For a few minutes they allowed that last phrase to settle, to reverberate: sow the seeds! What happens to those seeds is none of your business, but throw the seed anyway!

"Think also of Gandhi in India, British Empire," said Pam, "he saw a world he didn't like much, but he decided, okay, I'm going to create a better world and he had that clear intention! He stepped into that reality, as if it was happening right now, he lived it and changed the world! There's still more to change, but, boy, for one person, one skinny little Indian man, he did a lot… All of us have a role to play; all of us! If we can start to think more collectively and galactically, yes, we are all a piece of the puzzle! And how can each of us help this momentum to get towards new earth?

"I always say, before every video and also before every client session, let this be for the highest good of all. So, I set a clear intention: let this be for the highest good of all. I know we're not living in *la la land*; the world is very challenging right now. But I think that's our mastery… we have to see the difficulty, otherwise there's no mastery, you know? It's only by seeing the darkness and saying, okay, I see it, but I do not accept that as my reality, so I will integrate that into my knowing, but I will aim way higher than that. That's what great leaders did," said Pam.

"I have a dear friend, a Portuguese journalist, that created almost 15 years ago, a digital magazine, in English and Portuguese, to cover the best things in the world for a better world," said Helena. "It was the beginning of what's called 'solution journalism', to see problems through the lens of solutions.

"Everything you water, and pay attention to, becomes stronger, and with this medium the focus changed from fear to hope. Like you've said, we see the chaos, but we raise our frequency looking at so many people doing great work in every field!"

"I believe mainstream media is going to change dramatically," said Pam. "I believe that this is one of the key times when belief systems will be shaken to the core. Lifetime beliefs are going to be shaken, and there will be a whole series of peaks as we go through the next few years.

"Facts will become clear and, so, the people who are on a different trajectory will have to see them! Media is going to change. People are migrating to alternative channels, and independent journalists, probably like your friend, are getting their truth from elsewhere. And, ultimately, mainstream media has to either collapse completely, because that's also part of a system, or in some way dissolve and morph into something much more clean and benevolent, let's say that. So that's a huge part of this picture; huge because that's our normal way of getting information," said Pam.

"Still is..." said Helena.

"Now, everyone's reality is different," said Pam. "And because of this new photonic light pouring in the bandwidth, I believe the frequency is greater than we've ever had in history! I mean, this new light is taking people to higher frequencies, whereas, at this other level, things are really grim and dense and with much lower frequency."

Helena had often heard Pam talk about ejections of coronal mass happening with greater frequency, due to solar explosions that are also becoming more and more frequent, causing significant amounts of plasma to be released, along with the magnetic field accompanying it, from the sun's corona out into the solar wind. Some have even caused radio blackouts on Earth, as the material that is ejected by the Sun interacts with the atmosphere and the Earth's electromagnetic field, which can not only produce the beautiful Northern Lights, but also affect people on many levels, including mental, emotional, spiritual and physical.

The Earth is a sea of vibrations and frequencies. Humanity is good at creating and inventing devices in which there is a frequency of energy and vibration. These waves of energy are always moving through you. This planet is woven with these electronic frequencies. You just have to imagine threads of energy connecting all the power lines, electrical appliances, mobile phones, televisions and microwaves, to understand how tight this energy matrix really is, wrapping the planet in an energy web of discordant frequencies.

Most of humanity doesn't even think about this. Or do they? There is still this feeling of "out of sight, out of mind", but it isn't like that. These matrices of electronic frequencies are always affecting the body and the mental state, naturally, albeit imperceptibly.

Every time the Sun emits energy, it is also sending information through our Solar System, which, according to some experts, is like a cosmic energy impulse, a wake-up call for humanity. The vibrational energy currents from our sun flow to the planet and inside of us and, when the planet receives these coherent, high frequencies, it allows us to increase our own vibrations, forcing an adjustment of course, which many describe as the symptoms of light activation. Embracing more light, living life with higher, more coherent vibrations, was what Pam was talking about.

"Despite the cycles and repetitions, you also think we are living something completely new?" asked Helena.

"Yes, I do think this is the biggest evolutionary leap that humanity has ever made," answered Pam assertively. "This particular period in history has been predicted by many ancient philosophies, the Mayan, the Hopi, etc., and if you just simply look at the cosmology of what's happening, our earth moves through this particular area of space, called the photon belt, roughly every 12000 years; and we are entering that photon belt now! So this is a very specific time cosmologically, as well as spiritually, because the earth is upgrading as a result of all this high frequency light coming in.

"If we are able to hold more light in the body and benefit from that photonic energy that's coming in, then that will accelerate our trajectory as well. If we're able to hold more and more light in our bodies, then we're becoming increasingly crystalline, less carbon, and again shifting our timeline in every second. So, that's where it gets to be extremely exciting!" said Pam.

"A lot of people are waking up very quickly and the energies are definitely changing on this planet," said Sarita, "when I drop into meditation now is a whole another experience than two years ago. When I teach a complicated meditation, they have it in thirty minutes. Before, I would have had to teach them for a year. It is a quantum leap and we're all in a quantumltangle.

"I think that the more we just keep choosing every day to be expanded in our awareness, stuff comes: books arrive, little videos, you talk to somebody, they say one thing it just opens your mind, dreams, all that kind of stuff, because you're holding the intention to be aware of the truth," said Sarita.

"So how do you know that it is truth, when there is no proof?" Helena asked.

"Women are very intuitive," said Judith. "Your deep gut knowing is your best GPS system… Because it's always the truth of your soul that will tell you there, right in your gut, in your heart feeling, in your solar plexus area, when something is true or not, but most people have learned to ignore it."

"If you're genuinely authentic, when you hit a truth, your intuition becomes ignited," Sarita added, "it's like a deep knowing, but the problem is many of us have deep knowing from the space of our indoctrination. I'm calling it indoctrination, but you understand, it's a container of a lot of stuff, it's all the patterns and behaviours, the ideas about who you were told you are, your cellular memory, your ancestral trauma, all of your incarnations, your karmic footprint, all of that kind of stuff... so when you drop that, and something comes into the field of your reality, your intuition sparks, and you know it's the truth, but it's only the truth for you in this now of who you are.

"But if you really want to get to the truth of anything, you've got to be prepared to examine it from every angle, you have to be prepared to be wrong. And so, I think what happens in this work is: you strip the layers of all of that stuff that isn't really you, come into a truth, and then you realize there's more layers that you need to strip, and now there's a new truth revealing itself to you... It's like a meditation practice, you get good at a plateau and then, suddenly, this flame of intuition or truth arises, and you go up again and then you go up, so that's what I think is the journey...

"I think that we're all feeling truth through our perspective, our lens, our experience and everything, but I do believe there are some ultimate truths which cannot be bent or broken, like laws of the universe. A lot of people go "oh that's not true, everything is perspective" and yes that's true, but I think that there's the divine mind or the divine consciousness, if you will, the all that is, that holds some truths which are infallible, they can't be changed! I think those are the ones I'm trying to find out," said Sarita.

Helena looked at Pam.

"How do I know it's true? I think you really just feel that in your heart, you feel that in your knowingness," said Pam. "Also, if you're listening to external sources, teachers, mentors, whoever, and they raise your frequency, I always think that is loving to me they are speaking truth, and if they lower my frequency, I think I'm not so sure that's true, so I always bring it back to myself. I use a pendulum a lot, actually, which I think is just an extension of my intuition, to kind of get clarification on how I'm feeling in my heart, but I always bring it back to me, because I am the pendulum and earth energies and spiritual energies in every moment."

"All of you raise my frequency," Helena said, smiling at each of them and placing her hand on her heart. "I'm very aware of that, what that person makes me feel when I listen to her… It's so much simpler to navigate in this world on how you feel in this space, how you feel with this person, how you feel doing this..."

"That's it in a nutshell. I would agree a thousand percent," told Pam, "and checking on those feelings is, of course, checking in your frequency! Are you happy or sad? Are you joyful or depressed? It's that simple. But starting to become aware of that gives us that perspective on us, and how we're operating in our lives. That's one big step, as I say, towards higher consciousness.

"How do you spend your evenings and weekends that gives you joy? What lights you up? What do you love to do? What makes you sing? What makes you laugh? What lifts your heart? What subjects of books are on your bookshelves? Is it about cookery? Is it about gardening? Is it about fishing? What subjects do you focus on?

"You can start to become the observer with everything that happens in your day, with conversations you have, with things you read, stuff on the internet, just step back and observe: is that lifting my frequency and making me feel better? Or is that dropping my frequency?

"In this way, we start to practice our eagle's perch position, because in doing that, that is the first step in raising your consciousness, just having that slight objectivity and perspective on who you are, what doesn't interest you at all, and what lifts your heart when you hear about it! Is it always about gardening? Is it always about cooking? Is it always about singing? Is it always about dancing? That thing you wanted to do when you're a child and your parents said 'No, you've got to be a bank manager,' you know? It's rediscovering those passions, because every single person has that.

"Of course, in a birth chart, those are pretty easy to identify, but without doing that, you can just do those really simple things," said Pam.

"And you, Marin?" asked Helena.

"For me, the very best thing that anybody can give to themselves is the direct knowing. Gnosis. That's what the Essenes were able to hold," Marin shared. "The gnostic gospels come from that place of divine direct knowing of the mystery. We're never going to be able to understand different people's perspectives, or what's the truth in these realms, there is no truth, everybody has their own experience. The truth comes from the divine, the truth comes from beyond this world, and in order to access that, I have found, anyway, that really letting myself quiet, be still in my body, nice deep long breaths, our breaths are like a bridge, they're embedded in our body; God gave us this beautiful technology of breathing, inhaling and exhaling; we close our eyes, it brings us from the outer world right into the inner realms, into the inner temple, it's brilliant and beautiful!

"Getting out into nature that's another respite; here we are in this beautiful planet and we have not only the ability to go in, but the ability to go into the God frequency right here, if we get in nature, to get out of all the noise, putting ourselves in that, primes us for a direct experience with the mystical. And I have found that, if you can open up and have a direct experience, mystical, it doesn't matter who's saying what, you just know. But you don't know like here," continued Marin, pointing to the head. "You know here," said with one hand on her heart and other on her womb. "And that's the experience that I've had with my mystical experiences: they anchor a knowing inside of you that no one can take away…

"Mothers kind of understand this, if they've had a positive, natural or empowering birth experience. They know something about themselves, about their power, they know something about the rightness of their body that's beyond what anybody could tell them, because they've had a direct experience with the mystical to bring a baby into the world. That's what I would say is the number one thing: set yourself up to have that direct experience!" said Marin.

"Could you share more about your experiences in altered states of consciousness? Or non-ordinary, I never know what's the best word for it," asked Helena.

"I'll start by saying that what led me to those experiences was a deep trust, and a deep relationship with silence and stillness," Marin started, "and when I really began to understand the value of the other side of things: of being and not just doing! We are indoctrinated in a culture where we give so much value to doing, success, proving ourselves, creating things, and once I really got on the priestess path, and began to understand the essence of the Divine Mother, the essence of the Divine Feminine, and how important that was, I began to really embrace it.

"So I had years of meditation behind me, in other words, I'm a very experienced meditator, and it's not about a technique, it's just I was very comfortable releasing, softening into the unknown. That said, when I did that at these two different events, with plant medicine and with the techniques at the Dr Joe Dispenza event, what happened for me was as if I merged with the unknown, and suddenly began to feel this shimmer, this aliveness, this electricity, that was the force of life, the force of creation, and as I began to merge with it, and feel it, what happened particularly in the Dr Joe Dispenza retreat was that every single one of my cells aligned with this frequency, that was the frequency of love really, the frequency of creator, frequency of mother, father, God and I saw every single one of my cells began to sing in this octave, this harmonious, angelic song… I saw it and I heard it, I experienced it and then I recognized that grid that is inside of me, which was all of my cells; they are their own grid, they work together. And then my awareness popped out and I saw that every single human being is a cell in one body, that we are each this ball, this flame of the light of God, underneath all the veils of our humanity, and all the patterns, and all the ego, every single one of us has that innocent, alive, sacred white flame of the divine, right inside us! And it's part of a larger body, it's part of a larger grid! And then my awareness went beyond that and I saw that every single one of the stars is also part of the grid, and that God, the force of nature, is just… it's all this, one big beautiful grid that is constantly pulsing, expansion and contraction, this in and out flow, just like our breath, and I experienced total and complete oneness!

"Once I experienced that, it was like there's no words to describe it… it was bliss, it was beyond bliss, it just was everything! And, when I was in that, it was if there was a circular portal above me that opened, and all of a sudden the shower of this pearlescent diamond light came down upon me! And I was also at the time having a Kundalini experience, so my physical body was sort of, you know, doing this," explained Marin shaking her whole body, "like when you see videos of people that are having like the experience of rapture, you know, it was absolutely that… and I saw that there was a dove that came down through the portal, spinning, and she went right in my heart and my heart burst open!

"And all of the lifetimes, and all of the past memories that I had as a child of shutting my heart down, putting a wall around my heart, building armour, this dove, the power of love is really I think what that dove was, just exploded and all of that just left my body, and my heart was so open… and when my heart was so open, the best way I can describe, it's like there's an eye in your heart or something, it's hard to explain, but suddenly my heart could see… and I saw every single person is this innocent being, underneath all of the defences, and the armour and the mask… like we are all just these innocent, I guess children is the right word, we are innocence in our essence, that's the purity of us. And it lasted for almost a month, where I literally could see that, whiteness that flame, that innocence in everybody. Since that time, it's kind of faded, but it's still in me, I can still go back to it if I close my eyes and tune in," said Marin.

"What an experience!" Helena murmured, without finding good words to describe what she felt.

"It caused me to be able to keep my heart open, even when people are acting in ways that are in judgment of me, even if they do things that I don't necessarily agree with, I'm able to see that there's a difference between how they're acting within their pain body and who they really are. It's just given me a great freedom to be able to just keep my heart open, be neutral, and unconditional to the best of my ability with people, with humanity, with the circumstances of life," said Marin.

A silence lingered. Helena was profoundly moved.

"I don't even have words. I'm so moved that the tears won't stop... my whole body is shaking, as if I'm living a little bit of your experience... that resonates so much with me. What a poem!" said Helena.

"You are everything, you are the galaxies, you are the stars, you are every atom and every molecule, you are every living thing, you are the tree, you are the flower, you are the rock, you are the sky, you are the earth, there's nothing you are not, because you are everywhere, but you have a manifested side here on earth, and you have an unmanifested side, you have the visible and the invisible, and the invisible is more real than the reality, in fact we create our own reality," said Judith, as if reciting a poem.

"Here, with you, I feel blessed and profoundly inspired," Helena thanked them. "And in your sharing there are always many questions that come to me like waves coming ashore. I wonder, for example, about the true value of certain jobs, trips, retreats, if we're not able to bring this wisdom we receive to our day-to-day, to our actions, or even to our thoughts, to when we're driving in traffic, with our neighbours, relatives, work colleagues, the people we meet, in the supermarket, in the café, in the street, when we are confronted with difficult situations, with ideas that we don't like, when we have choices to make... I wonder what's the point of having certain experiences, if we aren't capable of integrating them in how we live our everyday lives, how we give ourselves to the world? I think about this, because I also wonder, at this key moment in my life, how far will I be able to integrate everything I have experienced and the huge knowledge that has come my way. I feel transformed, but how transformed will I really be? What will I do when the time comes? Hence the question. How can I bring this wisdom into my daily existence? What should I do?" asked Helena.

"I understand what you're asking," Marin began. "I'm actually just going to say one quick thing about leaving a retreat, and maintaining and retaining what you experience there, because I think that this is important and then I'm going to answer your question.

"Tribal cultures have a wonderful way of teaching their young through stories and mythology. In our culture, we teach our children through facts and knowledge, information, and any of us can go back to school, fourth grade, fifth grade, and we can't remember a thing, because that information went in and then it went out. But we remember stories, if someone tells you a good story that touches you. You remember it, because the story is experienced by the heart, not just the head.

"So when you go to a retreat like I went to, with that week-long Dr. Joe Dispenza retreat, and I had that experience that was able to go beyond just my head, and down to my heart, those are experiences that you will always take with you and remember, and be changed by. Because it's not just knowledge, that can be retained or not. When we bring our brain and heart into coherence, and the brain and heart begins to become one again in that sacred union of Divine Feminine and Divine Masculine, we can become frequency holders of a particular frequency, higher frequency, than what our culture is based on, which is really the frequency of fear, the frequency of scarcity, the frequency of lack, the frequency of separation, the frequency of suffering.

"One of the things that I've recognized in my priestess work is so many people think of their greatest contribution, their sole purpose, as something that they're supposed to do: write a book, give a talk, start a business, and that might be in alignment for them, but I think that our greatest contribution is to maintain, embody a frequency that is higher than the frequency that the world lives in.

"You cannot solve any problem, Einstein said, at the energy that it was created. So, our greatest contribution is breaking through the network of the matrix, the mind narrative of the matrix that is based on fear; if we can break through that, and hold that new frequency, maintain it, anchor it within our transmitting tower that is our human body, we could walk down a grocery store and we are emitting that tone, that octave, other people are going to feel that, and they may not even understand what's happening, but I do believe that that's the way that we're going to change the world!" Marin concluded, with a huge smile.

"I hear you," Helena softly intoned.

"We as woman now have got this gospel of love that we need to bring up, because women are love, they cannot be anything else but love," Judith reminded. "I had a beautiful conversation with one of my friends the other day, and he said to me, "Judith, do you know how difficult it is for men to open their hearts?". So we've also got to slowly, but surely, bring them back to their heart."

"The heart was always meant to lead, then the thought gives us the how to take the action," said Marin. "In other words, the masculine energy is set up in great design to serve the feminine. No way do I mean that men are supposed to serve women, but the masculine energy, the way that it comes into union with the feminine is that it is meant to serve.

"The reason we've created such chaos in our life is because we've cut off from our heart, we've left the head by itself to have to figure things out, and we've created a mess. So this return to the heart is what brings everything back into divine order. I think the masculine's job is to hold the space so that the feminine can blossom, open like the rose, so that she's in the vibrational field of complete holding protection and safety," said Marin.

"The union of the masculine and feminine beautifully balanced creates that fire," said Judith, "the gnosis, the flame, the shekinah; you can only live your truth, if this is firmly anchored inside your soul, so that you embrace the divinity that is your soul.

"If you cannot be safe with somebody speaking your truth without being judged, without being criticized, without being fixed or changed, you will not trust; you can only develop that, if both are willing to open their hearts and speak their truth, being safe with one another. There lies the greatest lesson, because once you are safe with each other, and you trust and respect each other, you will walk the path together, but you also need a vision and a calling which is greater than the sum of self," said Judith.

"I see men who are really in their divine masculine," Sarita assured. "They don't need to be violent or domineering or whatever these ideas we have about the masculine are; they're loving, contained, focused, presence which is soft, because it's incredibly sharp, you know what I mean, it's so strong, it's not in fear, so it doesn't need to react that way, or to project that way, or to abuse that way."

"I have a divine partnership," said Marin. "My husband does not meet me at this level of conversation and this frequency the way that you and I can have, but he is a pillar of divine masculine that bows, honours, and reveres the divine feminine, even though he doesn't understand. He doesn't meet me here, and I believe that in the great intelligence, and in the great unfolding of this thing that we call sacred union, it's not two people walking the exact same path, it's people getting into the vibration of absolute effulgence of the divine feminine, absolute unfolding of the divine masculine and, eventually, when the women are able to hold this frequency, the masculine whose job has been holding us so that we can open to this degree, they are going to naturally enfold and that's the sacred union.

"I believe that the divine masculine, when he is truly in his masculine, has a much different role to this role of opening like the rose, his role is to hold, protect, honour, revere, and allow the feminine to feel safe to do the work of that unfolding," said Marin.

Helena thought of Thomas again.

"So much to think about… And how about your perception of the divine, of God?" asked Helena.

"I see God in nature," answered Pam, "and I see a kind of divine intelligence in every moment of my day, whether is seeing an acorn grow into an oak tree or whether it's studying a birth chart with pattern and rhythm and depth and sacredness, you know? There's divine intelligence in everything and that to me is God. In every tiny piece of consciousness, that is God… We are all divine sparks, divine pieces of that divine consciousness. I believe in the coming years that connection to source, connection to God, however you define it, is getting stronger and higher, that's my feeling.

"I see the birth charts and that birth chart will never be repeated in history again, for anyone! So you know we are completely unique! And it's in discovering that uniqueness that also gives us our anchor," said Pam.

"And how do you feel when working with charts?" asked Helena.

"I'm an interpreter, a translator," answered Pam. "I'm not a psychic or a mystic. I'm a translator of symbolism and geometry. It's a language, but the more experienced you get with it, the more you start to read it as music and frequency and resonance… and what's the crucial thing now is frequency. I think our choices have to be led by our frequency, what gives us the highest frequency, not necessarily logic anymore. Because we're going to start to become much more aware of the universe just being vibrating energy and frequency, which it always has been, but we just haven't been aware of it.

"I mentioned recently that, with electricity, you can either torture people or bring light. Astrology is like that, it's just a language. You can focus on the very depressing and evil and ghastly things, but if I do that, I'll be taking people that listen to me down with me. So, my job is to help people to be the best they can be, but acknowledge what may be the most more challenging sides of whatever transits we're going through, and say yes this could manifest as overwhelming or confusion or flooding whatever, but it can also manifest as this, so let's focus on this, because this is going to take you to a higher state of being, this is going to take to a higher frequency!

"So, the more I can encourage more people to live the astrology at the highest level, then the faster we're going to get to a better place, because the destination for me is not under question… It's the speed that is affected by our collective frequency. That's why I really want to encourage people to get into this momentum of the power of the people, coming together in community, all supporting each other, whether it's digital or in person, and synchronicities happen. I mean, there are many big community events starting to happen, and the synchronicities are amazing, these beautiful synchronicities of being in the right place with the right person," said Pam.

"That's true. My life is full of amazing synchronicities. And with healing, Sarita? How it was for you?" asked Helena.

"I started healing," Sarita replied, "because I was just felt compelled to put hands on people, or whatever, and some people felt a little better from my healings. Then slowly, bit by bit, I began to see more and more miracles, until it became normal.

"So now, when I go to heal someone, I just know that they'll be changed, because it happens every time. I mean, that's a tricky one with healing… because in healing there's two parties, I mean, three, I guess the whole thing is there's a lot of entanglement going on, because I've healed people completely from long-term condition and then two weeks later it's all back, you know? Why does that happen? Because with healing, you have to believe you're worthy to be healed, your body is a record of everything that you think and feel, and it's literally showing you how you think and feel.

"Think about Louise Hay, she's never wrong with her diagnosis. You ask someone what's wrong with them, and it will be an absolute match. Ear problems, what they don't want to hear? What aren't they listening to? Did they hear something awful when they were in the womb? As a child? It's just extraordinary that your body is a record of everything you think and feel. So, when you're healing someone, it's not so much… do they believe they can be healed? Is more... Are they ready to let go of what they've been holding on to? As a shamanic practitioner, you apparently do the impossible, because they think they can't do it on their own, which they could, you're just doing it with them, but they really have to be at that place where they're ready to, not be in limitation. That's the problem, we hold on to limitation… I'm unworthy, I don't deserve to be free, I'm ugly, I don't know, people have many different ideas," said Sarita.

"Everybody wants to be loved for who and what they are, not for somebody's projection upon them," Judith added, "but we have always learned that "I love you if you do this or that, I love you if you look like this, I love you if you are like that..." So we have always put a condition on love, but in fact there is no condition on love. Often we have a harder time loving ourselves than loving anybody else, but the thing is, you will never believe that somebody can love you just the way you are, if you do not love yourself!

"I would say: Be true to yourself in the highest sense, the truth of your soul, and to live it, and not to pretend to be anything. We don't need masks. If you try to live to be somebody you're not, you will always feel you're living a lie, you'll feel empty inside... and many people try to live a life that their parents want them to live, try to be what their husbands want them to become, society wants them to become, I mean, we are constantly being bombarded, you've got to look like this, you've got to do this, you've got to drive this car, you've got to wear these clothes, you've got to be this and that, that's all nonsense! Be yourself in the truth of your soul and love yourself in the deepest sense! You can't be anything else, but the truth of who you are," said Judith.

"That's quite a journey," said Helena, like in a whisper.

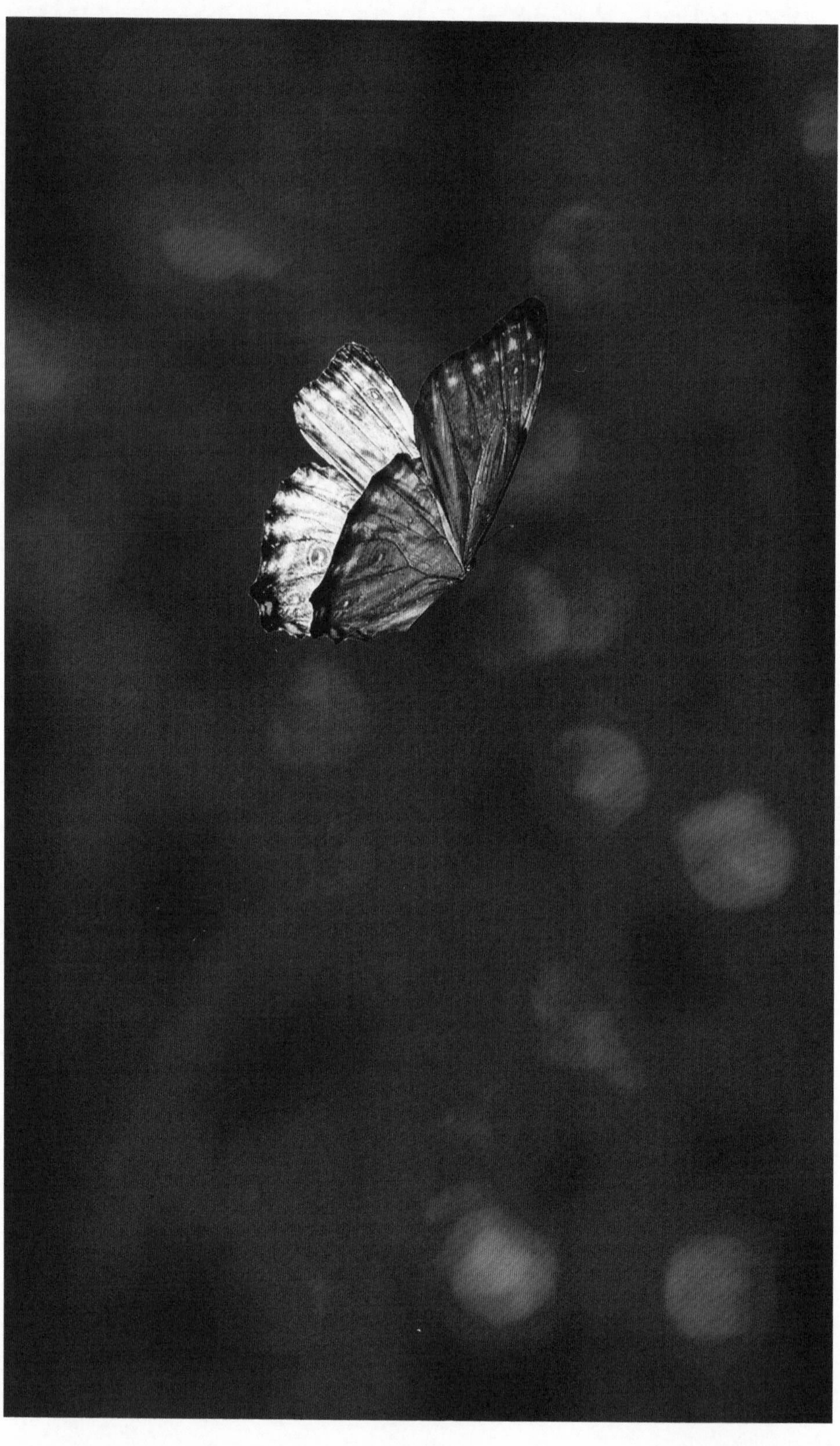

Rue de Changes, 30

On the train to Paris, making the most of the travelling time, and then on the train to Chartres, where her mother lived, Helena decided to listen to Anne Baring, another woman of great wisdom, talking about the construction of the gothic cathedral there, its mysteries and teachings.

She hadn't wanted to warn her mother of her arrival, despite having her telephone number, because there was a part of her that wanted to be sure, and she would only know in the exact moment, if she wanted to go ahead with it or not. Having arrived in Chartres, she followed the GPS on her phone, feeling the irony of her mother living at Rue de Changes, nº 30. She thought she might visit the cathedral first, but she didn't want to put off the moment any longer, now that she was there. She buzzed on her mother's number, but nobody answered. While she was waiting at the entrance, wondering what to do, a woman came out of the building, and holding the door asked if she wanted to go in.

"No, thank you. I'm looking for Débora, I buzzed but I don't think she's in," Helena said, her French a little shaky with nerves.

"Ah, look in L'Estaminet, it's just around the corner, she should be having her lunch there."

Helena did just that. In just a few steps, she was in sight of the street terrace of L'Estaminet. She had never seen a photo of her mother, she hadn't asked her father for one, she didn't know why, but it all clicked into place as she looked at the small yet full terrace.

She moved closer, until she was right in front of the terrace and, felt a gaze on her, a gaze she realised was that of a woman, sitting alone at the table at the end. When she saw her, she had no doubts. Her face was Helena's, only older. When she realised this, her heart stopped. She felt like fleeing but was frozen to the spot. A waiter came to ask if she would like a table and it was Débora who answered him:

"Josephe, she's here for me. Bring us another plate, please."

Débora got up, standing at her place. Helena walked towards her. They stood, face to face, each on their own side of the table.

"I didn't know you were pregnant."

Helena placed her hand on her belly, already very large for its six months. She smiled. She sat down, still a little awkward, not knowing what to say.

"Would like to eat? A salad perhaps?" asked Débora.

"Yes, that would be good."

"Josephe, the same as I'm having," she said to the waiter.

They sat for a few minutes looking at each other, seeing the similarities in their faces, familiarity and strangeness mingling within them.

"I'd been expecting you for some time. In fact, I'd been expecting some months back. It's been so long I thought you weren't coming."

"It was a long journey to get here," said Helena.

"38 years."

"Indeed..."

"It was 38 years for me too," said Débora.

"Yes... but it was your decision," Helena said coldly. "I'd just like to know why."

"By now, you surely know that life isn't black and white."

"But choice is sacrosanct. It belongs to us alone," Helena retorted.

"Yes, that's true. It was my choice."

"So... why?"

"I've come up with a thousand speeches for this moment, and now none of them seems to fit. 39 years ago, I was a very happy woman. I was pregnant by a man I loved dearly, one of those loves that doesn't bend with time or distance; we had a wonderful life ahead of us. We had bought a house in the country, in Provence, in front of a beautiful vineyard, we had lovingly decorated a room for the two of you..."

"The two of us?"

"For you and for Laura."

"Laura?"

"Yes, your twin sister."

When she finally found out about me, from our mother, an icy wind swept over her body. She felt a strange contraction in her belly. She thought back to Egypt. She smiled a little, as she relived what she had felt back then, understanding that it was me, her sister, that she had felt, when for the first time she hadn't felt the emptiness she had always felt before, accompanied in that loving darkness; I smiled too. Helena returned to the conversation.

"I didn't know that..." said Helena.

"I'm sorry it came out like that, I thought you already knew."

"I don't know anything."

"It was just as we left the hospital, on the way home, that we had the accident. Jonas, your father, was driving. It wasn't his fault. Another car swerved into our lane and hit us head-on. He and your sister, who was on his side of the car, they died instantly... from what I was told, later on, in the hospital. I was seriously hurt, with several injuries, to the head, spine, the possibility of being paralysed; you alone survived practically unscathed."

Helena was almost in a state of shock, tears running endlessly down her face.

"I'm sorry to say it here, like this..." said Débora.

"There's no good way to do it," Helena replied coldly.

"Yes, but let's go to my place. You'll feel more at ease there."

"There's no need," Helena said, wiping away the tears. "I want to know everything."

"There's not much to know. I saw the fact that you came out of such a catastrophe without a scratch as a sign, a sign of life. And there was only death there. I was dead too at that time."

"Death and rebirth are intertwined."

"I'm not saying they aren't. But, back then, I was too young to know it. I was just 22 years old and, for me, my life was over."

"And your parents?"

"They weren't part of my life either, back then. They'd wanted me to have an abortion and I refused, and distanced myself from them. They said being a mother so young, and with twins on top of that, would jeopardise a brilliant future. For them, it was all wrong. Marrying a farmer. Going to live in the country. Giving up my career before it had even begun, going to look after two children, without any notion of responsibility. You can imagine. The usual scenario, recreated so many times in films. An only child. Excellent student. Heiress to a great fortune... I was casting aside all their dreams, in their view, of course.

"But despite being young, and the fact that we hadn't planned it this way, I was so happy to be pregnant, so certain of that love, so in love with the simple idea of a life in the country, a happy family, which is something that I had never known," Débora explained, a new glow to her face, full of emotion. "They put pressure on me, threatening that 'I would be on my own' if I decided to marry and have you both. I married and wanted to have you. Jonas had already been working for some years, it was with his savings that we bought the land and the house, he was nine years older than me, well-known in organic farming, bio-construction. We made so many plans about living in harmony with nature, so many evenings cuddled up on the sofa or in bed planning our happy future...

"With what happened, all prospects of a future, bright or happy, were lost. Death had taken its place. It was more than likely that I would never walk again. My disinterest in life was so great that not even this bothered me. I remember, when they placed you next to me in the hospital, after the accident, and they told me about everything that had happened, I looked at you and I knew immediately that I couldn't keep you, if I truly cared for you. And I did care for you. I think you were the only thing I cared about in the midst of not caring about anything.

"I had your father's number, I mean Julian's, because he had worked for my father, on something to do with the university, and I had had to meet up with him, I knew what I was doing, and he was the only person I could think of calling, to save you, before I lost control of the situation.

"It was only much later on that I became aware of how life had brought all of this together. How it had brought me into contact with him, through my father, in such an unusual situation, a year prior to this... how it coincided with such a painful situation in his own life, enabling you to be welcomed in a home that truly wanted you, to have a mother, a father...

"At the time, all I wanted was for him to make sure that you wouldn't end up with my parents, who had never wanted you, or in a home, care of the social services, or with me, there in hospital, all the alternatives had the stench of brutal unhappiness... And you, so tiny, so perfect and so tiny... Obviously when I called him, I could never have imagined the uncanny timing of it all. But it was another sign that I was doing the right thing."

"And Jonas' parents?" asked Helena.

"He was an orphan."

"Ah... And then, how did it go?"

"How did it go? It all happened really quickly. I handed you over to Julian and he took care of everything. I don't know what he did, but he did it. No one has ever asked me about you. When he left with you in his arms, I closed my eyes and felt a great sense of relief, I can't deny it, it was if I could die now. But I didn't. A path of great suffering was coming my way. I stayed in that hospital for a couple of months, then I went back to my parents' house. They wanted it that way and I had no alternative. I was constantly back and forth to the hospital, a different private one, where I underwent many operations and rehabilitation.

I shut myself off from the world for many years. The first years were spent healing my body. I was a wreck, afflicted with so many physical ailments. And, when my body started getting better, I then started to focus on other cures, and these lasted many years more."

"Did you never regret what you did?" asked Helena.

"No. I know that it was the best thing to do."

"For who?"

"For both of us," Débora said assertively. "Yes, at the time I was giving myself the chance to die in peace, but what drove me was you being able to have a happy life. When I began to rise back to the surface, more than a decade of your life has already passed. You were a happy girl; I knew that instinctively. You were living with a family that seemed wonderful to me. Julian always sent me news about you, with photos, and that was enough for me. Entering your life would mean revisiting a life that I had never had, nor could I ever have again, and ruin yours, the only one you had known and in which you were happy. I never wanted that. My love for you would never allow me to.

"It was also around that time that I came into some money, inheriting it from an aunt of mine, and I decided to travel around the world. This was when the new Débora started to be born."

"What did you do?" asked Helena.

"Long story and long trip, too long to be able to tell you like that... But for 15 years I lived in different places, experiencing so many realities and I ended up here, in France, where I've lived for ten years or so."

"And the house in Provence?"

"It's still there," said Débora.

"You didn't sell it."

"No. I didn't sell it or use it."

"You never went back there?"

"No."

"Do you have anything else to tell me?" asked Helena.

Débora fell silent for a moment, looking downwards. Then, she lifted her face and looked at Helena in the eyes.

"Listen to me with your heart and you will know that it is true," said Débora. "My love for you has always guided me. That unconditional love is umbilically connected to the happiest moment of my life.

"You were the fruit of love, you lived nine months next to your sister in a state of grace, inside me, in the tender embrace of your father... Now that you're pregnant I imagine that you can understand what I'm saying... What happened afterwards, that choice, it was the greatest act of love that I could make. For you. And, deep down, maybe that wisdom was coming from a place that I didn't know how to recognise at that time. Mother and father aren't just biological. Family isn't just blood ties. That's why we find family, a family of friends, with whom we share more than blood ties. We share our lives. I gave you all the love in the world when you were inside me, and I gave you all the love in the world when I handed you over to Julian, your father, and Ingrid, your mother. Weren't they your parents?"

Listening with her heart, she recognised the truth. Believing in the intelligence and love of the Divine Weaver, how could she not believe that all those intersections had been for the best. For her? For everyone?

Helena had the best memories of her childhood. And now she understood the emptiness, the lack of her twin sister, it was if she could already connect with me from that place of knowledge, intentionally, opening the doors of her heart to receive my love, sending hers.

"Yes, they were," she ended up saying.

They looked deeply into each other's eyes.

"Have you visited the cathedral yet?" Débora asked, finally.

"Not yet."

"Shall we go together?"

"Yes, why not?" said Helena.

On leaving the restaurant, Helena saw Débora's walking stick and how she was still walking with some difficulty.

"Do you need any help?" she asked.

"No, I'm fine, but if you want to give me your other arm, I'd just love that!"

Helena gave Débora her arm and arm in arm they made their way to the cathedral. Débora noticed Helena's concern.

"Oh, don't get upset," Débora said, gently. "Twenty years ago, I was much worse and that didn't stop me from going round the world. Our greatest limitations are to be found here," she added, pointing to her head with the hand holding the stick. "Now, most of the time I don't even remember. I've got used to doing everything slowly... you wouldn't believe the time this has given me," she said, laughing, "contrary to what you might think."

"I understand you better than you could imagine," Helena said softly, looking ahead, taking in the spectacle of the magnificent gothic cathedral.

"I never imagined that I would be able to do this labyrinth with you..." Débora told her, nonjudgmentally. "Have you ever listened to Anne Baring?" she asked.

"I was listening to her on the train," Helena replied, noting the sheer serendipity. "We hear the unspoken, see the unrevealed, do what has never been done before. That's how change happens. That's how we're doing it, the two of us."

Débora laughed.

"You listened to her closely."

When they reached the entrance, they remained there, in silence, soaking up the magnitude and grandeur through their senses.

"Three men working on building site," Débora recounted, looking at the façade. "A passer-by stops to ask them: What are you doing? I'm earning my living, said the first. I'm doing my job, said the second. I'm making a cathedral, said the third. The latter is a stonemason, someone who knows how to use the compass."

They entered arm in arm, gazing raptly at it all and all its details, feeling that the stone that had seemed heavy in other places was somehow made light here. Magically, everything that was heavy seemed to be able to fly, enabling the passage from one world to another. There was a celestial harmony enlivening the material and, entering into dialogue with it, you could weep with wonder and amazement, discovering every one of its hidden secrets.

"I enter the cathedral almost every day, and every time I see different things. Chartres is truly phenomenal proof of the creative power of the human imagination, a bridge between earth and sky, the temporal and the eternal. Sometimes I sit here for an hour and take with me that question that she asked... We exist on a tiny planet in the middle of a cosmos of staggering immensity and extraordinary beauty. What could its dream be? Thinking about the Earth's dream, thinking about the dream of the Cosmos, as hope, that hope they carry has brought me countless reflections... sometimes I seem to hear the cosmos telling me its story through the symbols of the cathedral... through its rose windows...

"I have searched for many years for a new image of myself. It was only when I reconciled myself with who I am, not the idealized version of myself I once had, that I broke free and began dreaming again, said Débora."

They stopped in front of the labyrinth.

"Daedalus, the master engineer and mason of the island of Crete, had built a labyrinth to house the fearsome Minotaur," Débora began to tell, with that mysterious and exciting tone of the great storytellers. "Theseus was one of the seven young men and seven maidens who were to be offered as a sacrifice to this terrifying monster, half bull and half man.

"Ariadne, daughter of the king of Crete, but in love with Theseus, begged Daedalus to give her something that could get him safely out of the labyrinth. He gave her a ball of twine and with that, Theseus was able to find his way back to the entrance after killing the Minotaur. This was the myth that gave birth to this labyrinth. In fact, there was even a copper plate at the centre of the labyrinth with the image of the Minotaur, Theseus and Ariadne, with the twine ball. But during the Napoleonic Wars, it was removed and melted down."

Débora and Helena, arm in arm, in front of the entrance to the labyrinth.

"The questions remain," Débora continued. "What is the thread of Ariadne? Love? Spiritual guidance? What is the labyrinth? What is it like to confront the Minotaur? What is it like to return to the world again?

"This path has 12 dimensions, including the centre, the twelve constellations that influence our life, and 28 folds, like the lunar month. And the great rose window corresponds exactly to the dimensions of the labyrinth itself, as if telling you: walk, but hold the awareness of the divine world."

Once again Helena remembered the experience in Edfu and how remarkable the journey between the 12 rooms had been, having taken her back to the uterine experience, together with her sister. Now, here she was with the woman who had brought her into this world, at the entrance to the labyrinth.

"Symbols give their secret away to those who contemplate them," said Débora softly.

Helena separated from her mother and entered the labyrinth. She got barefoot and advanced slowly. There were very few people that day, so she dared to close her eyes when she reached the centre and stood there in meditation; she concentrated on the breath, made the connection to the earth and the central sun, tuned into the presence and rhythm of her heart, breathing in and out through it, accompanying with the mantra "I Am", open to receive what was hers to receive, and open to release what no longer served her or belonged to her.

She felt a very strong energy on her, as if she was wearing a robe of white light that floated over her skin. Helena was this vessel of light and love, and she too could free herself and others through compassion.

As she walked the path back into the world, she made the connection between what she had received and what she could take back from the world of eternity into the world of the here and now. She stopped in front of her mother who was still waiting for her by the entrance.

"To help heal humanity's wounded heart, we must first heal our own," Débora said, facing Helena, ready to receive her. Helena hugged her. Débora took her in her arms as if for the first time. Here, too, she was being born again.

"All evolution is an alchemical process, a continuous process of creation and transformation, of dissolution and regeneration. Whatever the difficulties of the path, the intricacies and circumvolutions of our life, everything helps us to discover our true direction and who we really are," said Helena, still half in a trance, washed in tears, still holding hands with his mother Débora, and looking into her eyes.

"We dream the dreams that our ancestors dreamt for us. And when we look at our own children, we dream those dreams for them. All of humanity becomes a sea of great dreams," returned Débora, herself with thick tears streaming down her cheeks.

After leaving the labyrinth, they stopped again in the middle point where the transepts cross the nave, this convergence of lines and proportions. There they let themselves receive all the alchemical force of the light that emanated from the three rose windows. They felt a fire envelop them, in the place where time and eternity meet. Feeling their heart in tune with the heart of the Cathedral.

"Do you remember Solomon's verses?" Débora asked. "You stir not up, nor awake my beloved, until the appropriate time"; "Do not arouse or awaken love until it so desires."

Helena hugged her again spontaneously. She could perfectly understand what she meant, she could feel this waiting or surrendering of Débora, of the strength of her love, surrendering any longing to the wisdom of the time, to the path and to the sacred choice of Helena.

It was true, they knew it from experience: every being who entered Chartres left there different, perhaps even those who did not realize it. With them, too, the Cathedral had worked its magic, but they made a point of leaving arm in arm, just as they had entered.

Débora invited her to stay with her, to sleep at her house, but Helena wanted to return to Les Contes. She told her the magic of that space and how it worked daily miracles, just as she had felt in the cathedral.

She laughed in a complicit manner. She had to integrate that meeting, which would not be her last, she assured her. Doing the night trip seemed fine to her, she enjoyed night trips and could even rest. Débora did not object and accompanied her to the train station.

"*Don't be a stranger*," she said in English, asking her not to disappear from her life.

"*Je ne pourrais pas,*" Helena replied in French, smiling tenderly. "Your blood runs through my veins."

"Thomas reached out to me. He was here with me," her mother Débora said, before Helena got on the train.

She felt a leap in her heart. Breath stuck.

"I didn't know if I should have told you, but I felt like I had to do it now. Julian gave him my address. He came on an impulse, he wanted to talk to me... understand more, while waiting for you. He's not well. The poor guy hasn't even been able to find comfort in the stars. I feel like he is waiting for you to tell him something... so that he can come to meet you."

Helena lowered her eyes.

"I already said."

"Good. I really enjoyed meeting him," and looking at Helena's belly. "He´s the father, isn't he?"

"Yes."

"Does he know?"

" Not yet," said Helena.

Débora shook her head in understanding.

"Everything has its timing," Débora said.

They hugged, at length.

"This day will last forever," Débora told her.

Helena got on the train. The train departed. Helena used that night to cry alone.

Sacred Theatre: the 12 houses

When she got back to her apartment at Les Contes, something had changed. The stones on the path were , just like those in the cathedral. Now she felt she was flying, even on them. She craved Thomas' presence, without feeling any doubt or repulsion. She wrote to him that she would return to Italy soon, to meet up , but that she still had to stay a few more days in Les Contes, France. Aniya had told her about an event that was going to take place two days later and that there was no way she should miss it. A Sacred Theatre event. She remembered Ariel had raved about the Sacred Theatre and it sounded like something she couldn't possibly miss.

"It sounds wonderful. What should I know about it?"

"Oh, the less you know, the better a participant you will be," Aniya explained to her. "In the Sacred Theatre we are all actors, there is no script. Everything will take place here. We walk around and let everything develop naturally. There will be twelve paths leading from the centre, and you will encounter different mythical and archetypal dimensions of being. We have also invited twelve astrologers, one for each sign and in each space. They too will have no script. Different artists have also been invited, who may or may not bring their art to the space. We have invited people of different nationalities, like you to take part. To celebrate, dance and cultivate the seeds of consciousness growing in ecstasy together."

"Very interesting. I will gladly be an open book... I already feel inspired!" said Helena.

Everything around her was a hive of activity in the days leading up to the Sacred Theatre. There were people building, creating, getting the space ready and, despite the commotion, everything seemed to move in harmony, as if expertly orchestrated by divine will. Her childlike eyes grew wide, and everything seemed beautiful, enchanting, like in a fairy tale. Even so, when she went outside first thing in the morning, she couldn't believe the magic that had happened during the night.

Several campervans had arrived without her having noticed and, every hour, more bird-people were arriving, as in a migration to the same nest. They flew in from around the globe, colourfully and highly creatively dressed, reminiscent of festivalgoers at *Burning Man*, all of them smiling as they passed, chatting as if they had known each other for a long time. She was mesmerised by the spectacle around her, whisking her off to be in a theatrical play. Enraptured by the atmosphere, she ran back to her apartment, hunting through her things for a dress that would evoke a fairy spirit. She came across her white, billowy dress, that had been part of that unforgettable day with Thomas and which, thanks to its flexible material, could accommodate her pregnant belly. She got dressed, did her make-up, and at the appointed time gathered with all the other participants, in a large circle.

When she looked around her, at each face that appeared, she was fascinated to recognise such human diversity. Every person so different, so full of hidden stories that no one could even imagine at first glance, so many lives in each heart beating there, individually, but almost in unison...

A large circle formed the centre of the Sacred Theatre, like a stage in an open-air amphitheatre. From it led twelve paths, each with different contours. A beautiful woman, with long, dark hair, that Helena had never seen before, stood in the centre of the circle. She was wearing a short, white summer dress, sandals, a red scarf over her head and a baby secured in a highly colourful cloth across her front. When she started to talk, in a calm, deep voice, everyone fell silent.

"Even though we don't know the script in advance, every day we perform in the film of our lives."

Helena felt a shiver run through her body. That's just how it was.

"Some are more aware of their roles than others. Others are totally unaware of their important role in this great play. What we give, what we think, what we say, what we do, depends on us and, each of us is an important being in the universal web of consciousness.

"In this space created by the Sacred Theatre, we are all conscious dreamers, creating our own realities, and we all contribute to the greater dream that will emerge. On the treasure map outlined in this space, you can touch different fields of experience, embody different archetypes, see what is blocked or hidden in your lives, you can receive signs, or clues, which may free you from restrictive patterns and help you to enter the path of beauty. Anyone walking this path, embraces the ability to see the intrinsic beauty within themselves and in all things. But don't forget... on this path, you need to stay connected to all your beauty and power. And, from that place, others will also feel invited to be all that they are.

"In the Sacred Theatre, as in Aboriginal dreamtime, there are no distinctions between the then and now, real or imaginary, dream or dreamer. Here, all things are not only possible, but also constantly in the process of creation. Here we experience the evolving game of all possibilities and, in it, as in the age of renewal, resistance to the new and unknown can lead you into darkness.

"Nevertheless, in this sacred space, as in life, you will always find lights to guide you in the direction of wholeness and fulfilment. Symbolically, you will find many intertwining, even labyrinthine paths, which can lead you to the twelve halls of mirrors, which is what I like to call them as they are no more than spaces in which you can face your own reflection and see the truth about yourself. Or not. Despite the world being a mirror so that you can truly see and be, what you see or not is down to you. Look around you for a few minutes."

The silence and depth of those gazes brought a chimera-like dimension to the moment.

"What glasses are you wearing? Do you remember the Hawkins scale? The world seems different on the different frequency levels we find ourselves in, because our life is also the mirror of our vibration. For a person with a frequency of 50, the world seems desolate. The person with 75 sees sadness wherever they look. A person with a frequency level of 200 sees the world as more hopeful and positive, while a person with a frequency of more than 500 observes the world as a loving, beautiful place. And, even so, it is the same world in which we are all in touch with reality and observing it!

"It's not easy to be a pioneer. It's not easy to be a trailblazer, to break through the layers of veils that distance us from our truth. We are too attached to certain truths; they bring us comfort. But the word for courage in French means "to be in the heart". So, find the courage to move through what seems hard and uncomfortable. You always have the power of forgiveness, and of acceptance, to let loose something that you might judge to be, or see as, imperfect. And use and abuse the power of love like an electric current to power the light."

With a gentle bow she left the centre to join the circle and, with their eyes closed and holding hands, they listened to the musical piece *Metamorphosis*, voiced by Darpan, in a communion that had no name. At the end of eight minutes, they gently let go of each other's hands and each of them followed their path, opening the Sacred Theatre, which would run for the rest of the day and night.

Helena stood there in the circle for some time. Her hands massaging her belly without thinking. There were tears and smiles on her face and a glimmer of intense hope deep within her. She looked around, saw the twelve paths, but didn't decide on one. The choice was made by her ears. She followed the sound of distant drumming. The dirt path was long and increasingly narrow, lined with lit torches, which, with the occasional gusts of wind, created a certain sense of danger, as the dancing flames seemed to reach out and touch her ; mainly because there were many people on this same path, in front of her, and some had decided to stop to play with the fire. Helena hesitated. She didn't know if she should stop where she was or try to go round them, knowing she would then get closer to the flames. She also didn't want to interrupt them either, as she felt she would be depriving them of their freedom. Then she laughed and realised that she was already in the game of life, reflecting it. She decided to accept the moment and to watch the four boys. They were testing who could get closest to the flame and, with each gust of wind, every movement of the flame, they marvelled at their ability to escape danger. They laughed so much, at their faces, their movements, at the fear they felt at times. Real children.

She too felt like laughing and, at the same time, she understood how she was being hampered by rules, how she had assumed that she would have to stay on the path that had been made. She saw what she had to do and, moving one of the torches out of the way, she headed out into the countryside. She followed the drumming all the same, away from the line of torches, on muddier ground, but her child's heart was excited to have been so daring.

Making her way through some trees, she came to a tribal circle, where everyone was dancing and playing drums and other instruments. The atmosphere was powerful, energetic, too much even, for what she was looking for.

Unexpectedly someone whispered in her ear:

"We are so conditioned by our short-term memory that we talk of first times... But if it's true that we have lived so many other lives we no longer remember, what was the first time? What was the first time like? If you gave me a kiss now, would it be the first time?"

Helena looked at the man who was whispering to her, a tangle of golden curls, piercing blue eyes like her father's, a young man, with tempting, thick, well-defined lips.

And if I didn't give you one, would that be the first time?" she replied, smiling, looking at his lips and then his eyes.

They laughed. It was good to be unattached. Just flirting. Creating little sparks.

"Do you know where the astrologer is?" Helena asked him.

"Over there," he said, pointing to the other side of the tribal circle, "on top of that big rock".

Helena saw an old man, his white hair tied in a ponytail, holding a staff, with several people around him, chatting. But she didn't feel like staying in that house. There was too much noise.

Once she'd left that space there was a choice of paths again, but Helena continued with her preferred shortcuts, through the trees, passing by the stream and entering a thicker part of the forest. Scarves had been hung in some of the trees, some of the rocks had been marked with colours and, without understanding quite how, Helena came across a small clearing, with wooden benches forming a circle and, in the centre, there was a totem pole, candles, and various musical instruments. There were few people sat there and one of them was playing the guitar. The atmosphere was very cosy. As she approached, she saw a delightful scene: six people swinging gently on a huge wooden swing. Every now and then one of them would jump off and head to the vegetable garden to plant something. It was entertaining to watch that sowing process. Further on, in a small greenhouse, tea was being brewed.

"What type of tea is it?" Helena asked the two young women who were standing there. They were both dressed in Red Indian garb, their hair in plaits, their faces painted, long, bright-coloured necklaces around their necks.

"Ginger, I think. Are you going to have some too?" one of them asked her.

"Yes."

"Pregnant?"

"Is ginger tea harmful?" she asked, confused.

They laughed. They pointed to the capsules in a bowl nearby.

"Mushroom micro dose."

Helena laughed too.

"I don't think such a small dose would harm Thaís. But I don't want to take anything during the pregnancy," said Helena.

"Thaís?"

"My daughter," she replied, touching her belly.

"Ah, what a beautiful name. But, come with us anyway. This isn't a trip," she said emptying a capsule into her tea, "just a light boost to the senses."

"And creative energy," the second woman added. "We are in the house of spring here, earth element. Let us lose ourselves in the embrace of nature. Connect with all the senses."

Helena readily agreed, very keen to immerse herself in nature. And she wandered around with them, aimlessly, but not at all worried, feeling light and relaxed, as if she had taken something herself, inhaling the aromas in the air, playing games, hugging trees, stopping to admire all the flowers that dotted the space. They barely spoke, rather calling out to each other with the constant refrain, "look at this!" Helena liked this visual communion, recalling the words about the path of beauty. Everything was beautiful to them and, in that presence, Helena was reminded of how she had gained that huge space within herself, that of allowing contemplation, without pursuing results.

After a while they came to another hall, with a huge white lino rolled out on the ground, and on it many tables and chairs, almost like a café terrace. There was a white screen at the back onto which many images were being projected, of people, buildings, the planet, constructions... The rest of the group went back. Helena stayed. She wandered around the tables, becoming aware that whenever they were talking louder at one of the tables, all the others got loud too. The cacophony of countless conversations was impressive. Even in the open air.

She remained there, moving from table to table, as if she were at a casino watching the games. She had become aware that each of the tables had a word placed in the centre indicating the subject of the conversations to be held at that table. She was drawn to the word freedom, pulled up an empty chair and sat there for a while, listening to the heated conversation that was already taking place.

"I can't remember who said that, when people reveal the desire to save humanity, it's almost always a sneaky way of governing it, controlling it," one man said.

"Tell me about it... and the strange thing is, without being funny at all, is that many people readily give up their freedom in favour of temporary security!"

"But isn't it also freedom to be able to give up your freedom?"

They looked at each other, smiling.

"But just what does freedom mean for you? Physical freedom?" asked another.

"No. Nelson Mandela is a good example of a man who was free even when imprisoned. Free to think."

"But are we really free to think? Aren't we unconsciously programmed? Things that we learn one way and follow with our eyes closed without questioning... Is that being free?"

"Free if you can understand what you are, what you really believe, or what has been instilled in you."

"Jim Morrison said that the greatest freedom is being ourselves. But who can achieve that?"

"We're all caged birds without realising it."

"You're being a bit excessive..."

"Am I?"

Suddenly, one of the women who was watching the conversation, without having spoken, burst into tears. Everyone stopped and looked at her.

"What happened?"

Wide-eyed and teary, her eyes raw with a mix of pain and fire, she cried out:

"You talk of freedom and I don't even know what that is. I've never been free. Ironically, I'm a prison guard and the prisoner. I've stopped myself from doing almost everything I truly want to do. For this reason or that, what difference does it make? I think I have lived my entire life in a cast, with my movement controlled by someone else's expectations, barely breathing.

"This is the first time I am where I want to be. I can no longer tolerate these walls, these ropes that bind me, this plaster I've encased myself in. I feel my body groan when I hear you speaking. Or maybe it's screaming! The time has come to tear things down, rip things apart, to shatter the plaster and pull down this cage... to break through and fly..."

And with these words yelled at the top of her lungs, she ran from the table, stripping as she went, until she was almost naked. The other people at the table jumped up with their arms in the air, shouting after her, cheering her on, as if they were her freedom fighters. The other tables looked at them for a moment, making them sit back down, their faces flushed with contentment.

Helena, inspired, returned to wandering around the tables, before taking a seat at the table of love, the subject that warmed her heart. The table was packed with people, with various rows of chairs in a spiral. Frozen in time, Helena delighted in hearing love stories. Romantic love, paternal and maternal love, love for animals, and animals' love for humans, love for the planet and for humanity, divine love, many stories of love that they were sharing as in a storytelling session. Hypnotised by all those stories of life, she heard behind her, at the end of an intoxicating account, a familiar voice that caused her pulse to race. Her heart seemed to burst out of her chest, her body trembling as she recognised Thomas' voice saying:

"Love is a light so strong that it can dispel the darkness of ignorance and of oblivion, which no other light could. Love is an axe so large that it could cut the samsara root, which no ordinary axe ever could. It is a broom so large that you could sweep up the dust of all suffering, which no other broom ever could. It is a fire so intense that it could burn down the entire forest of confusion, which no other fire ever could. It is a remedy so powerful that it can cure the chronic illness of afflicted emotions, which no other remedy ever could. Love is a sword so large that it can cut the web of duality, which no normal sword every could..."

Helena saw everyone's eyes locked on him, who spoke so powerfully, but her body was afraid to turn around, until she could stand it no longer and turned, dazzled by the uncompromising beauty of Thomas reading these powerful words from a book he was holding. As soon as Helena turned around Thomas lowered the book to look at her. And when Helena got up, he could finally see her huge belly in that dress that he knew so well. The book fell from his hands. Tears burst from his eyes, running down his cheeks without stopping. The people remained in silence, watching them there, face to face, a few chairs between them, understanding they were witnessing something magical, without knowing what. A thousand thoughts flew through her tumultuous mind and, at the same time, everything seemed empty in that distance.

"Our love lives within me," Helena repeated the words she had written, touching her belly.

Thomas broke down even more, in a mixture of laughter and tears, exposed in all his fragility and luminosity. Helena moved towards him, passing between the chairs until she was right in front of him, a belly away. Thomas' trembling hand reached out to her dress, slowly caressing the fruit of their last encounter. He felt Thaís kick and burst out laughing. He seemed like a child overcome with joy. Helena took his hand and they left in silence. They walked for a long time, in silence still, through labyrinthine pathways until they reached a space full of tents, children playing with their families, picnic rugs on the ground with some baskets where was still some fruit left. There was also a water area, where the astrologist was sat, surrounded by women and their birth charts.

"When is the birth due?" Thomas asked as they were crossing the family space.

"Early August."

"Leo, like its dad."

"If it doesn't come early," said Helena, smiling.

"Do you have a name? Do you know yet?"

"Thaís."

"Ah, it's a girl," he said to himself, a broad smile erupting on this face.

"Do your parents know?"

"No."

"Your mother Débora?"

"Yes, I was with her."

"When?" Thomas asked.

"A few days ago."

"So, you already know I went to see her."

"Yes, she told me."

"Sorry, I felt compelled to do so. I was lost and didn't know what to do. How have you been?" he asked.

"It was a long journey," Helena replied, lowering her eyes.

"I have not been well at all... but now I can't even remember the torment I was going through. What a gift!" Thomas said with joy.

They continued walking, hand in hand, heading out of the tented area along a path where they were many people collecting stones of different shapes, sizes and colours, before heading to a large lawn further on, where they were making fantastic stone sculptures, in the most improbable shapes, in an exercise of balance and patience, creating a fantasy setting reminiscent of *Alice in Wonderland*. There were dozens and dozens of rock sculptures, hundreds of stones piled up in a magical equilibrium, some defying gravity, creating a wave of vertical structures of varying proportions and guises, with many new artists in the middle of the lawn showing their self-control and desire to outdo the heights already reached.

"Isn't that Michael Grab?" Helena asked, pointing to a young man who was putting the final stone in a gigantic stone sculpture, larger than him, impossibly balanced, surrounded by people watching.

"If it isn't him, he looks like him... and his sculpture is outstanding!"

"Yeah! This is full of natural stacking artists," she said amazed. "What an amazing sight!"

"Do you want to make one?" asked Thomas. "We have some loose stones over there."

"We have a lot of unturned stones, you mean," she replied in a serious tone.

"None of that now. Come on!" he said, bending down to pick up some stones.

Together they carefully piled up many of these stones, and with each stone they managed to balance, they became more focused, more present and more playful, more spontaneous. They created new and daring shapes and, when they started to feel that they were getting the hang of it and at ease, they became aware of the peace that had taken hold of them.

They continued on their way, contemplating that world of stones dancing in the air.

Leaving the lawn, they stopped in another space, surrounded by fluttering red cloths, in which different artists were merging their arts. Some of them were playing music, others were painting large canvases to the sound of music and others were dancing. The ensemble was of rare beauty and, around the same space, there were different four-poster beds also decked in colourful fluttering cloths, where some couples or groups of people were enjoying the moment. There was an astrologer on one of these beds, with a couple. Another couple was waiting beside it. Helena and Thomas spontaneously headed in that direction, and sat down with them.

"Have you come for synastry too?"

"No, we didn't even know, it was just by chance."

The other couple laughed.

"Yes, we know, nothing is by chance," said Helena, smiling.

"This is the house of Libra. Relationships," said the woman, who was very pale, with grey eyes, but who had a special sparkle in her smile, as if she were ill, but because of that illness she had a special light within.

"Interesting. Do you want to stay?" Thomas asked Helena.

"Does it take long?" Helena asked the couple.

"It depends. There is no exact time."

"Depends on what?"

"On the couple. On their history. He does karmic astrology. He's a great Jung scholar. When he gets inspired it seems like he is connected up there, literally," said the woman, looking to the sky.

Thomas and Helena smiled.

"We'll stay, then."

They lay back, looking up at the sky. The sun was setting. That gesture and the magic of the orange-blue sky made them recall certain moments on their trip, when, in that lying back there was a growing, transcendent desire taking hold. They turned towards one another. For a long time, they looked deeply into each other's eyes, as the day turned to evening, forgetting all that was around them, entering this space that was theirs alone; a love that was healing itself. When they awoke from their trance, someone with a candle was watching them. It was the astrologer.

"Come, we're going over there," said the astrologer to them.

They followed him to a small wooden house, similar to a mountain hut. Inside the atmosphere was a palette of calming colours, inviting them to relax. It was lit in a subdued way and empty. They sat down on some cushions on the floor.

"Oh, a place just for us," said Helena, delighted.

"I alone have the key. Don't give away the secret," the astrologer replied, with a hearty laugh.

His laughter came out of nowhere, loud, energetic and exhilarating. They felt immediately like laughing with him. He laughed like this several times, taking up the whole space with this youthful joy, contrasting with the wrinkles on his face and the deeply serious voice when he spoke.

Thomas and Helena gave him the dates and places of their births, which he entered into his laptop, looking at the screen for some time in silence, with no discernible expression on his face.

"It's funny because I only found out my actual date of birth a few days ago," she commented.

Thomas held her hand, supporting her. The astrologer nodded, saying yes repeatedly.

"Well, you know that I would need a great deal of time to study your charts in detail. There are so many layers, so many approaches we could make! So, in these circumstances, I just allow myself to be guided by the question: where am I called to delve? And with you I am called to delve into mystery and potentiality. There is nothing conventional in your relationship and on the day in which you try to place it in a box, it will die. You're together to accomplish something greater than yourselves. But between what is possible and what will be, there lies a field of infinite possibilities. It's been a long time since I've seen something so open and unpredictable.

"At the same time, I find myself marvelling like a child. What an intense connection of souls you have... There are very ancient songs being sung between you both. Did you not feel that you'd been waiting your entire lives to meet?" asked the astrologer.

Helena and Thomas looked at each other, knowingly.

"Look, I could go on for hours about your connection, but I would rather leave it in the mystery that it is. Sorry. That's how I feel. All I will tell you is that this love of yours lives in the past, present and future, but as time is malleable, and everything happens at the same time, you now have the opportunity to touch the same time line and compose new music. You have already loved each other greatly in many lifetimes, but you have also suffered even more. There are deep wounds yet to close... that's why the here and now can be deeply cathartic.

"As I see it today, you clearly wanted to continue on this earthly odyssey and give yourself this opportunity to heal, for transformation and evolution, even though you knew that you could fall into a place of even greater pain. The challenge remains. This is the sacred choice of travellers. If they make the journey, the butterfly that emerges will be of incandescent beauty, so radiant that the world will not be left indifferent. If the obstacles seem insurmountable, if the path is too hard and, for some reason, you do not want to climb to the top of the mountain, don't want to take the trouble, you won't understand the wings that you have.

"This is all I can tell you."

Thomas and Helena looked at each other, with questions hanging on their lips.

"May we ask any questions?" asked Thomas.

"You may, it's just I can't answer them. I've already said all I can. The rest is part of the mystery of your choices."

They thanked him and went out into the night.

"I'm starving. I have to go and eat something," Helena told Thomas.

Thomas turned on the torch on his mobile and they set off without really knowing where they were going. They passed a group of people and Thomas asked them where they could get something to eat. One of them pointed in the direction in which they were heading. The darkness seemed to grow in intensity the further they walked and, without the light from the mobile, they wouldn't have been able to see a thing. At one point, heading down a small hill, they found a spot where people were dancing in the dark, some blindfolded, others with their eyes closed in a kind of trance.

There was a DJ playing music, almost underground, completely oblivious to what was going on around him. They looked around in search of food, but could only find a table with lots of empty plates, with nothing but crumbs and the remains of a cake on one of them. They headed towards it.

"I'll take anything at the moment," Helena said, eating the leftover piece.

"Come on, let's look for something healthier for you..." Thomas replied, taking her hand so they could leave.

In the darkness, they started to see fireworks in the sky. They thought this might be a good indicator of where there might be a food stall. It was still a while off, but it meant they could head in that direction more easily.

"If we don't find anything, I can always go back to the apartment. I have food already made there," said Helena.

Then, as they were walking in the direction of the lights in the sky, she started feeling strange, half-seasick, half-dizzy. She thought it might be out of hunger and asked Thomas to stop. They sat down next to a tree. Helena closed her eyes and leaned her head against Thomas, but whenever she closed her eyes, clear images appeared before her.

"Maybe it was something I ate," Helena thought out loud. "Maybe it was not just cake!"

"I'd have to go and ask, but I don't want to leave you here on your own. Lie down for a little, until you feel better. Put your head on my lap. We'll stay here as long as necessary. You ate the tiniest piece... If there was something in it, it'll soon be over. Everyone dancing there must have eaten some," Thomas assured her, trying to put Helena's mind at rest, but he too was worried about the situation.

Thomas spread his jacket out on the floor, and Helena lay down on it, placing her head in Thomas' lap and, feeling protected by him, closed her eyes and surrendered to the moment.

Letting go of her fear, she lost all sense of dizziness, but the images became stronger; she could perfectly see a huge mountain before her. She was down there, at the foot of the mountain and the mountain was inviting her to climb up. It seemed a heroic task to her, but at the same time a journey that was unavoidable. There was a path skirting the mountain in a spiral.

She headed up. When she started the climb, she realised there were people on either side of the path, as if forming a tunnel through which she was passing. They were all people she knew. All the people who had marked her childhood, family, friends, the friends of her parents and their children, teachers and, as she passed them, they offered words of praise, of encouragement, smiles, gestures of affection, but there was also rejection, people turning away, derision and cursing. It was strange to see the people from her life all crammed together there, even those that had been part of it fleetingly, yet memorably. Helena didn't interact with them, she just looked, listened, remembered, felt and carried on climbing, coming across more people, from different times, from her adolescence, from her adult years, friends, passions, loves, colleagues, interviewees, people she had met in the different countries she had visited... It was if her memory had been given access to a programme and was downloading all the people she had ever met in her life, with whom she had formed a connection in one way or another, men and women that had influenced the moments, choices, experiences that made her who she was.

And she carried on climbing the mountain along the spiral path, seeing all these people again, a treasure chest of memories opening as if by magic, realising how huge a number of people were part of her, the enormous number of interactions, conversations, looks, common projects, jobs, trips, shared experiences, loves, collaborations, laughter, tears, sleepless nights, parties, farewells, meetings and reunions. And her parents who were always there with her, at the foot of the mountain, along the ascent, appearing and disappearing, full of love, always with positive words, kisses, gestures of affection, admiration.

Helena was gaining strength as she climbed. You could have thought that she would become tired given the steepness, but instead she grew in energy, the urge to continue, spiralling around, up and up, always seeing the people from her life on either side of the path.

When she saw Thomas before her, for the first time, the sensation was so strong that it seemed as if her body wouldn't be able to cope, that the human heart is too fragile for such a strong feeling. Behind him she could see many people, almost in single file; and, despite being different, Helena knew they were all Thomas, other lives perhaps, all deeply connected to her. On this section of the path, there were many deep, dangerous holes; she had the feeling that if she were to fall into one, she would never get out. The climb had become steeper too. Helena hesitated, even when she saw Thomas on the other side, climbing alone, closer to the peak. Very cautiously, scared out of her wits, hugging the mountain wall, she tried to get round these openings in the ground, step by step, slowly, keeping clear of the cliff's edge, and sidestepping as much she could the many obstacles appearing in her path. That was when she started seeing people that she had met on that trip, one after the other, reminding her to connect deeply with her heart. She was the waking dreamer creating her reality. And recalling that power, the realisation that while awake in the dream she could do anything, just as had happened in lucid dreams, brought her the courage to move with conviction towards the holes, which, magically began to close as she passed. From then onwards, it seemed as if her entire body was fired up, connected to an endless energy.

Opening her eyes, she took Thomas' hand, got up and started to run in the dark, without fear, towards the lights in the sky, as she had done on the top of the mountain. As she ran, she felt as if her body was transforming, that wings were sprouting from her back. When they arrived at this brightly lit place, there was a ball, with a band playing folk music and many people dancing. Helena grabbed Thomas and started spinning around and around without stopping. As they danced, her head pressed against Thomas' chest, she closed her eyes again and let herself go, rising up as she transformed into a bird. As she was spinning on the ground, she could perfectly feel her bird-being flying, soaring through the skies with lightness. From up high, she could take in her magical mountain, her life, all those people connected to her, who were also part of her; from up high she could see that that mountain was connected to many other mountains just like hers, connected by golden threads that formed a giant mandala, a flower of life seen from the sky.

It was so beautiful that she felt tears running down her cheeks as she spun, while she heard Thomas' heart beating in harmony with the music, the desire to love him forever. When the music stopped, and they stopped, Helena felt wonderfully well, revived, reborn and clear.

She pulled Thomas towards her apartment. On the way they noticed a clearing in which a group of people, methodical and organised, were about to finish the construction of a geodesic dome. They stopped for a moment to take in the elegant structure. Then, further on, they came across different circles of people in the landscape. Some seemed to be seated, in council, in a deep moment of sharing, reviving this ancient practice, others were singing around a campfire, and further still there was a large group lost in joyful musical improvisation.

They followed the path, before spotting the Les Contes building, where calm and silence prevailed, contrasting with everything else. Helena took Thomas to look at the chapel, where some people were sitting meditating or praying.

They then went to the apartment. Helena pounced on the food she had kept in the fridge as if there was no tomorrow and, when she finally started to breathe between forkfuls, she told Thomas about her trip up the mountain.

"I still need to find out what was in that cake. What a trip! Words fail me, all those people, seeing them again, navigating through all those memories, feeling them as part of me, knowing that I am all of them! Being awake in the dream makes all the difference. The confidence in what we can do and overcome, there's no better way to explain it, gave me a strength, a feeling for everything! All that interconnection... And my parents, their love so present, and you... when I held your hand, I felt, I knew. Sometimes our mind plays so many tricks on us, places so many obstacles in our way, creates so many false holes... How did I manage to spend so long without you, I'm asking myself now?! How could I think that living with you would be impossible, because of the constant reminder of what I am not?

"Pain, anger, disappointment, bring us so many veils of deception. These are the feelings, together with fear, guilt, shame, jealousy, humiliation, that push our eyes into those dark holes. How we perceive everything around us, and even ourselves, becomes seriously contaminated.

"The universe is strange and has this mysterious way of operating," Helena continued with excitement. "I was looking for the truth, I was challenged in my perception, and what I took to be a lie, now I see as the truth. My parents haven't changed. My parents really are my parents in this life. I understood just how much I was being trapped by labels, forgetting about contracts between souls and the power of love.

Contained love is what makes the truth. We go round and round and we always go back to the words of Castañeda, whose books I read in my mother's library: does this path have a heart? That's all that matters.

"You are my heart. Thaís is my heart. My parents are my heart. All those people... Your mother was right. We are all connected with golden threads, invisible to the eye. And you know those Mexican waves that the crowd makes at football matches? The more of us that lift up this wave of love, the more beautiful life will be! For everyone! And for those yet to come," she finished, placing her hands on her belly, her face flushed, her gleaming eyes locked on Thomas.

Thomas felt no desire to say anything. His desire for her was consuming his words. He picked her up and carried her to the bed. Since their reunion they were yet to kiss, and that kiss that their mouths were demanding, breathlessly, transformed into an endless current of pleasure, in a sacred ritual celebrating that union.

Until the sun rose, they made love as if they were dancing, rocked by the music of an intense desire, hopeful-travellers in the harbour of happiness, reborn, full of wonder and amazement.

They had suffered through solitude, passed through storms, eaten dust and pain, but now, having finally reached the land of their bodies, stumbling still, they wiped away the pain of their yearning, exchanging dreams with each other through affection. Helena allowed him to drink in the petals of her being, and Thomas entered this deep and sweet portal with a love that was so powerful and indecipherable that it burst in his belly. It was life they were giving each other in that transfusion of love.

That night they experienced fullness in every embrace, expressed the thirst of humanity in every kiss, felt like children of the stars in that mythical universe of the heavens, their smiles gleaming white, a desire to be boundless in the constant galloping of their uncontrollable hearts; and when the first rays of sunlight came in through the window, they both knew that they were no longer the same, they couldn't be, transformed as they were by their reunion. Their light was so expansive that it could have been their light coming in through the window with the sun.

Falling asleep from exhaustion in the middle of a kiss, they woke with their lips still close, so happy that there was no way to contain it. Helena looked out of the window, to see what was happening outside and saw many people walking in the same direction, as if they were being called by church bells. Still sleepy, they got dressed in yesterday's clothes, a piece of fruit in their hands and, without a thought for appearances, they went outside, following the sea of people. They came to a large amphitheatre, already full, with a stage at the front, yet unoccupied, but with a beautiful bonfire burning on a huge iron base.

"You know, I had a feeling I'd missed the house of Leo," Helena said, chuckling.

"All in good time," Thomas replied smugly, looking at her playfully. "Thaís and I deserve this moment!"

"You don't even give her a chance to be born any other time!"

Thomas laughed.

"What are we waiting for?" Helena asked a woman beside her.

"The closing of the Sacred Theatre."

The woman who had been in the centre of the circle, appeared on stage, behind the bonfire and, behind her, a semicircle of men and women, a huge feather in their hair and one in their hands.

"I'll be brief," the woman began, this time without her child in her arms. "The time has come for us to return to our homes, to take in what has happened to us, the experiences we have had in this sacred theatre. There was drumming, the sound of flutes, dancing, crying, many visions, brilliant embroidered impressive images... people talked to each other, received precious information, meditated, cleansed themselves in the waters, took part in ceremonies, gathered in prayer, created a great deal, contemplated, felt the force of nature, felt ecstasy, joy, many will have cried out many times: "This is so beautiful; too beautiful for any person", but many others found themselves grieving, feeling devastated, trapped in the deepest darkness, howling inside and out...

"There has been love, so much love... timeless connections, abundance and the deepest of gratitude. Almost everyone has been able to witness the invisible web of the love that holds everything together. There have been moments of self-reflection, many journeys, eyes open, eyes closed, a great deal of revelry, celebration, revelations, merging with the most divine light, movement, excitement, giving and receiving. There has been co-creation of magic. The magic of which life, all of existence, is made. I thank you all for being here at this Sacred Theatre. I don't think any of us will ever forget this day."

The people in the semicircle behind her were waving up and down the feather they had in their hands.

"To finish off, I would like to evoke a practice of the Q'ero shaman tribe of the high Andes of Peru, which is an offering to the Earth and to the Heavens, which we have adapted for this closing. At the beginning of each row, you'll find little pieces of paper. Each person should take three. Without thinking about it, spontaneously, full of everything that you have experienced here, on one of the pieces of paper write down the three most important things in your life, on the other what you want to let go off and on the third what you want to bring to your lives now. Once you have done this, each in your own time, come up to the stage and throw these three pieces of paper into the fire and then return to your seat until everyone has done the same. These gestures will be accompanied by our prayers and chanting of thanks for what we are happy to let go, for what we are happy to have and for what we are happy to bring to our lives.

"At the end of this ceremony, together, I would like us to ensure that our passage here leaves behind no visible trace, only memories of our butterfly wings emerging from the cocoon. To this end, after you've thrown your little pieces of paper into the fire, please take a paper from the tombola, which will tell you a place and task you can contribute to cleaning the whole space. Then we'll all go home. Ok?"

A huge OK echoed out.

Thomas went to get them paper and pencils and they sat reflecting silently next to each other. The chanting of gratitude to the heavens filled the space with a deeply warming vibration. Helena looked around her, smiling, seeing all those people silently reflecting on what was most important to them, on what they wanted to let go of and what they wanted to let enter their lives. That ritual was truly beautiful. And, slowly, in a graceful movement, the fire seemed to greet each of the participants that passed by, the flames growing larger with the burning of the papers.

Once again, Helena felt she was witnessing human beauty, the magnificence of nature, the power of creation, the divine grace enshrined in every life, in every passage. In that moment, it was clear to her that being a witness to the life journey of someone else and being witnessed on her own journey by that same person, in absolute presence and love, was one of the most wonderful experiences she could ever imagine.

A witness to places of pain, places of doubt, to wings unfurling, to conquests, journeys, to eyes brimming with big tears, to lips bursting with smiles, to words, silence, to voids, insecurities, to backsliding and racing forward, singular gestures, gazes only rarely revealed, to flushed cheeks and moments of surrender. Witnessing the scars, the madness, the constrictions, the transformation of the body and mind, the expansion of the heart and of intuition, the earthly expression of the purpose of the soul, the creation, the path of connection with the whole, the opening to the invisible. Witnessing their different facets, their self-discovery, the courage to be true and be part of truth, the path of self-love, of liberation of their voice. Being a witness to the everyday, to repetitive gestures never repeated, and to be the witness to the dance back home, to their heart. Thinking of this filled her chest with ecstasy, her eyes with tears of emotion and, at the same time, it brought her back to the thought that her parents were those people, the ones who had been the witnesses to her life, to her ups and downs, to her bad things and others that are beautiful and magical, constant witnesses to her 38 years of life, to the transformation of her body and of her being, and that it was them, biological parents or not, who had been her parents in the greatest sense of that word. They who had loved her since the first days of her life, given their time, their knowledge, they who had been present through sickness and health, who had done their best, even making many mistakes like any human being, like her, witnesses like she would like to be to Thomas and to her daughter Thaís until the end of her days. A witness to all small and large things, to every moment of her journey and transformation, in love, deep love.

Orderly, gently and gracefully, everything that had appeared in the space was taken away. They were like magicians removing structures, storing material, smoothing out the land, cleaning away any traces. In a few hours, Les Contes returned to its usual form. Only the bodies of the people and the earth retained the luminous memory of that passage through the Sacred Theatre. And just as they arrived, the campervans left, the people flew back to their countries, and Helena and Thomas were also ready to leave, they just didn't know where to.

In the kingdom of her heart

France lay between Italy and Portugal; and it was where they had also found each other again, and where Helena felt at peace, in a deep connection with the divine and with herself. There was a secret desire to give birth in those lands where Mary Magdalene had left such a lasting mark. Out of the blue, the house that her biological mother had bought for them to live in Provence, a house that had never been lived in, came into her thoughts. She thought that that house - which had been designed for her, for me, her twin sister, for our parents, for that love - had never been filled with the happiness she had dreamed of. When she mentioned it to Thomas, Helena was entranced by his spontaneous smile as if saying yes intuitively. Both of them felt that it was a way of unifying all those events. Of reconciliation too. When they talked to her about this idea, Débora was thrilled to the core. She immediately gave them the key and, with few words, explained simply how to get there and the contact details of the couple that had rented the vineyard for local production. And seized by a happiness and youthful enthusiasm, Débora said assertively:

"You can visit it at your leisure and decide what to do. It's yours if you want it."

The house was in the Vaucluse area, considered the beating heart of Provence, and they quickly realised why. The fresh, soft, bright air gently filled their lungs. Their eyes lapped up the patchwork of orchards, olive groves and vineyards, interspersed with rugged mountains and hilltop villages. There, between the spring and summer, the blend of colours was glorious, from the almond, cherry and apricot trees, alongside fields of electric-blue lavender, dazzling sunflowers and scarlet poppies.

Later, when they arrived at the house, Helena burst into tears on recognising the house from her dream. For a long time, she was unable to say a word, overwhelmed by the feeling of déjà-vu. The house showed no signs that it had been abandoned decades beforehand; only later did they find out the deal Débora had made with the couple, allowing them to run the vineyard in exchange for maintaining the house: the beautiful stone house with white shutters, the rose garden, the huge outdoor terrace, with an iron table and chairs under a grape vine and a view to the small vineyard. The certainty that they should stay, at least until Thaís was born, was so clear to them that there was little to discuss.

It was from this same terrace that Helena called her mother, Ingrid, after so many months of absence. Strangely, her mother didn't bombard her with questions about her absence, as if she knew everything and Helena, overwhelmed by that gesture of unconditional love, felt compelled, even if on a video call, to show her belly and say she was going to be a grandmother. She realised that she had never seen her mother cry so much as she did at that moment. Overcome with the purest of joy. And when her father joined the call, Helena invited them to come visit them in Provence.

If Julian, her father, knew about the existence of that house, he never mentioned it at any moment. And when they both arrived, two weeks later, just as summer was beginning, the moment was so tender, so joyful, so natural, that it seemed as if nothing that had happened in those months had created any rift, quite the contrary, never before had that connection been so solid and true.

They spent days along forest footpaths, bird watching; strolling around the vineyards and farmland; exploring small villages and their wonderful markets. Long days that always ended with a well-deserved meal at sunset. At first, it was a little strange for Helena to see Julian and

Thomas together. But soon, it became a delightful picture of growing closeness. At times, when out on their walks, Julian would slow down, until he was by Helena's side, leaning against her gently, inviting her to take his arm as was his custom ever since she was a little girl, and the first time Helena did it again she felt the emotion unblocking both of their hearts.

In the house there was always the scent of lavender or flowers. Helena and her mother spent a lot of time together in the kitchen, making the delicious food they would later relish on the terrace. On one such occasion, her mother placed her hand on Helena's tummy and left it there, so as to feel Thaís kicking, as if they were lovingly communicating in morse code.

"I can remember this phase of pregnancy so vividly. I was so happy and radiant... Like you, daughter," she said, her eyes brimming with tears. "It's so great being your mother!"

Helena froze for a moment, her heart pounding unconsciously. Then she came round, becoming aware of the exact words that had been said and, for a while, gazed at her mother in admiration. Her mother gazed back, smiling, and Helena knew deep down what was being said to her. What she was being told between the unsaid words, in that majestic gaze in which a past sadness reigned and the unconditional love for the daughter that been brought to her arms and had revived her. Helena didn't know how she knew, but she was now certain that she knew, in a silent complicity, founded on love and on presence. Those very eyes that had watched her since she was a baby, which complemented the journey of her ever-changing being. That day, over dinner, between the stories and laughter shared between Thomas and Julian, Helena and her mother looked at other, smiling, aware of this complicity and of the love burning in their chests.

After a week, her parents returned to Portugal.

"Let them enjoy this last month in peace. Afterwards, nothing will be the same again," her mother said.

"Make the most of it," their father added, while embracing Helena and Thomas together. "And keep us informed about everything! We want to come and help when our granddaughter arrives!"

When they had left, a huge sense of calm and silence filled the house. Helena sat down on one of the chairs on the terrace, Thomas by her side, both of them looking out over the vineyard. They sat there until nightfall, caught in the moment, in contemplation and their thoughts. Me too. Thoughts in dialogue between twin sisters, telepathic, from a place of union and love that crosses space instantly.

I thought: Helena had sailed far from the safe harbour, caught the prevailing winds in her sails, explored, discovered, battled the most violent storms, walked through the dark night of the soul and emerged stronger, with a sense of propriety and authenticity never experienced before. That was it. She had experienced her strength as though from an epiphany.

Helena thought back: Adriana told me that I would come out stronger the other side. Life is peculiar. What seemed the most terrifying chaos, now seems the path to another level of order. As much in me, as in the world.

Me: I flew through the cosmos, recalling when Mike Brown and other astronomers discovered Sedna, the largest celestial body found in the Kuiper Belt and the most distant ever known to mankind, they wrote that it was "the coldest and most distant object known to orbit the Sun". So far away that it takes the equivalent of 10,500 earth years to complete one single orbit of the Sun, and is so distant from the sun that it freezes at an average temperature of minus 240 degrees centigrade. Later, when someone asked astrologist Melanie Reinhart, a major researcher of these objects in the Kuiper Belt, what discovering Sedna might mean, she replied:

"Even in the face of unrelenting trauma and suffering, we can, indeed must, beat our drum and sing to life. This is not a plea for escapism, but rather an acknowledgement that the Work is about keeping our heart open in hell. Sedna's story is about acknowledging just how bad things really feel, and starting from there. Radical acceptance is demanded.

Allowing love and harmony into our lives (symbolized by the Star of David, or the Harmonic Concordance) may mean opening up to the frozen places inside where we are conflicted and feel unloving."

Helena had felt frozen places in her, in the midst of that personal hell, and the path to acceptance and opening of the heart had transformed everything.

She knew that no one outside could define who she was, not even her parents. Her truth lived independently of all this, in her. She was love in search of herself. She was love in search of being experienced in her most diverse expressions and facets, even in her shadows, thorns, pains and challenges.

Helena seemed to reply to me: time needs heart and we need time to truly hear its intuitive guidance. It was a profound journey, but what seemed to be ending is only a beginning. How many lives will be needed to explore new truths on existence and who I really am? Or to free me of beliefs, perceptions and emotions that make no sense to me?

I can already look and see all my landscapes. Tomorrow I will find more, if I look and listen carefully. Where I feel peace, I remember myself, my light. I remember that, hidden behind all the noise and chaos, there lies this secret and silent path, inwards, to where I can connect myself to everything there is.

If I were to be asked the same questions today that I asked, like recognising the truth in my experiences, like trusting my inner knowledge, like knowing that I am living my own truth, today I would say that I have fine-tuned myself by the barometer of the truth, through a deeper connection with my heart. But that quest for the truth is something on going, which will never stop, which requires sacrifice, effort, willingness and altruistic determination, for having to always be ready to abandon belief systems, ideas, knowledge and personal preferences, independent of personal cost, as Blavatsky wrote in the preface to *The Key to Theosophy*.

Me: to be able to tune into her own truth, Helena had turned to the "know thyself" of the Delphic oracle, which the shaman and Ariel had reminded her of so well. The treasure map was laid out inside of her.

Helena closed her eyes. I did too.

Thomas thought that he was a wave of energy interacting with the environment. The environment, for him, was everything from the very core of his being all the way to the edge of the universe. He knew that, without his eyes being able to see it, the atoms in his body were receiving energy from that same environment and sending it out, at the same time, in an invisible dance. His vibrations in that instant were of love, the common agent in the divine equation, the magnetism that makes the proton, the neutron and the electron stay together. The environment radiated back a sweet and majestic music, full of harmonies, through the soul of things.

For a good student, all beings are teachers, as all of them have a piece of truth. We learn from nature, from the cosmos, we learn from people, we learn from difficult experiences, we learn from mistakes and failures. Love, like pain, plays a fundamental role in conservation, cohesion and renewal, and is an integral part of the organic functioning of the universe. Life, eager to expand and evolve, opens its arms wide to environmental forces, which are introduced in great quantities; reactions multiply and consciousness, eager for sensations, is enriched and perfected. The being becomes even wiser for having lived, for the experiences it has accumulated.

Often, he felt tired too, languishing on the side of the road, too many labyrinths, too much pain, but when he looked up high, in silence, to the endlessness of space and of time, all he saw was that force, that immense wave of love that kept everything connected in harmony. It was the sublime word of love that the colossal components of the universe repeated to themselves, in unison, right down to the lost voice of the tiniest being. The universe does not have a single heart, rather billions and billions, he could feel it! And he imagined his heart in unison with that of the universe, guided by that great conductor called love, and he hummed softly, happy to bring a little of the sky to the earth.

That's how it was for him, how it had always been for as long as he could remember, even in the face of the tangled plot of human destinies: when he could smell the perfume and poetry of love, the maelstrom in his heart subsided and the journey no longer seemed so long, so convoluted, because his heart knew the meaning of profound peace.

Like there, in that exact moment.

Without turning round to her, with his eyes still fixed on the horizon, on the vineyard before them, Thomas placed his hand on Helena's belly. He felt Thaís.

Helena smiled, she thought about that poem, which describes how, when a woman of an African tribe discovers she is pregnant, she goes to the jungle with other women and, together, they talk, they share, they sit in silence and meditate until, naturally, the song of the new person emerges and expresses itself. When the baby is born, the community comes together and they sing that song to it, the one that represents it essence. They do the same at every important moment in its life, but most importantly when the person is lost, when they feel ugly and worthless, so that, through love and recollection of their true identity, they can recall all of their beauty, their integrity, their innocence, their true essence. Their truth.

Maybe that was her song that she had heard on this journey. And although she was yet to know the art of living that well, she was open to walking the path with her hands open; to just let go. She knew just how difficult it was to stop wanting to be right, to stop wanting to be in control, to stop being afraid of discomfort, afraid of uncertainty, afraid of failure, afraid of boredom, afraid of the unknown, but she didn't need nor want to build her cathedral in one day. One day at a time, one stone at a time, one brushstroke at a time, making adjustments and readjustments, realising that the journey itself, with all the surprises, wonders, falls, rocks, injuries, exhaustion, fatigue, doubts, surrender, love, joy, ecstasy, was also the destination. And, looking back, with humility and pride, she now saw that she had already built so much.

She smiled one of those smiles that remain etched on the memory of time.

I smiled with her.

She knew, in the kingdom of her heart, that even if she harboured great dreams and expectations, she only had to do her part and step aside, accepting whatever the results might be, because a soul with greater wisdom was expressing itself through her.

She also wanted to pay close attention to the song of Thaís, this was absolutely fundamental, in that she never wanted to impose her own vision on her. And, when one day Thaís said to her, "No, that's not how it is for me", and her ego ached a little, she wanted to remember this journey and how truth is that multifaceted gem, the facets of which are impossible to perceive all at once. Different views enabled access to different reflections, parts of a greater whole. One didn't need to cancel out the other, both could be held in acceptance and respect through the heart. Through love. Through remembering that what connects is much greater than what separates us.

She placed her hand on Thomas' hand on her belly. Other on her heart. Completely surrendering to love, in all its simplicity and greatness.

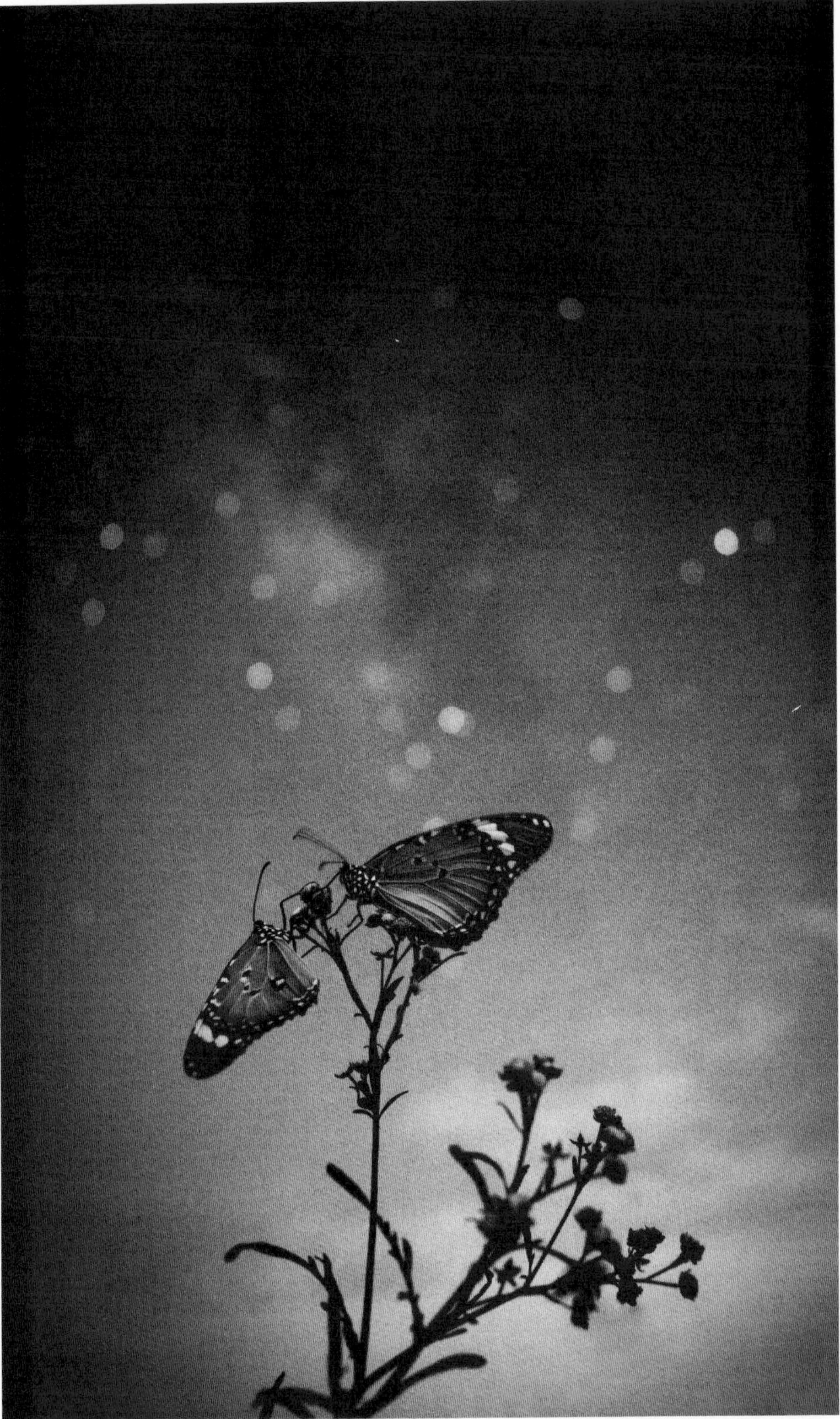